S0-BSJ-705

on

Charles R. Hoffer
Indiana University

Wadsworth Publishing Company, Inc., Belmont, California

Production Editor: Sandra Craig
Designer: Nancy Benedict

Printed in the United States of America
1 2 3 4 5 6 7 8 9 10—83 82 81 80 79

**Library of Congress Cataloging in Publication
Data**

Hoffer, Charles R
  A concise introduction to music listening.

  Includes index.
  1. Music—Analysis, appreciation. I. Title.
MT6.H565C6 1979   780'.15   78-24313
ISBN 0-534-00627-2

Available from your bookstore:

Record Album (a five-disk set prepared by Columbia Special Products, CBS Records, a Division of CBS Inc.)
Study Guide and Scores

Acknowledgments

Music examples are used with permission from the following sources:

Béla Bartók, *Concerto for Orchestra*. Copyright 1946 by Hawkes & Son (London) Ltd.; renewed 1973. Reprinted by permission of Boosey & Hawkes, Inc.

Benjamin Britten, *The Young Person's Guide to the Orchestra*. Copyright 1946 by Hawkes & Son (London) Ltd.; renewed 1973. Reprinted by permission of Boosey & Hawkes, Inc.

Aaron Copland, *Rodeo*. Copyright 1946 by Aaron Copland; renewed 1973. Reprinted by permission of Aaron Copland and Boosey & Hawkes, Inc., sole licensee and publishers.

George Crumb, *Night of the Four Moons*. Copyright © 1971 by C. F. Peters Corporation, 373 Park Avenue South, New York, New York 10016. Reprinted by permission of C. F. Peters Corporation.

Paul Hindemith, *Kleine Kammermusik*. Copyright 1922 by B. Schott's Söhne, Mainz; renewed 1949 by Schott & Co., London. Reprinted by permission of Belwin-Mills Publishing Corp.

Gian-Carlo Menotti, *The Medium*. Copyright 1947, 1967 by G. Schirmer, Inc. Reprinted by permission of G. Schrimer, Inc.

Arnold Schoenberg, *Four Songs for Mixed Chorus*. Copyright 1953 by Gertrud Schoenberg. Reprinted by permission of Belmont Music Publishers, Los Angeles, California 90049.

William Schuman, *New England Triptych*. Copyright © 1957 by Merion Music, Inc. Reprinted by permission of Theodore Presser Co.

Igor Stravinsky, *The Rite of Spring*. Copyright 1921 by Edition Russe de Musique. Copyright assigned 1947 to Boosey & Hawkes, Inc. Reprinted by permission of Boosey & Hawkes, Inc.

Igor Stravinsky, *Symphony of Psalms*. Copyright 1931 by Edition Russe de Musique; renewed 1958. Copyright and renewal assigned to Boosey & Hawkes, Inc. Revised edition copyright 1948 by Boosey & Hawkes, Inc. Reprinted by permission of Boosey & Hawkes, Inc.

Heitor Villa-Lobos, *Bachianas Brasileiras No. 5*. Copyright © 1948 Associated Music Publishers, Inc. Reprinted by permission of Associated Music Publishers, Inc.

William Walton, *Belshazzar's Feast*. © Oxford University Press. Reprinted by permission of Oxford University Press, London.

Anton von Webern, *Concerto for Nine Instruments*. © Universal Editions. Reprinted by permission of Theodore Presser Co.

To the Armers:
Bob, Clarice, Andy, and Erica

Contents

Preface

The Second Edition of *A Concise Introduction to Music Listening* tries not only to present the subject of music but to make its content relevant to the reader. It builds on what the students are most likely to know when they enter the course by beginning with an example of music in a popular style.

This edition strikes a balance between the presentation of information and the development of listening skills. Although all music appreciation books urge the reader to listen better, little provision is made for accomplishing this. On the other hand, a few music appreciation textbooks require the use of a particular set of recordings and focus attention on listening, but they fail to provide sufficient information to aid the student in understanding what is heard.

The four questions around which the book is organized give readers an approach that is useful for all types of music—past, present, and future; simple and complex; Western and non-Western. They are not confined to certain musical works and styles. Those four questions are:

1. What is music?
2. What is music made of?
3. What forms does music take?
4. What kinds of music have been created at various times and places?

After chapters on the nature of music and on listening, the book's first large section presents the basic elements of which music is made. The second major section examines the various forms music takes—songs, symphonies, keyboard works, and so on. The third section covers the stylistic periods of music and explores some significant types of music, including folk, jazz, and American music.

The Second Edition maintains the features of the First Edition. It attempts to be more concise than most other music appreciation textbooks. Also, the information has been pared down as much as possible without omitting important topics. The most significant change in the Second Edition is the way in which listening skill development is encouraged. Many students have no trouble following a work in class while the instructor points out its features but flounder without such help. The new edition provides sixteen Listening Guides for various works of music. These guides "walk" students through the music, helping them hear the features of the work and follow its basic form.

Another major improvement concerns the supplementary *Record Album*. It has been enlarged to five discs and now includes every work for which there is a Listening Guide and for which a simplified "line" score is provided in the supplementary *Study Guide and Scores*.

A number of smaller adjustments have also been made in the Second Edition to provide more balanced coverage, to improve clarity, and to update information.

For their reviews of the manuscript I would like to thank Nicholas Bridges, Northern Illinois University; Richard C. Cole, Virginia Polytechnic Institute; Raymond V. Gill, Grand Rapids Junior College; James C. Guerriero, West Liberty State College; William Kaplan, University of Illinois, Chicago Circle; Larry D. Lowder, Fullerton College; James A. Starr, Emporia State University; Dora Wilson, California State University, Long Beach.

Charles R. Hoffer

One

Music and People

Each year people all over the world spend countless hours listening to music and performing it, and they spend vast amounts of money for instruments, records, and record-playing equipment. People dance, sing lullabies, and whistle as they walk along in just about every part of the globe. In the United States an estimated 30 million people play musical instruments regularly. Americans spend more money on music than on spectator sports. At weddings, ship launchings, and ball games, music is present.

Reasons for Music

Why is music so vital in the lives of people? There are many reasons. First, it can be a background accompaniment for activity. It provides an environment of sound in the same way that wallpaper provides a visual environment. Some people want sound around them almost all the time. If their portable radios or record players were taken away, they would feel uncomfortable.

Another use of music is to provide a particular atmosphere for a nonmusical situation. An example of this use is the presence of music in motion pictures. The musical score enhances the mood created by the dramatic action, and by so doing it increases the impact of the story.

In a similar way sacred music promotes a feeling of worship in religious ceremonies. It is designed to encourage an attitude of devotion and commitment to religious beliefs.

Music is also used to promote a feeling of group identity. People often prefer a type of music (or clothing or hair style) because it associates them with certain people or ideas. Those who want to be considered "intellectuals" may let their friends know that they like Bartók's string quartets and sophisticated jazz renditions, while the truck driver may put money in the juke box to play some country music. When examined closely, some musical activities turn out to be largely social in nature.

Music is often used as emotional release. People vent their feelings about all sorts of things through the medium of music. It seems to make the world a little brighter and to ease the hurts of life. Folk music often provides such a release of feelings. For example, the American folk song "The Praties* They Grow Small," which was sung in the 1840s by Irish immigrants, has these words:

*Potatoes.

O, I wish that we were geese, night and
     morn, night and morn,
O, I wish that we were geese, for they fly
     and take their ease,
And they live and die in peace eatin'
     corn, eatin' corn.
O, we're trampled in the dust over here,
     over here,
O, we're trampled in the dust, but the
     Lord in whom we trust
Will give us crumb for crust, over here,
     over here.

Love songs and lullabies are also expressions of deep and personal feelings.

Music is often used as recreation; a song sung for the sheer fun of it is one example. There is a difference between recreational music and the expression of feelings that were just described. Emotional release implies the easing of some deep psychological need, while recreation implies refreshing or relaxing activity—mere diversion or frivolity. Here is an example from folk music:

O, the deacon went down to the cellar to
     pray,
He found a jug and stayed all day.
O, the Deacon went down to the cellar to
     pray,
He found a jug and he stayed all day.
I won't grieve my Lord no more.
I ain't a-gonna grieve my Lord no more.
     (repeat two more times)

The use of music to accompany work is less common in the United States than in some other cultures. In Africa songs are an accompaniment to almost all activities, including paddling a canoe and hunting animals. The music provides rhythmic support for a recurrent physical action.

Another use of music is to invoke divine action. The rain dance of the American Indian is one example of this. The difference between this type of music and the music that contributes to an atmosphere of worship is the fact that the rain dance is believed to have magical significance and is expected to yield a certain result.

Background music in a motion picture, the chant at a rain dance, the hymn and anthem in a religious service, a popular song, the song calling for social action, and the ever-present music in public places all have a purpose that is easy to understand. That purpose is to fulfill some need apart from the music itself—to produce rain, to promote social justice, to express feelings, and so on. The quality of the music is considered secondary to the desired outcome. If one long monotonous sound will bring rain or inspire people onward in a cause, then one long sound will be considered sufficiently musical to do the job.

Art Music

There is a type of music that does not have the easily understood goals described so far. It is music that people listen to because they find it intellectually fascinating and psychologically satisfying. It is music that is contemplated; it is thought about studiously and considered with undivided attention. This "music for listening" is generally referred to as *art music*. The term does not mean music that is associated with paintings or sculpture; *art* has a broader meaning than that. The term *fine arts* refers to objects that are created simply for the visual or aural satisfaction they offer. There is no practical reason for the existence of art music and no extramusical purpose that it's supposed to achieve. It exists solely for what it is.

Something that has no practical value and is important in and of itself—many people find this hard to understand. How can something have value if it doesn't do anything for us? Most things are created because we have some use for them. We say they are *functional*, because they do a definite job. But with music and the other fine arts it's different. Painting, sculpture, ballet, poetry, literature, and music exist only for the interest and fascination they hold for people. They have psychological—not functional—relevance.

Why do people create nonfunctional objects whose value lies in the intellectual and psychological satisfaction people find in them? That is a difficult question to answer. There are a number of speculative theories. One thing is known, however. Such creation is a distinctly *human* activity; it's one aspect of living that makes humans different from the animals. The valuing of an object for its intellectual and psychological satisfaction seems to call for a higher form of mental activity than animals possess. As far as can be determined, animals have no sonnets, sonatas, or sculptures.

The difference between humans and animals is the difference between the words *exist* and *live*. Somehow people want to do more than exist. They don't want to merely survive in a cave and grub roots for food. The fine arts help make a difference between existing and living. Humans notice sights and sounds and have feelings about them. And they find life richer because of these feelings.

The arts are not humans' only attempt to live rather than exist. Recreation—playing tennis or cards, for example—is also an attempt to enjoy life. The difference between recreation and contemplation of the arts is that the fine arts involve a type of thinking. The arts call for mentally standing off and contemplating an object.

Why is the word *fine* coupled with the term *arts*? To answer that question think back to your elementary school days when you decorated a paper plate or carved a figure on a potato for block printing. Would you consider these efforts to be fine works of art? Probably not. Why? Weren't they sincere human creations? Well, yes, but they weren't really *that* good. Most people can do much the same thing. The arts-crafts project didn't represent unusual skill, devotion, or talent, at least not enough to be considered "fine" or to be valued as being above and beyond the ordinary. If nearly everyone can do something, it may be art, but it is not fine art. Epic poems, symphonies, and marble sculptures, when skillfully created, are of value partly because very few people have the talent and energy to create them.

Music and Culture

Music and the other arts are created by people for people. The patterns of sound called *music* were not preordained in the dim past, with the musician's task being the discovery of those patterns. A search for the perfect melody or the lost chord is about as likely to succeed as a search for the pot of gold at the end of the rainbow. People do not look for music; they create it.

Since music is a human creation, it is a part of culture. This means that understanding a culture requires at least some understanding of that culture's music, and vice versa. The interrelationships between the fine arts and culture are important to the extent that if a person is ignorant of his or her culture, he or she is not in the mainstream of its life and feels alien and out of place. Suppose that you move to India. Like most Americans, you would probably find Indian music difficult to understand. But if you are going to live there, you should learn something about the music. If you don't, to that extent you will be more of an outsider in that society. You will find your life in India a little duller, shallower, and less satisfying.

It is to your advantage to learn as much as possible about the music and other fine arts of your culture. And in a day of jet airplanes and instant communication, it is good to learn a little bit about the music and arts of other cultures as well.

"I Know What I Like"

It's a fact: We don't all like the same foods, clothes, cars, or music. Should your preferences in music be strictly a personal matter? In one sense the answer is yes. Feelings are private and personal, and they cannot successfully be imposed or dictated, even in totalitarian societies. And there seems little danger that today's college students will accept without question the opinions of "authorities" about what music is "good" and what isn't.

But the question is more complicated than just personal preferences because people generally like what they know and dislike what they don't know. If there is truth in the phrase "I know what I like," there is also truth in the words "I like what I know." Not only is familiar music enjoyed more, it is heard more fully and accurately. People unfamiliar with a particular type of music simply don't hear some of its subtleties. Music is very much intertwined with culture, and culture is the product of a large group of people. So while each person has feelings about what he or she hears, these feelings are strongly influenced by cultural conditioning.

To demonstrate the effect of a familiar style on one's reaction to music, the *Record Album* that supplements this book contains two versions of the same music, "Bourrée" (pronounced boo-*ray*) by J. S. Bach. The original version is played on a keyboard instrument called the harpsichord (discussed more fully in Chapter 7) and has no accompanying instruments providing a rhythmic backup. The other version was devised for a vocal group called The Swingle Singers, who have performed contemporary-sounding renditions of many "classical" numbers, including this Bourrée (which they titled "Bourrée for Bach"). This version does have a rhythmic backup, what many people call a "beat," and the singers sing the melody on modern-sounding syllables such as doo-ba, doo-ba. Essentially, the use of the syllables and the backup rhythm are the only differences from the original, but chances are that the vocal version sounds more familiar, and therefore will be liked better, than the original harpsichord version. It is interesting to compare your reactions to the two versions and to consider analytically what the musical differences are. The original harpsichord version will be discussed again in Chapter 13.

The fact that knowledge and preference are two sides of the same coin has some important implications. First, it means that you should know something about a type of music before you make up your mind about whether or not you like it. You should be a student first and a judge second. Next, it means that there are no inherently inferior types of music, only types that are unknown to you. (Individual pieces within a certain type may be inferior.) Third, part of the knowledge to be acquired about music is that some kinds are created chiefly for listening, while other types exist mainly to advance nonmusical outcomes. Music is used for a variety of purposes. This information should affect how you consider a particular type of music. Fourth, when some musical works seem more worthy of careful attention than others, the difference usually lies in terms of a particular culture and in the purpose of the music. Few pieces of art music are suitable for performance at a pep rally or singing around a campfire, and few school fight songs or campfire songs are fascinating pieces for careful listening. Arabian or Japanese music doesn't fit American concepts of music and vice versa.

Usually the musical works that offer the greatest listening rewards are those that require some effort to get to know. Pieces that are easily comprehended on one or two hearings are usually too superficial and trite to hold our attention, and we soon become bored with them. Musical works that will live for more than a few months need to contain qualities that are familiar to us, but at the same time they must have something that doesn't follow exactly expected patterns. Of course, if there is nothing the listener recognizes as being musical, then the sounds are just a jumble. (If the listener becomes familiar with the work, it may turn out to be a meaningful piece of music, but this isn't always true.) A good piece—one that is satisfying and interesting to listen to—contains a balanced mixture of something familiar and something unfamiliar.

Although it is perfectly natural to like some musical works better than others, personal preferences should not keep you from music that you might find interesting and satisfying if you knew about it. Personal preferences should not be so narrow that you are left out of a portion of your society and culture.

Music and the Fine Arts

There are two reasons for considering music and the other fine arts together. Most important is the fact that they exist for essentially the same reason: their ability to be interesting and satisfying in and of themselves for purposes of contemplation. We look at a painting for much the same reason that we listen to a piece of music or view and listen to a ballet. A similar mental outlook is required for each.

The second reason for grouping the arts together is the fact that they are all products of culture. Works of art created under similar cultures and circumstances often show similar characteristics. For example, people in the twentieth century are fascinated with machines; this fascination is evident to some degree in the arts. There are the metal sculptures of Alexander Calder (this page) and others, the architectural paintings of Piet Mondrian (whose painting "Broadway Boogie-Woogie" is colorplate IV), and the musical sounds created by synthesizers and unconventional instruments such as brake drums. To understand one art is, to a limited degree, to understand the other arts. These commonly held outlooks are explored and explained at various points in this book, especially in the chapters on style periods.

Sometimes the arts are linked together in ways that are inaccurate. One such way is to draw misleading parallels among factors in the arts. For example, you sometimes encounter statements such as, "just as the vaulting arch rests upon the columns, so melody unfolds above the supporting chords." To begin with, melody can exist perfectly well by itself without chords. Sometimes the melody is in the middle of the chords or below them. Besides, chords are pitches sounded simultaneously, so the appearance of the notes stacked up vertically on a page of music is merely the way our culture notates music, not a representation of an architectural support. Simultaneous sounds can't hold up anything.

Music exists in time, and visual arts exist in space; time and space are two different dimensions. We cannot establish a direct relationship between them any more than we can draw a picture of two minutes of time. A composer of music works with sounds in time; the painter paints on a two-dimensional surface; the sculptor works in three-dimensional space. All of these creative artists manipulate their materials for artistic purposes. This they have in common, but not the dimension of their work.

The Redskin by Alexander Calder. This stabile stands in front of the Musical Arts Center, Indiana University, Bloomington, Indiana.

Many of the terms are used differently among the arts. For example, rhythm in music is merely the ongoing movement of the sounds in terms of time. In art it is a repeated pattern. A line in music is a series of pitches with one sounding after the other; in art it is a distinct mark of some length, or a direction in which the eye is encouraged to travel. The word *color* is used by both artists and musicians, but no direct relationship is possible —a clarinet tone is not the color green, for example.

Each art has techniques and challenges that aren't found in other arts. Outlooks and values may carry from one to another, and culture may exert influence in a particular direction. But an attempt to draw direct parallels is misleading and will cause you to miss out on some of what each art can offer.

Copyright © 1958 by United Feature Syndicate, Inc. Used by permission.

Hearing and/or Listening to Music

As has been pointed out, music is a very common commodity in America today, and people desire and use it for many reasons. A crucial question is: Which use of music requires careful listening and giving total and undivided attention to the musical sounds? When music is used as background or atmosphere, it is regarded superficially if at all. So we don't give careful and undivided attention to music that is played for us in an air terminal or that comes over the radio as we clean the house. When music is used as group identification, the musical sounds themselves are less important than what they represent. When music serves as recreation, emotional release, or an invocation for divine action, one doesn't usually contemplate its sounds carefully. When music is intended as an object of contemplation, however, it should be given undivided attention. Listening is the only reason for the existence of this type of music.

There is a difference between *hearing* and *listening*. When trained musicians use the word *listen*, they do not mean merely hearing, just being aware of sound. They refer to an activity involving keen concentration.

It is clear that most of the music heard every day doesn't need to be listened to carefully, although of course we can listen to it carefully if we want to. Most of it is not meant to be given undivided attention. Most of the music that surrounds us fulfills its function without the listener's being particularly aware of its properties.

Because skill in listening is vital if you are to understand and enjoy art music, this book devotes an entire chapter to the topic. In addition, it includes Listening Guides designed to develop listening skills. Further aids are the supplementary materials entitled *A Concise Introduction to Music Listening Record Album* and *Study Guide and Scores for A Concise Introduction to Music Listening*.

Two

Learning to Listen

While in college I had the good fortune to take an art appreciation course. One day the instructor projected a Rembrandt painting on the wall and proceeded to point out Rembrandt's genius in his treatment of light and shadow, the overall design, the brushwork for the hands of one of the figures, and similar features. After 15 or 20 minutes I was struck by the fact that every feature of the painting was there when I had first looked at it. They were there before his explanation, but I hadn't been aware of them; I had looked but not really seen. I realized then that I needed to be taught to see all that a fine painting has to offer.

It is similar with music. Most people need to be educated to hear what a fine piece of music has to offer in terms of listening satisfaction. The purpose of this chapter is to provide such help.

Attitude

It may seem strange to make attitude a prime requisite for appreciation of an art. But it is essential. You are the only person who can make yourself pay attention, who can center your listening on one part of the music, who can make yourself remember a musical pattern. No book or instructor can do this for you.

What makes up the attitude necessary for increased musical understanding? One part of it is the willingness to make an effort. It requires effort to move beyond a superficial acquaintance with music and to understand what it has to offer. Diligence and concentration are necessary while learning.

A second aspect of attitude is the acknowledgement that you are dealing with something subtle and complex. If music were too simple, too obvious, it would not be successful art music. Certainly an art that reaches to the very roots of people's psychological nature isn't going to be understood all at once.

Another feature of proper attitude is tolerance toward all music. Some of the music discussed in this book may be new to you and some of it may seem strange. But if you are openminded, if you assume the integrity of the creative artist and give yourself a chance to understand the work, your chances of growing to like the music are greatly increased.

Perhaps the most fundamental feature of attitude is a basic interest in hearing and understanding what composers do with sound. How do they organize it? What are they trying to do? Factual knowledge may help you answer these questions, but it can't replace careful listening.

Learning to listen is a matter more of wanting to understand the music than learning the techniques for understanding music. Without the desire and effort no amount of technique will succeed.

Types of Listening

There are three somewhat interrelated types of listening. The first can be termed *sensuous*. This delicious word means "of or appealing to the senses." In music it refers to the purely physical effect that music has on its listeners —the chill running up the spine, the tapping of the foot, the sheer pleasure of a beautiful sound.

Hearing is an action involving a sense organ. Sounds are physical in nature. So the sensuous pleasures of music aren't intellectually profound. They aren't to be downgraded, however. There is real pleasure to be gained from listening to even a single long tone on a violin or a French horn, just as there is pleasure in looking at a beautiful blue color in a picture. Sensuous pleasures are one of music's attractions, and the more you are aware of them the more you will enjoy music.

It is a mistake to think that sensuous effects are the main thing in music. An emphasis solely on sensuous qualities eliminates from consideration many musical works of much merit. What's worse, dependence on sheer sensuous effects leads to a dead end. The listener grows accustomed to one effect and so searches for another piece with even greater physical impact. This cycle leads finally to music that is simply orgiastic. When music reaches this point, it has lost most of its artistic quality. Music of lasting value is more than an aural roller-coaster ride or cold shower.

The second type of listening involves feeling or mood. It is sometimes called the *expressive* level. There can be little doubt that music has expressive power. Music frequently can relate to something the listener thinks or feels. A particular phrase may evoke a psychological reaction nearly identical to the reaction to some event in life. But music is limited in its ability to designate specific thoughts that can be interpreted in words. For example, music may give an impression of sadness, but it cannot describe what is causing the feeling. Nor can it define objects. For most people, one sound does not represent *clouds*, another *bread*, and another *wheel*. Music can provide general moods, but not specific thoughts.

The indefiniteness of music is to its advantage. One musical work may be heard by a thousand people, but each will hear it in a slightly different way, depending on the individual's inclinations. But even more important, music can break through the barrier of words. Words are too brittle, too inflexible, too conventional to allow for full expression. Between the words *anger* and *rage,* for example, there are infinite shades of meaning. Also, anger is usually coupled with frustration or sadness, or both. As a feeling becomes more complex, it is harder to describe. When a loved one dies, a person feels emptiness, grief, remorse, and powerlessness. But these feelings cannot be fully communicated to someone else, no matter how many words are used or how carefully the words are chosen.

The third type of listening involves concentrating on what happens in the music—what notes are being played, at what speed, in combination with what other notes, on what instruments in what range, and so on. It is often called the *musical* level, and it is in this type of listening that the more musical values are realized. It's here that the listener reaches the most sophisticated stage of musical experience, a stage in which understanding of the sounds and their characteristics is unhampered by physical response or a search for expressive meaning. Achievement of this type of listening requires more education, but it also offers greater rewards. So this book concentrates primarily on developing this type of listening.

Improving Listening Skill

There are several things you can do to increase your listening ability. The suggestions here are general, and they are not presented in order of importance.

1. Improve your memory for music.   Memory is absolutely necessary for the comprehension of music. At any particular instant all that can be heard is one sound. This may be a single tone or several tones occurring simultaneously. In any case, it can be perceived only briefly, for time moves on, and other sounds are heard in succeeding moments. The only way to make sense out of these brief and apparently isolated aural experiences is to use the phenomena of memory and anticipation. Even anticipation is a memory activity in that it involves a prediction of what will happen in the future based on what has happened in the past.

Visual experiences don't rely basically on the element of time. The graphic arts, for example, aren't involved in time. An entire picture can be seen in a moment. (Closer analysis and full appreciation will require a longer period of viewing, of course.) But suppose that memory and anticipation are made an integral part of the viewing experience. It might be done as follows: Assume you are to see an unfamiliar picture that is entirely covered except for a thin slit running vertically. Then the slit is drawn slowly across the picture. Your knowledge of the picture will have to be derived solely from (1) your memory of what you have seen, (2) the slit-sized portion you are presently viewing, and (3) your guess as to what will be revealed in succeeding moments. Difficult? Yes. But that's the way music is perceived. That's why memory is so necessary in understanding it.

As a general rule, the more frequently you engage in an activity involving memory, the better your skill at recall will become. Think again of the picture analogy. The fifth time the slit is drawn across the picture, you will have a much clearer idea of what the picture is like. The same is true of music. The more you hear a piece, the better you will remember it and the more fully you will understand it. Repeated hearing of a musical work is about the surest way to gain greater understanding

of it. In fact, with many musically interesting works, repeated hearings are necessary in order to reach a satisfactory degree of understanding.

Sometime when you are listening to a recording by yourself, select short portions for repeated listening. This practice is especially useful in places that sound like a jumble of sound to you. Between playings attempt to run through the portion in your mind. Shut your eyes and try to rehear in your own mind what you previously heard. Repeat this process of actual and imagined hearings, several times if necessary, until your mental rendition of the portion is accurate.

2. Concentrate on main themes and the important musical ideas.   When listening to a work that is new to you, especially if you are not particularly experienced at listening to art music, don't try to comprehend everything the first time. Learning to listen is like learning to drive a car. When you first learn to drive, your total attention is directed toward executing a few basic actions; your primary goal is to keep the car on the road and avoid hitting other cars or pedestrians. With increased experience, however, you find you can safely do other things —glance at the scenery or carry on a conversation with a passenger. Had you tried to do all this too early in your training, a catastrophe might have occurred!

How can you distinguish the important features of a piece before hearing it? In this book the main themes and sections are indicated for you. A "roadmap" or "guided tour" of the composition is provided in 16 Listening Guides. If you are listening at a concert or to a recording of a work not covered in these books, you can read the notes on the concert program or record jacket. Such commentary can be extremely helpful, if it is well written.

3. Hear as much detail as possible.   Although following single aspects of the music is helpful, don't stop there. Musical works written for artistic reasons have many inflections, many subtleties. And as in other phases of life, it's often the little things that make the difference.

A slightly changed chord, a brief interruption of the rhythmic pattern, a new combination of instruments, the sounding of a fragment of the theme—such apparently insignificant techniques can spell the difference between an ordinary piece and an exceptional one.

The overriding reason for hearing as much as possible in a musical work is that the composer intends for *everything* to be heard.

4. Encourage your reactions to music. This suggestion should *not* be taken to mean that

---

Listening Guide

Copland: *Rodeo*

"Hoe-Down"

0:00   Orchestra begins at loud dynamic level and fast tempo; repeats the following figure several times:

0:04   Trumpets and violins exchange a short figure.

0:14   Orchestra plays opening figure again at loud dynamic level.

0:18   Piano and strings play plucked notes patterns that emphasize note off the beat and simple chord changes; woodblock heard.

0:40   First phrase of first theme *(A)* played by upper strings, clarinets, and xylophone; theme includes opening figure:

0:48   Violins begin a "square dance"–like phrase of the melody; brasses and low strings sound chords in off-beat pattern:

0:56   First phrase of theme returns, played by upper strings and xylophone.

---

you should emote or talk to yourself when hearing a piece. Rather, be aware of your feelings about what you hear and let them be active. Consciously notice your responses while listening.

To notice your own reactions to sounds, try this experiment. In a quiet place play on a piano or guitar a series of three or four sounds. Listen for about 3 seconds between groups of sounds to allow you to contemplate what you heard. You probably won't be able to describe exactly what you feel about the

1:04   Second phrase of theme played at high pitch level by violins; followed by oboe and then orchestra; chords off the beat are also heard in brasses and low strings.

1:20   First phrase played again by upper strings, clarinets, and xylophone.

1:36   Opening figure played several times by orchestra.

1:40   Trumpet solo, answered by upper strings, is new theme *(B):*

1:48   Oboe, violins, and clarinet solos continue the *B* theme, followed by trumpet and violins.

2:04   Winds play off-beat figure; answered by violins; idea repeated three more times.

2:14   Violins, oboes, and clarinets begin a second "square-dance" tune; music increases in intensity leading to a sudden break.

2:36   Piano and plucked strings play short section heard very early in the work; music grows softer, slower, and descends in pitch.

2:51   *A* theme, first phrase, returns in violins, xylophone, and clarinets; loud dynamic level.

2:59   Second phrase of theme *A* played at loud level by strings and oboe; brasses and low strings sound chords in off-beat pattern.

3:12   First phrase of *A* theme played again by upper strings; followed by off-beat notes for low strings and French horns and xylophone, and then by even notes for strings and trumpet.

3:30   Closes with same note sounded rapidly and loudly three times.

sounds, but you will have some response. Experiencing your reactions when you listen is one of music's fascinations. In musical compositions, of course, the sounds come at you rapidly, with few silent spots in which to analyze your reactions. Single sounds heard in a gapped series soon become boring.

5. Do not attempt to visualize specific scenes or fantasize. Sometimes students in elementary school are given listening lessons dealing almost exclusively with "program" music—music in which the composer consciously attempts to associate the work with a particular story or scene. This type of music is in many ways well suited to the requirements of guided listening experiences in the early grades. Unfortunately, however, students sometimes begin to assume that for every piece there must be a picture or story. They conclude that music is incomplete or inadequate if it exists alone.

As was pointed out earlier, the best music is most fascinating in terms of sheer sound. Trying to conjure a tender love scene or the image of a ship plowing through the waves only distracts the listener's attention from the sound of the music itself. Instead of listening, the mind is engaged in creating fantasies. Pictorial association can easily become an invitation to daydream. Only keen concentration on the music itself will lead to an understanding of it.

6. Acquire some different listening habits and expectations. By the time they are 18 or so, most people have become very good at *not* listening carefully to music. Music is around us everywhere—in supermarkets, airports, our cars; even the home or dormitory is not without the radio or record player going as dishes are washed or studying attempted. The trouble is that we learn not to pay attention to all that music and sound; we would be mentally exhausted if we tried.

People have also acquired expectations about what music is like. It contains a steady background rhythm, is quite loud, lasts about 2 minutes and 30 seconds, states its musical ideas right off and does not attempt to develop or vary them to any extent. However, many works of music, especially art music, violate all these expectations. Musical ideas are strung out over many minutes, as if the music were progressing in slow motion. The music is often soft and subtle. Musical ideas are not stated obviously, and they are often subjected to all sorts of manipulation and variation. Therefore, if you are going to listen to art music more effectively in the future, it will be necessary to shake off some of the habits and expectations that you have acquired about music over the past 15 or more years.

7. Apply the knowledge your acquire about music to the music you hear. Information about musical forms, styles, compositional devices, and the like helps one to listen more effectively to music. Knowledge *and* listening skill are both needed.

Information about music will also help you avoid the disappointment of trying to find a quality in a musical work that is not supposed to be there in the first place. For example, Mozart wrote music that is tasteful, well designed, and beautiful. He lived in an age that esteemed the tasteful, the well designed, and the beautiful; flamboyant emotional display wasn't in style. So if you listen to his music expecting to be overwhelmed by lush harmonies and sensuous melodies, you will be disappointed.

8. Practice learning to listen to music more effectively. If you have decided that you want to improve your skill in listening to music (the matter of attitude mentioned earlier in the chapter), you need to practice listening just as you would need to practice tennis if you wanted to improve your tennis game. This book offers two ways to practice listening. The 16 Listening Guides that appear at various places in the book provide an outline of the main features of a work, such as changes of melody, prominent solos, and so on. On the left-hand side of the guide appears the time at which the feature will appear in the recording in the supplementary *Record Album.** Other

---

*Time notations are given in minutes and seconds. For example, 2:30 means 2 minutes, 30 seconds.

recordings will have similar but not identical timings. (Whether you follow a watch or clock as you listen is a matter of personal preference.) Listen to the recording while following the Listening Guide as many times as you need to be able to follow along without losing your place. When you can listen and keep your place in the guide, you can be reasonably sure that you are hearing the main features of the work, although the more subtle aspects may remain to be uncovered by later listening efforts. Probably it is not wise to listen to any work more than twice in one day; spread the listening practice out over a number of days by doing a little bit each day rather than "cramming" immediately before examinations.

The first Listening Guide, on pages 10–11, is for Aaron Copland's "Hoe-Down" from his ballet *Rodeo*. That work will be discussed in more detail in Chapter 15, but you can begin listening practice now with this work.

The second way this book helps you practice listening is through the simplified line scores that appear in the supplementary *Study Guide and Scores*. These scores take the 20 or more lines of an orchestral score and reduce them to one or sometimes two lines that present the most noticeable and significant aspect of the music at that point. Also, they indicate the instruments heard most clearly and describe the form and other features. While you may not be able to read music, you will probably be able to follow a line score as you listen. As with the Listening Guides, it is suggested that you listen as many times as needed until you can follow the music without getting lost.

Tests of Good Listening

How can you tell if you are hearing a piece of music fully and accurately? There's no easy answer, but you can ask yourself these practical questions:

Does the music seem sensible in its own way?

Does it move along without seeming dead and stagnant?

Am I hearing specific details of form, rhythm, and melody?

Have I kept my attention focused on the music all the time?

Do I get some reactions or feelings from the music as I hear it?

Do I like to listen to the music? Do I enjoy it? Does it seem interesting?

Do I want to hear the work again?

If your answer to all these questions is yes, there can be little doubt that you are hearing the music. Composers intend for their music to be enjoyed, to be found interesting and meaningful. They mean for their skill at handling music to be appreciated, and they want to produce something that will have lasting attraction. In most cases they realize that music will cause reactions in the listener. When you hear the music fully and with feeling, you are understanding it.

The Descent from the Cross *by Rembrandt van Ryn. (Widener Collection, National Gallery of Art, Washington, D.C.)*

Section One

What Music Is Made Of

The question of what music is made of is a logical place to begin a study of the subject. Since you already know something about music, you might try this short quiz about the elements that are combined to form music. Decide whether the following statements are true or false.

1. A musical work must include high and low notes. *T F*

2. All music proceeds through a period of time. *T F*

3. All musical works tell a story or describe something in everyday life. *T F*

4. Every sound has some level of loudness. *T F*

5. In order to be considered "music," sounds must be written down in notation. *T F*

6. All sounds have some type of tone quality. *T F*

7. Musical sounds must be organized. *T F*

8. Music must have a pulse or throb that you can tap your foot to. *T F*

9. A change in any element of music (speed, tone quality, loudness, etc.) affects the overall impression of the music. *T F*

10. Because the physical properties of sound can be measured scientifically, music can be judged scientifically. *T F*

Five of the statements are true and five are false. Each one will be answered at an appropriate place in Chapter 3. What is significant here is that each item relates to what is necessary for music. An understanding of each musical element aids in knowing more about music. So the first section of this book discusses each element in some detail.

Three

The Material of Music

Music is one form of sound. Quite a lot is known about sound. A stimulus acts to set in motion the molecules in the air. The molecules bump into one another, something like billiard balls on a table, each setting the next in motion. This chain reaction continues until the molecules strike the eardrum, where the nervous system picks up the impulses and transmits them to the brain. But not all sounds are music. So merely exploring the physical nature of sound isn't going to answer the question of what is necessary for music.

Pitch and Melody

Music usually (but not always) contains sounds of different *pitch*. Pitch in music refers to the quality of highness or lowness of sound. It depends on the frequency of the molecular vibrations. The faster the motion of the molecules, the higher the pitch is.

A *melody* is a cohesive series or line of pitches. These pitches must "hang together" if the melody is to be any good. Not any series of pitches will do. Whether a series of pitches seems cohesive or not depends on the perception and mental ability of the individual hearing the sounds and not on some law in nature.

Since no one understands the processes of the brain precisely, it is impossible to determine scientifically if a series of pitches forms a melody. So statement 10 on page 10 is false. Music has physical properties that can be measured scientifically, but it's much more than that.

When some people think of music, they think first of a tune or melody. In one sense they are right, because most music does have a melody. Although most music involves different pitches and some type of melody, these elements aren't necessary in every musical work. Some sounds of indefinite pitch have been placed on tape as musical compositions. Also, some musical instruments, such as snare drums, have no definite pitch, as is mentioned in Chapter 7, yet they can play solos of considerable complexity and interest. So the first statement is false. Most compositions have higher and lower notes, but they are not always necessary.

Melodies are affected by a number of musical factors. First, melodies are played on an instrument or sung. The features of the voice or instrument—its tone quality and adaptability to the requirements of the melody—contribute to or detract from the effect of the melody itself. Second, since melodies must exist in a dimension of time, they all have rhythm. Third, most melodies tend to center about one particular pitch. There is a sense in which music moves away from and returns to a "home" pitch. More will be said about this important fact in the discussion of harmony later in this chapter. Fourth, other music usually precedes and follows the melody, and this musical context influences the listener's impression of the melody. Fifth, almost all melodies have other pitches sounded with them. The kind of accompaniment or the nature of melodies occurring at the same time can make a big difference in the musical results. So statement 9 on page 15 is true.

Counterpoint

Pitches are frequently sounded together in music. One way in which this happens is for two melodies to be sounded at the same time, or for the same melody to be sounded at two slightly different times, as in *rounds* such as "Row, Row, Row Your Boat" and "Are You Sleeping?" The term for such simultaneous sounding of two or more melodies is *counterpoint*. *Counter* implies contrary or contrasting, and *point* is a carryover from hundreds of years ago when musical notes were called points. The adjective form of counterpoint is *contrapuntal*.

Harmony

The other way to sound pitches together is to create *harmony*. Harmony is somewhat like a backdrop on a stage. It adds to the total effect, but your main attention isn't centered on it. Most of the melodies we know are *harmonized*—given a backdrop of other pitches to make the music sound more complete. Harmony doesn't mean that the combination of pitches is necessarily pleasing. So the use of the word in music differs from its use in everyday life.

Harmony refers to the combination of pitches at any given instant, while counterpoint implies attention to lines as they progress together. In both harmony and counter-point pitches sound at the same instant, and yet they also progress in terms of time. The difference between them is one of viewpoint.

Most harmony consists of *chords*—three or more pitches sounded together. These pitches are usually selected according to a definite pattern. The most common pattern involves every other note above a basic sound, somewhat in the manner of the black and red squares on a checkerboard. Generally the melody is in the higher pitches in a piece, while the harmony is in the lower pitches.

Most music in Western civilization (Europe and America) starts from and returns to a tonal center, which is called the *tonic*. This tonic is something like the home office of a business concern. There may be branch offices at other places, but the activity of the company is centered at the home office. In music the identity of the tonic, and the activity going to and from it, create the feeling of *key* or *tonality*. Tonality is the framework within which harmonic motion occurs, and it's what makes a chord seem logical or illogical.

The key can change during a piece, and often it does. The term for a change of key is *modulation*. If handled properly, changes of key make the music more interesting and "fresh." The continuous use of one tonal center becomes tiring, a problem apparent in Scottish bagpipe music because the instrument can't play in more than one key. Modulation should not be confused with changes of chords. Chords change often within a key; a modulation occurs only when there is a definite movement to another tonal center.

Time

Music has been described as a "time art." That is, it exists in a span of time, not in physical space as do arts such as painting and sculpture. Therefore, statement 2 on page 15 is true. All musical works do move through a period of time.

The word that refers to the flow of music in terms of time is *rhythm*. It does not refer only to a recurrent pattern, orderly movement, or a repeated situation, as it sometimes does in everyday usage. The word *rhythm* is a broad term that has several aspects.

One such aspect is *beat*, which many people incorrectly consider a synonym for rhythm. The beat is the recurrent throb or pulse that makes you want to move along with the music. The beat is more strongly felt in some pieces than in others, but it's present most of the time. In fact, if by some mechanical means "Hoe-Down" were to be produced without a feeling of beat, the listener would tend to put one there. If you have any trouble feeling the beat in music, play the opening of "Hoe-Down" again and tap along with your finger or foot.

Beats can be fast, slow, or moderate. The musical term for the speed of the beat (not the speed of the notes) is *tempo*. The word in Italian literally means time. The composer suggests the desired tempo, but the performer can interpret it somewhat differently. For example, some pieces can be thought of in a pattern of two slow beats, or four fast beats. In either case the music consumes the same amount of time. The listener's impression of the music is changed slightly, however.

Most beats in music are steady for relatively long periods of time (a minute or more). There are changes from section to section and some gradual changes in the music, but certainly the beat is not erratic, with frequent starting and stopping. In only a few styles is much irregularity allowed, and even there its use is limited. Erratic changes in tempo sound disorganized and are annoying.

The beat is the unit of measurement by which the duration of a musical tone is judged. In music a tone is not designated as lasting for three seconds or one half minute. It is thought of as lasting for several beats, one beat, or a fraction of a beat.

In most music, beats are organized into patterns called *meter*. There is a natural human tendency to organize sounds into patterns. The sound of a clock becomes "tick-tock" in our minds, even when all the sounds are the same. Meters are created by emphasizing certain beats: "ONE–two, ONE–two" gives the listener a two-beat pattern; "ONE–two–three, ONE–two–three" gives a three-beat feeling,

and so on. Poetry often reveals patterns (called iambic, trochaic, etc.). Here is an example from Stephen Vincent Benét's "The Ballad of William Sycamore":*

> My fáther, he wás a móuntaineer,
>
> His físt was a knótty hámmer;
>
> He was quíck on his féet as a rúnning
>   deer,
>
> And he spóke with a Yánkee stámmer.

Each metrical pattern in music is called a *measure*, with the emphasized beat being the first of each measure. Short pieces may have 16 measures or fewer, while longer pieces have hundreds of measures.

Not all pieces of music need to have a beat or meter. Therefore, statement 8 on page 15 is false. Those pieces for tape recorders that were mentioned earlier often have no beat. Neither does some folk music, especially that from the Orient. And there are several types of music in our culture that have no regular beat.

Dynamics

All sounds have some degree of loudness and softness. Statement 4 on page 15 is true. The musical term for the levels of loudness and softness is *dynamics*. In most music the level of dynamics is constantly changing, something like the surface of the ocean. The term for a gradual buildup of sound is *crescendo*, and its opposite is *decrescendo*. These are Italian words that mean simply to get louder and to get softer.

Dynamics is an important aspect of *phrasing*. The term *phrasing* refers to the way that musical segments, called *phrases*, are presented by a performer. The phrases in music are somewhat comparable to the phrases and clauses in language. By skillful gradation of

---

*From *Ballads and Poems: 1915–1930* by Stephen Vincent Benét. Copyright 1913 by Stephen Vincent Benét. Copyright © 1959 by Rosemary Carr Benét. Reprinted by permission of Holt, Rinehart and Winston, Inc.

dynamics, by emphasizing some notes more than others, and by subtle changes of speed in music, the performer can give a more meaningful performance of the music.

Timbre

Every sound has a distinctive quality to it, which makes statement 6 on page 15 also true. In musical terminology the word for tone quality is *timbre* (pronounced *tam*-ber or *tim*-ber). Each voice and each type of musical instrument has its own unique tone "color." Three people singing the same note in the same way will each produce a different quality. The same is true when different types of musical instruments sound an identical pitch.

Timbre is an important musical element. Often the most significant difference among types of music is not in the rhythm or the melody but in the timbre. In recent years composers have become even more intrigued with timbre. They are exploring sounds other than those made on conventional musical instruments, which already offer a myriad of possibilities. Different qualities of sound can form the basis of entire pieces of music that contain little else except tone colors produced in a planned order and span of time. Although such pieces may seem strange the first time you hear them, they demonstrate the inventiveness of the human mind and the vast possibilities available through the use of tone color.

Organized Sounds: Music

So far it has been pointed out that musical sounds possess duration, dynamic level, timbre, and usually pitch. What else is necessary? One more thing: the *sounds must be organized*. Statement 7 on page 15 is true—definitely. This point was briefly mentioned in the discussion of melody, but it also applies to the larger concept of music. In 1962 the British Broadcasting Company played a deliberate trick on its listeners. It announced that it would play a work by an unknown Polish composer named Zak. Then for some minutes the studio technicians walked around banging and rattling whatever they could. Fortunately for their professional reputations, the critics thought the piece was awful. Why weren't "Zak's" sounds really music? They had no structure, no organization, no plan.

A sense of organization is the essential ingredient in making music. Composers or creators of the music must put all the elements together. If they don't, they have produced another "Zak" composition. Clearly, this quality of organization can't be measured, so statement 10 is false, as was pointed out earlier.

The elements that constitute music have now been presented. With this information in mind, we can identify two more false answers on page 15. Statement 3 is false because mere sound cannot tell a story, a point already made in Chapter 2—only words can tell a story. And statement 5 is false because notation is merely a way of symbolizing sound. It can't replace sound.

There's a type of psychology called Gestalt that states as its maxim, "The whole is greater than the sum of its parts." This idea certainly applies to music. So the seventh is the most important true statement in the quiz. Each element is important, but for music to come into being, the elements must be organized into a logical and interesting whole.

Four

Musical Rhythm

Music rhythm is basically a physical phenomenon; it is felt. To know that the beat is a recurrent pulse in music is a long way from feeling it as a driving force in a musical work. Rhythm, like life itself, is something that one experiences. While this is true of nearly everything in music, it is especially true of rhythm.

Beats and Notes

The speed of the beats and the speed of the notes are not the same thing. They are related, of course. A fast tempo usually has more notes in a given span of time, but not always. Even though a piece may have a rapid tempo, the sounds may be in long note values, giving an impression of slowness. And the opposite can happen: A phrase of music with a slow tempo may have short note values and appear to be quite fast. Other things being equal, a note will last longer at a slow tempo than at a fast tempo.

In most music the sounding of the notes themselves provides the only clue as to where the beats occur. A drum doesn't need to tap out the beat so that the listener can feel the pulse of the music. Most of the time the note patterns fit the underlying metrical pattern. If

this doesn't happen, the music has been incorrectly written. Putting the measure lines in the wrong place is like putting the periods and commas in the wrong place when writing a paragraph. Imagine reading: "The music of Bach is. Very interesting to, hear it makes much. Use of. . . ."

But if a piece of music always follows a predictable pattern, it doesn't have much rhythmic interest. In such music the composer must make sure there is enough that is interesting in the harmony and melody so that the listener will want to hear it. Much of this chapter is concerned with how musicians create deviations in the regular rhythmic patterns to make the music more exciting and fascinating to hear.

Syncopation

Sometimes the composer or performer deliberately misplaces the rhythmic emphasis and puts emphasis—called *accent* in music—where it's not expected or removes it where it is expected. This alteration of the accents is termed *syncopation*. It appears in most types of music to some extent, but it's especially prominent in jazz and twentieth-century music. In the song

"Dixie" there is syncopation on that word in the phrase "I wish I was in Dixie." If you sing the word *Dixie* in that phrase so that the second syllable occurs exactly on the second beat, it will be a duller piece of music.

Many popular songs contain a kind of syncopation. The normal pattern for accented and unaccented beats in two- and four-beat meter is *1 2 3 4,* or *1 and 2 and.* However, many popular songs have those beats performed 1 2 3 4, or 1 *and* 2 *and.* The first theme in the first movement of Beethoven's *Pathétique* Sonata (page 110) contains syncopation when the second note in the third measure occurs off the beat.

Alterations in Regular Meter

Sometimes composers choose not to follow a regular metrical pattern. To achieve rhythmic interest, they establish a somewhat regular pattern, then change it just enough to make the music more interesting. Not all music that maintains a regular beat is dull; not by any means. But something different is nice once in a while, too. A good example of the technique of *mixed meter* can be seen in *The Rite of Spring* by Igor Stravinsky. A simplified score for this music appears in the back of the *Study Guide and Scores* that supplements this book. At about measure 248 (the measure numbers appear for every 10 measures in small boxes above the line) a section called "Dance of Abduction" begins. The work is also included in the *Record Album* that supplements this book.

Notice how at about measure 280 the meter changes with almost every measure.

It's possible to combine two or more melodies that have different patterns of accents. When two rhythmic patterns are combined without any consistent change of meter, the result is called *polyrhythm.* If the meter is changed for several measures, it is called *polymeter.* The difference between the two terms is slight. For example, the melody of a piece may not follow the same metrical pattern as the accompanying chords. They might be in a steady four-beat pattern, while the melody is in a three-beat pattern or changes meter every so often. The effect of polyrhythm or polymeter can be quite exciting. And it's a challenge for a pianist when one meter is played in the right hand and another meter in the left.

"Mambo" and "Cha-Cha" from West Side Story

Almost no single musical work includes all the different aspects of rhythm discussed in this chapter, but Leonard Bernstein's two dances from *West Side Story* are excellent examples with which to summarize a discussion of rhythm. Both "Mambo" and "Cha-Cha" are Latin American dance patterns, and both are incorporated in the original Broadway version of the musical in a dance sequence called "The Dance at the Gym."

"Mambo" certainly demonstrates the excitement that rhythm can create. It achieves this partly through a rather fast tempo, although that is not the main reason for the tremendous energy of the music. The more important causes are the simultaneous appearance of more than one rhythmic pattern and the frequent and rapid use of syncopation. The color provided by the trumpets, voices, and percussion also contribute to the overall sense of excitement.

"Mambo" is filled with examples of interesting rhythmic writing, but perhaps the best one appears at about 1:11 into the recording in the *Record Album*. In this example the notes are placed so that the progression of sound at any point can be seen from the pat-

tern of sixteenth notes at the top. These fly by at the rate of *four* in *less* than *half a second!* (The chevron-shaped mark indicates an accented note.)

The "Cha-Cha" is the opposite of "Mambo." It contains a little syncopation, but it is quite subtle. The four-beat meter is followed regularly. Actually, much of the rhythmic interest of "Cha-Cha" lies in the rests, in which finger snapping takes place on the recording in the *Record Album*. The melody, by the way, is a version of the song "Maria," which appears a little later in the musical.

Five

Melodies and Scales

Scales and melodies both involve the linear aspect of music. They are the sounding of pitches one after another. But the two words are not synonymous. As was pointed out in Chapter 3, a melody is a cohesive series of pitches; it is a group of notes that seems to "hang together." A *scale* is a series of pitches that proceeds upward or downward according to a prescribed pattern of intervals. It's the underlying pattern or "skeleton" of pitches on which the music is built. A scale can be extracted from the music, but it seldom appears intact in a melody. (One exception is "Joy to the World.") The most prominent note in a scale—step 1 in most scales—is the key center.

Scales

Some pieces are known by the name of their key—Prelude in F Sharp Minor, for example. This is a means of identification, and it indicates the importance with which keys were regarded at one time in the history of music. The ability to play scales well is an important part of an instrumentalist's development as a performer. (That's why instrumentalists practice scales so much.) Although the listener doesn't need a detailed knowledge of scales, some in-

formation about them does aid in understanding music.

Theoretically, thousands of scales are possible, but only a few are prevalent today. The basis of these standard scales is the *octave*. An octave is distance between two pitches, one being either double or half the number of vibrations of the other pitch. Not only do the notes of an octave sound similar, they also bear the same letter name. This is why only seven letters of the alphabet are needed for note names. The eighth note in an eight-tone scale must match the first in sound and name, no matter on what note the scale begins. An octave can be split up into any number of pitches, but in the music of Western civilization the division of an octave into 12 equal parts or half steps has been standard for the last several hundred years.

A scale composed of all 12 tones is called a *chromatic* scale. None of its notes is more important than another. Because it conveys no feeling of tonic or "home," the chromatic scale is never the basis for an entire piece of music. (Some styles make use of all 12 tones equally, but they are not built on the chromatic scale, and they have no tonic.)

The two scales most common in Western countries today each involve all seven letters of the musical alphabet in some form. The differences among scales result from adjustments in the pattern of these seven notes. The most frequent pattern is called *major*. It can be played on the piano by sounding consecutively all the white keys from C to C. If you look at the keyboard on page 281, you will see that the white keys E–F and B–C are not separated by a black key. This means they are closer together in pitch than the other white keys. The placement of these *half steps* or *semitones* determines the type of scale. In a major scale the half steps occur between the third and fourth notes and the seventh and eighth notes.

Every *minor* scale has a half step occurring between the second and third notes, rather than between the third and fourth notes. The basic form of a minor scale can be duplicated on the piano by playing on the white keys consecutively from one A to another A. This pattern of whole and half steps is called *natural minor*. There are other types of minor scales involving alterations of the sixth and seventh steps of the scale.

Other types of scale patterns using the same seven notes within the octave are heard in Western music. These patterns are called *modes*. Until about 1600 they were more common than major or minor, but they fell into disuse until the twentieth century. Today they are heard about as often as major and minor, and in popular songs they have regained the lead. The various modes can be played on the piano by sounding the white keys from D to D, E to E, F to F, G to G. (The mode from B to B is almost never used. Play it and you will hear why.)

Any scale or mode can be moved or *transposed* to notes other than the ones mentioned above as long as the pattern is retained. This requires adding one or more black keys and omitting one or more white keys.

Melody

For some pieces—especially pieces known as songs, including popular songs—the melody is synonymous with the piece itself. It *is* the piece. So the quality of the melody and the

quality of the music are often virtually the same thing. If the melody isn't attractive or can't be remembered, the piece simply doesn't make it as music. In art music this is less likely to be true. Art music composers are frequently more interested in the overall musical effect than in the quality of the melody; they are seeking to do something more than create a catchy tune. They see the melody as important not only for its own qualities but also for its potential manipulation.

A melody can be a unifying thread in a long musical work. Such a melody is often called a *theme*, to indicate its place as a central musical idea for a piece. A theme may or may not be a highly attractive series of pitches. The world of music contains many examples of average tunes that have become the central idea for great works. In other words, a theme is good not so much because of *what it is*, but because of *how it is developed and what it becomes*.

Melodies have several aspects that make them intriguing in themselves.

Range. The term *range* refers to the upper and lower pitch limits of a melody. Two extremes of range can be demonstrated by the two melodies in the first movement* of Igor Stravinsky's *Symphony of Psalms*, which is included in the *Record Album*. The first melody in this work begins in the singers' parts about 34 seconds into the music. (A fragment of it is heard earlier in the orchestra.) Its two different pitches are only a half step apart. The second theme also appears in the singers' parts about 1:41 from the beginning. It opens with a leap of an octave, and soon moves down nearly an octave. This is a wide range for a vocal melody, although "The Star-Spangled Banner" is even more extreme, with a range of 1½ octaves. Most songs stay within a range of an octave.

Register. The term *register* refers to the general pitch level of the melody. Some are in a low register, while others are in a high register. And of course, the same melody may appear

---

*A movement is a large independent section of a musical work.

in different registers at different times. This depends on the wishes of the composer-arranger. Some melodies seem more suited to one register than to another. A masculine melody seems out of character when played high, and a birdlike song seems inappropriate in a low register.

Length.   Melodies come in all sorts of lengths. Some are short, like the first theme from Stravinsky's *Symphony of Psalms.* The first theme from Brahms' Second Piano Concerto is longer. Some works have a melody that seems nearly continuous, yet it never quite repeats itself.

Contour.   Contour is the shape of a melody in terms of pitch. The contour of the first theme from the first movement of Brahms' Second Piano Concerto is (see page 89):

The contour for the first theme from the first movement of Stravinsky's *Symphony of Psalms* is:

As you can see from the contour drawings of these works, there is no one shape for a melody. Some are rough in contour, some are smooth. Some start high and end low, while others do just the opposite. Some don't move much at all, while others jump around.

Steps and leaps.   Melodies exhibit wide variety in their movement to other pitches. Some move largely to adjacent notes. Stravinsky's first theme from the *Symphony of Psalms* moves only by half steps. The second theme from that work demonstrates some wide leaps.

Prominence of melody.   There is also variance in the prominence given the melody in different musical works. Sometimes the melody is clearly heard, and the accompaniment stays very much in the background. At other times the melody is just part of a total fabric of sound.

Fragments and motives.   Some melodies seem to be made up of several small segments that have been combined to form a larger melody. As the music progresses, the composer takes one of the fragments and uses it as a unifying element in the composition. When a fragment is so treated, it is called a *motive.* To be musically effective, the motive needs to have a characteristic interval or rhythmic pattern that helps the listener to remember it. Many art music composers are gifted at pulling motives from melodies and unifying long pieces of music with them.

Embellishment.   Some melodies are as solid and basic as a rock of granite. Other melodies are laced with filigree and decoration. In some types of music the composer adds special symbols that call for decorative figures. The Sarabande from *English Suite No. 2* by J. S. Bach presents two versions of the same melody, one rather plain and the other much more decorated (see page 105).

Chord outline.   Chords are generally formed by combining the pitches of every other letter in the musical alphabet—A C E, D F A, E G B, and so on. Because this every-other pattern is such an integral aspect of music, it appears in melodies as well as in chords. Of course, in melodies the pitches are sounded one after another. Not all such melodies exhibit a chord outline so clearly as "The Star-Spangled Banner" or "The Blue Danube Waltz," but chords are sometimes rather strongly implied.

Style of performance.   The impression you get of a melody is affected a great deal by how it is performed. The opening solo in Brahms' Second Piano Concerto gives the impression of a flowing, songlike melody. But when the orchestra takes up the same theme after the piano solo, the music has a marchlike character. This change can be clearly heard in the recording in the *Record Album* at about 1:27 into the work. Brahms makes this change of style to achieve variety in his music.

The opening theme of Brahms' Second Piano Concerto can serve as a summary of the points presented in this chapter. The scale, which in this case is B flat, is not fully present, but it is strongly implied. All notes except two, A and G, are there. The half step occurs between the third and fourth steps (D and E flat in the key of B flat), so the music is in major.

The range is one octave, and the opening solo is in the middle register of the piano. The melody contains two phrases, with the second serving somewhat as an answer to the first. The first phrase ascends; the second descends. Each phrase has the same rhythmic pattern.

The melody is beautifully designed, with the two halves balancing each other and providing a symmetry in sound. The melody is of moderate length. Most of its movement is to adjacent notes except the leaps at the end of the first phrase and the opening and ending of the second. It is very prominent in the piece; in fact, it is the only thing going on for a while. Later in the work Brahms extracts a motive of the first three notes, the same three that begin the song "Do-Re-Mi." The melody doesn't outline a chord, but the notes that make up the tonic chord are strongly present. They are marked with an X in the example.

There is, however, something about a melody that defies analysis, something that goes beyond range, phrase design, and contour. A good melody contains just the right combination of rhythmic patterns, pitches, and all the other aspects. And on this last indefinable quality Brahms' melody scores easily as a musical entity of interest and substance.

This chapter has presented ten aspects of melody, which in turn is only one aspect of music. Melody is, in a sense, a microcosm of the infinite variety of music itself.

Six

Harmony and Counterpoint

The words *harmony* and *counterpoint* were presented in Chapter 3. Both refer to the simultaneous sounding of pitches, but counterpoint is the concept of independent lines of music sounding at the same time, while harmony implies clusters of simultaneous sounds to provide an enriching backdrop to a melody. Harmony occurs when a folk song is accompanied by a guitar. The song may be a nice melody, but if heard alone it can sound a bit barren. Harmonizing the melody—putting chords to it—provides an appropriate setting and enriches the effect of the music.

Intervals and Counterpoint

The word *interval* refers to the distance between two pitches. If the two notes are on the same line or space on the music, the interval is a prime or unison. If the two are on an adjoining line and space, an interval of a second exists. The interval from one line to the next or from one space to the next, either above or below, is a third, and so on. The designation of intervals is further refined by labels of *major* and *minor,* plus some other terms, but this additional designation is of little value to the nonmusician.

Counterpoint involves the combining of independent lines of music. Usually it's not as clear-cut as the appearance of two well-known songs at the same time. Sometimes one of the lines is harder to remember than the other. Sometimes the contrasting line is not a full-fledged melody but rather a repeated figure (ostinato); this is true of Stravinsky's *Symphony of Psalms.* When the first melody begins, the bassoons (the instruments playing the lowest notes during this portion of the music) repeat the figure five times in succession, and then return to it several more times before the first theme closes.

Often a line of counterpoint is added to a melody. The additional line contrasts with the main melody. If the notes of the melody are slow, the line of counterpoint often has faster moving notes; if the melody is plain and simple, the added contrapuntal line is more decorative.

A good example—one that is very easy to hear—is the fourth section of Bach's Cantata No. 140. It is presented on page 175. A simplified score is provided in the *Study Guide and Scores,* and a recording of it is included in the *Record Album.* The first melody appears in the violins. Although it is not a rapidly moving melody, it does flow along easily and beautifully. The contrasting melody is sturdy and solid; it's the notes to a church hymn sung by the men in the choir. Actually, the hymn is sung in long note values, which increases the differences between the two melodies.

Chord Structure

Harmony usually consists of chords—the simultaneous sounding of three or more pitches. (Two pitches sounded together are too ambiguous to be considered chords.) The most frequently used chord consists of three notes, each a third apart, and is called a *triad.* If you go to the piano and play every other white key, the first three sounds you play will form a triad of some type. The notation of such a chord can be written so that the notes appear line-line-line or space-space-space.

Sometimes the three notes in a chord are rearranged. For example, a low C may appear as a high C. This new arrangement may hide the alternating pattern of the chord from the eye of the person looking at the notation or seeing the notes played on the piano, but the ear can hear the similarity, and the chord is still essentially the same.

The two main types of triads in use today are *major* and *minor.* These terms refer to the placement of the middle note in the triad. The major triad can be heard by playing C E G on the piano. It can be made into a minor triad simply by moving the middle note, E, to the black key immediately to the left, E flat. This small change gives the chord a different sound. Several other types of triads and chords are possible, of course. Quite often chords consist of more than just three notes. A fourth tone can be added, and occasionally even a fifth or a sixth tone. Generally the every-other pattern is followed; for example, C E G can be expanded into C E G B flat. The addition of another pitch does not change the essential nature of the chord, but it does give a richer sound.

Most chords are constructed according to the every-other pattern already mentioned, but this isn't mandatory. Composers, especially in the twentieth century, have used some different chord structures. The notes of a chord can be placed two, four, or five notes apart. Or they can follow no particular pattern at all. These latter sounds are referred to as *tone clusters;* but more about them later.

Chords in Music

Seldom does a composer merely write out the basic chords to harmonize a melody. Basic chords without some elaboration are not very interesting. Usually chords are treated in a variety of ways to give the harmonizing part more appeal. So when you look at a piece of music, you may have some difficulty finding the basic chords, although you probably sense them when you hear the music performed. They are there, but they are not easily visible.

To compare how chords are used in musical works, listen to the songs by Aaron Copland ("Simple Gifts") and Charles Ives ("Autumn"), and the third movement of the *Pathétique* Sonata by Ludwig van Beethoven, all presented in the *Record Album.* Copland's accompanying music to the Shaker melody (presented on page 51) is designed to further the idea of simplicity that is central to the song. The chords appear in about as basic a form as they ever do in music. Also, the rate at which they change is quite slow. The first half of "Autumn" (page 56) also presents very simple chords. Most of the interest is achieved by having them occur off the beat. As the song gains in intensity, however, the chords are repeated more often, and sometimes the notes are not all sounded at the same time. Beethoven's piano sonata (page 112) presents chords with the notes sounded one after the other in "harp style" (the musical term is *arpeggio,* pronounced with soft *g*'s) instead of simultaneously. The basic harmony is not changed when this is done. The third movement of the Beethoven sonata changes chords more rapidly and frequently than do either the Copland or Ives songs, partly because the tempo is faster.

Consonance–Dissonance

If musical sounds give the listener an impression of repose, equilibrium, or agreement, they are called *consonant*. If they give an impression of harshness, tension, or disequilibrium, they are called *dissonant*. But words are inadequate to describe these two concepts. They must be heard in actual chords, and even then there is no clear-cut distinction between consonance and dissonance. Since any judgment of these elements must be subjective, involving individual impressions, it's more accurate to speak of degrees of consonance and dissonance.

Chords are heard not only as units containing greater or lesser tension but also as single sensations of sound. Composers, especially in the last 100 years, have sometimes added tones to chords to achieve a desired "color." An example of this practice occurs in some arrangements of popular songs for large stage or dance bands; sometimes the piece ends with a big colorful chord. The effect is one of enriched sound rather than tension.

Generally music has increased in dissonance over the centuries. What was considered a dissonance in the thirteenth century had become a consonance in the sixteenth, and what was considered a cruel clash of tones in the sixteenth century has become commonplace in the twentieth.

The impression should not be left here that dissonance is necessarily disagreeable and should be avoided. Because contrast is needed if music is to be interesting, both consonance and dissonance are vital. The composer considers the amount of dissonance contained in the various chords and then balances these with more conventional sounds to get the desired effect.

Tonality

As was pointed out in Chapter 3, most music has a key center, or tonic, that the harmony moves to and from. Through skillful choice of chords the composer can "punctuate" the music—that is, suggest varying degrees of tension and repose comparable to clauses and sentences in language.

One of the ways a composer establishes key and punctuates the music is by using patterns of two chords called *cadences*. (The word as used in harmony has little to do with a cadence in marching.) Cadences appear at the ends of phrases, and they contribute much to the feeling that the music should either move on or stop, depending on the chords in the cadence. The type of cadence that gives a sense of stopping can be compared to a period on the printed page, and the kind that gives a feeling that the music should move on can be compared to a comma. One cadence that may be familiar is the "Amen" conclusion of hymns in Protestant churches. Cadences are not usually so obvious, however.

Not all music must be in a key. At one time the establishing of a key was mandatory, but over the years composers became more free in their treatment of keys. They modulated more frequently and didn't establish the key as thoroughly as had composers in earlier centuries. The result was a general weakening of key center, and by the end of the nineteenth century some music was being written that could not be designated in any key. In musical terms it is *atonal*—without tonality.

Harmonic Progressions

Chords move to other chords during successive moments of time. In so doing, the harmonies convey a sense of progression, just as do other aspects of music. The logic of harmonic progression is probably culturally learned, although it may be based partly on the physical laws of sound. No one really knows whether nature or nurture is more important in this matter.

Traditionally the chord that seemed most logically to lead to the tonic was the V, or *dominant*, chord. The Roman numeral comes from the fact that a chord can be built on any degree of a scale. A chord built on the first degree—the tonic chord—is labeled I. A chord built on the second degree of the scale is labeled II. Similar labeling identifies the chords built on the remaining notes of the scale. The VII chord, like V, also leads strongly to the tonic. The II and IV chords can move to the tonic, but they seem more inclined to move to the V. The most remote in terms of leading to the tonic are the III and VI chords. Folk and popular music in recent years has tended to break down this expectation of harmonic progression that had existed for 250 years. The progressions in popular music seldom move in the traditional I-IV-V-I; instead they sometimes move I-IV-II-I, or use other harmonic patterns. This gives the music a different sound from traditional art music, and these progressions do have a quality that is appealing and interesting.

The "punctuation" of music through chord progressions and cadences can be easily heard in Copland's arrangement of "Simple Gifts," which is included in the *Record Album.* The chord for the words ". . . gift to be simple . . ." is the home, or tonic, chord. The chords work away from the home chord but return briefly on the words ". . . when we find ourselves. . . ." Although there is a held note on "right," which might be expected to be a good place to end, the chord does not give the impression that the music will end—and it doesn't. The end of the phrase comes with the words ". . . love and delight." At that point the second portion or half of the song begins. Another cadence is clearly presented in the final chords of the song.

Seven

Musical Instruments

There are hundreds of different kinds of instruments in the world, and they can be grouped in a variety of ways. One way is to discuss them according to the type of music they perform; this chapter is so organized.

Orchestral Instruments

The instruments of the symphony orchestra can be divided into "families" on the basis of similar design and principles of sound production. There are four families: strings, woodwinds, brasses, and percussion.

Strings. The strings are the backbone of the orchestra. They constitute about half its membership. The violin, viola (vee-*o*-la), cello (*chel*-lo; officially the violoncello), and the string bass have essentially the same design. The main difference among them is one of size and consequently the general pitch level at which they play. The player produces tone by plucking the strings with the finger or, most often, by drawing a horsehair bow across the strings. When the hair of the bow is examined under a microscope, tiny depressions can be seen. The uneven surface catches on the string to set it vibrating. The player also applies rosin to the bow to help it sound the string.

The body of the instrument is largely hollow. The wooden bridge visible on the top of the instrument props up the strings and transmits their vibrations to the body, which amplifies the sound and provides the distinctive tone quality of the instrument.

Extending out from the body of the stringed instrument is the neck, on which is glued the black fingerboard. The player presses the string down firmly on the fingerboard to change the pitch. The shorter the string—that is, the smaller the distance between bridge and finger—the higher the pitch. The four strings are of different materials, thicknesses, and tension. Tension is regulated by the pegs at the scroll end of the instrument. When the player tunes, a tightening of the string produces a higher pitch; loosening the tension causes a lowering of pitch. The instruments are tuned so that there is an interval of a fifth between the pitch of each string and the one adjacent to it; on the string bass the interval is a fourth.

It is possible to play two or even three notes at one time, a technique called *double* (or *triple*) *stops*. In this instance the bow is drawn across adjacent strings in a single stroke so that they vibrate simultaneously.

While pitch is controlled by the fingers of the player's left hand, volume and phrasing

The violin. Isaac Stern, concert violinist.

The cello.

are manipulated by the bow held in the right hand. The more pressure applied to the bow, and the faster it is drawn over the strings, the louder the tone will be. The player can bow smoothly, or can separate the strokes to produce a variety of styles.

All good string players vibrate the left hand in a slight, rapid motion when playing. This motion creates *vibrato,* which adds warmth to the tone by causing rapid but very small changes of pitch. The tone can be made softer and more mellow by the use of a mute—a wood or plastic device that is fitted over the bridge.

The violin is the smallest and highest pitched of the four instruments. Its range covers well over four octaves from its lowest note, which is G below middle C. There are two sec-

tions of violins in the orchestra: first and second. There is no difference in the instruments themselves; the distinction lies in the way the music is written for them. The first violin part is generally higher, more difficult, and more easily heard in the total orchestral sound.

The viola is somewhat larger than the violin, but it is also held under the chin. Its general range is about five notes lower than the violin's.

The cello rests on the floor and is supported lightly between the player's knees. It is pitched an octave below the viola. In general, its range is comparable to that of a baritone singer, so it is especially well suited for warm, melodious passages.

The string bass is known by several other names: contrabass, double bass, and bass viol.

Oboe and bassoon reeds.

Clarinet reed and mouthpiece.

When playing, the performer either stands or partially rests on a high stool. The string bass is seldom heard alone, although its tone is not unpleasant in the slightest. The instrument contributes substantially to the important low sounds of the orchestra.

The harp is also a member of the string family. Its sounds are made by plucking the strings with the hands. There are only about half as many strings on a harp as there are keys on a piano. But the harp compensates by means of a pedal mechanism, which can change the length of the strings almost instantaneously to provide any necessary pitches.

Woodwinds. As their family name implies, these instruments use wind to produce the tone and are (or were) made of wood. Their strong point is the varied timbres they provide. Usually two flutes and a piccolo, two oboes and an English horn, two clarinets and a bass clarinet, and two bassoons and a contrabassoon are found in a symphony orchestra. Saxophones seldom appear in a symphony orchestra.

All woodwinds are alike in that their bodies are hollow tubes. Holes along the length of the tube are opened and closed either by the fingers or by small pads attached to key mechanisms. As the holes are opened

closer toward the source of air, the pitch gets higher because the tube is being "shortened." At a certain point a key is opened to permit the instrument to move into a still higher range, and the holes and keys can be used for a new set of pitches. Tones are started and stopped by the player's tongue, and each instrument can usually produce only one note at a time.

The flute changed its wooden body early in the twentieth century in favor of a metal one, which is usually of a silver-nickel alloy. The metal construction gives the instrument a more brilliant tone. The flute and its diminutive version, the piccolo, are unique in that they produce sound on the stopped-pipe principle. Many a youngster has made a sound by blowing across an empty pop bottle; the flute operates in a similar way. What happens is that the air going into the pipe collides with the air returning from the stopped end, and a sound results. The flute's range is from middle C up about three octaves, and the piccolo's range is one octave higher.

The oboe is made of wood that, like the wood in the clarinet and the bassoon, has been carefully treated to prevent warping and cracking. The distinctive tone of the oboe is produced by a double reed. The reed is similar to bamboo cane. It is shaved, and the two small reeds are wired together. The instrument does

Doc Severinsen playing the trumpet (Courtesy The Getzen Company, Elkhorn, Wisconsin).

not have a wide range; it extends only a little over two octaves. Its best notes lie around an octave above middle C, where they can be easily heard. The English horn is neither horn nor English. It is basically a large oboe with a bulb-shaped bell.

The bassoon is also a double-reed instrument. It can play from more than two octaves below middle C to at least one octave above it. Its tone is highly distinctive but not powerful. The range of the contrabassoon is an octave lower; its lowest pitch reaches almost to the lowest note on the piano.

The clarinet has the most varied timbre in its more than three-octave range. Its low notes have a quality quite different from its high notes. It has only one reed, which is placed on a mouthpiece. Clarinets come in a variety of sizes, but only three are found regularly in the symphony orchestra: the B flat and A soprano, and the B flat bass, which looks like a black wooden saxophone.

The saxophone is the newest instrument in the woodwind family. There are eight different-sized saxophones. The saxophone is used only occasionally in orchestral music but is a regular member of concert and jazz bands.

Brasses. The sound on brass instruments is produced by a "buzzing" or vibrating of the lip membranes on a cup-shaped mouthpiece. This buzzing sound is then amplified through a metal tube with a flared bell at the end. Today all brass instruments have curves in them so

The trombone.

Six-valve F tuba and C tuba held by Abe Torchinsky.

that they can be held more easily. Also, all of the orchestral brasses have some means of changing the length of the tube.

A bugle is not an orchestral instrument, but it can illustrate an important principle of brass playing. The bugle has no valves, so all its different pitches must be produced solely by changes of tension in the player's lips. This limitation means that the bugle can produce only a certain series of pitches, the familiar ones heard in bugle calls. All brass instruments achieve these different pitches by lip manipulation, but if pitches outside the series are desired, the length of the tube must be changed so that a new series is possible—one that contains the desired pitch. This is the function of the valves on most orchestral brasses: By pushing down various combinations of valves, the player opens or closes different portions of tubing so that the air column can be made the desired length for a new series.

Like the woodwind instruments, the brasses are articulated by the player's tongue.

(Left to Right) Trumpet, French horn, trombone, and tuba mouthpieces.

(Left to Right) Xylophone, vibraphone, and Chinese temple blocks.

Generally an orchestra uses three trumpets, four French horns, two tenor trombones, one bass trombone, and one tuba.

The trumpet is the highest pitched brass instrument. It has three piston valves, which, when activated, change the length of tube in varying amounts. Its range is not extremely wide, extending from a few notes below middle C up somewhat over two octaves. What the instrument lacks in range it makes up in power. The cornet is similar to the trumpet except for the conical tapering of its tube or bore. (The trumpet bore is more cylindrical.) Differences in the shape of the bore account for the mellower sound of the cornet. A mute for cornet or trumpet can be inserted into the bell to soften the tone and make it sound more pinched. The most common is a fiber mute, although there are other materials and several variations of the basic mute.

Extreme accuracy of lip tension is required in order to produce the desired note on the French horn. It can sound more than an octave lower than the trumpet, and its overall range is wider. Its valves, operated by the player's left hand, are of a rotary type. The valve mechanism turns to open up lengths of tubing. The player inserts the right hand into the bell to control the tone somewhat. A mute is occasionally used.

The trombone is an octave lower than the trumpet. It is unique in that it has a slide to regulate the length of its tubing. The trombone has great power. The bass trombone is somewhat larger than the usual tenor trombone and plays a few notes lower.

The tuba is comparable to the string bass in its musical function. It seldom gets to play a solo.

Percussion. All percussion instruments produce sound by being struck or rattled. They may be further grouped into those that play definite pitches and those that don't. First to be considered are those that can produce definite pitch.

A kettledrum is a large copper bowl over which is stretched a calfskin head. Around the rim is a ring that regulates the tension of the head when the small protruding handles are adjusted: the tighter the drumhead, the higher the pitch. The problem with this procedure is that it takes a minute or two, which means the performer must stop playing for that period of time. Until the middle of the last century, composers had to consider the inconvenience of retuning when they wrote for the instrument. Today there is a pedal mechanism that regulates pitch very quickly. The sticks have padded rounded heads on the end. To permit a variety of tone qualities, the player has available several pairs, each having a different firmness.

Kettledrums do not appear singly. A minimum of two is required, and more are often used, each of a different size and tuned

Timpani. The pedal for each drum is at the side of the instrument.

to a different pitch. The name *timpani* is plural and is synonymous with kettledrums. The timpanist positions the instruments in semicircular fashion for ease of playing.

The glockenspiel, xylophone, marimba, and vibraphone are similar. All have tuned bars arranged to resemble a piano keyboard, and the player strikes them with mallets. The glockenspiel is highest in pitch and has metal bars that produce a light, tinkling sound. The xylophone has wooden bars and produces a dry, brittle tone. The marimba also has wooden bars, but below them hang hollow metal tubes that permit the sound to resonate for a few moments after a bar is struck. The vibraphone also has tubes, but has in addition an electrically powered device that produces a vibrato in the tone.

The piano and celesta are keyboard instruments. The piano tone is produced when a felt hammer, activated when the player pushes a key, strikes the strings. Because of this striking action, the piano is included among the percussion instruments despite the fact that its tones are produced by the vibration of strings. The celesta looks like a small spinet piano, but it is essentially a glockenspiel operated from a keyboard. Its steel plates are struck by hammers.

The chimes also produce definite pitches. The player hits near the top of a hollow metal tube with a wooden hammer.

Percussion instruments of indefinite pitch are many in number. Most important is the snáre drum. It is hollow, with calfskin or plastic heads stretched over both top and bottom. On the underside are several strands of wire that rattle against the lower head when they are tightened sufficiently to touch it. These are the snares, and they give the drum its characteristic crisp sound. The snare drum is played with a pair of wooden sticks.

The bass drum is the largest percussion instrument; it is placed upright on its side for playing. It is struck with a single stick or "beater" with a rounded head. When hit hard, the bass drum has tremendous power.

The cymbals are large metal discs that are often struck together as a pair. A cymbal also can be suspended from its center and struck with a stick. A gong is a large metal disc of thicker metal than a cymbal. It is suspended from one edge and struck with a beater.

The triangle is a three-sided metal frame suspended from one corner. A small metal beater activates the sound. The player can produce single strokes on one of the sides or can produce a more sustained effect by placing the beater inside one of the angles and moving it rapidly back and forth between the two adjacent sides.

The tambourine has a calfskin head stretching over a wood or metal rim, around which are placed small metal discs that rattle. The player shakes the instrument or taps it against the hand. Castanets are hollow pieces of wood or plastic that are clicked against each other.

Percussion players are assigned many unusual instruments. They hit the woodblock, crack a whip (which consists of two large, flat wood pieces that are slapped together), shake maracas (hollow, dry gourds in which metal pellets have been placed), and even get to blow on whistles.

Britten's The Young Person's Guide to the Orchestra

To become acquainted with the sounds of the various musical instruments that make up the orchestra, there is no better work than *The Young Person's Guide to the Orchestra* by Benjamin Britten, a twentieth-century English composer. In spite of its title, the work is *not* juvenile in any sense. For the theme of this work Britten chose a melody by the most esteemed English composer of the seventeenth century, Henry Purcell.

The first section of the work is a set of variations on Purcell's theme. Britten makes it especially easy to follow the instruments because he first introduces the full orchestra, then the woodwinds, then the brasses, then the strings, and finally the percussion. He closes this section with the full orchestra again. Having presented the full orchestra and each family of instruments, he proceeds through each section from the highest pitched instrument to the lowest.

The last section of *The Young Person's Guide to the Orchestra* is a fugue (pronounced *fewg*). The fugue form will be discussed in greater detail in Chapter 13, but the idea can be introduced here by stating that it is somewhat on the order of an intellectual round. The main theme (called the *subject*) is presented, then

Suggestions for Listening to Orchestral Instruments

Flute
Bach, Sonatas for Flute and Harpsichord (any of seven)
Griffes, *Poem for Flute and Orchestra*
Mozart, Concerto for Flute (K. 313 or K. 314)

Oboe
Handel, Concerto for Oboe (any of three)
Mozart, Concerto in C Major for Oboe, K. 314
Poulenc, Sonata for Oboe and Piano

Clarinet
Brahms, Sonatas for Clarinet and Piano, Opus 120, Nos. 1 and 2*

Debussy, *Première Rapsodie for Clarinet and Piano*
Mozart, Concerto in A Major for Clarinet, K. 622

Bassoon
Hindemith, Sonata for Bassoon and Piano
Mozart, Concerto in B Flat Major for Bassoon, K. 191
Vivaldi, Concertos for Bassoon and Orchestra (any of several)

Saxophone
Debussy, *Rapsodie for Saxophone and Orchestra*
Glazounov, Concerto for Saxophone
Ibert, *Concertino da Camera, for Saxophone and Chamber Orchestra*

Trumpet
Haydn, Concerto in E Flat Major for Trumpet and Orchestra
Hindemith, Sonata for Trumpet and Piano
Purcell, Sonata for Trumpet and Strings

French Horn
Hindemith, Sonata for Four Horns

*The word *opus*, meaning *work*, is put on compositions by the composer (or publisher) to indicate the general order in which works were written. The practice began early in the seventeenth century, but only since the mid-nineteenth century have opus numbers been applied consistently to new compositions.

other instruments enter in imitation of that main theme. In the fugue Britten presents each section and instrument in the same order in which he featured them in the variations, which means that the subject is introduced by the piccolo. The music closes with the full orchestra sounding Purcell's theme.

A Listening Guide for *The Young Person's Guide to the Orchestra* appears on pages 40–41.

Band Instruments

Band instrumentation is far less standardized than orchestral instrumentation. Several instruments have been tried out in bands at various places and times and have been dropped from the organization—the flügelhorn, the saxhorn, the bass saxophone, and others. Bands vary tremendously in size. Some are as small as 30 players, while others run well over

100 players. Arrangers and composers cannot be sure of what kind or size group will play their band arrangements or compositions.

Although the wind band has a long tradition running from the courts of kings to the touring band of John Philip Sousa, most people tended to think of bands in "town band" terms; that is, a small but noisy group that existed primarily to give concerts on hot summer nights in a park. Nobody took the group very seriously. Following World War I and on into the 1940s, the band took on a new dimension. It became a much larger organization and played a heavy diet of transcriptions of orchestral music. When the band was good, the effect was something like the sound of a mighty pipe organ. Since World War II another idea has appeared in bands and band music. Often called a *wind ensemble*, this concept strongly favors original compositions and a much smaller group. Gone are the romantic

---

Mozart, Concerto for Horn (K. 412, K. 417, K. 447, or K. 495)
Strauss, Concerto for Horn (either of two)

Trombone
Hindemith, Sonata for Trombone and Piano
Poulenc, Sonata for Trumpet, Trombone, and French Horn
Rimsky-Korsakov, Concerto for Trombone and Band

Tuba
Vaughan Williams, Concerto for Bass Tuba and Orchestra

Percussion
Chavez, *Toccata for Percussion*
Harrison, *Canticle No. 3 for Percussion*
Milhaud, Concerto for Percussion and Small Orchestra

Harp
Handel, Concertos for Harp, Op. 4, Nos. 5 and 6
Hindemith, Sonata for Harp

Ravel, *Introduction and Allegro for Harp, Flute, Clarinet, and String Quartet*

Violin
Beethoven, Concerto in D Major for Violin, Op. 61
Chausson, *Poème for Violin and Orchestra*, Op. 25
Prokofiev, Concerto No. 2 in G Minor for Violin, Op. 63

Viola
Bartók, Concerto for Viola and Orchestra
Berlioz, *Harold in Italy*, Op. 16
Hindemith, *Trauermusik for Viola and Strings*

Cello
Block, *Schelomo*, Rhapsody for Cello and Orchestra
Haydn, Concerto in D Major for Cello, Op. 101
Schumann, Concerto for Cello

String Bass
Dittersdorf, Concerto in E for Double Bass
Koussevitzky, Concerto for Double Bass

Listening Guide

Britten: *The Young Person's Guide to the Orchestra*, Op. 34

"Variations and Fugue on a Theme by Purcell"

Theme and Variations

0:00   Theme presented at loud dynamic level by orchestra; a stately, solid melody:

0:28   Theme played by woodwinds.

0:54   Theme played by brasses.

1:17   Theme played by strings.

1:38   Theme played by percussion, especially timpani.

1:57   Theme repeated by entire orchestra.

2:20   Variation 1—flutes and piccolo; playful, with many notes.

2:53   Variation 2—oboes; plaintive, songlike melody.

3:50   Variation 3—clarinets; many arpeggios and runs.

4:30   Variation 4—bassoons; marchlike, with a little songlike melody.

5:24   Variation 5—violins; rhythmic accompaniment and dancelike melody.

5:59   Variation 6—violas; songlike melody with a wide range.

7:01   Variation 7—cellos; rich, flowing melody.

8:14   Variation 8—string basses; melody in which the three-note pattern ascends one note with each appearance; after the middle it basically descends one note each time.

9:13   Variation 9—harp; presents the theme upside down (inversion).

10:00   Variation 10—French horns; variation built around chords.

10:53   Variation 11—trumpets; marchlike figures.

11:23   Variation 12—trombones and tuba; heavy and majestic.

12:40 Variation 13—percussion; timpani opens with portion of theme; followed by bass drum and cymbal, tambourine, triangle, snare drum, Chinese blocks, xylophone, castinets, gong, and finally the whip.

Fugue

14:32 Subject played by piccolo:

14:38 Subject played by flutes.

14:47 Subject played by oboes.

14:52 Subject played by clarinets.

15:03 Subject played by bassoons.

15:13 Subject played by first violins.

15:15 Subject played by second violins.

15:23 Subject played by violas.

15:29 Subject played by cellos.

15:33 Subject played by string basses.

15:45 Subject played by harp.

15:57 Subject played by French horns.

16:03 Subject played by trumpets.

16:11 Subject played by trombones and tuba.

16:17 Subject played by percussion.

16:27 Purcell's theme played loudly in long notes by brasses; upper strings and woodwinds continue contrasting material based on fugue.

16:57 Percussion enters loudly.

17:16 Closes with long, full-sounding chord.

sounds of yesteryear, replaced by a more intellectual and detached kind of music.

Until well into the twentieth century, the band suffered from a serious lack of quality music written for it. Very few of the great "name" composers wrote much music for a group of wind and percussion instruments. And of the few works that were available, none were considered major contributions of the composer. Some improvement is evident in the last 50 years, however. Several outstanding contemporary composers have been commissioned to write works for wind band, and a few are making it their primary medium of musical expression.

The concert band is largely an American institution. Very few bands are found in schools and colleges in the rest of the world. Most bands in Europe and Asia are adjuncts of military organizations. There are very few permanent professional bands in any country, except for the armed services bands. There is no "New York Philharmonic Band" or anything of that quality or permanence in any city of the United States or the world.

The main difference between the instrumentation of the band and the orchestra is that the band includes no violins, violas, or cellos. Larger concert bands often use one or two string basses. Bands use a greater variety of some of the instrument types: There are often cornets in addition to the usual trumpets, and tenor and baritone saxophones in addition to the alto saxophone. There is the regular clarinet, an alto clarinet, a bass clarinet, and sometimes even a contrabass clarinet. Bands are likely to include a baritone horn, which is almost never found in an orchestra. The baritone horn is in the same range as the trombone, but it has a slightly different bore and piston valves. Because tubas are extremely difficult to carry while marching, an instrument of a comparable range and sound was developed in the band of John Philip Sousa and appropriately named the sousaphone. The sousaphone is coiled over the player's shoulder and can be carried far more easily than the tuba. Sousaphones are the horns most evident in marching bands, and they are often used by school bands in concert as well.

Keyboard Instruments

Keyboard instruments that produce sounds with strings can be divided into two types. One produces the tone by means of a quill that plucks the string when the key is depressed. The other type produces sound when a key causes a hammer covered with felt to strike against the string.

Harpsichord.   The harpsichord and virginal both operate on the principle of the plucked string. The main difference between these two instruments is that the virginal is a smaller, simpler instrument. It looks somewhat like a box that sits on a table. It was probably intended to be an instrument befitting a young lady, due to its rather delicate tone. The first piece of virginal music was published in England, and the cover featured a young lady playing the instrument.

The harpsichord looks somewhat like a grand piano. The case or body is much the same, and the keyboard is composed of the usual black and white keys in the same arrangement. Later harpsichords, built in the seventeenth century, had two keyboards plus stop knobs. These knobs allowed other notes to sound with those the player was performing and permitted the strings of the two keyboards to sound together.

Neither the harpsichord nor the virginal mechanism allows the player to alter the volume by the finger pressure applied to the keys. The only way to change the dynamic level is for the harpsichordist to play on the second keyboard or, on the more complicated harpsichords, to engage a knob that doubles the tones an octave higher or lower. In either case the change is abrupt because no gradual dynamic shadings are possible.

Clavichord.   The clavichord is basically a simple piano. It consists of a shallow box with strings running from left to right. The strings are secured on the left by pins in a block of wood and are sounded by brass tangents that strike the strings when depressed. The clavichord has a weak tone, but the player has some control of the musical expression.

Piano.   The piano came on the musical scene relatively late. It was first constructed in 1709, and the early models were not very impressive. The piano did not gain prominence until the last half of the eighteenth century.

If you don't know how a piano works, you may wish to lift up the top of one and take a look at its mechanism. Basically, the piano has a flat table of wood called the soundboard, the purpose of which is to amplify the sound from the strings. The strings themselves are strung over a cast iron frame. The cast iron frame is absolutely rigid, enabling the strings to stay in tune for relatively long periods of time. The strings are tuned by means of pins that are sunk in a block of wood. The tuner merely twists the pin with a wrench to raise or lower the pitch. The keyboard mechanism itself is more complicated than it appears to be, with about 27 pieces of metal and wood for each key. The most critical phase of the key's action is the movement of the hammer, which must leave the string immediately after striking it so that the string can vibrate freely.

The piano has two advantages over the other keyboard instruments mentioned previously. It has a much more powerful tone, and the player can make gradations in the dynamic level by the force with which the keys are struck. One pedal on the piano allows the sounds to ring even after the fingers have left the keys. Another pedal allows only certain strings to ring—those whose keys are depressed at the moment the pedal is activated. A third pedal moves the entire keyboard mechanism slightly so that the hammer cannot strike all the strings for each note, so a somewhat softer sound is produced. On upright pianos this pedal moves the hammers closer to the strings, weakening the hammers' strokes.

Pianos come in two types. The grand piano is long and flat, like a large table. Because of its large size, its sound is superior to the upright. The upright piano has its strings mounted vertically, and the low strings are shortened in order to fit into a smaller space. Therefore, it has a less powerful tone and is a little more difficult to keep in tune. Concert music is always performed publicly on a grand piano. Throughout history keyboards have been constructed with differing numbers of notes. The modern piano is standardized at 88 black and white keys.

Organ.   The sound of the organ is made when air is blown into pipes. Even a small change in the design of a pipe will cause a change of tone quality. Each timbre must have its own set or rank of pipes, one pipe for each pitch in the rank. A large organ can have as many as 100 ranks; medium-sized organs have 40 to 60. Each rank is brought into play by pulling a knob. Various knob combinations can be activated by pushing a button with the hand or foot. In the picture on page 44, the knobs are on both sides of the keyboards, and the buttons are below the keys and on both sides of the center pedals. So even when the organist depresses only one key, 50 or more pipes can be sounded, depending on which knobs have been activated.

Several keyboards are visible. An organ usually has at least two keyboards, called *manuals*. Each manual has 61 keys, which is less than the piano's 88. The different manuals facilitate the use of different ranks of pipes. There isn't time during the playing of a piece for the organist to adjust the knobs for each of the manuals; this work must be done ahead of time.

The organist's feet are nearly as important as the hands. As you can see in the picture, on the floor are black and blond wooden slats. The slats form another keyboard, the pedal board, which is played with the feet. Most tones sounded by the pedals are low in pitch. Playing music with the feet is not easy, but good organists can perform remarkably fast passages on the pedals.

Organ music utilizes three staves simultaneously: one in treble clef and two in bass clef. Generally, the organist plays the treble-clef part with the right hand, the upper bass-clef part with the left hand, and the lowest line with the feet on the pedals.

The twentieth century has brought forth many inventions, among them the electric organ. Many pipe organists object strenuously to the electric version. Their objection is based on the fact that the synthetic tones simply do not

The console of a pipe organ. Photo courtesy of Rogers Organ Company.

sound like an organ as it's traditionally conceived. It is generally conceded, however, that a *good* electric organ usually has a better sound than a *poor* pipe organ. In any case, the tone quality of most electric models is a far cry from the instrument of Bach. The organ of Bach's time is considered the standard for organs built today; modern quality pipe organs have copied it in nearly every detail. They are custom-made and extremely expensive.

Folk Instruments

Folk instruments can be grouped into four large categories. One is composed of those that are played with the breath. The most common instruments of this type are flutes. Some flutes are played sideways; others are played straight out from the player's mouth and are held like a recorder. The nose flute, a type of flute played by the natives of Oceania and Hawaii, is literally blown with the nose. There are double-reed instruments similar to the oboe and single-reed instruments similar to the clarinet. The *pungi* played by the snake charmers in India is another example in the reed category. A few simple brass folk instruments also exist.

A second classification involves percussion instruments other than drums. Included in it are bells, chimes, xylophones, rattles, and the Jew's harp, which is a flexible metal strip attached to a small horseshoe-shaped frame. Its name originally may have been *jaw's harp*.

A third group includes all kinds of drums, which involve a stretched membrane of some kind. Drums are constructed from many materials, including wood, metal, coconut, and gourd, and they come in shapes ranging from the hourglass drums of the Cameroons to friction drums, on which sound is made when a piece of hide is rubbed across the drum skin.

The fourth classification includes all the string instruments. Most of these are plucked —zithers, lyres, and harps, for example—but some are struck with mallets, and a few are bowed like a violin.

The instruments of a culture are usually constructed of materials readily available in that culture's area—animal horns or bones, skins, wood gourds, and so on. The availability and complexity of instruments also depend on the knowledge of such crafts as smelting metals and shaping wood. Some folk instruments are unreliable and have a weak tone.

Popular Instruments

Guitar. The ancestry of the guitar can probably be traced back to the Near East. The instrument was popular in France by the 1500s, and soon it became well known in Italy and Spain. Early guitars had only four strings, but today six is standard. Except for acoustical improvements the modern guitar has not changed much in the last several hundred years. The guitar has two somewhat different relatives. One is the ukulele, which is basically a small guitar. The other is the banjo, which has a parchment skin stretched over a hoop and no back. The banjo has a much more brilliant sound than the guitar. It may have come to America with the slaves from Africa, but its ancestry is probably Arabic.

Electric guitar. The electric guitar predominates in current popular music. Its timbre is the "sound" of rock. The electric guitar is only distantly related to the traditional acoustic guitar just described. Instead of having a hollow sound box that amplifies the sound, it has an artificial box that serves more for decoration and as a site for mounting the control knobs. The sound of the strumming is picked up and amplified by electronic means. By turning knobs the player can adjust the volume level,

change the timbre of the sounds, and produce a vibrato. The electric guitar comes in basically two sizes. Like the acoustic guitar, the electric guitar has metal strips that cross the fingerboard. These strips are called *frets,* and they help the player find where to place a finger to achieve a certain pitch.

Drums. The percussion used in pop groups usually consists of a drum set played by one player. The set includes one or two cymbals that are placed on top of a stand. They are activated by striking them with a stick or a brush. Often there are three or four drums, usually without snares. The absence of snares gives the drum a more "tubby" sound. The largest drum in the set is a small bass drum that the player hits by pressing a pedal mechanism with the foot. Often this drum has a felt pad braced against one side to muffle the sound and cut down the reverberation. Much showmanship is involved in such drumming.

Accordion. The accordion has enjoyed several waves of popularity in the United States, and it is still quite popular in some European countries. The accordion is constructed somewhat on the principle of an organ, in that the air is squeezed through the instrument to activate metal reeds. The accordion has a short keyboard for playing the melody. The accompanying chords are produced by pushing buttons that sound entire chords; there is one button for each type of chord in each key. In addition, when playing on a quality instrument, the accordionist may achieve different timbres by pushing different buttons. In a small way the varied timbres of the organ can be emulated.

Instruments of the Future

The most important new instrument is not an instrument at all in the usual sense of the word. It is the tone synthesizer—an electronic instrument that can produce all sorts of sounds and timbres and is sometimes used in conjunction with a tape recorder. The player-composer does not actually interpret a work while the audience listens. Instead, a piece is prepared

Electronic music studio.

on the synthesizer and recorded onto a tape. Then the composer works with the tape to produce the composition.

Synthesizers are extremely complex, as the picture on this page indicates. One almost has to be an electrical engineer and acoustician to develop music for it. Synthesizer and tape compositions are usually "solo" endeavors. That is, they are seldom combined in an ensemble, as one might combine a violin and a piano.

Like the synthesizer, the tape recorder is not an instrument in the usual sense of the word. It can only reproduce sounds that are fed into it. The composer's job is, of course, to decide which sounds should be recorded. One of the chief sources of sound for the tape re-

corder in contemporary music—in addition to the tone synthesizer—is the world of commonplace, everyday sound: the cry of a baby, the chirp of a bird, the drip of a faucet. Sounds from conventional instruments are also used. The performer-composer then manipulates the tape by increasing or slowing down the speed, by splicing the tape, by rerecording sounds on top of one another. The composer experiments freely to create radically different sounds. This type of music has been called *musique concrète*. It alters natural sounds by means of the tape recorder itself.

Minor improvements in instruments will continue to be made, of course. Different materials will be tried and other refinements will be added.

A scene from Carmen.

Section Two

Musical Forms and Media

The elements of music discussed in Section One can be sounded in a variety of ways. One way is the voice. It is the first musical medium presented in this section. Following the presentation of music for solo voice comes the discussion of choral music—music for a number of singers.

Another means of musical expression is through instruments. One chapter is devoted to symphonic music, another to concertos, and another to music for small instrumental groups. Yet another chapter is devoted to keyboard music.

Some types of music are related to other fine arts. A chapter is devoted to opera, which is a unification of music and drama. The section concludes with a discussion of ballet, the bringing together of dance and music.

Eight

Songs and Singing

It is hard for contemporary Americans to realize the importance with which singing is regarded in many parts of the world and to appreciate the place it held in our society in the past. Most of the folk and ethnic music to be cited in Chapter 16 is vocal music, not instrumental. Much of it is sung by nearly everyone in the society. Until about 50 years ago singing was a more common means of expression than it is today.

One of the reasons singing seems to be less vital today is the advent of recordings and other means of producing music. In the past if you wanted to hear music, you or someone you knew had to make it. Every performance was a live performance. People often sang at square dances because they had to; without the singing there would have been only a little fiddle music. People heard little music that they or their acquaintances didn't produce.* Today it's very nearly the opposite; we hear only a small amount of music that we or our acquaintances produce.

The type of work we do today also discourages singing. The automobile assembly plant is hardly conducive to singing, and neither is an office filled with typewriters and a computer. If you were to sing on the subway or bus on your way home from work, fellow passengers would suspect either your sanity or your sobriety. And the romantic notion that a young man sings to his loved one seems as quaint as the custom of bringing her a box of candy and some flowers when calling on her in the parlor.

Singing is not going to pass from the face of the earth, however, because the use of voices to make music is too basic a means of expression. Nearly everyone has a voice, and through talking and singing people express themselves. Every so often there is a revival of interest in folk songs, and guitars to accompany them are sold by the thousands. These facts indicate that singing is by no means obsolete.

---

*Sometime before World War I my grandfather was the first in his area to buy a phonograph, a wind-up model with a long horn that played cylindrical records with what today we would consider poor fidelity. Nearly every evening for several winters, one or more of the neighboring families would call at his home to listen to the wonderful new machine that played music.

Folk Songs

Chapter 16 will present various types of folk music from around the world; this chapter deals with some of the types found in Western cultures.

Work songs. Work was a more integral part of life a few generations ago because many more hours of labor were required to maintain oneself and one's family. The sea chantey (pronounced *shantey*) "Haul Away Joe" is an example of a song to accompany work. Clearly, the words are of little importance.

Louis was the King of France before the Revolution,
    'Way, haul away, we'll haul away Joe.
King Louis got his head cut off which spoiled his constitution,
    'Way, haul away, we'll haul away Joe.

Dancing and recreation. A second type of folk song was intended to accompany dancing. In America this frequently meant square dancing. Again, the words were of little importance; some, in fact, were added just to fill out a phrase. A well-known example of this is "Turkey in the Straw," in which one verse is:

As I went out to milk, and I didn't know how;
I milked a goat instead of a cow.
A monkey sittin' on a pile of straw,
A-winkin' his eye at his mother-in-law.
Turkey in the hay, turkey in the straw,
The ole gray mare won't gee nor haw;
Roll 'em up and twist 'em up a high tuck-a-haw,
And hit 'em up a tune called Turkey in the Straw.

Some "fun" songs were not for dancing. "The Deacon Went Down" cited in Chapter 1 is one example.

Storytelling. Many English and American folksongs tell a story. "Careless Love" has a story of woe that concludes:

Love, oh love, oh careless love,
See what careless love has done to me.

When my apron strings were long,
You passed my window with a song.

Now my apron strings won't tie,
You pass my cabin door right by.

Expression of feeling. Many songs, both folk and art, exist primarily to express feelings. The white spiritual is one example. The words to "The Wayfaring Stranger" are:

I'm just a poor, wayfaring stranger,
A-trav'ling through this world of woe,
Yet there's no sickness, no toil, no danger,
In that fair land to which I go.

I'm goin' there to see my mother,
I'm goin' there no more to roam,
I'm goin' over Jordan,
I'm just a-goin' over home.

Sometimes composers find songs that they consider worth arranging for concert or recital hall performance. They leave the original melody largely intact and devise an accompaniment for piano or orchestra. Aaron Copland did this with the Shaker song "Simple Gifts." The song originates from the period between 1837 and 1847, and the text expresses the Shaker ideal of the simple, orderly life.

'Tis the gift to be simple, 'tis the gift to be free,
'Tis the gift to come down where you ought to be,
And when we find ourselves in the place just right,
'Twill be in the valley of love and delight.

When true simplicity is gained,
To bow and to bend we shan't be ashamed,
To turn, turn will be our delight
'Till by turning, turning we come round right.

As was pointed out in Chapter 6, the setting of the melody for "Simple Gifts" is in keeping with the text and melody by being very open and uncluttered. There are only very brief introductory measures based on the melody for each half of the song. Sometimes the chords are sounded off the beat in a subtle syncopation, but generally everything is understated and plain.

Chant and Recitative

Chant is a style of singing that usually has no regular meter; its range is narrow, to suggest the inflections of speech. Frequently it is not very tuneful. Once it was quite important, but it is not common in the United States today. The style goes back at least to the ancient Greek poet Homer (about 850 B.C.), who recited his epic tales in a singsong fashion as he plucked out notes on an ancient guitarlike instrument. The word *psalm* means song, and the Biblical psalms were probably often recited in a singsong fashion, too. Chant is still a part of Judaic worship. The style was adapted by the early Christian Church and is heard today in some Roman Catholic churches and briefly in some Protestant worship services. Below is a portion of a "Credo" from a Mass. (The *Mass* is the central worship service of the Roman Catholic Church.) The words are the creed of the Christian Church: "I believe in God the Father Almighty," and so on.

The reciting style is also heard in many vocal works such as operas (see Chapter 14). The term for this kind of singing is *recitative*. It is especially suitable for telling the listener a lot in a short period of time. Long-flowing solos or choruses, on the other hand, usually cover only a small amount of text; the words are often repeated throughout the number. Another feature of recitative is that it can be very expressive. The composer of the music and the singer who performs it can adjust the melodic line to fit the mood suggested by the words. Recitative looks on a page of music as though it would be performed quite regularly. Tradition, however, allows the singer considerable freedom. The accompaniment is kept simple to allow the singer greater latitude of expression. Here is an example of a recitative from *Messiah* by George Frideric Handel:

Notice its simple accompaniment and the many repeated tones in the voice part.

Chant and recitative are types of singing, but they are not songs as we know them. The style has a certain haunting charm, and it is strangely effective in projecting the message of words.

Strophic Songs

Most of the songs we know consist of a melody and several verses of words. This type of music is called *strophic*. Church hymns, popular songs, and most folk and community songs are strophic, including our national anthem. The melody existed long before Francis Scott Key wrote his poem. If you have ever tried singing the second and third verses, you probably discovered that they do not fit the music too well at some points.

Strophic songs are made up of rather distinct units or phrases. A line of words must fit a line of music. As was pointed out in Chapter 3, phrases can be compared to clauses and sentences in language. The "punctuation" in music is done by shaping the melody, dynamics, and chord patterns. Try singing "When Johnny Comes Marching Home" to yourself. Notice that each of the four phrases seems

self-contained, like a rather complete musical statement, and yet only the last phrase suggests conclusion.

> *When Johnny comes marching home*
> *again, hurrah, hurrah!*
> *We'll give him the hearty welcome then,*
> *hurrah, hurrah!*
> *The men will cheer, the boys will shout,*
> *the ladies they will all turn out,*
> *And we'll all feel gay when Johnny comes*
> *marching home!*

Different sets of words can often be sung to the same melody. Most church hymnals contain an index that groups hymns according to meter. (The numbers in the index—8. 6. 8. 6., for example—refer to the number of syllables in each line.) All hymns grouped under a particular meter may exchange words or music. Words of nonsacred songs have been exchanged also ("America" and "God Save the King"), and *Mad* magazine regularly makes up humorous lyrics to familiar songs.

Many strophic songs include a refrain—a section of music with a single set of words—although the verses have changing words.

Strophic songs often display an overall musical design or *form*. Take, for example, "Deck the Halls":

The first line is:

Deck the halls with boughs of hol - ly, Fa la la la la, la la la la.

Let's label this line *a*. (If it were an extensive section of a long piece, it would be identified by a capital *A*.) The second line is:

'Tis the sea - son to be jol - ly, Fa la la la la, la la la la.

It's exactly like the first line, so it can also be labeled *a*. The third line is different:

Don   we now   our   gay   ap-par-el,   Fa___ la,   la___ la,   la   la   la,

Since it is different, it can be labeled *b*. The fourth line is like the first, except that it's altered somewhat toward the end.

Troll   the an-cient   Yule-tide car-ol,   Fa la la la la,   la   la   la   la.

It's best marked by *a'*. The prime mark (') denotes a slight alteration, but not enough to warrant a different letter. The form of "Deck the Halls," then, is *a a b a'*. This pattern is one of the most frequent in music. It seems to contain the best balance between familiar and contrasting material. The two basic song forms are *a b*, which is called *binary*, and *a b a*, which is called *ternary*. "Simple Gifts" is in binary form and "Deck the Halls" in a modified ternary form.

Music Written for One Set of Words

When composers want to give maximum expression to a set of words, they do not try to write a catchy tune. Rather, they design the music for one particular text so that each supports the impact of the other. No substitution of words is desirable; if it were done, it would probably not be musically effective.

The ability of music to enhance words was mentioned earlier, in the explanation of recitative. Handel wrote certain notes and rhythms for the singing of the words "Fear not" because he thought that they best expressed the feeling of those words in sound. A strophic song cannot do this. The same notes and rhythms are not equally suitable for words as varied as "He's going," "You villain!" or "I love you."

Another example of unity in words and music is the *art song*, which is primarily a nineteenth-century German development. In fact, this type of composition is often called a *lied* (plural *lieder*), the German word for song. It is usually written for one singer and piano accompaniment. The song is created mainly to express the idea of the words in music and only secondarily to provide a memorable melody. The accompaniment also contributes to the mood of the music and is nearly as important as the singer's part. The result is maximum musical expression of the words.

Some art songs are strophic to a degree, but many are *through-composed;* that is, there is no literal repeating of lines of music. One of the best known examples of a through-composed song is "The Erl King" (in German, *"Der Erlkönig"*) by the Austrian composer Franz Schubert (1797–1828). Schubert wrote this song when he was only 18. The text is by the great German poet Goethe, who lived from 1749 to 1832. The prevailing mood of the work is one of fear and suspense engendered by the Erl King, the mythical king of elves. According to the legend, whoever is touched by him must die. The singer is required to be narrator, father, child, and the Erl King—quite an assignment.

Because words and music are so closely related in the art song, translations from the original language are difficult. It is hard to retain the original meaning of the words and also make the emphasis of the translated words and the music coincide. Usually the songs are sung in the original language. Here is one translation:

Wer reitet so spät durch Nacht und Wind?   Who rides so late through night wind wild?
Es ist der Vater mit seinem Kind;   It is a father with his child.
Er hat den Knaben wohl in dem Arm,   He holds the boy securely with his arm,
Er fasst ihn sicher, er hält ihn warm.   He clasps him tightly, he keeps him warm.

"Mein Sohn, was birgst du so bang dein Gesicht?"   "My son, why hide your face in fear?"
"Siehst, Vater, du den Erlkönig nicht?   "See, father, isn't that the Erl King near?
Den Erlenkönig mit Kron' und Schweif?"   The Erl King with crown and shroud."

"Mein Sohn, es ist ein Nebelstreif."   "My son, it's only a misty cloud."

"Du liebes Kind, komm, geh' mit mir!   "You lovely child, come, go with me!
Gar schöne Spiele spiel' ich mit dir;   Such pleasant games I'll play with thee!
Manch' bunte Blumen sind an dem Strand,   The fields have flowers bright to behold,
Meine Mutter hat manch' gülden Gewand."   My mother has many a robe of gold."

"Mein Vater, mein Vater, und hörest du nicht,   "My father, my father, don't you hear
Was Erlenkönig mir leise verspricht?"   What the Erl King whispers in my ear?"

"Sei ruhig, bleibe ruhig, mein Kind;   "Be calm, be calm and still, my child;
In dürren Blättern säuselt der Wind."   It's only the leaves when wind blows wild."

"Willst, feiner Knabe, du mit mir geh'n?   "My lovely boy, won't you go with me?
Meine Töchter sollen dich warten schön;   My daughters all shall wait on thee,
Meine Töchter führen den nächtlichen Reih'n   My daughters nightly revels keep.
Und wiegen und tanzen und singen dich ein."   They'll sing and dance and rock thee to sleep."

"Mein Vater, mein Vater, und siehst du nicht dort   "My father, can't you see the face
Erlkönigs Töchter am düstern Ort?"   Of Erl King's daughters in that dark place?"

"Mein Sohn, mein Sohn, ich seh' es genau,   "My son, my son, all I can see
Es scheinen die alten Weiden so grau."   Is just the old gray willow tree."

"Ich liebe dich, mich reizt deine schöne Gestalt,   "I love thee, thy form enflames my sense;
Und bist du nicht willig, so brauch' ich Gewalt."   Since thou art not willing, I'll take thee hence!"

"Mein Vater, mein Vater, jetzt fasst er mich an!   "My father, my father, he is grabbing my arm,
Erlkönig hat mir ein Leid's gethan!"   The Erl King wants to do me harm!"
Dem Vater grauset's, er reitet geschwind,   The father shudders, he speeds through the cold,
Er hält in Armen das ächzende Kind,   His arms the moaning child enfold,
Erreicht den Hof mit Müh' und Noth;   He reaches home with pain and dread:
In seinen Armen das Kind war tot!   In his arms the child lay dead!

The accompaniment adds to the mood with an agitated figure of three notes per beat and a foreboding bass pattern:

Clashes of tones are heard as the child expresses fear, while the father's music has a reassuring quality about it. Notice how effectively Schubert ends the song. The piano stops, and the singer declaims, "In his arms the child"—a pause to allow anticipation to build up—"lay dead!"

A more contemporary example of art song is "Autumn," by the American Charles Ives, who wrote 114 songs. Written in 1908, this song is a setting of a short poem by Harmony Twichell Ives, the composer's wife. The text is:

Earth rests!
Her work is done, her fields lie bare,
and 'ere the night of winter comes
to hush her song and close her tired eyes,
She turns her face for the sun to smile upon
and radiantly, radiantly
thro' Falls' bright glow,
he smiles,
and brings the Peace of God!*

The music casts a feeling of calm and rest. As can be heard on the recording in the *Record Album*, the lower notes in the piano part throb smoothly off the beat in syncopated style for almost all the 23 measures of the song. The upper notes of the piano part present a contrasting melodic line that sounds many of the same melodic figures either before or after the singer. The word "radiantly" is an example of how a text is given a "customized" treatment by an art song composer. The music does seem

to radiate, especially the second time at which point the first note is raised a half step and the accompanying chord changed to major. The word "smiles" is given the highest pitch and loudest dynamic level in the singer's part. "The Peace of God" is written to be sung in a calm, slow, and reassuring manner.

Nineteenth-century art songs sometimes reveal an uneven quality of text, and they seem a trifle dated today. But such music has melodic appeal, and the accompaniment enhances the mood of the music in a beautiful and effective way. When a Schubert or Ives combines text, vocal line, and accompaniment, something of artistic worth is created. That "something" is not duplicated elsewhere in the world of music. Folk songs and songs from operas do not achieve the same kind of expression; they have other virtues. The art song is a high point in the expression of specific thoughts in music.

Singing Styles

Each type of song—folk, popular, art—is associated with a style of singing that seems most suitable for it. For example, to sing a popular song in the manner of an art song is as inappropriate as wearing a tuxedo at a picnic. And vice versa; singing an art song in a pop style is ineffective and out of place. Several factors make up a singing style—fluctuations of pitch, speed and size of vibrato, and the manner in which words are pronounced. But the most significant aspect of vocal style is timbre.

---

*© Copyright 1956 by Peer International Corporation. Used by permission.

Some styles call for a nasal quality, others for a light timbre, and others for a virile, powerful sound.

When you first listen to it, the singing style evident in art music may seem unnatural and a little contrived. It is not as natural as the style associated with folk songs. It's more trained, and it exhibits greater power, range, and technical skill. Very few pop or folk singers can even perform the notes called for in many works of art music, to say nothing of sounding good while doing so.

As for being contrived, almost all singing implies drama, which is a type of artificial situation. Certainly much singing in jazz, rock, and art songs sheds "crocodile tears" over lost loves and expresses exuberant joy over found ones (although for some reason there seem to be more songs about unhappy events than happy ones).

But contrived or not, natural or trained, folk, popular, or art—singing has an expressiveness about it that is fascinating. It is a very human activity.

Franz Schubert

Franz Schubert (1797–1828) was born into the family of a schoolteacher in a Vienna suburb. Young Schubert's creative talent was evident while he was still a boy. After completing school, he tried to follow in his father's footsteps, but he couldn't accept the routine involved in teaching. He preferred to spend his time writing music.

Schubert didn't adjust well to adult life. He never held a real position of employment; in fact, he made only halfhearted attempts to find one. He had a small circle of friends who appreciated his talents. They housed and fed him when he was in need, which was his normal condition. Schubert was incompetent in dealing with publishers, who made good profits on his music. He sold some pieces, later worth thousands of dollars, for the price of a meal.

As the years passed, he became lonelier and more discouraged. He was even unlucky in love. But his output of compositions never dwindled. He died of typhus at the age of 31,

leaving the world his clothing, his bedding, some manuscripts valued at 10 florins—and a vast store of beautiful music.

Schubert was a versatile composer. He wrote piano works, chamber music, and symphonies. Popular legend has falsely assumed that the familiar Symphony No. 8 *(Unfinished)* was left incomplete because of his death or because of his despair over a lost love. The real reason is less dramatic. The work was probably left unfinished because Schubert never got around to completing it. It is even conceivable that he had said all he intended to say in that particular work. In any event, the symphony was not curtailed by his premature death. He went on to compose and complete another long symphony.

In his instrumental works Schubert tended to be less subjective than in his vocal works. His vocal music, which included seven Masses and about 15 operas, was thoroughly Romantic. His 600 songs did much to assure his posthumous success and immortality.

Composers of Songs Presented Elsewhere

Charles Ives, page 262

Aaron Copland, page 140

Nine

Choral Music

Not all vocal music is intended to be sung by only one person at a time. Many vocal works are created for groups of singers, and such music is called *choral* music. This chapter explores the most important types of choral music. Some large choral works contain sections for soloists, but because these works require a number of singers performing together they are considered choral music. Let's begin by looking at the oratorio.

Oratorio

An oratorio is a long work for chorus, soloists, and orchestra, and it usually deals with a religious topic. It is generally performed without scenery, costumes, or actions in a concert hall. It's not written as part of a worship service but more as a concert. The text of an oratorio is dramatic (often taken from the Old Testament), and each soloist represents a specific character.

The man who developed the oratorio as it is known today was George Frideric Handel. Handel was born in Germany, and as a young man he moved to England to write Italian operas. (Things weren't always logical in the

eighteenth century, either.) When Italian operas went out of style in England, he developed a type of opera without staging, costumes, or actions. His new compositions were called *oratorio* and were very successful; some of them are still performed today.

Handel's Messiah

The oratorio *Messiah* is musically rather typical. It differs from other oratorios chiefly in that its text is taken entirely from the Bible and has no part for a narrator, who through singing describes the events of a story. *Messiah* is primarily a contemplation on Christian belief starting with a section on prophecy and Christ's birth, followed by His suffering and death, and concluding with the resurrection and redemption. Handel wrote its nearly three hours of music in the unbelievably short time of 24 days. As he wrote, he was aware that he was creating a great work. Afraid that if he stopped he might lose his momentum, he hardly slept, ate, or left his house for three weeks.

Messiah was well received by critics and the public at its first performance in Dublin. At the first performance in London on March 23, 1743, King George II was so awed by the "Hallelujah Chorus" that he rose and stood at his seat. And in those days, when the King stood, everyone stood. So the King's spontaneous action became a tradition that is still followed today.

Like other oratorios, *Messiah* contains many individual musical numbers—53 in all. Each number is one of three types: recitative, aria, or chorus.

Aria. An aria (pronounced *ar*-eeah) is a vocal solo of some length and complexity. It's not just a tune like "America" or "When Johnny Comes Marching Home." Like the art song, it's intended to be musically expressive, although often it doesn't cover as much text. The aria makes sizable demands on the performer's singing technique, with frequent passages of rapidly moving notes and a wide

---

Listening Guide

Handel: *Messiah*

Tenor Aria: "Every Valley Shall Be Exalted"

Form: *A B A B*

0:00   Orchestral ritornelli (refrain) playing main melodic ideas from both main portions of aria.

0:23   Solo tenor sings "Every valley shall be exalted" *(A)*; short responses by orchestra:

0:38   First long run on "exalted."

0:54   Second long run on "exalted."

1:02   Melodic and text ideas "and every mountain and hill made low," etc.; enter *B*:

1:54   Repeat of first melodic material, with some changes, and text *A*.

2:35   Repeat of second melodic ideas, with some changes, and text *B*.

3:12   Tempo slows much for last repeat of text and music, "and the rough places plain."

3:29   Orchestra repeats its opening nine measures exactly.

3:54   Conclusion.

range. Arias are often *virtuoso* music, music that requires a highly skilled performer. They are generally longer than art songs, and they are intended to be sung with orchestral accompaniment.

One of the first arias in *Messiah* is "Every valley shall be exalted." It is sung by the tenor soloist. A *Listening Guide* for this aria appears on page 59.

The soloist often has to sing rapidly moving notes or perform long phrases on a single word or syllable. The long runs of sixteenth notes such as appear on the word "exalted" illustrate the virtuoso singing typical of arias.

--- Listening Guide ---

Handel: *Messiah*

Chorus: "Hallelujah"

0:00   Short orchestral introduction.

0:07   Chorus sings together the word "Hallelujah" five times and then five times more.

0:27   Chorus sings together, "for the Lord God Omnipotent reigneth"; followed by four "Hallelujahs":

0:39   Altos, tenors, and basses repeat "for the Lord God . . ." phrase; followed by four "Hallelujahs."

0:52   Sopranos sing "for the Lord God . . ." phrase, with rest of chorus singing "Hallelujahs" forming counterpoint.

0:59   Tenors and basses take up "for the Lord God . . ." phrase, while sopranos and altos sing contrasting "Hallelujahs."

1:09   Altos and tenors sing "for the Lord God . . ." phrase, while sopranos and basses sing contrapuntal "Hallelujahs."

1:20   Chorus sings together with no counterpoint "The kingdom of this world is become the Kingdom of our Lord and of His Christ."

1:42   Basses begin new melody and text, "and He shall reign for ever and ever":

When arias were first written in oratorios and operas, they were intended to be pleasing and expressive solo songs. But soon the soloists began to add flashy runs and decorative notes. The custom snowballed until the composer's music became just a skeleton that the singers fleshed out as they wished. Astound-

ing singing resulted, but musical expressiveness and quality suffered. Some reform had taken place by Handel's time, but audiences still liked to hear virtuoso singing and expected some of it in arias.

In "Every valley," the runs do more than show off the singer's skill. Handel cleverly in-

1:47	Tenors sing "and He shall reign . . ."; basses sing free contrapuntal material.
1:53	Altos sing "and He shall reign . . ."; tenors and basses continue contrasting lines.
1:59	Sopranos sing "and He shall reign . . ."; other three parts continue in counterpoint.
2:06	Sopranos and altos sing "King of Kings," with second "Kings" held; basses and tenors sing "forever and ever, Hallelujah" and alternate with "Lord of Lords."
2:17	Same basic idea is repeated four more times, each time at a higher pitch level.
2:45	Sopranos reach highest pitch level for "and Lord of Lords"; are joined by other sections of chorus.
2:50	Basses begin "and He shall reign . . ." melody again; other sections sing contrasting imitative material.
2:56	Sopranos sing "and He shall reign . . ."; other sections sing contrasting imitative material.
3:03	Tenors sing "King of Kings"; other sections respond with "forever and ever" and "Hallelujah."
3:13	Chorus sings together (basses on melody) "and He shall reign . . ."; followed by "King of Kings." Same basic idea repeated, except sopranos sing "King of Kings."
3:56	Closes after four "Hallelujahs" and one long "Hallelujah."

tegrates them into the entire musical fabric so that they enhance the effect of the piece. For example, it's easy to imagine that the singer's runs are an instrument adding a counter-melody. Handel uses the runs to bring out the idea of the words. In this aria the word "exalted" is treated to the long runs. *Exalted,* meaning raised or lifted up in a spiritual sense, is the word that most appropriately expresses the main thought of the text. The low places will be raised up spiritually, says the poet in Isaiah 40:4. Not only does "exalted" have a crucial meaning within the text; it has an especially good vowel on which to sustain the singing: the *awe* or broad *a.*

Virtuoso passages are sometimes baffling and disturbing to nonmusicians. They cannot understand why a syllable is stretched out over 40 or more notes. Of course, "exalted" can be sung with just three notes, and these can even occur on a single pitch level. But the musical interest would be diminished. It's impressive to hear a skilled singer execute the long runs, and it's even more rewarding to hear the line fit into the music and to sense the emphasis that is given certain words. In everyday practical terms it's silly to use 40 notes to sing one word, but in terms of music it makes much sense.

The chorus. The word *chorus* has a double meaning in music. It can refer to a group that sings choral music or to the choral sections of an oratorio or opera. So a chorus sings a chorus.

In many ways the chorus portion of the music is similar to the aria. It is a rather lengthy section. It involves about the same amount of text and has frequent repetition of words. Metrical rhythmic patterns are followed strictly, and lines of music calling for considerable singing ability are found. The accompaniment may be heard alone in certain passages.

There is one fundamental difference between the chorus and aria, however. If you study the music for the "Hallelujah Chorus," you will observe that the parts are sometimes contrapuntal. This imitation tends to occur when a new section of text begins.

A Listening Guide for the "Hallelujah Chorus" appears on pages 60–61. As you listen to the "Hallelujah Chorus," notice how skillfully Handel has placed the words in regard to rhythmic accent. The word "Hallelujah" is written as one would say it when excited. In phrases such as "and He shall reign for ever and ever," the important words of the phrase land on the important beats and parts of the beat in the rhythmic pattern. It is interesting that Handel combined words and music so well in a language that he himself never learned to speak very well.

Walton's Belshazzar's Feast

William Walton was born in England in 1902. Unlike Handel, Walton spent two years on his oratorio *Belshazzar's Feast,* completing it in 1931. Like Handel, he uses a chorus, orchestra, soloist, and Biblical text (selected and arranged by Osbert Sitwell), but no costumes, scenery, or acting. Walton's forces are significantly larger. The chorus is a double chorus (eight parts instead of four), piano, organ, large percussion section, and two brass bands to be located at the sides of the hall to give a stereo effect. Two additional choirs are called for from the sides of the hall.

The music is not divided into separate movements but does fall into three broad sections. The first section describes the sorrows and suffering of the Jewish captives in Babylon. The chorus sings: "By the waters of Babylon, there we sat down, yea, we wept . . . How shall we sing the Lord's song in a strange land!"

The second section tells about the pagan worship of the false gods. "Babylon was a great city, her merchandise was of gold and silver . . . and the souls of men." Belshazzar orders a feast "to a thousand of his lords," and wine is brought forth in gold and silver stolen from Jerusalem by his father, Nebuchadnezzar. The king praises the god of gold and the gods of silver, iron, wood, stone, and brass. With harp and timbrel the guests extoll the king.

Then in the hour of revelry there is a chilling silent pause. The soloist grimly tells about the handwriting on the wall:

And in that same hour as they feasted came forth the fingers of a man's hand, and the king saw the part of the hand that wrote. And this was the writing that was written: "Mene, mene, tekel upharsin." "Thou art weighed in the balance and found wanting."

In that night was Belshazzar the King slain, and his Kingdom divided.

As the words about the handwriting on the wall are sung, the cymbal shakes, the gong sounds, the strings play dissonant clusters of notes, and the piccolo emits a high trill to give the music a spooky quality. The translation of the words by the chorus is preceded by a short, forceful fanfare figure from the trombones. After the words "slain" and "divided" the chorus or orchestra punches notes out of the silence almost as though they were kicking the body of Belshazzar.

The third section of the oratorio presents the rejoicing of the Israelites over the fall of Babylon:

The text is:

Then sing aloud to God our strength; make a joyful noise unto the God of Jacob. Take a psalm, bring hither the timbrel, blow up the trumpet in the new moon. Blow up the trumpet in Zion, for Babylon the Great is fallen. Alleluia!

After a while the text expresses some sympathy for the silent and dark Babylon. The oratorio concludes with words of praise to "the God of Jacob. Alleluia!"

Motet, Madrigal, and Cantata

Three other types of choral music are the motet, the madrigal, and the cantata. Because they are associated closely with a particular musical style, they are presented in Chapters 17 and 18 in conjunction with the Renaissance and Baroque periods. Both the madrigal and the motet are short, usually unaccompanied pieces for a small group of voices. Both contain much counterpoint. The main difference between the two vocal forms is that the motet is a religious work sung in Latin, while the madrigal is a nonreligious work in a language such as Italian, German, or English. The madrigal is also somewhat more liberal in its harmonies, texts, and rhythms.

The cantata is quite similar to the oratorio. The main difference is length; the cantata is much shorter. It often requires fewer performers and was composed for use in the worship service. Often cantatas use a church hymn tune (chorale) as a theme.

George Frideric Handel

Handel was born in 1685 in the city of Halle in Saxony, which is a part of Germany today. His father was a well-to-do barber-surgeon who didn't think music was a good career for his son, so he discouraged young George in music study. But the boy showed much ability in composing, and he played the harpsichord and organ well. He also studied oboe and violin. After a year in college, he went to Hamburg, where he took a job playing violin in the orchestra. Italian opera was extremely popular throughout Europe, and Handel quickly learned its style. By the age of 20 he had written his first opera.

Italy was the center of the musical world at that time, and Handel lived there for several years. He learned much, made many friends, and continued writing operas.

In 1710 he returned to Germany to be musical director of the Court at Hanover. During his two years there he managed to take two leaves of absence to go to London. His second visit was made on the condition that he return to Hanover "within a reasonable time." But he was still in London two years later when his employer, the Elector of Hanover, was proclaimed King George I of England. Just how Handel handled this embarrassing situation isn't known. One story has it that he composed a group of pieces to be played while the King sailed on the Thames River; thus the title for the *Water Music*.

From 1720 to 1728 Handel held an influential position in the musical life of London. His efforts during this time were spent in writing and presenting Italian operas. By 1728 this type of opera began to lose favor because of something called *The Beggar's Opera*, a satirical play with songs inserted. Stubborn and unrelenting, Handel kept on writing Italian operas, investing and losing money in the process. At the age of 52 his health broke, and he left the country to recover.

George Frideric Handel. Painting by Philip Mercier, formerly in Halle.

And recover he did. He tried opera again, without success, and then turned to a new form. Years before, he had written one or two works in operatic style but without scenery, costumes, or acting. Handel began writing oratorios again, and within a few years he was back on top of the English musical world. During the 1740s and 1750s he wrote an amazing number of oratorios, including *Messiah, Samson, Semele, Joseph and His Brethren, Hercules, Belshazzar, Judas Maccabaeus, Joshua, Susanna, Solomon, Jeptha*—over 26 in all.

In 1759 Handel collapsed after participating in a performance of *Messiah*. He died a few days later and was buried with state honors in Westminster Abbey in London.

William Walton

Walton was born in 1902 in Oldham, Lancashire, England. His father was a music teacher, and as a child Walton showed exceptional talent. He attended school at Christ Church in Oxford and later went to college there. Partly self-taught, he began publishing works when he was just past 20 years old. His earliest successful work was *Facade*, a recitation with music. *Belshazzar's Feast* was completed about five years later. Since that time he has composed a viola concerto, a violin concerto, a number of sizable works for orchestra, chamber music, choral music, and songs. Twice he has composed works for the coronation of British monarchs; *Crown Imperial* in 1937 for King George VI and *Orb and Scepter* in 1953 for Queen Elizabeth II. He has also composed a number of works for plays, films, and radio broadcasts. He was knighted by the King in 1951.

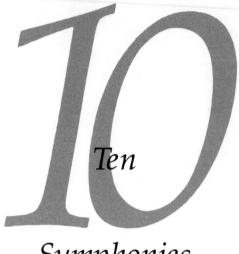

Ten

Symphonies

A *symphony* is a work for full orchestra. Usually it is rather long and divided into *movements,* which are large, independent sections of instrumental compositions. From about 1790 to 1920 symphonies were to musicians as novels were to writers: the largest and most significant creative effort in their art. A composer who brought forth a symphony was in effect saying, "This is an important creative effort." Johannes Brahms, one of the great German composers of the nineteenth century, fussed and fumed over his first symphony and did not bring it out until he was past 40 years of age.

In the last half of the eighteenth century, Haydn (the so-called father of the symphony) wrote 104 symphonies, of which only the last 16 or so are played with any frequency today. From that point on the numerical output declined. Mozart, who was 24 years younger than Haydn, composed 52 symphonies, but only 10 are played much today. In the next generation Beethoven composed 9, all of which are standard works in the current orchestral repertoire. Two generations later Brahms wrote only 4, and they too are all heard frequently today. Haydn's and Mozart's symphonies are shorter and lighter, while Beethoven and later composers regarded their symphonies as long and serious efforts.

A logical place to start an examination of the symphony is with the works of Haydn and Mozart. They did not originate the form, but their symphonies are the earliest examples to be maintained in the standard orchestral repertoire today.

Mozart's Symphony No. 40

Mozart's Symphony No. 40 in G Minor, K. 550, was written in the summer of 1788, along with two other symphonies, Symphony No. 39 and Symphony No. 41, the *Jupiter.* Little is known about the circumstances that encouraged the writing of these symphonies, but it is likely that Mozart never heard them performed. The instruments called for in Symphony No. 40 are violins, violas, cellos and string basses (separate parts were not yet written for the two instruments), a flute, two oboes, two bassoons, and two French horns. Mozart later added parts for two clarinets.

First movement—sonata form. The first movement of this symphony is in the usual form for first movements in the eighteenth century: it's called a *first-movement* or *sonata-allegro* or, more commonly, *sonata* form. With no introduction, the music opens at a moderately fast tempo with this theme:

Several things should be pointed out about these nine measures. First, the theme is divided into two equal parts, the second being nearly identical to the first but one note lower. Each half is further divided in half, the first part being on the order of a melodic statement and the second a sort of musical answer. So the melody is symmetrical in both its larger and smaller sections. The melody is not particularly singable, which indicates that it is designed for instruments. Also, and this is significant in the music of the eighteenth century, the melody is in a sense a collection of several melodic fragments. It is not sweeping, flowing, or overarching. It is neat and precise. Not only is this type of melody appropriate for the artistic goal of Mozart's times, it also subjects itself well to development, an important feature of sonata form to be mentioned shortly.

After a few closing chords, the theme begins to be repeated, but this time, halfway through, the music shifts to some firm chords and rapid running scales—a *transition* of 15 measures. The transition acts as a bridge to the second theme and a new key. It might seem that a transition doesn't need to have much musical interest in itself if its function is merely to join one theme to another. But a good composer can make a transition musically quite interesting. Later, composers in the nineteenth century became much more subtle in their handling of transitions, but Mozart wrote in such a way that the parts of sonata form are clearly delineated. In fact, the end of the transition is easily identified by its two closing chords followed by a measure of silence.

One function of a transition is to allow for modulation. If the first theme is in a major key, the second theme in sonata form will usually be in a key five notes higher, the *dominant* key. If the original key is in minor, as it is in the case of Symphony No. 40, the second theme is usually in the relative major (the major key that shares the same key signature but whose center is one and a half steps higher). The pattern of keys was quite significant to eighteenth century musicians, but by the middle of the nineteenth century, keys were treated more freely. Today the effect of key arrangements in long works is negligible. Another function of a transition is to allow time for the listener to absorb the first melody and get ready for the second. If one theme follows immediately upon another, this seems too obvious to be artistically desirable.

In this particular movement the second theme is played between the violins and woodwinds:

Even if you don't read music very well, you can see that the second theme doesn't look like the first. The second has longer note values, and it doesn't have the repeated rhythmic pattern. There are only a few skips up and down to other notes. The theme is also more difficult to remember than the first. In fact, it comes dangerously close to being insipid. But the two themes in sonata form are seldom similar in mood or style; one usually contrasts with the other.

After the second theme a transitionlike passage appears. Interspersed in it are fragments of the first theme. At this place in sonata form, composers have some options. Sometimes they introduce a third theme, at other times they engage in an extended transition, and occasionally they manipulate a fragment of one of the preceding themes, which is what Mozart does here.

The transitional section following the second theme concludes with a *codetta*. The term is derived from the word *coda*, meaning tail. The suffix is a diminutive ending suggesting shortness, so the codetta is simply a short wrap-up section, a concluding series of scales and chords. Often it has a brief melody associated with it.

Exposition.   So far only a third of the movement has been accounted for. The musical ideas of the composer for the movement have been presented, exposed. The section to this point, therefore, is called the *exposition.* It might help to diagram the pattern of the movement to this point:

EXPOSITION

First theme (in tonic key)	Transition	Second theme (in dominant key or relative major)	Transition	Codetta (in dominant key)

Normally a composer writing in this form indicated a repeat of the entire exposition. In performances today this sign is frequently ignored, and the music moves right into the next section, the development.

Development.   In music, *development* means manipulation of the themes. It demonstrates the composer's ability to present the themes in different and musically satisfying ways.

What does Mozart do in the development

section of the first movement of his Symphony No. 40? Basically, he subjects the first theme to three kinds of treatment:

1. He has the first half of the theme played three times, each time in a new key. Musical interest is achieved by shortening the theme and frequent key changes.

2. He adds counterpoint. While the lower strings play the first theme in a new key, the violins begin a countermelody of rapidly moving notes:

When the lower strings finish the first half of the first theme, they pick up the countermelody, while the violins play the theme in yet another key. A similar exchange occurs two more times, with each key center a note lower than its predecessor.

3. He further fragments the theme. The first few notes are tossed back and forth between the flute, clarinet, and violins. Again new keys are utilized, but the section is quiet compared to the busy, vigorous exchange that preceded it. Soon the answer in the wood-

winds is shortened further to include only the first three notes of the first theme. Several times the direction of the first two notes is inverted, so that they ascend in pitch rather than descend as in the original theme:

Theme fragmentation is so complete throughout this section that the first two descending eighth notes appear, at various pitches and in various instruments, in *all but the first two measures* of the development section. Fragmentation is also apparent in the transition leading from the development into the next main section of the sonata form.

In this particular development section Mozart works with only the first theme. He fragments it, uses frequent modulation, adds countermelodies, and inverts the direction of melodic intervals. These devices are typical of development sections in sonata form. He could have done more. He could have developed the second theme, or introduced an entirely new one. He might have altered the rhythm of the original theme, written different chords to harmonize it, or combined the two themes in a contrapuntal manner. The means of development are infinite.

Recapitulation. The term for the third section of sonata form, *recapitulation*, means literally return to the top. And sure enough, Mozart comes back to the same theme that began the movement. It is played by exactly the same instruments, with exactly the same accompaniment, and it involves exactly the same notes. The exact repetition is quite short.

As the music moves into the transition heading toward the second theme, some changes occur. The transition is longer than it was in the exposition. The second theme is not in a new key. It stays in the tonic. If the second theme were in a different key, the composer would find himself caught off base, away from the home key and near the end of the movement. He would need to get back to the tonic in a hurry and make the key change sound convincing—a difficult thing to do. Following the second theme the transitional music is similar to that found at the same place in the exposition.

The movement ends with a *coda*. The coda is like the codetta except that it is longer and provides the movement with a convincing conclusion. In the coda to this movement, Mozart again utilizes a fragment from the first theme, passing it to the violins, then to the violas, and finally to the woodwinds. Concluding chords alternate between dominant and tonic. So ends one movement of one symphony.

No two movements in sonata form are exactly alike. Each contains some small deviations from the form. In general, however, sonata form can be diagrammed as follows:

EXPOSITION					DEVELOPMENT	RECAPITULATION				
First theme (tonic)	Trans.	Second theme (dominant ....) (or relative major)	Trans.	Codetta	Working over of musical ideas. Rarely are new melodies introduced	First theme (tonic	Trans.	Second theme	Trans.	Coda)

An excellent way to gain a better understanding of sonata form and also improve listening skill is to follow the simplified score of the first movement of Mozart's Symphony No. 40 that appears at the back of the *Study Guide and Scores* for this book. All the parts of the form are labelled and instruments identified.

Second movement. The second movement of a symphony is usually slow and melodious, and its theme is not as easy to develop. So the presence of sonata form in this movement is somewhat unusual. This explains why the development section is very much abridged. The first theme starts with six equal soundings of the same pitch—hardly a melodious beginning.

But Mozart achieves interest by having the theme reenter in another instrument, and to balance the evenly spaced unison notes he concludes the theme with a gentle rocking melody.

The second theme, in good sonata-form tradition, contrasts with the first:

Notice that this theme is also symmetrical in design. Each short phrase in the first two measures is played twice; then the entire theme is played again. When the theme appears the second time, the third measure is embellished, but this version is easily heard as being related to the first.

Third movement. For the third movement of the work, Mozart composed the traditional *minuet and trio*. The movement begins at a moderately fast speed with this melody in the minor key of the symphony:

Next, a 13-measure section occurs that is quite similar to the first, but it is in the relative major key, B flat. The low strings and woodwinds play a two-measure segment much like the first, with this addition: The violins and bassoon play a downward pattern outlining the tonic chord, B flat major.

On its reappearance the theme is treated somewhat in imitation. The melodic lines are very similar to the original and to each other, but some liberties are taken with them. In this music one violin section enters, then the other.

The trio section derives its name from the fact that traditionally it contained only three instrumental parts: the bass or continuo plus two other instruments. As a result the sound was quieter than the preceding minuet. By the time Mozart wrote this symphony, custom no longer required such sparse instrumentation for the trio, but the change to a quieter mood was retained. The trio contrasts with the minuet not only in style but also in key; it is in G major. The first theme of the trio is:

The section is repeated. The second melody of the trio also outlines basic chords. In fact, it is so common a pattern that it is hardly distinguishable as melody. Then the first theme is heard again, with one change: Two French horns are added for contrast. This second section of the trio is repeated. The minuet is then played through again exactly, but without repeats.

The third movement is based on a strict formal structure:

| Minuet | Trio | Minuet |
A	B	A
aa ba' ba'	*aa ba' ba'*	*a b a'*

Like the first movement of this symphony, the third movement has been included in a simplified score in the *Study Guide and Scores.*

Fourth movement. As is typical of symphonies in this period, the last movement of Mozart's Symphony No. 40 is lively and brilliant. It moves at a rapid rate and provides an exhilarating finish to the work. In fact, Mozart marked the movement with the word *finale* (fee-*nahl*-ee) in addition to a tempo marking. When composers want a dashing conclusion to a symphony, they do not pour their most profound musical efforts into it. Instead, they tend to fall back on simpler ideas, common patterns, and technical brilliance. That's what Mozart did in this movement.

Final movements come in several forms, some of which will be presented later. Mozart on this occasion chooses—you guessed it— sonata form. The first theme is based on the notes of the G minor chord. The theme itself was not completely original with Mozart. Many composers of his time used a similar pattern; so many, in fact, that the theme has acquired a nickname—"the Mannheim rocket." (Mannheim, a city in southern Germany, had a famous symphony orchestra.) Like the

first theme in the first movement, the melody again follows a symmetrical statement-answer scheme:

The transition that follows is longer and more interesting than the transitions found in the other movements of the symphony. Again, the end of the transition is easily heard because of the clearly marked cadence followed by a rest.

The second theme, like that of the first movement, contains many chromatic notes and makes more use of the woodwinds. It's in the relative major key, B flat:

A melodic fragment from the first theme occurs frequently in the codetta that concludes the exposition.

The development is built around the first theme. It begins with harmonies that sound unsettled. Soon the "rocket" is passed back and forth between the violins and bassoon. Then the strings treat the theme in a manner that resembles a round. The appearances of the theme in the various string parts are not identical, but they are similar enough to suggest the theme strongly. The music modulates many times.

The recapitulation is conventional and faithful to the pattern of the form. The development and recapitulation are marked to be repeated—a direction that is somewhat unusual. The coda is almost identical to the codetta except for being slightly expanded.

Beethoven's Symphony No. 5

Beethoven's Fifth Symphony is probably the best known of any symphony ever written. It was composed in 1805, only about 15 years after Mozart's Symphony No. 40. How different Beethoven's music is!

The outline of the first movement and its sonata form is provided in the Listening Guide on pages 72–73. Therefore, the discussion here will concern the characteristics of Beethoven's music. One feature is the extreme contrasts he achieves. At times he erupts from a very soft section with a loud, accented chord (often indicated by a *sforzando* sign *sfz*). Or the music may suddenly shift from a rough, combative style to something very tender and lyrical.

A second characteristic is his fondness for and ability at developing themes. The first movement of the Fifth Symphony uses what has to be one of the least promising melodic ideas ever to grace a page of music; and yet what Beethoven makes out of that little idea is sheer genius. This example indicates how the same idea is repeated many times, each time at a different pitch level and all the time leading up to a climactic point in the music. Toward the end of this example he also turns the figure upside down, or uses what is termed *inversion:*

The love of developing musical material led to another Beethoven characteristic: an extended coda section. The coda grows from being a closing section to a second development section as long and as important as the exposition, development, or recapitulation sections.

A fourth characteristic is the sense of drive that can be sensed in many of Beethoven's musical works. At times he reaches the point of almost hammering notes with repeated blows. He makes much use of accent signs to tell the players to punch certain notes. The sense of drive can be seen in the preceding music example in the repeated notes and the way the music builds—three phrases each leading to a fuller chord, and each phrase leading to a yet more powerful phrase.

Second movement. The second movement shows another side of Beethoven's creative abilities—his skill at writing serene and lovely melodies. The movement is a theme and variations built on two melodic ideas. The first melody is:

It is played first by the violas and cellos. The second theme is:

As the movement progresses, Beethoven achieves variety in the themes by changing the melody and ornamenting it and by altering the harmony, rhythm, dynamics, tempo, registration, key, and type of accompaniment.

Third movement. The third movement is quite a change from the traditional minuet and trio of Haydn and Mozart. In its place Beethoven writes what he calls a *scherzo*, which in Italian means joke. No longer is the music refined and polished; it becomes more rollicking and dramatic. The initial theme is the "Mannheim rocket." This time, however, it's very smooth and pitched in the low strings so that it sounds more appropriate for Halloween than for the courts of nineteenth-century Austria.

The middle section of the scherzo is still called the trio, but it assumes a much more significant role in the movement. The opening figure is a lusty motive of running eighth notes played by the cellos and basses. In turn, the theme is played by the violas, second violins, and first violins.

The opening motive of the trio is treated to repetition at different pitch levels. The form of the minuet is retained as the original opening section, the *A* portion, returns in a modified version but with different orchestration. It's followed by a transitional passage that develops out of the scherzo theme and rhythm and is sounded by the timpani. The transition slowly accumulates power until it surges without a break into the fourth movement.

Fourth movement. The fourth movement is in sonata form and is of massive proportions, a characteristic that lasts for the rest of the nineteenth century among symphony writers. The movement is built around two themes. The opening one is based on the C major chord and scale:

The second main theme is:

The development section is marked by active rhythm and frequent changes of key. In it Beethoven does something rather unusual for his time—he brings back the initial motive from the first movement of the symphony. When themes from one movement are found in other movements, the treatment is referred to as *cyclical*. The recapitulation is followed by an extensive coda, which at times sounds as if Beethoven is having trouble deciding when to stop. The final result, though, is a monumental piece of music.

Listening Guide

Beethoven: Symphony No. 5 in C Minor, Op. 67

First Movement

Sonata Form

Exposition

0:00   First theme (form *A* of theme), with fourth note held, played by strings; loud:

0:06   First theme played quietly and repeatedly by strings; leads to held note by violins.

0:20   First theme played loudly by full orchestra; fourth note held.

0:22   Transition beginning with repeated playings of first theme; grows in volume and rises in pitch.

0:44   Vigorous short French horn solo based on first theme (form *B* of theme):

0:47   Second theme, in major key, played softly by violins; followed by other instruments; motive of first theme played softly every fourth measure by cellos and basses:

1:08   Codetta starts as smooth phrases of second theme end, and violins take up chord outlines in pattern of first theme; leads to playing of motive loudly by orchestra.

1:18   First theme idea reappears.

Development

1:27   First theme sounded loudly by French horns and then strings; fourth note held; followed by first theme, sometimes inverted, passed among sections of orchestra at soft dynamic level; music slowly increases in volume.

1:56   Full-sounding chords in winds; repeated notes and first theme in strings; followed by silent places.

2:04   Strings sound *B* form of first theme; first theme fragments passed among the woodwinds.

2:14   Two-note motive (circled in example) derived from *B* form of first theme predominates; later reduced to only one note exchanged between winds and strings.

2:37   Vigorous, loud sounding of *B* form of first theme, contrasted with softly played single notes.

2:45   Sudden loud appearance of first theme, form *A*.

Recapitulation

2:59   First theme played loudly by full orchestra; fourth note held.

3:10   Short oboe cadenza.

3:24   Transition growing out of first theme; music increases in volume and pitch.

3:46   French horns play the *B* form of the first theme.

3:50   Second theme, in tonic minor key, played softly by violins; transition based on portion of second theme; first theme sounded occasionally by lower strings.

4:14   Coda begins as smooth phrases of second theme end, and violins take up chord outlines in pattern of first theme.

4:32   Rhythmic pattern of first theme alternated between winds and strings; much repeating of notes; silent places follow.

4:47   *B* form of first theme played by low strings; two-note motive expanded and extended.

5:03   Four-note melodic idea, sometimes inverted, derived from second theme is played in ascending sequence by violins.

5:14   Woodwinds and strings alternately play four-note idea; fragmented to two notes as music progresses.

5:33   First theme pattern played loudly again by orchestra, leading twice to held notes.

5:48   Quiet appearances of first theme, then suddenly loud.

6:03   Closes with series of brusque chords.

Shostakovich's Symphony No. 5

Dimitri Shostakovich, a twentieth-century Russian composer, finished his Fifth Symphony in 1937. Although over a century later than Beethoven's Fifth Symphony, it stands in the same tradition, just as Walton's *Belshazzar's Feast* follows in the tradition of Handel's oratorios.

First movement. The first movement is in sonata form and begins with a violent-sounding theme that is treated in imitation:

A second portion of the first theme soon appears:

The next theme has a wide range and is presented over a throbbing rhythmic background:

Throughout the movement these themes are varied and combined with each other. The first movement is long by contemporary standards.

Shostakovich follows Beethoven's scherzo idea in the second movement, which is filled with humor and occasional satire. The cellos and string basses begin it in waltz tempo, but what they play is too jovial, too fat to be a waltz in the graceful Viennese tradition. It reminds one of music for a dancing bear in a circus. The tiny E flat clarinet wheezes out a little tune as though it were trying to take itself seriously. The bassoons burp out notes of the shortest possible length, and the solo violinist slides around on a glissando. A peculiar march starts up in the horns; instead of conventional two-beat meter, however, there is an extra beat in each measure, so that the music hobbles along with an uneven gait. At the very end, when the heavy chords suggest that something important is about to happen, a meek and plaintive oboe is heard, sounding as though it were apologizing for being there. The whole movement is filled with ideas, instrumentation, and rhythms that are incongruous when combined.

The third movement is impressive. It begins slowly with warm, romantic sounds from the strings. The themes have a chantlike quality about them:

The third theme is introduced by the oboe:

Throughout this portion of the music, the extremely transparent nature of Shostakovich's writing is evident. At times only one instrument is playing. After a while the first two themes are heard from the strings. The music then winds up to a tremendous climax of intensity, and the strings move higher and higher with an excited tremolo. At the climactic point the second part of the first theme is heard coming through the orchestra, its notes doubled by the xylophone. The cellos come in full force on the third theme. The movement closes with the same music that began it.

Fourth movement. In this movement Shostakovich follows in the symphonic tradition of Beethoven by his extensive manipulation of melodic and rhythmic motives. The music of Shostakovich sounds different, as could be expected of music composed 132 years later. But there is a similar sense of "drive" and a superb ability in handling musical ideas. To assist you in hearing Shostakovich's music better, a simplified score for the movement is provided in the *Study Guide and Scores* book. Themes, instruments, and compositional devices are indicated in that score.

The opening two pitches played repeatedly by the timpani are the opening interval of the first theme. The first four notes of that theme become the main motive for the movement; sometimes only the rhythmic pattern of it is used.

It is followed by an excited, energetic melody:

From this theme (and it is also present in the first theme) Shostakovich takes another four-note figure that is used as a motive, especially for transitions:

On first hearing the music may sound like a random jumble of sounds, as though just about any notes would make as much sense. Actually, just the opposite is true; the music is extremely well organized, so much so that one must know it very well before appreciating all the interrelationships it contains.

Not only does Shostakovich demonstrate a great ability to develop themes and motives, he also is able to give an overarching design to the movement in terms of intensity. The first portion is vibrant and vital. The middle section is more contemplative and quiet and lyric. The third portion brings a return of the themes from the first section and a return of its power and drive. The transition from the calmer middle portion to the third portion gradually leads up to a climactic point. Shostakovich's fondness for continuing one pitch (in this instance doubled in several octaves) can be heard in the powerful coda section. A number of higher pitched instruments in the strings and woodwinds repeat one pitch as the brasses sound the motive from the first theme in major (which sounds similar to the musical phrase "How dry I am").

Other Notable Symphonies

This chapter has discussed three well-known symphonies, but this introduction has only scratched the surface of the quantity of great works that carry the title. To acquaint you with some outstanding symphonies, the following list is offered:

Beethoven, Ludwig van
  All nine symphonies

Borodin, Alexander
  Symphony No. 2 in D Minor

Brahms, Johannes
  All four symphonies

Bruchner, Anton
  Symphony No. 4, *Romantic*

Dvořák, Antonin
  Symphony No. 8, Op. 88
  Symphony No. 9, Op. 95, *New World*

Franck, César
  Symphony in D Minor

Hanson, Howard
  Symphony No. 2, *Romantic*

Haydn, Franz Joseph
  Symphonies No. 94 through 104

Mahler, Gustav
  Symphony No. 4 in G Major

Mendelssohn, Felix
  Symphony No. 3, Op. 56, *Scotch*
  Symphony No. 4, Op. 90, *Italian*

Mozart, Wolfgang Amadeus
  Symphony No. 35, K. 385, *Haffner*
  Symphony No. 36, K. 425, *Linz*
  Symphony No. 38, K. 504, *Prague*
  Symphony No. 39, K. 543
  Symphony No. 41, K. 551, *Jupiter*

Prokofiev, Sergei
  Symphony No. 5, Op. 100

Schubert, Franz
  Symphony No. 8 in B Minor, *Unfinished*
  Symphony No. 9 in C Major, *The Great*

Schumann, Robert
  Symphony No. 1, Op. 38, *Spring*

Sibelius, Jean
  Symphony No. 1 in E Minor, Op. 39
  Symphony No. 2 in D Major, Op. 43
  Symphony No. 5 in E Flat Major, Op. 82

Tchaikovsky, Peter
  Symphony No. 4 in F Minor, Op. 36
  Symphony No. 5 in E Minor, Op. 64
  Symphony No. 6, Op. 74, *Pathétique*

Wolfgang Amadeus Mozart

Mozart was born in 1756 in Salzburg, Austria. His father, Leopold, was a recognized violinist and composer in the court of the Archbishop. The elder Mozart was quick to realize that his son had extraordinary talents and to capitalize on them. Under his father's tutelage young Mozart showed remarkable mastery of the piano and, to a lesser extent, the violin. By the time he was five he had composed his first pieces, and at six he performed at the court of the Empress Maria Theresa. When he was seven, Mozart and his sister, who was four years older, went on a grand tour of Europe that included Paris, London, and Munich. By the age of 13 he had written concertos, symphonies, and a comic opera; at 14 he was knighted by the Pope.

The most phenomenal aspect of Mozart's musical talent was his memory for music and his ability to work out whole pieces in his mind. He once wrote, "Though it be long, the work is complete and finished in my mind. I take out of the bag of my memory what has previously been collected into it. For this reason the committing to paper is done quickly enough. For everything is already finished, and it rarely differs on paper from what it was in my imagination."

Mozart never experienced the stability of a good appointment as a composer to a patron. For a while he worked for the Prince-Archbishop of Salzburg. The Archbishop was a difficult man, and the high-spirited Mozart resented the restrictions of the patronage system. (He wrote his father, "The two valets sit at the head of the table. I at least have the honor of sitting above the cooks.") He quarreled with the Archbishop and was dismissed. At the age of 25 he left Salzburg to pursue a career as a free musician in Vienna.

A year later he married Constanze Weber. Since Mozart didn't fare well under the patronage system, he spent the next—the last—ten years of his life, as he put it, "Hovering between hope and anxiety." Due in part to his impractical and overgenerous nature in finan-

Wolfgang Amadeus Mozart. An unfinished painting by Joseph Lange, his brother-in-law.

cial affairs, his only recourse was to eke out an existence by teaching, giving concerts, composing, and borrowing from friends.

In 1791, at the age of 35, Mozart died of uremic poisoning. Because he was so deeply in debt, he was given the cheapest funeral and buried in a pauper's grave.

Despite his short life and the disappointments that plagued him, Mozart composed over 600 complete works, including 22 operas, 25 piano concertos, 12 violin concertos, 14 concertos for other instruments, 24 string quartets, 60 solo works for piano, 27 choral works, and 52 symphonies. Mozart never used opus numbers, although some were added later by publishers. His works were catalogued by a Viennese botanist and amateur musician named Köchel, who assigned each composition a number on a generally chronological basis. So today every Mozart work is identified by a number (up to 626), preceded by the initial K, for Köchel (*Keh*-shul). A few Köchel numbers have been corrected on the basis of later musicological research.

Ludwig van Beethoven

Beethoven was born in 1770 into the family of a ne'er-do-well musician in Bonn, Germany. His father, a drunkard, observed the boy's talent and nourished dreams that he might have sired prodigy who, like the young Mozart, would bring in a good income from his performances. So Ludwig was pushed into music study, especially piano, viola, and organ. He also sang in the chapel choir at Bonn. Although talented, he never became the prodigy his father had hoped for. At the age of 22 Beethoven set off for Vienna to make his fortune in the world of music.

Beethoven had little formal academic schooling. He studied composition with several teachers, including Haydn, and made a name for himself as a pianist. He won friends and admirers among the aristocracy of Vienna, and within a decade he had established himself as a leading composer and performer whose services were in demand.

The musical training he received from Haydn and others was steeped in the careful, formal style of the times, which made a lasting impression on him. But there were other influences. One was the revolutionary spirit that was awakening in Europe. The spirit of independence was burning not only in Beethoven's music but in the works of other artists as well. The American and French revolutions both occurred while Beethoven was a young man, and he was inevitably affected by these forces.

Then there was Beethoven's own personality. Were he alive today, he would probably identify himself with humanitarian causes and social protest groups. He would insist on his rights as a person and on the rights of others. Two events give support to this view of the man. His Symphony No. 3, entitled *Eroica* (the "heroic" symphony), was originally dedicated to Napoleon. When Beethoven heard that

Ludwig van Beethoven composing his Missa Solemnis. *An 1819 painting by Josef Stieler.*

Napoleon had declared himself Emperor, he was disappointed to learn that his idol was just another ambitious soldier-politician, and he angrily tore up the dedication. In its place he wrote: "To the memory of a great man." Another example of Beethoven's belief concerns his Ninth Symphony. As early as 1792 he had thought of setting Schiller's *Ode to Joy* to music. The ethical ideals of the poem—the universal brotherhood of man and its basis in the love of a heavenly Father—had strong appeal to Beethoven.

Beethoven is probably the first composer

in history to be considered a "personality." His great and independent spirit fills his music. Haydn's music is sometimes difficult to distinguish from Mozart's, and Bach's from Telemann's. But Beethoven's mature works sound like no one else's music. And his personal life reflected this same desire for independence. He took orders from no one. He was successful enough at selling his music that he could remain free from worry about deadlines or patrons. He could afford to be a man unto himself.

In appearance he was described as "a short, stout man with a very red face, small piercing eyes, and bushy eyebrows, dressed in a long overcoat which reached nearly to his ankles. . . . Notwithstanding the high color of his cheeks and his general untidiness, there was in those small piercing eyes an expression which no painter could render. It was a feeling of sublimity and melancholy combined."*

Beethoven's personality was also affected by a hearing loss that eventually led to complete deafness. The condition was evident by the time he was 28, and it became progressively worse. After the first performance of his monumental Ninth Symphony, Beethoven didn't acknowledge the applause because he couldn't hear it. His attention was attracted by a tug on the sleeve, whereupon he turned and bowed to the cheering audience.

His deafness caused him to lose contact with others and to withdraw into himself, becoming more irritable, morose, and suspicious of people. His final compositions were products of this period of his life. They tend to be more personal, meditative, and abstract. His output of new works during the last 15 years of his life was not as large.

You may wonder how it was possible for the deaf Beethoven to write entire symphonies. The process becomes understandable when you look within your own experience. You can recall melodies and the sounds of people's voices in your memory, even though physically you hear nothing. Trained people can "think out" a sizable amount of music in their minds. And Beethoven was obviously a well-trained musician with more than average abilities.

There is a second reason for his success despite his disability. It has to do with the way he composed. It was his custom to write down themes in a sketchbook. Then he would work over the themes, revising and rewriting them, making slight alterations and trying them out to determine their suitability for the piece he had in mind. This trial-and-error process might be resumed intermittently over a period of years. So the thematic material for many of his later compositions had been worked out when he was still able to hear fairly well.

Beethoven poured strenuous effort into each measure of his music, for he was not the "natural" composer that Mozart was. Beethoven is reported to have compared the writing of a particular work, his opera *Fidelio*, with the bearing of a child. And with good reason. His manuscripts look "like a bloody record of a tremendous inner battle."**

He died in 1827 of jaundice and cholera. That his death occurred during a hailstorm was a coincidence that seems appropriate to the man and his life.

---

*From a description by Sir Julius Benedict (1823), quoted in Alexander Wheelock Thayer, *Life of Beethoven* (Princeton, N.J.: Princeton University Press, 1964), p. 873.

**From *The Joy of Music* by Leonard Bernstein (New York: Simon and Schuster, 1954), page 81.

Dimitri Shostakovich

Dimitri Shostakovich (1906–1975) received all of his musical training in Russia, and he spent very little time outside the country. He was born in St. Petersburg (Leningrad), and his mother was a well-trained pianist. At 13 he entered the Conservatory at St. Petersburg. In 1925, at the age of 19, he finished his First Symphony, which is a mature work that has become a part of the repertoire of most symphony orchestras. His career was off to an auspicious start.

In 1934 he ran into trouble with the Communist Party over an opera entitled *Lady Macbeth of ·Mzensk.* It was accused of being "formalistic," a vague charge meaning that the music was not sufficiently political or that it was too much like music of the Western world. He publicly promised to do better in the future. In 1937 he brought out his Fifth Symphony.

During World War II Shostakovich was not permitted to serve in the armed forces because he was considered so valuable a citizen. He spent the war years in Leningrad, where he remained even through the long siege of that city, writing his Seventh Symphony and serving as a volunteer fireman. He had another falling out with the Communist Party in 1948 when he was again accused of "musical formalism." A public apology and a new opera extricated him from the predicament. He came

Dimitri Shostakovich.

to be revered in his native land. His symphonies number 15, making him the first important composer since Beethoven to accomplish more than nine.

Eleven

Concertos

A concerto (con-*chair*-toh) exhibits some of the same features as symphonies and sonatas. It is a composition for instruments, usually consisting of several movements and utilizing traditional forms. The principle of a concerto is the contrast between groups of different size or instruments of different types.

Concerto Grosso

The *concerto grosso*—*grosso* meaning grand or big—was the first type of concerto to predominate in music history. It achieves contrast by pitting a small group against a larger one. There is little difference in instrumentation or in the music that each group performs. There is no attempt to have the small group "show off," as is true in later concertos. The small group remains seated and often plays along with the large group. Usually concerti grossi are composed for strings, with a harpsichord helping out on the harmonies. A few wind instruments are sometimes included in the small group. For example, four of the six frequently heard *Brandenburg Concertos* by Bach contain solo parts for winds.

The fact that the same or similar instruments play the same music sometimes makes it difficult to distinguish which group is playing. The orchestra of Bach's day was small, so the larger group was not large by today's standards. Also, three or four good string players can produce a healthy, vigorous sound. Recordings tend to make the groups less distinguishable by taking away most of the physical distance that is present in live performances.

Corelli's Christmas Concerto

Arcangelo Corelli's Concerto Grosso, Op. 6, No. 8, *Christmas Concerto*, is one of many concerti grossi written in the seventeenth and early eighteenth centuries. The "Christmas" part of the title comes from the inscription on the music: "Composed for the night of the Nativity, 1712." Corelli died the following year. Except for a movement marked *Pastorale*, there is no connection between the music and Christmas. The solo group consists of two violins and cello accompanied by a string orchestra and harpsichord, a typical instrumentation for a concerto grosso. It is typical also in the contrasting tempos that distinguish its various sections.

The first movement opens with a fast introduction that is followed by a slow, deliberate section featuring the full orchestra throughout:

The pattern of the first two pitches of the theme is imitated as the parts enter. The music is quite contrapuntal.

The first movement continues at a fast tempo, and it features the two solo violins. The melody is built around a short fragment that is only two measures long and contains only four different pitches:

The third and fourth measures are similar to the first two, except that most of the pitches are three notes higher than they were the first time. The immediate repeating of a pattern of notes at a different pitch level is called *sequence*. It can be heard often in music written between 1650 and 1750. In this particular movement the two violin parts weave around each other in contrapuntal fashion. Many times there is a dissonance that resolves to a consonance on the second half of the beat. To hear the interplay of consonance and dissonance is one of the pleasures of listening to this type of music.

The second movement consists of three sections in a slow-fast-slow pattern of tempos. Again the violins are featured, and again sequence can be heard. In the notation of the theme, a bracket has been put over the figure that appears at different pitch levels:

The theme is not heard immediately; the movement opens with an accompanying figure and also closes with one.

The other three movements, which make a total of five, continue the alternation between fast and slow tempos. This alternation is typical. None of the movements is long, at least by standards of art music. The longest takes about five minutes to perform and the shortest, about 1:25. The last movement is marked *Pastorale*, a restful type of music that was popular during the time of Corelli.

In music of this type the small group sometimes has a theme of its own that the orchestra never plays, and vice versa. In other movements there is alternation between the theme of the orchestra and the theme of the small group.

The Solo Concerto

Gradually the concerto grosso lost favor, and by 1750 it was replaced by the solo concerto. The newer form became so prevalent that the word *concerto* is understood today to mean a solo concerto. The part that the soloist plays in the solo concerto is intended for a virtuoso performer. It is much more difficult and showy than the parts assigned to the orchestra players. The orchestra serves largely as accompaniment.

Although three instruments have been especially favored by composers—piano, violin, and cello—a concerto can be written for any instrument. A trumpet concerto will be examined first.

Haydn's Concerto for Trumpet and Orchestra

Haydn's Trumpet Concerto in E Flat was composed in 1796 for a keyed (not valve) trumpet. The keys were added to the sides of the instrument somewhat like keys on clarinets and saxophones today. The valves, which are much superior, replaced the keys about 1813.

A keyed trumpet.

The work was written for the great trumpet virtuoso of the time, Anton Weidinger. He must have been quite a performer, because Haydn did not hesitate to write difficult passages for him to play.

First movement. Since the focus of this discussion is on the techniques involved in writing for a soloist and orchestra, the features of the particular sonata form need not receive detailed attention. Before the solo trumpet enters, the orchestra presents a shortened version of the exposition. The first and most important theme is:

A second theme is heard soon afterward. It is short and serves as a counterbalance to the first theme:

Toward the middle of the movement the trumpet presents a third theme, one that is derived from the first theme:

The soloist plays a few short passages before entering on the main theme, which occurs after 36 measures have passed. This concerto features the typical *double exposition,* one for the orchestra and one for the soloist. Except for the double exposition, the movement proceeds through the normal sonata form. The development section is shorter and simpler than was its counterpart in the G Minor Symphony. The concerto was written when neither Haydn nor sonata form had reached full musical maturity. The development section is more like the addition of different musical ideas than a true development.

There is another feature of the concerto that is not found in symphonies. Shortly before the end of the movement, the orchestra comes to a stop, and the soloist begins playing by himself a freely constructed and often technically difficult paraphrase of the preceding musical material. Many stops and starts are made, holds and altered tempos appear freely, and the rhythm is entirely flexible. This portion of a concerto is called a *cadenza.* It is usually found in one of three movements and permits the soloist to show off in terms of both playing and improvising.

Originally the cadenzas played were supposed to be a performer's own, and theoretically they were to be improvised, although one suspects that the performers must have thought out well in advance what to play for

_____ *Listening Guide* _____

Haydn: Concerto for Trumpet and Orchestra in E Flat Major

Third Movement

Rondo

0:00   Main theme *(A)* played by violins at rather soft dynamic level and rather fast tempo:

0:10   Main theme repeated by orchestra; louder.

0:22   First contrasting theme *(B)* played by violins:

0:28   Transition leading back to main theme.

0:38   Trumpet enters playing *A* theme.

0:48   Trumpet repeats *A* theme.

0:58   Transition leading to *B* theme.

the cadenza. Therefore, Haydn indicated only where the cadenzas were to be inserted in his music; he did not write them out for the performer.

Second movement.   The second movement is in the style of a pastorale, which is mentioned in conjunction with Corelli's *Christmas Concerto.* The mood is leisurely and the music melodious. The main theme is played first by the orchestra before the solo trumpet is given a turn at it.

The middle section of the movement contrasts with the main theme and modulates into a remote key. The overall form of the movement is *A B A.* It does not contain a cadenza.

1:08   Trumpet and violins alternate playing *B* theme in new key.

1:34   Second contrasting theme *(C)* played by violins and trumpet:

1:49   Trumpet plays *A* theme again.

1:59   Short development of *A* theme by trumpet and orchestra; several changes of key.

2:38   Trumpet plays *A* theme; some imitation of theme by violins.

2:55   Trumpet and violins play *B* theme again.

3:11   Portion of *C* theme played alternately by violins and woodwinds.

3:27   Trumpet plays first portion of *A* theme.

3:36   Portion of *C* theme played by violins and trumpet with trilled notes.

4:05   Coda begins with trumpet playing portion of *A* theme softly.

4:20   Closes after crescendo and full chord.

Third movement—rondo form. For the final movement of the concerto Haydn chose *rondo* form. The basis of the rondo idea is a melody that returns several times, with other musical material interspersed among its various appearances. Symbolically it can be represented *A B A C A D A* and so on. Theoretically there is no limit to the number of sections possible in a rondo, but a minimum of five sections is customary. Normally the main theme of a rondo is a distinctive melody that is easily remembered; the subordinate themes are less memorable. This characteristic holds true in the case of Haydn's rondo. One can easily miss the *B* and even more easily miss the *C* theme. In effect, they are as much contrasting material to the main theme as they are additional melodies.

A Listening Guide for the third movement is provided on pages 86–87.

Brahms' Piano Concerto No. 2

The first theme of the first movement of Brahms' Second Piano Concerto was presented in Chapter 5 as an example of good melodic writing. Finished in 1881, the concerto is of monumental size; it actually is more like a symphony, with four movements instead of the usual three. The first movement is about 17 minutes long. The music has a sweeping, rolling, robust quality. Even the chords the pianist must play are big (Brahms apparently had large hands), and the full range of the keyboard is exploited from one end to the other.

The music has a quality that is hard to put into words—optimistic, positive, and healthy come as close as any. There is an unabashed love of beautiful harmony and melody, and a quality that seems to say all will work out right in the end.

Brahms wrote this concerto when he was well established as a composer. It is typical of his well-conceived and careful approach to writing music. Brahms worked with most of the same forms that Haydn and Mozart had employed. By the time Brahms composed his music, however, such forms had become

passé, and he was considered hopelessly conservative by many of his contemporaries.

By nature Brahms was, in fact, conservative. But the combination of his rational approach to music and the emphasis on emotion and personal feelings that marked the nineteenth century produced just the right mixture for some enduring and beautiful music. Depending on your inclinations, you can listen to Brahms' music in one of two ways: You can simply enjoy the lush sounds and beautiful melodies, or you can admire his skill in manipulating themes and forms.

A typical technique of Brahms was to take fragments from a melody and then manipulate and develop them throughout an entire movement. As a result most of the time you are hearing a theme or fragment of a theme. The music sounds familiar, but it does not repeat itself literally. Brahms also blurred the changes from one part of the form to another so that the "seams" between the parts are difficult to detect.

First movement. A Listening Guide for the first movement appears on pages 89–91. Notice that the time dimensions for the movement are longer than for much of the music presented earlier in this book. Also, the movement contains a first theme with two distinct portions, a second theme, plus two other themes that appear as the music progresses. There is also a double exposition, as there is in the first movement of Haydn's Trumpet Concerto.

Second movement. The second movement is in a lusty $\frac{3}{4}$ meter. It is a sturdy-sounding scherzo. The opening theme is:

The second theme reminds one of a Viennese waltz:

Listening Guide

Brahms: Piano Concerto No. 2 in B Flat, Op. 83

First Movement

Sonata Form

Exposition I

0:00   First theme, first portion, played by French horn; piano answers the two phrases of the theme:

0:22   First theme, second portion, played by the woodwinds:

0:34   Cadenza for piano.

1:27   First portion of first theme played by orchestra; leads into transition; loud dynamic level.

2:16   Second theme, in minor key, played rather softly by violins:

2:38   Transition based on dotted-note figure; marchlike.

2:50   Codetta begins with loud statement of first theme; is followed by descending chromatic passages by strings and winds.

Exposition II

3:08   Piano begins with free-sounding solo but soon takes up first portion of first theme.

(Continued on page 90)

The third theme enters well along in the movement:

_____ *Listening Guide* _____

(Continued from page 89)

4:01   First theme, second portion, played smoothly by violins.

4:42   Transition containing free material for piano; fragments of first theme played by orchestra.

5:25   New theme introduced in transition section by French horns; is repeated several times by other instruments:

6:01   Two-note motive (circled in example) is repeated many times by orchestra and then piano.

6:35   Second theme played in rhapsodic style by piano alone.

6:57   Transition with dotted-note figure and marchlike melody played by piano.

7:47   Codetta begins with first part of first theme played loudly by orchestra; is followed soon by a portion of second theme played by violins and flutes; concluded with descending chromatic passages in violins and clarinets.

Development

8:25   French horn softly plays opening measures of first theme; is soon answered with the second measure from woodwinds.

8:59   Dotted-note figure is played by violins with rapidly outlined chords played by piano; tempo increases.

9:23   Piano plays chords off the beat as dotted-note figure continues in orchestra.

9:37   Episode: Marchlike melody based on dotted-note figure begins in piano; similar material is heard four more times, each time somewhat varied, and each time with runs by piano interspersed between the appearances:

It is given a varied rhythmic treatment, with an occasional meter of $\frac{2}{4}$ instead of $\frac{3}{4}$.

Third movement. The third movement is the slow and melodious one in this concerto. It is built on one theme that is introduced by a cello solo:

Fourth movement. The fourth movement is marked *Allegro grazioso* (allegro, gracefully). The opening theme is playful:

10:36   Opening notes of first theme sounded loudly by orchestra; free cadenzalike material for piano.

10:53   Opening three notes sounded loudly by orchestra again; three-note fragment of first theme, second portion, begins to appear in orchestra; piano has free material.

11:31   Calm, quiet chords held by orchestra, with alternating notes played by piano.

Recapitulation

11:44   French horn plays first theme, first portion, rather quietly.

12:05   Second portion of first theme played by woodwinds.

12:38   Theme from transition in second exposition played by woodwinds and used as transition.

13:15   Two-note motive from transition theme played by piano and later taken up by woodwinds.

13:49   Second theme played rhapsodically by piano alone.

14:11   Transition using dotted-note marchlike material; is developed somewhat.

15:05   Coda begins with playing of first theme, first portion, by French horn; piano continues free-sounding lines; music becomes calm.

15:30   First three notes of first theme played loudly by orchestra.

16:02   First theme, second portion, played by piano; soon other instruments take up this theme.

16:40   Suddenly music gets loud; second phrases of first portion of theme played by orchestra.

17:04   Closes with full-sounding chord.

p Piano

The second theme seems to be straight out of Vienna:

Woodwinds Strings

Two more themes are heard:

Piano

p

Piano

p

This is one of Brahms' most tuneful movements.

Brahms' Piano Concerto No. 2 is especially significant because it was by one of the master composers of the nineteenth century and also because that era is referred to as "the Golden Age of the piano." The peak period for the writing of piano concertos extended from the time of Mozart until about the beginning of the twentieth century.

Franz Joseph Haydn

One man who had much to do with the development of orchestral music was Franz Joseph Haydn (1732–1809). He was born in the same year as George Washington, in the town of Rohrau in eastern Austria. Unlike Mozart, he didn't have the advantage of early musical training. An uncle, with whom Haydn went to live at the age of six, gave him his first musical instruction. At eight he became a choirboy at the Cathedral of St. Stephen in Vienna, where he gained musical experience but little theoretical instruction. When his voice changed, he was dismissed. For the next few years he lived a precarious existence, doing odd jobs and teaching as well as studying music theory on his own initiative. In 1761, at the age of 29, Haydn was taken into the service of Prince Paul Anton Esterházy (*Ester-hahzy*), head of one of the richest and most powerful noble families in Hungary.

The next year Nicholas Esterházy succeeded his brother Paul Anton. Nicholas, besides being rich and powerful, was also a connoisseur of music. Most of the time he lived at a country estate at Eisenstadt, the sumptuous-

ness of which rivaled the French court at Versailles. On the estate were two beautiful concert halls and two theaters, one for opera and one for marionette plays.

Haydn both composed and conducted the performances, trained the musicians, and kept the instruments in repair. He had 25 *good* instrumentalists and a dozen or so fine singers.

Haydn's contract was typical. It required him "to produce at once any composition called for" and to smooth out all difficulties among the musicians. He was expected to present himself twice daily in the antechamber to await orders.

For the most part, Haydn's experience with the Esterházy family represented the patronage system at its best. Haydn liked them and they him.

After Haydn had been with the Esterházys for 30 years, Prince Nicholas died. Haydn subsequently made two visits to London in the 1790s. For each trip he composed six symphonies, which collectively are known as the London symphonies, numbers 92 to 104. They represent Haydn at his orchestral best. After

Arcangelo Corelli

Arcangelo Corelli, the leading exponent of Italian violin playing, lived from 1653 until 1713. Educated in Bologna, he spent most of his life in Rome, where he was much admired as a violinist and composer. His music promoted the technical and tonal capabilities of the instrument. His best works are sonatas and concerti grossi. His body lies in the Pantheon in Rome, not far from that of the painter Raphael.

Franz Joseph Haydn. Portrait by Thomas Hardy. Royal College of Music, London.

the London trips he returned to work for a while for Nicholas Esterházy II, who was not as interested in music as his father had been. Haydn then wrote mainly vocal works, including two oratorios, *The Creation* and *The Seasons*. He gradually retired from composing and died in 1809.

Haydn was recognized during his lifetime as a great composer by the public and by other musicians. He admired, and was in turn admired by, Mozart. The two learned from each other's music, a fact especially evident in Haydn's string quartets written after 1781. Beethoven also regarded Haydn with esteem.

Haydn is sometimes referred to as the "father" of the symphony, the string quartet, the modern orchestra, and instrumental music in general. Although such claims are exaggerated, they give some indication of his significance. What Haydn did was to work out a better balance for the new forms. For example, he developed the finale of the symphony. Prior to Haydn, the fourth movement had been only a frothy little section. Haydn expanded it into a movement with a definite form.

Johannes Brahms

Johannes Brahms (1833–1897) was the son of a musician, a somewhat shiftless string bass player in Hamburg, Germany. Young Brahms got his start by playing piano in the dance halls in the poorer sections of town. He demonstrated considerable talent, and by the age of 20 he was serving as piano accompanist to one of the better violinists of the day. He showed talent in composition as well and soon went to study with Robert Schumann. The Schumanns took the shy young man into their home. Schumann also published a magazine on music in which he praised Brahms' music, and before long Brahms was known throughout the musical world. He was a great help to the family when Schumann suffered a mental collapse and had to be hospitalized.

At first Brahms admired and then grew to love Clara Schumann, who was 14 years older than he and the mother of seven children. Because he had the highest regard for her husband, his ailing benefactor, the situation caused him much conflict. After Schumann died, Brahms should have felt free to follow through on his love for Clara and marry her; she was no longer the unattainable ideal. But somehow he could not bring himself to take a step that would have obligated him and limited his freedom. Later in life Brahms fell in

Johannes Brahms when a young man.

love with other women, but he chose never to marry.

Brahms reacted in a similar way to employment. He never accepted a position that made heavy demands on him. The one position Brahms coveted—conductorship of the orchestra in his native Hamburg—eluded him throughout his life. Apparently the directors of the orchestra couldn't forget that he started out as a waterfront musician. Most of his adult life, therefore, was spent in Vienna, where for short periods of time he directed various choral groups and a music society. Most of his income came from the sale of his compositions and from conducting.

Brahms was every bit a human being. A bachelor, he scrimped on buying food for himself but never failed to eat heartily if invited to someone's home for dinner. He was brusque, especially as he grew older, but he was also fond of children and enjoyed a good laugh.

Brahms was aware that he had extraordinary talent as a composer, and this was partially the reason for his wanting to be as free as possible. Unlike Beethoven, he left no rejected versions of his music for posterity to find. He wanted the world to know only his best work, so his rough sketches were carefully destroyed. It is said that he burned as many of his compositions as he allowed to be published.

Brahms composed almost every type of music and wrote with consistently high quality—symphonies, concertos, chamber music, piano works, songs, and choral music. One of his greatest compositions, *A German Requiem*, was written early in his career. This work for chorus, orchestra, and soprano and baritone soloists is one of the most profound in all music literature.

In spite of his demonstrated skill in writing for both the choral and strictly instrumental idioms, Brahms was not attracted to either opera or tone poems, and therefore he attempted neither. His coolness toward opera may have been partly due to the excessive competition raging between the followers of Brahms and those of the German opera composer Richard Wagner. In the second half of the nineteenth century, music lovers evidently felt obliged to choose sides between the two men. The division concerned the artistic role of music as much as it did personalities. The Wagnerites held that music was a medium for the expression of emotions and ideas. Brahms promoted the idea that music was an end in itself. Since there is truth in both views, the dispute has never been resolved to everyone's satisfaction. Brahms handled the matter sensibly: He ignored it as best he could and went about his composing.

Twelve

Chamber Music

Chamber music is distinguished by the fact that each part is performed by only one player. For instance, even though a string quartet contains two violins, in addition to a viola and a cello, each violin part is different. As long as each part is different, there could be ten violin parts and the result would still be chamber music (but not a quartet).

Because chamber music requires fewer instruments, it is more suitable for performance in a room than in a concert hall. (The word *chamber* comes from the French for room.) Musicians value chamber music because it permits a refinement and intimacy of expression that cannot be derived from a large group. An orchestra has power and color, while a string quartet provides a sense of involvement and clarity. One medium can be as effective as the other in the hands of a skilled composer.

Chamber music is an instrumental medium, although a few works include voices with the instruments. Chamber works usually contain several movements, employing sonata form, rondo, and other formal schemes. A few string quartets are almost as long as symphonies.

Almost every conceivable combination of instruments has had chamber music written for it. Certain groups are more frequently found, however. The most common are the sonata and the string quartet. Another likely string group involves two violins, two violas, and one or two cellos. The woodwind quintet is made up of a clarinet, oboe, bassoon, flute, and French horn. Although the French horn is a brass instrument, its timbre blends well with woodwinds, so composers have included it in this woodwind group. Brass ensembles have the least standardized instrumentation. Perhaps the quintet (two trumpets, French horn, trombone, and tuba) has most frequently drawn the attention of composers.

It is not unusual to find one nonstring instrument added to a string quartet. For example, a work for clarinet and string quartet is called a *clarinet quintet*, though only one clarinet is present. If a piano plus a string quartet is called for, the work is a *piano quintet*. A *piano trio* is a piano plus violin and cello. Apparently the presence of strings is taken for granted, so the unusual instrument is designated in the naming of the group.

Mozart's Clarinet Quintet

Mozart's Clarinet Quintet in A Major, K. 581, is a relatively late work, written after his Symphony No. 40. It is in the best "polished" style of the eighteenth century. The form is clearly delineated, the parts are well balanced, and everything is neat and enjoyable.

The first movement is in sonata form, of course. The first theme is:

Some runs for the clarinet are inserted after each of the initial appearances of the first theme, and these runs occur extensively in the development section. The second theme of the movement is:

The second movement is in three-part form and has many of the characteristics of an operatic aria. The main theme is:

The contrasting section consists of many scale-wise runs and decorative figures in the clarinet and first violin.

The third movement is a minuet and trio:

This minuet is unusual because it has two trios, one for the strings alone and a second one giving the clarinet a chance to show off its wide range.

The fourth movement is a *theme and variation*. Since this technique has not been presented thus far in this book, the movement will be given more space here. The theme is in two-part, or binary, form: *a b*. The last part of the *b* line is identical with the second line of *a*, a not unusual circumstance. The similarities make the theme easier to remember.

The first variation contains some of the melody in the violin but gives the clarinet a free-wheeling countermelody:

In the second variation the viola plays an ornamented version of the melody, while the violins have a counterfigure:

The third variation presents a change of mode from major to minor. The viola "sobs" out this melody:

The second half of the variation on the melody contains many chromatic notes.

The fourth variation returns to major and presents a decorative melodic line in the clarinet and first violin parts:

An adagio variation follows. It uses the figure played by the violins in Variation II. The harmony of the theme is preserved, but the original melody is only hinted at.

The theme is heard again as the coda for the movement.

In this movement of this quintet, Mozart varies the theme in three ways by (1) adding a countermelody, (2) ornamenting and decorating the theme, and (3) changing the harmony. He could also have altered the rhythm or combined any of these four types of variation. In Mozart's time composers stuck rather close to the original theme. (You can usually hum along on the theme while listening to a variation.) Later composers are much freer in their concept of variation, and at points in their variation material no recognizable connection with the theme can be found.

There is a difference between varying and developing a theme. Recall what Mozart does in developing the themes in his Fortieth Symphony, and contrast that with what he does in varying the theme in his Clarinet Quintet. Development involves fragmenting and remolding a theme. Variation consists of placing the theme in a new setting or giving it a new "costume"—adding a countermelody or altering its rhythmic pattern, for example.

The Sonata

Early eighteenth-century musicians did not use the word *sonata* consistently. Originally the word meant any piece for instruments. But a distinction was drawn between a *sonata da camera*, or chamber sonata, which was usually based on dances, and a *sonata da chiesa*, or church sonata, which was more serious and complex. Actually the two types of sonatas overlapped, and after 1750 the distinction was dropped altogether.

Many seventeenth- and eighteenth-century sonatas were for small ensembles, often four players. Frequently the music was written for three instruments plus keyboard, and it acquired the name *trio sonata*, even though more than three players usually performed the piece.

Solo sonatas were composed for only one instrument. Domenico Scarlatti (1685–1757), an Italian who spent much of his adult life in Spain, wrote over 500 solo keyboard pieces that he called sonatas. Bach wrote a number of solo sonatas for cello, flute, and violin, and more recent composers have written solo sonatas. The instrument most commonly used in a solo sonata is the piano. More will be said about the piano sonata in Chapter 13.

Early sonatas have short movements that alternate in tempo. Since the time of Mozart, the sonata (not to be confused with sonata form) has been a sizable work in three or four movements. The movements correspond to those found in the symphony, except that the minuet or third movement is often omitted. In tempo, form, and key relationships, each movement of the sonata tends to resemble its symphonic counterpart.

A sonata is usually a composition for two instruments: a piano and one other instrument. The two parts are considered to be of *equal* importance; in no sense is the piano accompanying the other instrument. As a matter of fact, the piano part often contains the more important musical idea, while the other instrument accompanies. Since the presence of the piano is assumed, the sonata is called by the name of the other instrument. So a violin sonata is for violin and piano.

Because the sonata is ensemble music, the players perform with the music before them. The custom of memorizing has come to be associated with solo playing, as when a soloist performs a difficult concerto. In chamber music, however, the individual must be subordinate to the ensemble, so memorizing is inappropriate. Furthermore, the complexity of the various lines and the number of players involved (two people for a sonata, more in other ensembles) make the memorized performance more susceptible to error. An exception is the solo sonata, which is usually played from memory.

Franck's Violin Sonata

One of the most famous sonatas for violin and piano is César Franck's Violin Sonata in A Major. Franck lived and wrote in the latter half of the nineteenth century, and his music is full of rich harmonies and luscious melodies. Franck himself was an organist, and his music shows an advanced knowledge of harmony.

The first movement of the sonata is in moderate tempo and presents two themes. The first theme has no distinct ending. Franck keeps the elements of a thematic idea going for quite a while and in so doing he transforms them into transitional material. He gives the impression of a brief development shortly after each presentation:

The second theme appears almost exclusively in the piano part. The movement is in a loose

sonata form, but there is little actual development.

The second movement is a dazzling allegro. A difficult and dynamic piano solo opens the movement. The piano is soon joined by the violin:

The second theme is far more lyric and smooth:

Again the music is in a loose sonata form.

The third movement is marked *Recitativo-Fantasia*. The word *recitative* should be familiar to you from Chapter 8 in this book. It is a free declamatory style that is featured in sections of operas and oratorios. Here Franck adapts that style for the solo violin. *Fantasy* indicates a free piece with no particular form. The second theme that appears in the fantasy is of interest because it appears again in the fourth movement:

For the final movement Franck combines a flowing melody with one of the oldest techniques in music, a *canon*. Canon (not to be confused with *cannon*, the old military weapon) refers to music in which one part enters after another, in strict imitation. The word literally means rule. It has fascinated composers since at least the year 1200.

The piano opens the movement and is followed in strict imitation by the violin, four counts later:

The movement is dominated by the main melody, but the appearance of the theme from the third movement provides the sonata with some cyclical writing, a favorite technique of Franck.

Dvořák's String Quartet No. 6

This quartet, Op. 96 of Antonin Dvořák, is often referred to as the "American" Quartet. The reason for this name is the fact that Dvořák composed it during the summer of 1893 in the little town of Spillville, Iowa. Dvořák was for three years Director of the Conservatory of Music in New York. He missed his native Bohemia very much, so he spent his summers living among the Czech-Bohemian people in Spillville. The music is largely Bohemian in character, not American. It has about it some of the qualities of Brahms' music—good cheer, enjoyment, optimism. It is not as complex as Brahms' music, however, although it may be just as enjoyable.

The first movement is presented in the Listening Guide on pages 102–103. As the Guide indicates, the movement is in sonata form.

Second movement.   This movement is in a large three-part form. It presents flowing, sentimental melodies. The melody for the *A* portion is:

The middle section of the movement is also melodic, with the first and second violins playing some of the time three notes apart. The gradual nursing of the music up to climactic points can be clearly heard. The movement closes with the cello restating the opening theme.

Third movement.   This movement contains some of the scherzo character found in Beethoven's Fifth Symphony; however, the pattern is extended to five sections: *A B A B A.* There is also some variation on the theme during the movement. The *A* theme begins in the cello. Like several other themes in the quartet, the *A* theme is basically pentatonic—based on a five-note scale:

Fourth movement.   The fourth movement is a rondo with a pattern of *A B A C A B A.* It is very lively and ends in a flourish of sound. The main theme is:

César Franck

Franck was born at Liege, Belgium, in 1822, and died in Paris in 1890. His father was a banker who had a keen love of music. He gave his two sons, Joseph and César, a good musical education. To make sure it was adequate, the family moved to Paris so that the boys could finish study at the Conservatory there. César won a number of prizes for his music abilities. He was a quiet, unassuming man who spent most of his adult life as the organist at St. Clotilde. At the age of 50 he was appointed organ professor at the Conservatory, but his music was little understood by his colleagues. His compositions received only modest acclaim during his lifetime. What success and recognition he did achieve came in the last few years of his life, and his best compositions were written after the age of 57: a piano quintet, a string quartet, his only symphony (which is performed frequently today), a set of variations for piano and orchestra, and the Violin Sonata discussed in this chapter.

Most of his music consists of compositions for organ and sacred choral works. Several of his techniques influenced later composers, especially Debussy.

Antonin Dvořák

Dvořák was born in 1841 into the family of a Bohemian innkeeper and amateur musician. Antonin grew up listening to the folk music of his native land. After several years of conflict between his music teacher, who wanted his talented pupil to go to Prague to study, and his father, who wanted him to become an innkeeper, an uncle provided Antonin the necessary funds for a year of music study in Prague. When the money ran out, Dvořák earned his living for the next 15 years by playing in café bands and the National Opera orchestra.

As he grew older, Dvořák became less satisfied with the prevailing German style and more determined to write Bohemian music. When he was about age 40, his fortunes changed. He submitted a composition to the Austrian Commission. Although the prize he won was small in monetary value, it gained him the devoted friendship and unsparing help of committee member Johannes Brahms. Brahms opened many doors to publishers, performers, and conductors for Dvořák, who was humble and grateful. He once wrote Brahms, ". . . all my life [I] owe you the deepest gratitude for your good and noble intentions toward me, which are worthy of a truly great artist and man."*

By 1885 Dvořák was esteemed throughout the world. A few years later he accepted the directorship of the National Conservatory of Music in New York at a salary over 20 times what he was earning in Prague. During his summer stays in Spillville, Iowa, he wrote some of his best works, including the *New World* Symphony (formerly numbered 5 but more recently designated as No. 9) and the Cello Concerto. He was introduced to black American music by Harry T. Burleigh, who was a pupil of his. He also became acquainted with the music of the American Indian. He was the first composer, native or foreign born, to recognize these great musical resources.

After three years in the United States, Dvořák returned to Bohemia, where he became director of the Prague Conservatory. In 1904 he collapsed and died of a stroke; in his honor a national day of mourning was declared.

*Milton Cross and David Ewen, *Encyclopedia of the Great Composers and Their Music*, vol. 1 (Garden City, N.Y.: Doubleday, 1953), p. 234.

Listening Guide

Dvořák: String Quartet in F Major, "American," Op. 96

First Movement

Sonata Form

Exposition

0:03   First theme played by viola:

0:12   First theme repeated by first violin.

0:20   Transition based on fourth measure of first theme; exchanged among other instruments.

0:50   Transition theme played by first violin; theme repeated several times:

1:07   Transition works up to a loud dynamic level; then gradually becomes softer and slower.

1:32   Second theme, in new key, played softly by first violin:

2:00   First three notes of second theme used to work into transition.

2:28   Codetta containing measures 1 and 2 of first theme; soft.

Development

2:38   First theme, somewhat changed, played by viola.

2:48   Measure 1 of first theme played by first violin.

2:56   Measure 3 of first theme played loudly by first violin.

3:15   Viola plays out melody based on measure 3 of first theme.

3:37   Cello plays out with measures 3 and 4 of first theme; is followed by first violin.

3:48   New melodic idea introduced; is imitated in fugal style starting with second violin, then first violin, viola, and cello:

Recapitulation

4:22   First theme played by viola.

4:31   First theme repeated by violin.

4:42   Transition based on fourth measure of first theme; music modulates and transition is longer than in exposition.

4:45   Brief cello countermelody.

5:18   Transition theme; repeated several times.

6:00   Second theme, in tonic key, played by first violin.

6:13   Second theme repeated by cello, dynamic level increases.

6:30   Climactic point; full dynamic level; music turns to softer and slower material.

6:56   Coda; measures 3 and 4 of first theme are played.

7:10   Closes on loud chords.

Thirteen

Keyboard Music

As was pointed out in Chapter 7, there are several types of keyboard instruments, the most important being the harpsichord, organ, and piano. The piano was the latest to arrive on the musical scene, and when it did, it surpassed the organ and supplanted the harpsichord in popularity. Before about 1750 composers did not specify which keyboard instrument should play a work. The word *clavier* meant any keyboard instrument and was considered a sufficient designation.

The fact that keyboard instruments can sound several pitches at the same time makes certain types of music especially suitable for them. This chapter examines some important types of keyboard music.

Suite

A *suite* (pronounced sweet) is a composition for keyboard or a group of instruments. The word *suite* simply means a collection or group of items that belong together. So we speak of a suite of rooms or a suite of furniture. In the time of Bach suite referred to a collection of dances that were intended for performance as a unified series.

The dances were *stylized;* that is, they were "dressed up" to make them attractive pieces for listening. The composer wrote original music for them, but in meter, tempo, and other characteristics, their similarity to known dance types was apparent. A modern-day composer might do the same thing by selecting a popular dance of a generation ago, say the fox trot or the Charleston, and writing similar music with more interesting melodies and harmonies while retaining the essential rhythm and style of the original dance. This is what Bach and other composers of his time did. They selected several contrasting dances that were no longer in vogue, then applied their compositional skills to stylizing them. The resulting music was for listening, not dancing.

Many different dances were incorporated into suites. The four most commonly found were the allemande, sarabande, courante, and gigue. The *allemande (ahla-*mahnd), which means *German* in French, probably came from Germany. It has a moderate tempo and a rather continuous movement of eighth or sixteenth notes. The *courante* (koo-*rahnt*) was French in origin. It moves a little more rapidly than the allemande. The *sarabande (sara-bahnd)* is a slow dance. It was probably imported by the Spaniards from Mexico. The *gigue* (zheeg) originated in Britain, where it was called *jig.* It is lively and is appropriately placed as the final dance in a suite. It also tends to be more contrapuntal in character than most dance types.

Other dances less frequently encountered in the suite are the bourrée, minuet, gavotte, louré, polonaise, and passapied. Often a composer wrote a *double*—a variation of the dance preceding it. Many times a suite was prefaced by a prelude or an overture. It was customary for all the dances in a suite to be written in the same key. The composer achieved variety by arranging the movements in a suite so that the faster dances contrasted with slower ones. Most dances were in two-part form, with each part repeated, although when they are played today, the performer sometimes omits the repeats and attaches the *double* to form a single piece.

Bach's Suite No. 2 of the *English Suites* is for solo keyboard instrument. Since the most prominent keyboard instrument of Bach's day was the harpsichord, the music is most authentically rendered on that instrument. The harpsichord has a light, brilliant sound and a mechanism that is conducive to playing rapid decorative notes. Therefore, composers often wrote highly decorative versions of a melody.

The example shows the unadorned and decorated versions of part of a sarabande from Bach's Suite:

unornamented

ornamented

In the bourrée (boo-*ray*), a lively dance with two beats per measure, Bach employs a running accompaniment in the left-hand, or lower, part. Instead of simple block chords, he takes the pitches of the chords and breaks them up or spreads them out. The broken chord is a different way to sound the harmony. Here is the opening portion of Bourrée I:

Bourrée II, which has been presented somewhat in Chapter 1, is similar to Bourrée I in tempo and character, but the key and manner of chord presentation are different:

Bourrée II

The other movements of the suite include a prelude, an allemande, a courante, and a gigue.

Some suites are for orchestra. One of the best known is Bach's Suite No. 3 for Orchestra, with its famous "Air," which is often heard alone under the title "Air for the G String." Other well-known orchestral suites are Handel's *Water Music,* composed for the King as he sailed down the Thames, and Handel's *Music for the Royal Fireworks.* The latter was written for a victory celebration, which went awry when the fireworks ignited the wooden pavilion and caused widespread panic.

Suites composed in the nineteenth and twentieth centuries departed from the eighteenth-century model of stylized dances. These later suites consist largely of a collection of orchestral pieces from an opera or ballet.

Fugue

A most important type of keyboard music in Bach's day was the *fugue* (fewg). The fugue, like most musical forms, did not appear full-blown. It evolved from less complex types of keyboard music. The fugue and its predecessors have one thing in common: They are conceived contrapuntally, with lines of music imitating one another.

J. S. Bach's Fugue in C Major is one third of a longer work that includes a toccata and an adagio. A Listening Guide containing the themes for the fugue appears on pages 108–109.

For the first nine measures only one melody is played. Although it is a single melody, it is divided into four distinct phrases, with rests between each phrase. Those rests may seem to interrupt the flow of the music, but Bach soon fills them with other music. This melody serves as the main theme for the fugue and is called the *subject.* At the tenth measure the subject begins in a second line. In fugues these lines are called *voices,* even though they are to be played, not sung.

While the second voice is sounding the subject in a key different from the first appearance, the first voice continues with a line of counterpoint. This line is somewhat of a melody, but is not as distinctive and easily remembered as the subject. Logically, it is called the *countersubject.* Notice that it is active at points where the subject has the rests, and vice versa.

At measure 19 the third voice enters, sounding the subject in the original key, while the second voice continues into the countersubject. The first voice begins free contrapuntal material. In this fugue the contrapuntal material actually is parallel with the subject, sounding two octaves and a third lower.

At measure 28 the fourth voice enters in the pedal part. The first and second voices continue in the free contrapuntal material, with the first voice somewhat parallel to the countersubject (which is in the third voice at this point) and the second voice parallel to the subject in the fourth voice.

The fourth voice completes the subject at the beginning of measure 37, marking the end of the *exposition*—the rather standard beginning section of a fugue. From that point until the end of the fugue, the subject appears in different keys and voices, free contrapuntal sections are included, and the subject and countersubject are combined in different ways. In this fugue Bach brings back the subject seven more times; some of these times the countersubject also appears with it. The final appearance of the subject is an especially healthy one in the pedals.

The basic design for the Fugue in C Major can be diagrammed:

	EXPOSITION				DEVELOPMENT	
Voice I	S	CS	FM		Return	Close
Voice II		S	CS	FM	and	with
Voice III			S	CS	development	subject
Voice IV				S	of	
					subject	
					and countersubject	

S = subject   CS = countersubject   FM = free contrapuntal material

This fugue has four voices. It could have had two, three, or five; more than five is not common. The order in which the voices enter is a matter of choice for the composer. Composers often vary the structure slightly to suit their desires for the piece.

What is necessary for the understanding of a fugue? Certainly knowing the plan of the exposition helps, but it doesn't guarantee that you will understand the music. More valuable is the ability to listen and think in linear, contrapuntal terms.

Remember that the subject is the unifying element of the fugue. The plan of the exposition makes it likely that you will recognize the subject when you hear it again. The interlacing of counterpoint around a central subject (with its contrasting countersubject added for interest) reminds one of a complicated mathematical formula working itself out to a beautifully correct conclusion.

Other Keyboard Forms

The fugue is not the only form that is well suited to the organ. Two others are based on the chorale. The plain, sturdy melody of a chorale makes it especially suitable as a theme for other works. One type of adaptation is called *chorale variation*. The other form is called a *chorale prelude*—a contrapuntal piece built around a chorale melody.

A third type of music well adapted to organ is the *passacaglia* (pah-sah-*cahl*-yah). It begins with a statement of the theme, usually in the bass and without accompaniment. This melody, in triple meter, is repeated over and over in its original form, but new variations are added in other voices each time. The melody is likely to stay in the bass throughout. (The pedals are ideal for maintaining the rather slow-moving melody, leaving the hands free to play the faster, higher-pitched lines of music.) The continuous repetition in the bass, combined with continuous variation in the upper parts, can build to a mighty climax. One of Bach's finest organ works is his *Passacaglia in C Minor.*

Some types of pieces that were common for the harpsichord were also written for organ. One such type is the *toccata*, a flashy work with many rapid scale passages. The *prelude* is another type. In the eighteenth century, it simply meant a short piece of instrumental music. A *fantasia* is supposed to give the impression of improvisation, with abrupt changes of mood and sound. An *invention* is a short contrapuntal piece for a keyboard instrument. Bach wrote several famous inventions to help his wife and children learn to play the harpsichord. Piano teachers use them often today. *Sinfonias* are *not* symphonies. Rather, they are overtures, or introductory movements to longer works. In a few cases the term is a synonym for invention.

Listening Guide

Bach: Toccata, Adagio, and Fugue in C Major, BWV 564

Fugue

Exposition

0:00   Subject, in four distinct phrases, is presented in first voice alone, at moderately high pitch level:

0:18   Subject presented in second voice (four notes lower than first voice); countersubject begins in first voice and appears largely between the phrases of subject:

0:36   Subject presented in third voice (five notes lower than second voice); second voice takes up countersubject; first voice begins free material, which in this fugue parallels subject at a higher pitch level.

0:54   Subject starts in fourth voice (four notes lower than third voice), played on pedalboard; third voice presents countersubject; second voice parallels subject, and first voice somewhat parallels countersubject at higher pitch levels.

Piano Music

The piano is credited to Bartolomeo Cristofori (1655–1731) of Florence, Italy, who produced the first such instrument in 1709. It did not become popular until after 1770, when its key action was improved. Even then the piano did not sound like today's instrument. The tone was softer, lighter, and a bit duller. A significant improvement was made about 1820, with the addition of the cast iron frame, which allowed the strings to be given more tension and

End of Exposition

1:12   Episode begins with upper voice sounding fast-moving notes in sequence by raising the pitch level one step with each appearance.

1:24   Subject played in middle pitch range in third voice; countersubject in first voice.

1:45   Subject played in fourth voice (pedals); countersubject played in third voice.

2:04   Subject played in first voice at high pitch level; new contrapuntal material in third and fourth voices.

2:25   Episode similar to first episode, with third voice sounding rapidly moving notes sequentially.

2:38   Subject played in second voice; first voice has running notes derived from countersubject.

2:56   Subject played in third voice (in minor key); second voice partially imitates subject one measure later; first voice continues running notes in sequence.

3:15   Episode uses figures in sequence, outlining chords similar to free material appearing earlier with subject, except that patterns basically ascend instead of descend.

3:22   Subject returns in fourth voice (pedals) at rather loud dynamic level; countersubject in third voice.

3:40   Episode begins in first voice, with fast notes in sequence; very similar to initial episode; followed by sequence that descends.

4:09   Subject makes final appearance in fourth voice, doubled with low pitch level at loud dynamic level; other three voices sound free material.

4:27   Free material containing a figure repeated in sequence; long, low pedal tone sustained until nearly the conclusion.

4:56   Closes with a rather low-pitched chord.

enabled them to produce a bigger sound. Also during the nineteenth century the action was improved, and pedals were added to sustain tone and alter dynamic level.

Today the piano is the most frequently played instrument. Over 14 million Americans play it, as compared to 7 million who play guitar, the next most popular instrument in the United States. The piano has had a huge amount of music written for it, ranging from short simple pieces to long works of terrifying complexity. Virtually every significant composer since 1770 has written piano music, and so have many not-so-significant composers. The remainder of this chapter is devoted to examining three works that represent the main trends of nineteenth-century piano music.

Beethoven's Pathétique Sonata

The Piano Sonata in C Minor, Op. 13 (No. 8) was named *Pathétique* by Beethoven himself. The *No. 8* comes from the order of the sonata among the 32 piano sonatas Beethoven composed. It is a relatively early sonata, dating from 1799.

First movement.   It was probably the introduction to the first movement that suggested the idea of *Pathétique*. It is marked *Grave* (solemn), and sounds like a brooding fantasy. Each measure begins on a loud chord and is followed by a dotted rhythm at a soft dynamic level:

Contrary motion can be seen and heard between the treble and bass parts.

The sonata-form portion of the movement is marked to be played fast and vigorously:

Typically, the second theme is in contrast to the first:

It is in E flat minor. There is a third theme and a codetta. The introduction returns just prior to the development section. In the development Beethoven combines the first theme with the theme from the introduction. Before the end of the movement, the slow introduction appears once more, adding a sense of drama to the entire movement.

Second movement.   The second movement is songlike. Its main melody opens on middle C, and is heard over a typical accompaniment figure of the eighteenth century. The melody is repeated one octave higher, and then contrasting sections are heard.

The overall form is *A B A C A*, which gives it the form but not the spirit of a rondo. The *C* section is especially dramatic, with sudden changes of dynamics and a triple meter.

Third movement. The third movement is the final one, thus following the classical pattern for a sonata. Also typical is its rondo form. Although in minor, the theme is not as somber as the minor theme in the first movement. The form for the entire movement is *A B A C A B A*. This arrangement shows the eighteenth-century fondness for symmetry. There is a codetta after the first *B* section and a coda at the end of the movement, producing a form that combines rondo and sonata—logically called rondo-sonata by some musicians.

A Listening Guide for the third movement appears on pages 112–113.

Chopin's Fantasie-Impromptu, *Op. 66*

Chopin was the leader of the "intimate-sensitive" school of piano music and performance. He was not fond of the concert hall; he preferred to play for his friends in the more intimate atmosphere of a parlor. He treated rhythm more freely than did other pianists. He was sometimes criticized for doing this, and one contemporary of his even complained that Chopin couldn't keep time. Undoubtedly he could, but he chose not to.

The *Fantasie-Impromptu* is typical of the free-form *character piece* of the nineteenth century. Although it bears the name *Impromptu,* it's not actually improvised. Chopin and other nineteenth-century composers worked very hard at sounding casual.

The first large section of the work (below)

has the left-hand, bass-clef line contined entirely to broken chords. The right-hand, treble-clef part contains a rippling melody made up exclusively of sixteenth notes. There are many accidentals, indicating many harmonic changes. Of interest also is the extensive use of three notes in the left hand against four in the right. The combination of patterns tends to blur the rhythmic effect of each.

The notation frequently includes the symbol *Ped.* This mark tells the pianist to depress the sustaining pedal, thereby lifting the dampers and allowing the strings to ring freely. The effect adds richness to the music by prolonging the sounds, which would otherwise be immediately curtailed by the dampers. Proper pedaling also contributes to smooth and lyrical phrasing. The composer and/or performer

---

Listening Guide

Beethoven: Piano Sonata, Op. 13, No. 8, *Pathétique*

Third Movement

Rondo—*A B A C A B A*

0:00   Main theme *(A)* in major played in the upper notes at soft dynamic level:

0:17   Extension of main theme begins after short silence following two decisive chords.

0:34   Transition using triplet patterns takes over in rapidly moving notes.

0:45   First subordinate theme *(B)* in new major key; a return of the triplet figures follows:

must plan carefully for the use of the pedal, since dissonant notes that are allowed to ring simultaneously have a chaotic effect.

The middle section of the piece changes character by becoming much more lyrical. In fact, the melody is so singable that it was made into a successful popular song under the title "I'm Always Chasing Rainbows." Chopin confines his ornamentation of the melody to a few five-note turns and *trills* (rapid alternation between two adjacent pitches):

1:04　　Main theme *(A)* starts again at soft dynamic level in the same key as its first appearance.

1:21　　Second subordinate theme *(C)* begins in new major key and is repeated a number of times, some of the time in imitation:

1:50　　Transition of rapidly moving notes that become triplets used for earlier transition.

2:05　　Main theme *(A)* starts again after long, loud chord followed by a short silence.

2:27　　Transition containing the rapidly moving notes in triplets.

2:38　　Second subordinate theme *(B)* returns in different major key; modulates several times.

2:58　　Main theme *(A)* returns at soft dynamic level in original major key.

3:10　　Coda begins with triplet figures leading up to short "punched out" chords; music increases in intensity; key changes to minor.

3:32　　First portion of main theme appears at soft dynamic level after long, loud chord.

3:42　　Closes with a series of rapidly moving notes and a short chord.

Again the pedal is employed as an integral part of the music. Chopin indicates that the melody should be played *sotto voce* (so-toh *vo-chay*), literally under the voice, or in a subdued manner.

The first section is repeated, this time with an extended coda at the end. The ending seems to fade away. Nineteenth-century composers favored one of two endings, both of which tend to be "effects." One is the glorious, full-blown climax of sound. The other is its opposite: the quiet fade-out.

Bach, Handel, Mozart, Haydn, Beethoven, and Schubert were all extremely versatile composers. They wrote successfully in nearly every medium, vocal and instrumental, solo and ensemble. Chopin was different. He was the first of the "specialist" composers, who tended to limit their writing to one or two areas. Although Chopin attempted a few other media, the bulk of his effort was directed toward his piano works, and through them he earned his reputation as a composer.

Liszt's Mephisto Waltz

Franz Liszt was the opposite of Chopin in many respects. Liszt was fond of the concert hall and was the outstanding piano virtuoso of his day. He succeeded in dazzling his audiences with his piano-playing ability.

Mephisto Waltz is program music—music written to be associated with a nonmusical idea. The story for this work was suggested by an excerpt from Nikolaus Lenau's poem *Faust.* Faust is the man who makes a bargain with the devil, Mephistopheles. In this section of the poem, called "The dance at the village inn," Mephistopheles and Faust wander through the countryside looking for pleasure. They come upon a dance at a local inn. Faust is attracted to one of the girls but is afraid to ask her to dance. Mephistopheles scornfully seizes a violin and plays so beautifully that no one there is able to resist the music. Faust and the girl dance together and then disappear into the night.

Frédéric Chopin

Frédéric Chopin (*Show*-pan; 1810–1849) was the son of a French father and Polish mother. He showed considerable talent at an early age and received his musical education at the conservatory in Warsaw. Before he was 20, he set out to make his way in the world. Shortly after his departure from Poland, the Poles revolted against the Russians and their Tsar. In time the Russians crushed the revolt, an event that caused Chopin much anguish.

He traveled extensively and then reached Paris, the city that was to become his adopted home. His skill as a pianist and composer made him a sought-after musician. Soon he began to move in a circle of artistic friends, through whom he met Mme. Aurore Dude-

vant, who wrote novels under the pen name of George Sand. She had an unusual personality and a penchant for smoking cigars and wearing masculine clothing. She was considerably older than Chopin. They lived together for several years, and her domineering personality seemed to suit Chopin's need to be governed. The years were productive ones for him.

In time his health began to fail, and the relationship with Mme. Dudevant became strained. Finally they parted in bitterness, and with this event his creative energy seemed to weaken. At the age of 39 Chopin died of tuberculosis. Symbolically, his heart was returned to Poland, and the rest of his body stayed in Paris.

A Listening Guide for *Mephisto Waltz* appears on pages 116–117.

Mephisto Waltz is not a polished and proper waltz, such as Johann Strauss, composer of "The Blue Danube" and other waltzes, might have written. In fact, some sections of *Mephisto Waltz* are in $\frac{2}{4}$ meter. Obviously the work is for listening, not dancing.

One purpose of the piece is to show off the virtuoso technique of the pianist who plays it. Liszt wrote most of his piano music for his own performances, and he surely gave himself plenty of opportunities to show off. *Mephisto Waltz* is filled with rapidly repeated notes and chords, passages with hands crossing at great speed, extremely rapid scales and arpeggios (chords outlined with consecutive notes), many decorative trills and other figures, and the full range of the piano employed from the lowest to the highest notes. It's the type of piece that only a very accomplished pianist can undertake.

Since the nineteenth century, composers have certainly not stopped writing for piano, but piano music did seem to reach the high point of its development during that time. For range, power, and musical versatility, the piano is almost unexcelled as a solo instrument.

Franz Liszt

Franz Liszt (1811–1886) was a varied and complex man. The son of servants of the Esterházy family in Hungary, he was sent to Paris to study under a scholarship arrangement. While there he attended a concert by the spectacular Italian violinist Niccolo Paganini. The 19-year-old Liszt was so impressed by the performance that he became determined to do for the piano what Paganini had done for the violin. He spent hours practicing flashy techniques. He even imitated Paganini's dramatic appearance and mannerisms: the black tight-fitting clothes and tossing hair. Liszt became a dazzling performer, and he wrote pieces to demonstrate his ability. He was one of the first soloists to turn the piano to one side so that the audience could see the performer's hands. Before this soloists had turned their backs to the audience.

Liszt loved life and people and was a man of generous disposition. He had great admiration for Beethoven and tried to promote his music. He helped many musicians, including Wagner and Berlioz, to get their works performed. His career was a success in every way, and he wrote some fine piano music full of

Franz Liszt. Early daguerreotype.

originality and musical invention. In the last years of his life he took minor orders in the church and was known as Abbé Liszt.

─────── *Listening Guide* ───────

Liszt: *Mephisto Waltz*

0:00   Rapid, low, repeated notes; more notes appear as music progresses; short figure soon added in upper notes.

0:14   After a short silence, four quick figures are played, leading into opening repeated-note material.

0:31   After another short silence and four quick figures, the pitch level ascends as the intensity of music increases.

0:42   More repeated chords and notes; music grows louder and heavier.

0:55   First theme *(A)* is played at rather low pitch level:

1:08   Section sounding somewhat like scherzo begins; opening figure played several times in lower notes.

1:44   After a very rapid ascending scale and repeated notes, *A* theme is played in lower notes.

1:57   Scherzolike material returns.

2:17   Rapid and loud sounding of chords, two to the beat instead of usual three; noticeable key changes.

2:31   *A* theme returns in upper notes; music gradually grows softer and calmer.

2:56   Second theme *(B)* appears; music is slower and calmer. Motive (circled in the example) sounding somewhat like a sigh is used extensively as music progresses:

3:09   *B* theme repeated one note higher.

3:39   Motive and phrases from *B* theme appear as music slowly grows louder and more passionate.

4:21   After a silent place playful theme *(C)* appears; played rather softly at high pitch level:

4:34   After a short silence phrase from *B* theme is played in upper notes over runs in lower notes; music grows slowly more intense and louder.

5:05   *C* theme is played softly.

5:23   After two silences and ascending run, *B* theme is played rather smoothly and somewhat softly in high repeated notes.

6:05   Descending phrases repeated and phrases from *B* theme heard again in repeated notes.

6:19   *A* theme returns at low pitch level; rather soft.

6:34   After a long descending run of notes, portion of *B* theme is played in lower notes below dazzling chord outlines in upper notes.

6:52   "Sigh" motive from *B* theme played in upper notes; loud repeated chords and increasing tempo lead to silent measure.

7:12   Very fast, loud section; alternates notes between player's hands; some of *B* theme and "sigh" motive used.

7:30   Scherzolike section; softer and lighter, with certain chords accented; phrase from *B* theme in middle notes.

7:52   "Sigh" motive appears below very fast runs in higher notes.

8:13   Free, cadenzalike runs.

8:25   *C* theme played softly in upper notes.

8:45   Portion of *B* theme played slowly and softly; free rhythm as in a cadenza.

9:49   Coda starts softly and builds quickly to climactic point; repeated notes and rapid alternation between hands.

10:13   Closes with two short chords.

Johann Sebastian Bach

Johann Sebastian Bach (1685–1750) lived an uneventful life, one not very different from that of many successful musicians of his time. The most notable feature about him was his lineage—he was one of a gifted musical family. Over a period of about six generations, from 1580 to 1845, more than 60 Bachs were musicians of some sort, and at least 38 of these attained eminence as musicians. Included among the latter were several of J. S. Bach's own sons.

Bach, the son of a town musician, was born in Eisenach, Germany, in 1685. When the boy was ten, his father died. Johann's musical training was taken over by his older brother, who was an organist. During his lifetime Bach was known more as an organ virtuoso than as a composer. After two short-lived positions as organist, Bach, at the age of 23, was appointed to his first significant post—court organist and chamber musician to the Duke of Weimar (*Vy*-mar). He stayed nine years. It was during his Weimar years that he concentrated on the organ, as both performer and composer.

When the Duke failed to advance him, Bach accepted another position at Cöthen. The prince at Cöthen was interested in chamber music, so the versatile Bach turned from writing church and organ music to composing primarily for instruments other than the organ.

Johann Sebastian Bach. Mezzotint by E. G. Haussmann.

It was during this time that he wrote the famous Brandenburg Concertos. After the death of his wife, Maria Barbara, he remarried. He immortalized his second wife, Anna Magdalena, by writing a book of keyboard music for her.

The third and last portion of Bach's life began with his appointment in 1723 as Cantor of St. Thomas Church in Leipzig. It was one of the more important musical posts in Germany, but it demanded that he teach the choir boys music and nonmusical subjects (and "in case they do not wish to obey, chastise them with moderation"). He was required to "so manage the music that it shall not last too long, and shall be of such a nature as not to make an operatic impression, but rather incite the listeners to devotion."

Bach was not the first choice for the position. A member of the town council is reported to have said, "Since the best man could not be obtained, lesser ones will have to be accepted." The Leipzig position required the writing and direction of church music, so Bach again complied by changing the emphasis of his composing. Not only were the Leipzig city fathers unaware of his genius; they were stingy. They paid him a poor salary and provided him with a choir of about 30 singers, few of whom were competent musicians.

In spite of the annoyances of the position at Leipzig and tragedy in his personal life (six of his first eight children born in Leipzig died),

Bach continued his endless stream of compositions. Late in life he suffered a stroke and became blind. In 1750 he died, with his stature as a composer still unrecognized. His music went largely unnoticed until 1829, when young Felix Mendelssohn rediscovered the *St. Matthew Passion*.

Except for brief journeys in Germany, Bach knew little of the world outside his native country. He was neither well read nor well educated. He was religious almost to the point of superstition. He created no new musical forms and instituted no new techniques of composing. His music was seldom heard outside of Leipzig during his lifetime, and even there it was probably not performed well.

Why is it that Bach is so dominating a figure in music? Simply because he wrote with such effectiveness and skill. Words are not adequate to describe his genius. Perhaps the late Dag Hammarskjöld, Secretary General of the United Nations, expressed it best. In speaking of Bach and Vivaldi, another Baroque composer, he said, "Both have a beautiful way of creating order in the brain."

All of Bach's music is catalogued with the letters BWV, an abbreviation of the German title of the thematic list of Bach's music edited in the twentieth century by Wolfgang Schmieder.

Opera

Opera includes several artistic elements in addition to music. Opera takes place on a stage, so it is a form of theater, requiring eye appeal and action. The success of opera depends to some extent on its staging—the scenery, costumes, and actors' movements. As drama, it must present a story and delineate and project the feelings of various characters. Frequently dancing is integrated into the production. Opera, then, involves many things: literature, drama, vocal and instrumental music, staging, and dancing. It's the great union of the arts. For that very reason opera presents the composer and performer with the greatest opportunities and the most difficulties of any type of music.

The Elements of Opera

Believability is hard to achieve because, although the stage action attempts to duplicate the realism of human life, the participants communicate through singing rather than through speech. Normally a phrase such as "John will be here at nine o'clock" would be spoken. Singing it would probably cause people to wonder. But suppose the sentence about John's arrival is in an opera. If the singer

sings the words with a minimum of musical expressiveness, the music won't be very interesting. The drama may have been preserved, but at the expense of the music. On the other hand, if the composer writes a beautiful melody to these words, then realism and believability have been sacrificed.

The element of time is a factor, also. Stage action can proceed normally if "John will be here at nine o'clock" is spoken in the routine manner of real life. But if an aria is developed from these words, the forward motion of the plot will have to be suspended for its duration. If interesting music is to be included, therefore, the drama will have to be abbreviated to accommodate the pressures of time, and it will have to be interrupted occasionally to allow for artistic balance between drama and music.

The impression of realism has been further hampered by the style of singing that has evolved, of necessity, within the operatic tradition. This style was developed in the centuries before recordings and mechanical amplification were available. Above all, a singer had to be heard—clearly—all the way to the last row of the balcony. If the style was somewhat unnatural, it was at least powerful.

The drama-music dilemma has a bearing on the appearance and acting ability of the opera singer. Some outstanding singers of the past were either not interested in acting or not talented in it. Because of the great vocal demands of opera, it's difficult to find people who can both sing and act with skill. The roles are lengthy and difficult to learn, and years of experience are required to do them justice. Fortunately, opera companies today are aware of the need for a more natural vocal sound and appropriate appearance and acting ability, and are casting accordingly.

Another distracting problem in opera is understanding the words. Even when sung in English, the words may not be easily comprehended. The problem is magnified when the opera is written in a foreign language. Operas can be translated and sung in English, but should they be? Although translation is difficult, involving correct numbers of syllables, natural accents, shades of meaning, and rhyme schemes, the answer is probably yes.

It must also be admitted that some opera plots are hardly fascinating. Many of the stories make no attempt to be believable, or they try to be realistic and fail. Others are dated and quaint.

Opera companies, if they want to remain solvent, must attract an audience, which means that certain favorite operas are performed year after year, often to the exclusion of new operas. Financial considerations as well as audience preference tend to work against the performance of a new opera. The cost of producing an opera is very high, and for this reason few opera company managers wish to undertake the risk and expense of trying a new work.

Appreciating Opera

Despite the obstacles to creating a successful opera, this musical medium often achieves a tremendous artistic impact. The drama provides the composer with situations that are ripe for musical expression. Some operatic "I-love-yous" encourage a sensuous reaction best described as "goosepimply." There is also pageantry and action, as well as both vocal and instrumental music.

An appreciation of opera can be increased by accepting the same limitations on realism that are accepted for a play. For example, in a play interior scenes are designed to suggest four-walled rooms, even though one wall must be missing so the audience can watch. People accept the fact that time in a play or movie is not measured in absolute terms. Months or years are presumed to have elapsed during a ten-minute intermission. To such limitations accepted for dramas, add two more for opera: the singing of the lines and the shortened attention to plot and character development.

As with any type of music, the more you know about opera, the greater the chances are that you will like it.

Early Opera

Opera began in Florence, Italy, shortly before 1600. It was an attempt to re-create ancient Greek drama. At first it was almost entirely recitative, but opera composers soon became more concerned with melody and less concerned with dramatic declamation. By the time the first public opera house opened in Venice in 1637, the artistic ideals of reestablishing Greek drama had been largely forgotten. The stories were burdened by the addition of irrelevant incidents, spectacular scenes, and incongruous comedy episodes. But other changes were more constructive. Arias, duets, and ensembles evolved, and the orchestra took on more prominence.

As opera spread throughout Europe, its dramatic element became less and less important. The singer reigned supreme. In their desire to hold the center of the stage, soloists added all kinds of embellishments to the melody to show off their virtuosity. The situation deteriorated so much that Christoph Willibald von Gluck (1714–1787) felt compelled to lead a reform movement. Gluck had written many operas himself, so he knew the field and was undeniably right when he said that opera was in need of correction. He tried to bring back its dramatic integrity by making the music serve the text. Everything in the opera, including ballet, was to be an integral part of the drama. Gluck wrote several operas that demonstrated his reforms.

In the decades following the opening of the opera house in Venice, opera evolved into two rather distinct styles. One was *opera seria*, which was of a serious nature more like the original dramatic purpose of the first operas. The other was *opera buffa* (*boo*-fa), which was lighter opera of a comic nature. Mozart wrote both kinds of opera, but his greatest public successes were of the *buffa* type.

Mozart's Don Giovanni

The title of the work *Don Giovanni (Don Juan)* reveals its language to be Italian, although Mozart's native language was German. Mozart had made several journeys to Italy and knew the language, but the *libretto* (opera text) was written by the Italian Lorenzo da Ponte, the best librettist of his day. The selection of an Italian text was a happy choice for the additional reason that opera was a thoroughly Italian product, and audiences in Vienna were more accustomed to hearing opera in Italian than in their own language.

Basically, *Don Giovanni* is *opera seria*. It contains some humorous moments, but it has a serious outlook. Because of the opera's length, the discussion here is limited mainly to its last portion. The plot is intricate, so the opera should be listened to with libretto in hand.

The opera opens with a typical overture. (It's claimed that Mozart composed the overture the night before the first performance and completed the copying only half an hour before the opening curtain.) The stage action starts as Don Giovanni begins his adventures with Ottavio's fiancee, Donna Anna. She refuses his advances, and her father, the Commendatore (the Commander), is killed by Don Giovanni in a duel while defending the honor of his daughter. At a village wedding Don Giovanni attempts to seduce Zerlina, the bride of the peasant Masetto. Act I ends with a ball given for the peasants by Don Giovanni, during which he makes a more blatant attempt on Zerlina's virtue.

Later he plays a cruel trick on Donna El-

vira, whom he had seduced long ago and deserted. She pursues Don Giovanni to Seville, and he disguises his servant Leporello in his own clothes so that he can pretend to be in love with her and thus get her out of the way for a while. In the meantime, Don Giovanni pursues other adventures and pleasures. During one of his escapades he takes refuge in a cemetery, where he discovers the statue of the Commendatore and mockingly invites it to dinner. The statue nods its head in acceptance.

The final scene is the banquet hall in Don Giovanni's palace. The gay and bouncy music tells us immediately that the Don isn't worried. In fact, he seems to have forgotten all about the graveyard and the statue. He commands his private orchestra to play some dinner music. A wind ensemble plays a song from a popular opera of the day:

Leporello serves the table and looks hungrily at the food. "What a greedy appetite," he complains as he watches Don Giovanni down one mouthful after another.

A second piece is heard from the wind ensemble:

Leporello pours the Don some wine, and thinking that he won't be seen, he stuffs some food into his mouth. As the third number begins—"Non piu andai"

from Mozart's own *Marriage of Figaro*— Leporello helps himself to more food. The Don, realizing that Leporello's mouth is full, asks him to whistle along with the selection from *Figaro*. Poor Leporello is forced to admit that he's been snitching. The whole scene bubbles along like champagne.

Donna Elvira breaks the spell as she rushes in and throws herself at Don Giovanni's feet. She begs her former lover to give up his evil ways. Leporello is moved, but not Don Giovanni. He mocks Donna Elvira by proposing a toast to her. ("Long live women and good wine!") Angered and humiliated, she turns from him and runs out the door. Just as she leaves, she emits a piercing scream. "Go and see what's the matter," the Don orders his servant. Leporello does as he's told, only to shriek in terror himself and slam the door shut. "For God's sake, don't go out there," he implores Don Giovanni. Leporello has seen the stone guest advancing to keep his dinner appointment. Terrified, Leporello even tries to imitate the sound of the statue's footsteps. "You're crazy," the Don scoffs. But suddenly the orchestra drowns out the sound of a stone fist striking the door. "Open the door!" Don Giovanni shouts to Leporello, who refuses. "I'll go myself," sneers the Don, and he opens the door.

Two huge chords are heard from the orchestra, and the great white statue of the slain Commendatore enters the room. The whole scene suggests inevitable doom. The statue speaks: "Don Giovanni! You invited me to dine with you. And I am here."

For the first time, Don Giovanni seems shaken. His words are brave, but the music from the orchestra reveals his fear. Brazenly he orders Leporello to set another place. The statue declines "mortal food"; he has come for another reason. A brief trio begins. Mozart keeps each part distinct, according to what the character feels. Leporello sings a quick patter that gives evidence of his terror and his desire to make himself invisible. Don Giovanni's lines are brief, patient, and defiant. The stone guest sings most of his words on a few unyielding tones:

The orchestra music becomes more chilling, and the statue invites Don Giovanni to return the courtesy and dine with him. Leporello pleads with his master to say no. The Don hesitates a moment, then with true bravado says, "I'll come!" The statue offers his hand to seal the agreement. When Don Giovanni grasps it, he cries out in pain. The stone hand is as crushing and cold as death itself. Again and again the statue calls on him to repent ("Pentiti"). Each time Don Giovanni refuses. Finally he pulls his hand away. "Your time has run out," the statue tells him. Then all hell breaks loose; flames leap up, flashes of light are seen, and the orchestra plays rapidly moving notes as Don Giovanni writhes in agony. Slowly he sinks to his death as an offstage chorus sings.

Abruptly the mood changes from tragedy to comedy. Donna Anna, Donna Elvira, and Zerlina rush in, followed by Ottavio and Masetto. They find Leporello crawling about on the floor and demand to know what's happened. Leporello stammers out the tale of what he has just witnessed. The music is again filled with wit and sparkle. Don Giovanni is already just a memory. In a brief duet Donna Anna and Ottavio tell of their plan to marry after her year of mourning for her father is over. Donna Elvira pledges to end her days in a cloister. Zerlina and Masetto are impatient to be off so they can have dinner. And Leporello sets about finding himself a new master. As the six singers face the audience, they deliver the moral of the opera. The whole scene is so mischievous that one wonders whether Mozart was not really attempting to have the last laugh in the moralizing. The sextet sings:

> *Such is the end*
> *Of those who do evil.*
> *The death of the wicked*
> *Always matches their life.*

Interestingly, the last scene—the moralizing by the sextet—has often been omitted from the opera. In the nineteenth century it was felt that adding such a finale after the damnation scene was inappropriate. Mozart himself approved its deletion the second time it was staged. In this century, however, the scene has been reinstated.

The music in Mozart's operas represents the eighteenth-century style, which exhibits good taste and a control of emotions. True, the librettos of his comic operas are sometimes spiced with *double entendres,* and the singers' emotions are exaggerated for comic effect. The situations in his serious operas often suggest strong emotions and drama. But the music is handled with a restraint that contrasts nicely with any incongruities of text or action. Even in serious moments he does not allow the music to become bombastic or sentimental. There is about his operatic writing a "light touch," an awareness that music can be valid even when conceived as entertainment.

Bizet's Carmen

The opera *Carmen* did not enjoy initial success. Its failure was a bitter blow to Bizet (Bee-zay), who died of a heart attack three months after the first performance. Perhaps in 1875 the audience at the opera-comique, which was a family theater, thought there was too much passion in the opera. Whatever the reason for their coolness, later opera-goers have made up for the early lack of enthusiasm. The color and tunefulness of the music have won it a permanent place in the repertoire of almost all opera companies.

The Prelude forecasts the music and the moods of the opera. The opening theme returns in the final scene outside the bull ring at Seville:

Also heard in the Prelude is the Fate motive. Its ominous sound predicts the final disaster:

The opera opens on a square in Seville, where soldiers are standing around the guardhouse. Micaela, Don José's fiancée, appears and asks about him. The soldiers are quite flirtatious, and Micaela leaves. A trumpet in the distance announces the changing of the guard. The relieving company is accompanied by a crowd of urchins as they enter to the strains of a captivating march. As the clock strikes 12, the women who work in the cigarette factory emerge. The entrance of Carmen, one of the women who work there, is heralded by a rhythmic transformation of a Fate motive.

Her character is established when she begins to sing the Habañera, a Spanish dance. Its characteristic rhythm is heard in the accompaniment:

Then comes the familiar Toreador Song:

bel - le Que nul ne peut ap - pri - voi -
free, A bird that none can hope to

Don José, waiting for Micaela to return, seems lost in his own thoughts and ignores Carmen. This irritates her; she takes a flower from her dress and throws it at him. As he picks it up, the orchestra sounds the Fate motive. The clock strikes again, and the women go back into the factory. Micaela enters with a letter from Don José's mother, and a duet follows.

Micaela's exit is followed by a quarrel in the factory between Carmen and another woman. At once the stage is filled with two groups of chattering women. Carmen is led in—insolent and cocky, as usual. She strikes one of the women, who demands that she be sent to jail. The soldiers arrest Carmen, tie her hands behind her back and put her in the custody of Don José.

She loses no time in exerting her charms. She sings, "Close to the walls of Seville, with my good friend Lillas Pastia, I will soon dance the gay seguidilla."

Près des rem - parts de Sé - vil - le,
Close to the walls of Se - vil - le,

Chez mon a - mi Lil - las Pas - tia,
With my good friend Lil - las Pas - tia,

Not only will she do the seguidilla, she intends to dance it with Don José. Of course, Carmen points out, to do the dance she has to be free.

At first Don José resists her temptations, but the final outcome is certain. By the time the soldiers come back, Carmen's wrists have been freed. (Don José isn't really very clever.) She is marched off to jail, but at a prearranged point she knocks Don José down and escapes.

The Prelude to Act II opens with a lovely melody. The scene is Lillas Pastia's tavern. Carmen's song celebrates the joy of gypsy life:

Les trin - gles des sis - tres tin - taient A -
The gyp - sy drums were beat - ing loud, And

vec un é - clat mé - tal - li - que Et
tam - bour - ines re - sound - ed bright - ly, And

sur cette é - tran - ge mu - si - que
when they heard this mu - sic surg - ing,

One of the soldiers presses for Carmen's attention. She learns from him that Don José was sentenced to two months in jail for allowing her escape, but he's just been set free. Soon Escamillo, the champion bullfighter, arrives and offers his swaggering Toreador Song. He's obviously attracted to Carmen.

A quintet follows, in which some smugglers invite Carmen and her friends to join them in a little matter of thievery that evening. The friends accept happily, but Carmen declines because Don José is coming. His voice is heard in the distance, singing the same melody that opened the act. The scene between Carmen and Don José covers a wide range of feelings. She begins by dancing for him and playing the castanets. Don José is enthralled. When the trumpet sounds retreat, he prepares to leave. Carmen is infuriated that anyone would put duty above her; she mocks him and finally urges him to go. Don José takes from his pocket the flower that he has treasured during the two months he's been in jail. He sings the famous Flower aria for her:

Now Carmen realizes her hold on Don José. She decides to lure him into the smugglers' band by describing the life of freedom they'll lead. When the lieutenant comes for him, the two men quarrel and are finally separated by the gypsies. The lieutenant is hustled out by Carmen's friends. The die is now cast for Don José: He has attacked an officer and can no longer return to military life.

The Prelude to Act III consists of a lovely flute solo with harp accompaniment. The curtain rises on the hideout of the smugglers. Don José gloomily reflects on his situation and the fact that his mother still thinks he is a good man. Carmen has already grown bored with him, and she urges him to return to the village. They quarrel, and the Fate motive is heard again. The Card Trio, one of the highlights of the opera, follows. Two of Carmen's friends tell their fortunes; the cards promise to one a young lover, to the other a rich old husband. Carmen cuts the cards and draws the ace of spades: death.

Micaela enters, looking for Don José. She sings one of the loveliest arias in the opera:

Escamillo enters, eager for Carmen. A fight develops between him and the jealous Don José, but the two men are eventually separated. Don José learns from Micaela that his mother is dying, and he's persuaded to leave to see her. "We will meet again!" he warns Carmen as the Fate motive is heard once more from the orchestra.

The Prelude to Act IV is a somber melody played by the oboe. The curtain rises on a brilliant scene outside the arena in Seville. The crowd hails the various bullfighters who march by. Finally Escamillo enters with Carmen holding onto his arm. The crowd accompanies him into the ring and Carmen remains alone to face Don José.

Their encounter is tense and bitter. He urges her to go with him, but she refuses. "Then you don't love me anymore?" he asks. "No," Carmen replies. Don José cries, "But I still love you!" Finally he reaches the breaking point as the happy strains of the chorus in the arena are heard in the background. He demands again that Carmen come with him, and again she refuses. He then pulls a knife and stabs her as the Toreador Song rises from the crowd in the bull ring. Don José kneels beside her body, and the Fate motive is heard again as the curtain falls.

German Romantic Opera

In the nineteenth century, opera tended to divide into a German type and an Italian type, both of which differed from their eighteenth-century predecessors. In 1821 Carl Maria von Weber (*Vay*-ber; 1786–1826) wrote *Der Freischutz* (The Free-Shooter), an opera based on German folklore. The story concerns a marksman who receives from the black huntsman (that is, the devil) seven magic bullets; six of them do as he wills, but the seventh does as the devil wills. The devil also gets the soul of the one who receives the bullets. Besides mysticism, the opera features peasants, rustic scenes, and hunting horns. Weber completed two more operas before his early death. Although they are seldom performed today, they exerted a significant influence on Richard

Wagner (*Ree*-kard *Vahg*-ner, 1813–1883), one of the musical giants of the nineteenth century.

Wagner's Music Dramas

It's hard to know where to begin or end in discussing the music of Wagner. Entire books have been written on one or another of his operas. In fact, each of his operas has a score the size of a large book. His music is awe-inspiring, profound and pompous, fantastic and forceful. He was a complex musician and a complex personality, with one of history's more massive egos.

More than any previous opera composer, Wagner consciously tackled the dilemma of balance between music and drama. In his lengthy philosophical discourses he often indicated his belief that poetry and music should be one. To meet his artistic goals, he created a different kind of opera, one that he called *music drama* instead of opera.

Music drama required a new and different approach to the concept of libretto, so Wagner wrote his own texts. The topics were mythological because he felt that such stories best appealed to the emotions. For poetry he revived an old German alliterative form, of which the following is an example:

Die Liebe bringt Lust und Leid
Doch in ihr Weh auch webt sie Wonne.

(Thus love doth lighten loss,
For 'tis from woe she weaves her wonder.)

Wagner's favorite libretto themes were not only mythological; they were also rich with philosophical overtones—the struggle between good and evil, the contest between the physical and spiritual, and the idea of redemption through love. Because these overarching themes are present, the characters in the music dramas are not personalities but more nearly symbols or pawns being pushed about by irresistible forces. In this respect, Wagner approaches the drama of the ancient Greeks.

Wagner refined a technique that Weber had used and that Richard Strauss was later to utilize in *Don Juan.* The technique is to associate a musical motive with a particular character, emotion, or idea; the concept is called *leitmotiv*, or leading motive. As soon as various motives are established, Wagner weaves them in and out of the music at appropriate times to enhance the intrigue of the plot and to provide unity. Such use of motives also permits the orchestra to assume a more vital role in the music drama, since it can expand on people and ideas referred to in the text.

Since the division of music into recitatives, arias, and choruses interrupts the forward motion of the drama, Wagner eliminates these forms as independent sections. Instead he creates a flowing, melodious line to serve as an unending melody. The vocal line emphasizes the expression of the words being sung. With its continuous interweaving of motives, the orchestra contributes to the impression of never-ending motion. It's incorrect to say that there are no arias in Wagner's music dramas; there are, but they are woven into the continuously flowing music.

To heighten the impression that a musical work is "seamless," Wagner emphasizes chromatic harmony. That is, by making half-step alterations of chords, he weakens the "magnetic pull" of chords toward a tonic. The absence of a strong tonic means that the music seldom arrives at a cadence point or musical "stopping place," so the feeling of key is nebulous.

Wagner does not treat the orchestra as mere accompaniment for the singers on stage. The importance of the orchestra in his works equals, perhaps exceeds, that of the singers. In a real sense his orchestra is symphonic, both in its size and in its ability to stand almost without the vocal parts. In fact, many portions of his operas are performed today as concert pieces without singers. Probably Wagner's greatest genius was his ability to exploit the full resources of the orchestra. He made it produce effects that had previously not been dreamed of—brilliant light as well as dark, somber colors; overwhelming force and sensuous intimacy.

Wagner's most ambitious achievement was a cycle of four complete operas entitled *Der Ring des Nibelungen* (The Ring of the Nibelung).

The four operas in the cycle are *Das Rheingold* (The Gold of the Rhine), *Die Walküre* (The Valkyries), *Siegfried,* and *Götterdämmerung* (The Twilight of the Gods).

The story of the cycle of operas is built around some gold supposedly guarded by the Rhine maidens in the Rhine river. The gold is stolen and a curse put on it. (In nineteenth-century operas the direction of events often hinges on curses and magic potions.) The curse states that if the possessor will renounce love, he will rule the world. The result is a chain of misfortunes affecting all the characters in the drama.

Because in many ways Richard Wagner and his music are the epitome of nineteenth-century romanticism, his *Siegfried's Rhine Journey* is presented in Chapter 20, which discusses that period and style.

Italian Romantic Opera

At the beginning of the nineteenth century, Italian opera was in the style of Mozart. Gioacchino Rossini (1792–1868) even based his opera *The Barber of Seville* on the same characters found in Mozart's opera *The Marriage of Figaro.* With Vincenzo Bellini (1801–1835) Italian opera reached a high point of interest in melody. The arias in his operas, such as *Norma,* emphasize beautiful singing (*bel canto* in Italian) through technically demanding melodic lines, cadenzas, and ornamentation. Gaetano Donizetti (1797–1848) also contributed to the *bel canto* style of opera. Although these early operas often lack convincing dramatic qualities, the brilliance of the soloists' lines and the beauty of the melodies make for very enjoyable listening.

The most important Italian opera composers in the latter half of the nineteenth century were Giuseppe Verdi and Giacomo Puccini. Both of them greatly improved the dramatic quality of their operas. Verdi insisted on having a good libretto and used the finest literature—Schiller, Victor Hugo, Dumas, Shakespeare. Both Verdi and Puccini contributed more realism to the opera. Their characters were neither stock roles, as had often been the case in the preceding century, nor symbols, which they tended to be in Wagner's operas. They tended to be more like real people interacting with people and events. Also the recitatives stopped being just filler that provided a great deal of text. Instead they became more melodious and expressive. Finally, both Verdi and Puccini utilized the orchestra very effectively to back up the singing and actions on the stage. The titles of Verdi's and Puccini's better known operas are cited in their biographies on pages 131 and 133.

Menotti's The Medium

The Medium by Gian-Carlo Menotti was first performed in 1946 in New York. It was commissioned by and premiered at Columbia University.

Menotti was born in 1911 in Italy, but he has lived in the United States since the age of 16. His many successful operas include *The Old Maid and the Thief, The Telephone* (a short comic opera that is often coupled with *The Medium* on the same program), *The Consul, The Saint of Bleeker Street,* and *Amahl and the Night Visitors,* which was commissioned for television. He writes the librettos as well as the music for his operas.

The cast of *The Medium* is small. There are only six characters, one of whom is mute, and three have rather minor roles. There is no chorus. The presentation, then, contrasts sharply with the large casts and choruses found in most nineteenth-century operas. Other differences can be observed. Only one stage setting is required for the opera's two acts. Furthermore, the entire opera takes less than one hour to perform. The shortness is a distinct reversal of nineteenth-century tendencies; three or more hours is not an unusual length for an opera of that century.

Menotti's orchestra is also much smaller, and the piano is given a prominent part in the accompaniment. Gone are the lush sounds of the nineteenth century, although the orchestra does provide coloristic effects to augment the meaning of the singer's words. For instance, at one point in this opera, Madame Flora is sick with fear. As she wails out the word "afraid," the strings sound rapidly repeating notes as though to suggest trembling.

The story, which takes place in New York, is about a devious old lady (Madame Flora, known to her family as Baba) who dupes bereaved people into thinking that she can serve as a medium between themselves and the dead. She is assisted in this hoax by her daughter Monica, a sheltered girl of 17, and by a mute orphan, Toby, whom she once picked off the streets of Budapest.

The curtain opens on Madame Flora's weird and shabby parlor. The apartment is arranged according to the stage sketch shown below.

Monica sings to Toby as they indulge in one of their fantasy games, in which he is an oriental king. Madame Flora enters, irked that nothing is ready for the evening seance. Quickly all is made ready—the wires that move the table, the lights, and the curtain behind which Monica imitates the voices of the dead loved ones. Mr. and Mrs. Gobineau enter; they have been attending seances for two years. Soon Mrs. Nolan arrives. It's her first experience with Madame Flora, and she is understandably nervous. The Gobineaus and Mrs. Nolan exchange information about the tragedies that have brought them there.

Finally the seance begins. The lights are dimmed, and an eerie wailing is evident. Soon a haunting motive ("Mother, Mother, are you there?") is heard coming from behind the screen, where Monica is impersonating Mrs. Nolan's daughter:

Moth - er, moth - er, are you there?

Monica and Mrs. Nolan converse for a while, and Monica sings some wonderfully warm, reassuring melodies:

Mum - my, Mummy dear, you must not cry for me.

I'm still with you. What is death but a

sweet-er change, there's no part-ing, there's no end.

She encourages Mrs. Nolan to give away her daughter's personal effects, no doubt mostly to Madame Flora. She mentions a locket. "I have no locket," says Mrs. Nolan. Suddenly the image behind the curtain begins to disappear, and Mrs. Nolan runs to the screen. She is stopped and calmed down.

Next it is the Gobineaus' turn. They talk with their dead two-year-old son and take comfort from his happy laughter. Suddenly Madame Flora screams. A cold hand has touched her throat! But who or what? The persons involved in the seance were touching hands at all times. Toby and Monica were behind the screen. Madame Flora abruptly ends the seance and rudely dismisses the customers. As they slowly climb the stairs, bewildered and accusing, they sing a chantlike melody to her: "Why be afraid of our dead?" As the act closes, Monica is trying to calm her mother by singing an old gypsy ballad. Madame Flora, terribly shaken, mumbles superstitiously and whispers her rosary in a distracted manner.

The actions of the second act parallel the events of the first; so does some of the music. A week has passed. Monica sings a song, actually an aria, and improvises a dance for Toby. Suddenly the game is no longer childlike. Monica asks, "Toby, what is it you want to tell me?" Toby, the mute, doesn't need a tongue; the orchestra answers for him with intense, impassioned chords that can only mean love. As Monica's aria continues, she sings both Toby's role and her own. Throughout the scene, much tenderness is added by Monica's gentle caressing of Toby's head. Her lines end, "Why, Toby! You're not crying are you? Toby, I want you to know that you have the most beautiful voice in the world!"

The mood changes abruptly when Madame Flora enters, disheveled and carrying a bottle; she is obviously still tormented by the memory of the hand that touched her throat at the seance. She pulls every known trick—emotional blackmail, bribes, threats, and love—to get Toby to admit that he was responsible. Toby's inability to answer only frustrates her further. Madame Flora sings "Toby, you know that I love you," but the orchestral accompaniment is tense and dissonant. It seems to reveal the falseness of her words. Before she is through with Toby, she loses her temper and begins hitting him.

The doorbell rings. Still breathless, Madame Flora answers. It's the Gobineaus and Mrs. Nolan arriving for their weekly seance. To ease her conscience, she offers to return their money and explains how she tricked them, but they refuse to believe her. Mrs. Nolan has even found the locket! They plead

for another seance, but in a rage Madame Flora orders them out. Then, despite Monica's pleadings to the contrary, her mother orders Toby to leave and sends Monica to her room and locks her in.

Madame Flora seats herself at the table. The haunting "Mother, Mother" motive is heard. Her shouting can't seem to stop it. She tries to reassure herself; she has seen many horrors in her lifetime, and *they* have never bothered her. She prays. She laughs at her fears. She prays again. Finally, she becomes drowsy and lays her head on the table.

Silently Toby reenters the apartment. He tries Monica's door but it's locked. He opens a trunk but the lid drops, making a sharp noise. Madame Flora wakens as Toby scampers behind the screen. "Who's there?" she cries, "Speak out or I'll shoot!" Toby can't answer, of course. Madame Flora pulls out a gun she has been carrying and fires at the screen. Silence follows, then blood begins running down the white curtain. Finally Toby's body falls headlong into the room. Madame Flora unlocks Monica's door, exclaiming "I've killed the ghost!" Monica, horrified, sees what has happened. She cries for help and then runs out into the night. Madame Flora kneels over Toby's body, still questioning, "Was it you? Was it you?"

Here the opera ends, with its situations unresolved. The audience has looked on the tangled emotions of people under stress. As in other twentieth-century operas, considerable psychological depth is imparted to the characters. People are complex mixtures of fear, gullibility, tenderness, guilt, and childlishness. No longer are their emotions as simple as love or anger. Their feelings are sometimes mixed and their motives uncertain. Freudian thinking has, in effect, moved onto the opera stage. *The Medium* might be described as a "psychological opera." Madame Flora, it might be said, is suffering from hallucinations caused by extreme feelings of guilt. Menotti treats her tortured existence with insight.

Menotti and several other twentieth-century opera composers have faced the economic realities of opera production. Their operas are small in scope, the staging simpler.

These composers know that there is little chance for a new opera with a huge cast and extensive scenery to be produced; it's just too expensive. Opera companies can hardly make ends meet even when they confine themselves to the standard repertoire. Besides, most modern opera composers are not at all sure that the grandiose opera is what they want to write or what the public wants to hear. They think that perhaps opera comes across best in a more intimate situation. Although a few operas on a large scale are still being written and produced, with varying degrees of success, there does seem to be a trend toward the smaller, more down-to-earth opera.

Georges Bizet

Georges Bizet (1838–1875) was born in Paris and lived most of his life there. Young Georges wanted to become a musician, and his parents supported the idea—quite a change from the situations of Handel, Dvořák, Berlioz, and others. He won the Prix de Rome, which afforded him a three-year stay in Rome. He composed a symphony and a few other works, but opera seemed to be his primary interest. *The Pearl Fishers*, written in 1863, is a drama of love and life in Ceylon. Four years later he wrote another opera, *The Fair Maid of Perth*, and later an opera named *Djanileh*, which is set in Cairo. None of these operas proved especially successful, and they are rarely performed today. One of Bizet's better works is the incidental music to the drama *L'Arlesienne* *(The Woman of Arles)*, which was written in 1872.

Most of Bizet's fame is the result of his opera *Carmen*. Its initial performances were largely failures. (One critic wrote: "If the devil were to write an opera, it would probably come out sounding very much like *Carmen*.") He had poured enormous effort into its writing and production. Worn out by months of rehearsal and tension, he wasn't prepared to take the blow of its failure. He died at the age of 37, exactly three months after the premiere of the opera. Today, *Carmen* is perhaps the best known and best loved opera in the world.

Giacomo Puccini

Giacomo Puccini (1858–1924) was not as sophisticated a composer as Verdi. He did possess, however, a wonderful gift of melody and an instinct for what would be successful on stage. His operas are as popular as Verdi's.

Puccini belonged to a group of opera composers who stressed *verismo* (realism). He drew material from everyday life, rejecting heroic or exalted themes from mythology and history. He was fond of parallel chord movement and selected chords for their particular sound as well as for their harmonic function.

Puccini's best known operas include *La Bohème* (1896); *Tosca* (1900); *Madame Butterfly* (1904), which is a story about the marriage of an American naval lieutenant and a Japanese girl; and *Turandot* (1926), which was completed by a friend after Puccini's death.

Richard Wagner

Richard Wagner (1813–1883) is an artistic phenomenon. Born in Leipzig, he was the son of a minor police official who died when Richard was still an infant. His mother married a talented actor and playwright, who encouraged his stepson along similar lines. For most of his career Wagner was largely self-taught. At 20 he obtained a post as chorus master in a small opera house in Leipzig and produced his first operas.

Success was slow, and for the next ten years it looked as though Wagner would spend his life hovering on the edge of poverty. His first successful opera was *Rienzi,* which earned him a position as conductor for the King of Saxony. Other successful operas followed in the 1840s: *The Flying Dutchman, Tannhauser,* and *Lohengrin.* The latter two operas derive their subjects from medieval German epic stories, with emphasis on supernatural elements and glorification of the German people.

In 1848 Wagner became associated with the political uprisings that were taking place in Europe. He even published two articles in a magazine that advocated anarchy. A revolution broke out in Dresden in 1849, and the king and his court fled. Wagner was forced to escape to the home of his friend Franz Liszt at Weimar. Since there was a warrant out for his arrest, Wagner soon fled on over the border into Switzerland. At that point he seemed a ruined man. But he was helped by some willing patrons, and the years in Switzerland were some of his most productive. It was during this time that he began work on *The Ring of the Nibelung.*

In the 1850s he composed *Tristan and Isolde,* and in the early 1860s *The Meistersingers of Nurenberg.* Wagner became estranged from his wife, who had grown unsympathetic to his artistic aims and desires. He became involved with a succession of married women. In 1864 again all seemed lost.

At this point fate seemed to step in. A 19-year-old who was an admirer of Wagner's music ascended to the throne in Bavaria. He

Richard Wagner

was Ludwig II, known as "Mad Ludwig." He summoned Wagner to Munich, where Wagner resumed work on *The Ring of the Nibelung.* In time he married Cosima, the daughter of Franz Liszt. Unfortunately, at the time their affair began, Cosima was already married to Hans von Bülow, the most famous conductor of the nineteenth century.

By 1876 Wagner had reached the top of the artistic world. It was during that year that he opened his first Bayreuth (*By*-royt) festival. Later he built an opera house there, and the Bayreuth festivals continue today. It is the only theater in the world that is devoted exclusively to the music of one person. His last opera was *Parsifal,* which is a legend based on the Holy Grail. It was finished shortly before he died. He is buried at Bayreuth, which in a sense is his monument.

Giuseppe Verdi

Verdi was born in 1813 in a small town in northern Italy. His father was a poor innkeeper. Giuseppe probably wouldn't have had a musical education had it not been for the support of a prosperous merchant who paid for two years' study in Milan. When Giuseppe returned, he fell in love with the wealthy merchant's daughter. The marriage was a happy one, but misfortune began to plague the family. His two children and his young wife died within a three-year span.

Although his first opera had been a moderate success, the next one was not. That failure, coupled with the tragedies in his family, caused him to give up composing for about a year. Finally the manager of the La Scala opera in Milan persuaded him to write an opera on Nebuchadnezzar, which Verdi shortened to *Nabucco*. It was an immediate success, and it launched him on a long and outstanding career as an opera composer.

In the late 1840s the Italians were having trouble with the Austrians. Verdi associated himself with Italian nationalism, and some of his operas were thinly veiled protests against the Austrian monarchy. Cries of "Viva Verdi" rang out in Italian opera houses, symbolizing both admiration for the man and his music and love for Italy. To many patriots the letters of his name represented "*Victor Emmanuel, Rex d'Italia.*"

In spite of his fame, Verdi remained a simple man who preferred the quiet of his farm to the pressures of society. His second wife was a sensitive and intelligent woman who encouraged his work. After Italian independence, in addition to sitting in the newly founded chamber of deputies, he wrote many successful operas: *Macbeth, La Traviata, Un Ballo in machera* (A Masked Ball), *La Forza del destino* (The Force of Destiny), *Aida*, and—after the age of 70—*Otello* and *Falstaff*. He died in 1901.

Fifteen

Ballet and Ballet Music

Like opera, dance involves both visual and aural aspects; it's a combination of arts. Appropriate music contributes to a good ballet, and in turn dancing has inspired the creation of some fascinating music. Although dancing is nearly universal, the discussion here is of ballet and the modern dance as they exist in Western civilization.

Ballet

Classical ballet began in the courts of Europe, especially France, about three hundred years ago. Its main goal was grace and courtliness. Deportment and etiquette were supreme virtues among the aristocracy. In the court of Louis XIV, for example, *everyone* took dancing lessons. What did people learn in these lessons? One thing was proper ballet posture; another was a balance of footwork and elevation—the ability to rise on the toes and to leap gracefully. They learned a posture that was based on a straight and quiet spine, a stiffened, straight knee, and a level hip line—the hips were not to lift, thrust out, or rotate. The shoulders were not to ripple.

From such instruction there developed a systemized set of positions and steps that are basic in classical ballet. Many of the positions, with their French names, are shown in the pictures on pages 136–137. From these positions a *choreographer* (designer of dances) plans routines and sequences for a complete scene.

The art of ballet remained relatively unchanged until the twentieth century. It was (and is) a beautiful art, but it was also artificial. The first revolt against these artificialities occurred at about the turn of the twentieth century, when Isadora Duncan threw off her corset and shoes and danced barefoot throughout Europe. She believed that dancing should be harmonious and simple, with no ornaments. Although she devised no new techniques, she gave ballet a more natural look. Her ideas were adapted by Michael Fokine, Ruth St. Denis, Martha Graham, Agnes de Mille, and others.

This chapter discusses the music of two well-known ballets: *Swan Lake*, which is in the classical ballet tradition, and *Rodeo*, which is more modern in concept.

Tchaikovsky's Swan Lake

Swan Lake was given its premiere performance at the Bolshoi Theater in Moscow in March 1877. Tchaikovsky's interest in the story began in 1871, when he was visiting his sister's children in the country. He composed for them some pieces based on a legend from *A Thousand and One Nights*. The tale involves a woman who magically becomes a bird. Four years later Tchaikovsky was commissioned to create a ballet on the story. Its initial reception was rather discouraging. The merits of the ballet were not fully appreciated until the production was presented in St. Petersburg in 1895. Since that time it has remained one of the most beloved ballets in the repertoire. George Balanchine, one of the great choreographers of ballet living today, has written: "To succeed in *Swan Lake* is to become overnight a ballerina. All leading dancers want to dance *Swan Lake* at least once in their careers."

The story is pure magic. Prince Siegfried is approaching his twenty-first birthday. His mother plans to hold a great ball at which he will select the most pleasing young woman to be his bride. On the day before the ball the prince and some of his friends go into the country to hunt swans. They come upon these glorious white birds, and the prince notices one that is obviously their Queen. (In the ballet she usually wears a diamondlike crown.) She is a ravishing creature, but is she a swan or a woman? Siegfried finally soothes the creature into telling him that a sorcerer named von Rothbart has transformed her into Odette, Queen of the Swans, and that she must remain that way forever—except between midnight and dawn. The spell can be broken only by a man who loves her, marries her, and never loves another. Siegfried immediately wants Odette to come to tomorrow's ball.

The third act of the ballet takes place at the ball. Siegfried is melancholy because he is afraid he has lost Odette. Six of the most beautiful young women in the kingdom dance for Siegfried, and he mimes that he can't marry any of them because he loves another. Soon the lights dim and a dark beauty is led forward by the Knight of the Black Swan. She is Odile, but Siegfried knows only that she is the image of Odette. Odile's dancing enchants Siegfried and she leads him into the garden. In the meantime the guests are honored by dances from foreign lands—Spain, Hungary, Poland.

Odile reappears to do the final dance. With the Prince she performs the brilliant Black Swan Pas de deux. Siegfried is so taken with her that he swears eternal faithfulness to her, still believing her to be Odette. Now the spell cannot be broken; von Rothbart has tricked Siegfried.

In the fourth act the Queen of the Swans appears, sobbing and insisting that she must die. The Prince arrives, swears his eternal love, and embraces her. She believes him, but tells him that only death will break the dreadful spell. Odette and Siegfried, wishing to drown, fling themselves into the lake. Love triumphs, von Rothbart dies, and the spell is broken. Odette and Siegfried glide on a jeweled ship into the ever-after.

Tchaikovsky arranged a suite from the music that he composed for *Swan Lake*. He did the same with his other well-known ballets, *The Nutcracker* and *The Sleeping Beauty*. The music in the suite does not appear in the same order as in the ballet because in the suite Tchaikovsky does not need to follow the story line. Also, the suite contains only a portion of the music that appears in the ballet. The first movement of the suite contains the most prominent theme from the ballet. It appears at various times in both major and minor.

The second movement is built around the waltz:

The third movement contains the theme for the dance of the swans:

Vocabulary of the Classical Ballet

First Position

Second Position

Third Position

Fourth Position

Fifth Position

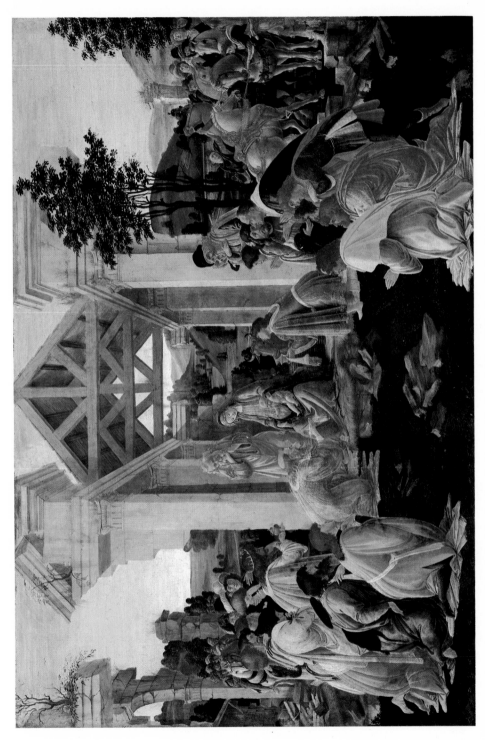

Plate 1. The Adoration of the Magi by Sandro Botticelli. *(Andrew Mellon Collection, National Gallery of Art, Washington, D.C.)*

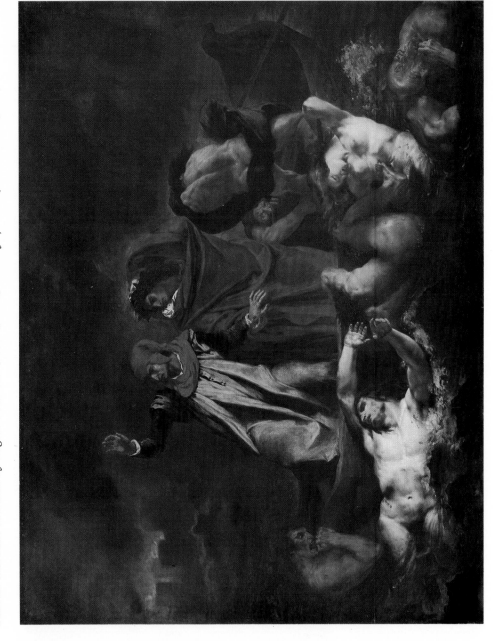

Plate 2. The Bark of Dante by Eugène Delacroix. (Louvre, Paris, Courtesy of Art Reference Bureau, Inc.)

Plate 4. Broadway Boogie Woogie *by Piet Mondrian. (Collection, The Museum of Modern Art, New York)*

Pas Poisson

Pas de Chat

Attitude

Petits Battements

Arabesque Penchée

Pirouette

Arabesque

Pas Ballonné

Attitude

The fourth movement features a harp cadenza followed by a violin solo. A Hungarian dance called the czardas (*char*-das) appears in the fifth movement. The czardas has a slow beginning, followed by furiously paced music. Traditionally the dancers move as fast as possible. The two themes associated with this movement are:

Allegro moderato

Vivace

A sixth movement provides a brilliant ending to the suite.

Tchaikovsky's style of music is especially well suited to ballet. His music has a lilting quality that seems to inspire graceful movement.

Copland's Rodeo

Rodeo was first presented by Agnes de Mille and the Ballet Russe de Monte Carlo in 1942, and it soon became a standard work in the repertoire of ballet companies. The music is most often heard in a suite with these four parts: "Buckaroo Holiday," "Corral Nocturne," "Saturday Night Waltz," and "Hoe-Down."

The ballet tells the story of the young Cowgirl who has been a tomboy. Suddenly she becomes aware of men and romance. She tries to impress the Head Wrangler (her favorite) and the Champion Roper with her ability as a rider. The Cowgirl is in the corral with the men, but they pay little attention, concentrating instead on their own work and riding. They finally gallop off without even noticing her, and she in turn rides away in anger and tears. The section opens with this spirited theme:

Allegro con spirito

Later two American folk tunes are heard: "If He Be a Buckaroo by His Trade" and "Sis Joe."

"Buckaroo Holiday" employs several rhythmic figures that suggest dances associated with the old American West.

The music for "Corral Nocturne" contains no folk tunes. City girls wearing pretty dresses instead of jeans have come to visit the Rancher's Daughter and to enjoy the Saturday night dance. Once more the Cowgirl is ignored. She simply can't compete with feminine frills. A tranquil, somewhat sad mood is set by this melody:

Moderato

The couples move off, eager for the dance, and the Cowgirl is left behind again.

Saturday night at the ranch is a time for dancing. The Cowgirl, still in jeans and boots, sits alone watching the festivities. The Roper and the Wrangler take pity on her and ask her to dance. She is too shy and misses the opportunity. As the "Saturday Night Waltz" begins—it contains the song "Old Paint"—the Roper insists that the Cowgirl dance. She wants to but then sees the Wrangler dancing with the Rancher's Daughter. Jealous and confused, she stands motionless among the dancers. Annoyed, the Roper turns and leaves, and the Cowgirl runs from the floor.

The dancing reaches a climax in the riotous "Hoe-Down," which is based partly on the folk melody "Bonyparte." (The Listening Guide for "Hoe-Down" appears on pages 10–11.) The Cowgirl reappears, this time wearing a party dress. She is vivacious and pretty, and she soon becomes the center of attention. The

Roper again asks her to dance. Though she would rather have the Wrangler, she accepts the Roper and joins the others in the wild dancing as the ballet ends.

As you can tell, *Rodeo* is quite different from *Swan Lake*. No longer does the plot rely on magical events, and no longer is the main goal etiquette and courtliness. The dancing is natural, and the story is realistic. The music often draws on folk sources, and the choreography is also based on folk dancing, especially the "Hoe-Down."

Both *Swan Lake* and *Rodeo* are fascinating ballets with attractive music. Their diversity shows the wide spectrum of styles that can be encompassed by artistic dancing.

Peter Ilich Tchaikovsky

Until early adulthood, Tchaikovsky (Chy-*kuff*-skee, 1840–1893) seemed destined to follow in his father's footsteps by working in a governmental position. At the age of 23, however, he decided to become a musician, so he resigned his job and entered the newly founded Conservatory of St. Petersburg (now Leningrad). He did well, and in three years he had finished his course and was recommended for a teaching position in the new Conservatory of Moscow. He taught harmony there for 12 years.

Throughout his life, Tchaikovsky was plagued by the fact that he was a homosexual. He once described his existence as "regretting the past, hoping for the future, without ever being satisfied with the present." He married a Conservatory student, a rather unstable girl who was madly in love with him. He could feel only pity for her and despair for himself. The marriage was a disaster. Finally, on the verge of a complete mental breakdown, he went to live with his brothers in St. Petersburg.

At this point in his life entered Nadezhda von Meck, a wealthy widow who, though a recluse, successfully ran her inherited business empire and the lives of her 11 children. She was impressed by the beauty of Tchaikovsky's music and decided to support him financially. There was, however, one unusual twist to the arrangement. So that she could be sure she was supporting a composer and not a personal friend, she stipulated that they should never

Peter Ilich Tchaikovsky

meet. And so it was. For 13 years Mme. von Meck and Tchaikovsky carried on intense and devoted contact—all by letter.

In 1891 he accepted an invitation to America, where he participated in the opening of Carnegie Hall in New York. According to his letters, he liked Americans and was gratified by the fact that they appreciated his music. In 1893, while in St. Petersburg to conduct his Sixth Symphony, he contracted cholera and died at the age of 53.

Aaron Copland

Aaron Copland was born in Brooklyn in 1900 of Russian-Jewish immigrant parents. He attended the New York City public schools, worked in his father's department store, and took his first piano lessons from his older sister. After graduation from high school, he studied piano and harmony in New York and spent much time studying scores at the public library. In 1921 he went to the American School of Music at Fontainebleau in France. The teacher there was a remarkable woman named Mlle. Nadia Boulanger (Boo-lahn-*zhay*). Copland became the first of a long list of young American composers to study with her. When she was invited to give some concerts in the United States, she asked Copland to compose a work for performance on her tour. The work he provided was the *Symphony for Organ and Orchestra*. It was first performed in New York in 1925.

Copland became interested in jazz in the late 1920s, and several of his compositions show the jazz influence. *Music for the Theater* and *Symphonic Ode* are from this period. His works in the early 1930s tend to be more abstract, as is revealed in his *Piano Variations* and *Short Symphony*. In the late 1930s he composed two works for performance by school groups: *The Second Hurricane* and *Outdoor Overture*. *A Lincoln Portrait* is a tremendously exciting work. It includes a part for a narrator and is centered on the quotations of Abraham Lincoln. *El Salón México* is a rhythmic rhapsody on Mexican tunes.

In three of his works, all ballets, Copland exploits American folk music: *Billy the Kid* (1938), *Rodeo* (1942), and *Appalachian Spring* (1943–1944). In them he reaches a happy medium between retaining the interest and respect

Aaron Copland. Photo by C.B.S., courtesy of Boosey & Hawkes.

of the trained musician and at the same time pleasing the public. Not many twentieth-century composers have been able to attain this balance.

Since the late 1940s his music has become a bit more intellectual. With Roger Sessions, another able American composer, Copland organized a series of concerts to promote new music in America. He is the author of several interesting books for the musical layman. He has lectured at many universities and has written several film scores.

The Lovers by Pablo Picasso. Courtesy of the National Gallery of Art, Washington, D.C. (Chester Dale Collection).

Section Three

Musical Types and Styles

So far this book has discussed the elements of music and the more important forms and media. It now turns to considering the varying types of music that have been created around the world over the course of history. First it looks at folk-ethnic music. In a day of instant communication and easy world travel, people are becoming more aware of the riches of folk-ethnic music. Next the book briefly traces the development of music in Western civilization up to and through the Renaissance period.

When several composers organize sounds in a similar way, they are said to be writing in the same *style*. Style refers mainly to musical qualities, not to a period of time or a geographical place. Even after a style has passed the peak of its popularity, composers occasionally return to it, sometimes centuries later. And elements of one style can appear in music of other styles.

Although a style of music is not confined to a particular time and place, it is named for the historical period in which it was most clearly prominent. The designation of periods can be made only after the actual years have passed because such categorizing requires historical perspective. In no case can the dates of a period be stated precisely; they must always be approximate.

Despite its limitations, a concept of style is useful in learning music. It helps you organize your thinking about what you hear. When you understand what constitutes musical style, you are learning the very stuff of music. An understanding of style helps you listen for the right things. Knowing that the Renaissance ideal was purity and restraint of sound, you won't be surprised by the lack of volume and flashing brilliance in Renaissance music. You will be able to listen with more realistic expectations and greater reward.

For this reason, Chapters 16 to 26 discuss significant musical styles—Baroque, Classical, Neo-Classical, Nationalism, and so on. Chapter 27 presents some thoughts about music as it exists now.

Because American music is of special interest and importance to Americans, a chapter is devoted to it. The last chapter considers America's popular music and jazz.

Sixteen

Music Throughout the World

Music is found in every part of the world. It is universal among human beings. No one knows how much folk music there is, but the amount must be tremendous. The forms and styles of the music people produce are as varied as their languages and ways of life. Folk music is a fascinating and significant area of the world of music.

What Is Folk Music?

The words *folk* and *ethnic* are not synonymous. *Ethnic* refers to music identified with a particular race or group of people. *Folk* refers only to music actually adopted by the common people. A Hungarian peasant song about harvesting hay is a folk song. And because it is characteristic of that country, it is also ethnic music. The *raga* of India is not folk music; it is not the music of the common people but rather of a highly trained musical elite. It is characteristic of India, though, so it is ethnic music. All folk music is ethnic, but not all ethnic music is folk music.

Folk-ethnic music is not created "by committee"—by a group of people sitting

around a campfire or marching into battle. Individuals create ethnic music, just as individuals compose art music; but there the similarity ends. The creator of ethnic music is almost always unknown. In fact, the individual might not admit to the accomplishment even if he or she could be located. In many areas of the world, songs are considered gifts from the gods revealed in dreams or visions or created on "orders" from a supernatural being. Besides, in most cultures people neither care nor remember who was first responsible for providing a song.

Once created, the music is perpetuated through *oral tradition*, whereby individuals hear the music, remember it, and perform it for others. If no one except the originator likes the song, it passes into oblivion. This tradition insures the survival of only those songs that are liked by the particular culture. Oral tradition also means that the music is subject to many changes.

Nonliterate societies have no system of musical notation. Even in the advanced societies of ancient India and China, only a system of visual cues was developed. Without a system of notation or recordings, music cannot be preserved accurately. For this reason folk music is always changing, which may be one of its strengths. It is both traditional and contemporary; it represents the heritage of the people and their current tastes.

A thorough study of ethnic and folk music is an enormously involved undertaking. The musical aspects are only the beginning. The total culture must be included—language, customs, thought forms, and so on. Ethnic music cannot be separated from the culture in which it exists.

Most of the folk-ethnic music of the world is less complex than art music. Why? First, most of it is confined to short works, usually songs. True, some African rituals last for hours, but the same music tends to be repeated over and over, with only slight variations. The Indian *raga* is also long, but it's an exceptional kind of music. Without a system of notation, musical works are usually rather short, because most people cannot remember long complex works accurately. The short length allows for little formal or thematic development, something that is important to art music.

When ethnic music does display complexity, such as the rhythm of African music, it tends to do so with only one aspect of the music, leaving the other aspects relatively undeveloped. By contrast, art music, especially in the twentieth century, displays involved combinations of pitch, harmony, rhythm, timbre, dynamics, and form.

Listening to Folk Music

Several suggestions beyond those made in Chapter 2 can be made for listening to folk-ethnic music. Listen to examples of the more significant types—African, Arabian, Latin American, and so on. Learn to identify each from listening in terms of its overall quality. Compare and contrast the timbres, rhythmic structures, instruments, singing style, melodic patterns, and other aspects of the music. While listening, keep in mind the cultural setting of the music in terms of its purpose in that society.

Characteristics of Non-Western Music

What makes much of the ethnic music found throughout the world different from most of the music familiar to us? Let's start with rhythm.

Rhythm. As was pointed out in Chapter 4, most rhythms in the music of Western civilization have regular patterns of accented and unaccented beats. Measure is linked to measure, something like beads on a string. But much of the world's music exhibits unequal rhythmic patterns. Sometimes the rhythm is very free. Frequently it conforms to natural speech patterns, so that the text is not adapted to a given metrical pattern, as is usually true of the music we know.

Melodic structure. Two important differences exist between most Western music and other types of music. One concerns the exact tuning of pitches. The octave has a solid basis in the physical laws of sound, and it appears throughout the world. The higher of the two pitches is produced by twice as many vibrations as the pitch an octave lower. All other intervals in Western music are adjusted to approximate the present system of keyboard tuning. Even the splitting of the octave into 12 equal parts is an arbitrary decision by Western musicians. Non-Western music generally does not divide the octave into 12 equal half steps. *Microtones*, which are pitches less than a half step apart, are found in the Near East and Far East and, to some extent, in Africa. The octave is divided into 22 parts in India; in the Moslem world it has been variously divided into 25, 17, and 15 parts. To a listener unaccustomed to them, microtones can sound hauntingly expressive or just plain out of tune.

The other difference is the type of scale on which the music is based. A scale is a series of ascending and descending tones that follow a specific pattern of intervals. Usually the top and bottom notes are one octave apart. A scale with all its pitches sounded in order seldom appears in a melody. A scale is the underlying "formula" for the pitches appearing in a particular section of music. The major and minor scale patterns are predominant in Western music today, although other seven-note scales called modes are favored in folk and popular songs. A common scale in non-Western folk music is the *pentatonic* scale, a five-note pattern that duplicates the pitches of the black keys on the piano keyboard. (*Penta* means five.) Many other scales are found throughout the world.

Add to the variable tuning of notes and the wide diversity of scales the fact that, in some musical systems, certain notes can be altered or ornamented by the performer, and you can see why genuine ethnic music sounds different to our ears.

Harmony. Most of the world's music contains very little harmony. Some melodies are never intended to have other sounds occurring with them. When harmony is found, it is usually in one of two forms. One is a *drone*, a single continuous sound lasting throughout a piece. The Scottish bagpipe produces one of the few examples of a drone in Western music. The other type of harmony is produced by adding a duplicate melodic line that moves along strictly parallel to the original melody. This harmony part is often a fourth or fifth above or below the melody. Sometimes it is a third, which is the usual interval in Western harmony.

Form. Most ethnic songs are too brief to allow for much formal development, but short sections are often arranged in various patterns. One type is the leader-response found in African music. The result is a game of "musical tennis," in which lines of music alternate between a soloist and the group. In many parts of the world, music is subjected to a simple variation treatment in which the basic melody is varied slightly and repeated many times.

Improvisation. Almost all art music is written out. The performer's main task is to re-create the notes on the page and follow the composer's intent. Not so with most ethnic music. No accurate system of notation exists outside the West, and most composers of ethnic music are unknown, so the performer is encouraged to make up new music while playing or sing-

ing. This art of performing music spontaneously, without the aid of notes, is called improvisation. The performer does not often improvise "out of thin air"—that is, without any guidelines at all. Melodic or rhythmic patterns and performance customs act as guidelines.

In contrast to art music, in which the ideas of the composer prevail, most ethnic music is geared to the performer. Improvised performances are never quite the same twice. They reflect the inspiration of the moment.

Instruments. Folk instruments were described in Chapter 7.

Some Significant Types of Ethnic Music

The topic of ethnic music is so vast that it could occupy many volumes. To keep the chapter within reasonable limits, it is necessary to leave out music from many areas of the world.

Europe. As might be expected, the folk music of Europe resembles Western art music more closely than does other ethnic music. Wide differences can be found within the European continent, however, especially in isolated rural areas.

One characteristic of European folk music is the singing of different lines of words, each time to the same melody. Some pentatonic scales are encountered, especially in Hungary and eastern Europe, but major and minor scales and modes predominate. The rhythm is metrical, with somewhat more freedom of meter in eastern European music.

The topics found in European folksongs include a greater percentage of epic-narrative tales and love sentiments than do the songs of other cultures. There are some folk hymns and songs about turning points in a person's life, such as birth or marriage.

India. Probably the most sophisticated music outside of Western civilization is found in India. The music described here is not folk music, but an ethnic music that requires much training for both performer and listener.

Musical instruments of India. (Front to Back) Sitar, tabla (smaller drum) and bayan (larger drum), and tambura.

Indian music is very much intertwined with religious belief and practice. It began at least a thousand years B.C., and it continues today. Despite pressures from the Near East, invasions by the Mohammedans a thousand years ago, and British occupation in the nineteenth and twentieth centuries, it is believed that the music has not changed much since its inception.

At the heart of Indian music is the *raga*, a melodic formula resembling a scale. But it also embraces important Indian religious concepts. The performers believe that its vibrations must be in tune with the universe, and that other arts such as poetry and painting must fit with music into the great cosmic scheme. For example, there are *ragas* that should be performed only in the morning, others only in the evening, others only in the rainy season, and so on. Theoretically, thousands of *ragas* exist, but only about 50 are used frequently. *Ragas* vary in length; the average is about 20 to 25 notes. Two tones tend to stand out in each *raga*, one being a fourth or fifth higher than the other.

The next significant element in Indian music is its rhythm, which is built around the *tala*. Each *tala* is a rhythmic cycle of from 3 to 128 beats; most are from 5 to 8 beats long. Each *tala* is divided into smaller groups. A *tala* is not a measure, as was described in Chapter 4; it's a pattern. For example, a seven-beat *tala* might be made up of 3 beats + 2 beats + 2 beats. If an Indian musician taps his foot as he plays, it is not a steady tapping but an indication of the unequal divisions of the *tala*. Furthermore, the first beat in a *tala* should not be accented more heavily than the other beats. Like each *raga*, each *tala* is named.

With the *raga* and *tala* as their guides, the performers improvise as they sing a religious poem from one of the holy books. Because the musical system is so complicated, they have a dazzling array of melodic and rhythmic possibilities—enough to last a lifetime. The pleasure for the listener lies in hearing performers create their own music within the guidelines of the system.

Indian musicians use some instruments: hand drums, simple flutes and double reed instruments, and *sitars*. The *sitar* is a complicated string instrument with five melodic strings, two drones, and 13 more strings that sound in sympathy with the melodic strings. It looks like a large guitar with pegs along the neck of the instrument.

China.   China's musical heritage is as old as India's. Although China had no system of writing music, accurate verbal accounts are available about music throughout its history. Like Indian music, Chinese music was closely related to philosophy and religion.

The Chinese developed a system that included the 12 pitches that appear within the octave in Western music. Although they had more than five pitches, their basic melodic tool was the pentatonic scale.

The Chinese developed several exotic instruments. One was a model of a crouching tiger with a serrated ridge or set of wooden slats along its backbone. It was sounded by

dragging a bamboo stick across the bumps or slats. Another instrument was a mouth organ with 17 bamboo pipes.

In some periods of China's history, music thrived; in other eras it hardly survived. Much of the music was created for the official court, often for banquets. A few large orchestras existed in China—a situation that was rare outside of the West. Many theatrical, operalike productions were presented also.

In 1911 the last Chinese dynasty fell, and the country was declared a republic. The ensuing years have been hard ones for music, largely because of internal strife and repression. Since 1949 the Communist Party has controlled the mainland, and sophisticated music has been discouraged. More in favor is the unison singing of politically oriented songs such as "Up the Mountain Come the Manure Carriers" and "Hearts of the Frontier Guards Turn to the Party," actual titles of songs heard in China in 1973. Some of the old Chinese musical tradition is being preserved on Formosa, but the influence of Western music is strongly felt there.

Arabian music.   The Arabian world extends 4,000 miles from the north coast of Africa (just across the Strait of Gibraltar from Spain) eastward to the borders of Pakistan. Although most Arabs share the same religious faith—Islam—their culture and music have never been well unified. Four main groupings of Arabian music can be identified. One is Persian, which centers in Iran. A second is Arab, centering in Egypt and Saudi Arabia. A third is Andalusian; it exists mostly in North Africa. The fourth is Turkish. To further complicate matters, Arabian music has intricate and confusing music theories that vary from country to country. And when performed, the music often differs from the stated musical theories.

Much music from the Arabian world is vocal and is characterized by a tense, nasal quality. Some call-and-response between soloist and chorus is found. Accompaniment often consists of hand claps or tambourines—small hoops with a hide stretched over one side and metal jingles in the hoop. Mohammed, the prophet of Islam, did not approve of music in the mosque, so it is restricted in orthodox Islamic worship. A few restrained prayers and chants are "sung" in the mosque, but they are not officially considered to be music, so they are acceptable.

In Iran the basic feature is a *gushe*, which is similar to the Indian *raga*. Usually playing a flute, the performer improvises a highly decorated line based on the *gushe*. The rhythm is free, allowing performers to follow their musical inclinations.

Important Arabian instruments include the *tombak*—a drum in the shape of an hourglass, which is played with the hand and fingers; the *ud*—a string instrument with a pear-shaped body; and the *rebab*—a direct ancestor of the violin.

Although there are some professional musicians in the Arabian countries, there are few concerts in the Western sense of the word. Cafés are the usual setting for music performances, and people may listen or sip a drink as they wish. As an added attraction the more thoughtful numbers may be interspersed with the gyrating female dancers for which the Arabian world is noted. Artistic musical standards are difficult to maintain against such competition, and they seem often to be abandoned.

Jewish music in Israel. Because the Jews were dispersed throughout the world for so long, their nonreligious music has assimilated many regional characteristics. Even the pre-Christian music of the Jews was influenced by both the East and the West, primarily because Jerusalem was a crossroads for caravans traveling between the two worlds. The Arabian culture, which almost surrounds Israel, has also exerted its influence. Many Jews, however, sing Arabian songs in a style different from the one they use for Jewish music.

Jewish religious music has remained rather consistent in form and content. Judaism was not as evangelistic as Christianity; it tended to keep its faith within the group, and it seldom incorporated local music into its worship. Its religious music consists of sung prayers and invocations, not anthems such as are found in many Protestant churches. The use and type of music varies according to the degree of orthodoxy. The more orthodox congregations permit only unaccompanied chanting by cantors, with a free rhythm and some decorative notes. More liberal congregations often employ non-Jewish instrumentalists and singers to perform adaptations of music written for Christian worship.

Since the establishing of modern Israel in 1948, attempts have been made to create new folk traditions to help unify a multiethnic nation whose bonds are largely religious and political. New popular songs have been composed about economic and political topics. Arabian tambourines and hourglass drums, as well as guitars and accordions, are used for accompaniment. Arabian-type scales are often harmonized with Western chords. Like its people, Israel's music is highly cosmopolitan.

Latin-American music. The term *Latin-American* includes a wide variety of music. To begin with, the music of Spain itself is immensely varied. It includes the music of the Spanish gypsies and of the Basque people of northern Spain; it exhibits Arabian influence resulting from 600 years of occupation by the Moors. With the Spanish conquests in the New World, elements of Spanish music were transplanted to the Americas. Here it was mixed with native Indian music and the music of the blacks, especially in Cuba, Brazil, and the West Indies.

In the centuries since the Spanish entered Latin America, their music has been adapted so extensively that it has become impossible in many cases to identify the source of a particular song. Some Spanish dances have been adapted, also. For example, the *bolero* was originally Spanish, but in Cuba its rhythm became more complex. Elements of Latin-American rhythms appear in jazz. Among other features carried over from Spanish music into Latin-American music are the frequent use of meters having three notes to the beat, the presence of a line moving in parallel thirds with the melody, and melodies with a rather narrow range.

Mexican music is largely Spanish in character, more so than most other Latin-American music. Some Mexican Indians have retained their own music, but the Indian influence is not significant in Mexico's music. The Mexicans have a narrative type of song called a *corrido*, which relates an event or tells a story. Instruments play an important role in Mexican music and are sometimes featured in instrumental interludes. The often-heard *mariachi* band consists of from three to twelve people playing violins, guitars, brasses, and other instruments. Some of the band music has a complex rhythmic structure.

Latin-American music enjoys considerable favor in the United States. Much of it, however, is commercial music created for nightclubs and cocktail lounges. It's not authentic, and to a musician it's less interesting than the legitimate music of the Latin-American peoples. Fortunately, some Latin-American folk songs have been incorporated into the musical heritage of the United States, and Latin-American people have preserved some of their distinctive songs.

Africa south of the Sahara.   The areas north of the vast Sahara desert are largely Arabian in character. To the south are the provinces of the black peoples, and it is their music that will be discussed here. For the sake of brevity, the term will be shortened to Africa.

Music for the African is more important, more an integral part of life, than it is for many of the peoples of the world. Music is called upon to cure illness, appease gods, and celebrate the birth of a baby. Some music is sheerly for entertainment and is performed by men whose livelihood comes from their music making. In some tribes there is a small musical elite, usually drummers, who practice their trade from youth. They spend most of their childhood learning how to drum and do not perform publicly until they are young adults.

The Western idea of a performer and a passive group of listeners is unusual in Africa. An African musical performance is truly a participatory event in which everyone sings, claps, or dances. Furthermore, African musicians want the music to have an impact on the listeners. They do not particularly care whether they consider the music "beautiful," but they do want them to share their feelings.

Music is even used for signaling. Sometimes the drum rhythms resemble a simplified Morse code, but the signals are also related to the pitch structure of the language. Many African languages are tonal. A sound, *ba* for example, takes on a different meaning depending on the pitch level at which it is spoken. As many as four pitch levels are found in some languages. A drummer then approximates the pitch of the word being signaled by playing different-sized drums or hitting a log drum at different places.

Form in African music is based on a short phrase that is repeated, varied slightly, or alternated with group response. The call-and-response technique between leader and group is central to African music. It assures the participation of which Africans are so fond.

Improvisation is common in African styles. The variations of the short musical unit are improvised. Not only does the leader improvise; in some tribes, the group members improvise simultaneously among themselves, so that several lines of music are being sounded at the same time.

Melodically, African music is not far different from Western music. The underlying scale contains seven different notes—the pattern described in Chapter 5. But more use is made of microtones and the pentatonic scale. Glides and other ornaments are incorporated into the singing, and this sometimes disguises the true pitch of a note.

The main feature of African music is its rhythm. The fact that it does not follow a regular pattern has already been mentioned. A feature of West African music is the musician's ability to maintain a steady tempo for minutes or even hours. Western musicians keep a generally steady tempo, but they make slight fluctuations in it. The exactness of the tempo in African music makes it easier to emphasize the irregular accents and rhythmic patterns.

A more spectacular feature of African rhythm is the sounding of two or more rhythms at the same time—a technique that occurs most often in drumming, but also appears in other types of music. Some works contain as many as six different rhythmic parts sounding simultaneously. The effect can be truly exciting.

African music includes some simple types of harmony and counterpoint. One type is the parallel movement created by a melodic line and its duplicate on a different pitch. There are also some two-part rounds. These rounds may have developed from instances in which either the leader or chorus was overly anxious and began its part before the other had finished. Accompaniment is evident in African music. Instruments such as the xylophone or harp sometimes accompany a melody by persistently repeating a short melodic phrase that contrasts with the melody.

American Folk Music

The English heritage. The main source of American folk music is the British Isles. Many songs were imported intact from Britain, and others have been patterned after British types.

The most significant type of British folk song is the *ballad*. It is a narrative song ranging from 5 to 20 stanzas in length. Traditionally the ballad had iambic meter and stanzas of four lines, in which a four-foot line alternates with a three-foot line. Here is an American example:

> *When John Henry was a little baby*
> *sitting on his pappy's knee,*
> *He grabbed a hammer and a little piece of*
> *steel,*
> *said, "This hammer'll be the death of me."*

Ballad stories are often tragic. In "John Henry" the hero dies with a hammer in his hand.

In a ballad the narrator-singer is a third person relating a tale, so he or she is not personally involved. The music usually reflects this by a calm and detached attitude.

In older ballads the music often reveals a seven-note modal scale, not the major-minor system of today. Some, such as "John Henry," conform to the pentatonic scale. The rhythm depends primarily on the text, which means that a regular pattern is followed. Much of the ballad singing in the United States is unaccompanied, although in Kentucky an accom-

paniment is taken for granted and is provided by a banjo, guitar, or dulcimer. The dulcimer looks like a long, flat violin with three strings. It is laid on the player's lap and plucked with a quill. Two of its strings produce a drone, which was a common feature of ballad accompaniment.

The ballad style is evident in many American folk songs associated with occupations—seafaring, cattle herding, forestry, mining, farming, railroading, and so on. "John Henry" is such a song. The ballad's influence can also be observed in American religious hymns. It has been estimated that most songs in the English heritage descended from about 55 tunes or "tune families."

Non-British music also came to the United States with various immigrant groups, and in a few cases such songs were incorporated into the culture and stand along with the British-style music: "Du, du liegst mir im Herzen" is a German song that has been adopted into the culture; "Alouette" is a French-Canadian example; and "Chiapanecas" (sometimes called "The Mexican Clapping Song") is a Latin-American contribution that is clapped and stomped at many major league ballparks. Some of these songs have had new words put to the music. Unfortunately, much non-British music was lost in the New World.

American Indian music. The functional nature of American Indian music is apparent in the names given to the ritual procedures. As the titles imply, a sun dance or rabbit dance is created for a specific purpose.

Traditionally, Indian instruments consisted of a variety of drums, usually played with sticks. Sometimes kettledrums were filled with water or the drum head was moistened before playing to achieve the pitch desired by the performer—a practice that indicates some musical sophistication. Many types of rattles were developed. Several types of flutes were played, especially by the men, who performed love music on them to impress their chosen young women.

The Indian population was never large (not more than one or two million in all of North America), and it was spread over a vast land area. As a result, musical styles differed widely among the various tribes, a fact that is also true in Africa.

Indian music has not had a significant effect on other American music for two reasons. First, most Indians do not live in close proximity to non-Indians. They have been set apart on reservations, and their music tends to remain there. Second, Indian music is quite different from Western music. In some respects it is more oriental than Western. When one culture incorporates music from another, the two styles are likely to be somewhat similar. Some change, but not too much, is accepted in music. In the few instances in which Indian music has been incorporated into art music, it has been changed freely and westernized.

Occupational songs.   An important contribution to America's folk-music heritage can be heard in songs about various occupations. In many cowboy songs the text and music are often tinged with loneliness and melancholy, reflecting the fact that life on the frontier was not an easy or particularly happy existence. Some of the cowboy tunes originally had other words before they were adapted by the cowboy. Such adaptations are common in folk music.

The development of the railroad provided another source for occupational songs. Some of these songs are about the men who worked the railroads ("Drill Ye Tarriers, Drill"), some describe famous personalities ("John Henry" and "Casey Jones"), and others tell about trains themselves ("The Wabash Cannonball"). Sailors have also provided songs. But today's computers and assembly lines do not encourage the development of song literature. One doesn't sing to a computer, and the noise of an assembly line drowns out other sounds. So the occupational song may have become a thing of the past.

Afro-American music.   It is difficult to determine which aspects of Afro-American music were transplanted from Africa and which were developed in America. In a complex and pluralistic society, the sources of a cultural merger are hard to assess. In any case, some of the African rhythmic ideas, the call-and-response patterns, the love of instruments, and improvisation are now a part of American music.

The African influence has been felt most in the area of performance; the spiritual is a good example. Actually, the spiritual, which is so widely associated with the American black, is largely borrowed from southern rural whites. In text and melodic ideas, black and white spirituals are almost identical. The difference between the two kinds of spirituals is in the way they are sung. The black spiritual is more rhythmic and stresses call-and-response, with some improvisation; the white version is more lyric and less exuberant. Performance differences are also apparent in other types of black folk music: work songs, love songs, ballads, and lullabies. Some were originated by blacks, but many were simply taken from the American culture. The songs may look similar in notation, but in performance the Afro-American qualities become evident.

Another performance area in which the influence of African music is evident is the variety of singing style. African singers produce more varied sounds when singing. Some tones are purposely harsh and raucous in order to imitate animals; some are tense, and some are throaty, but generally the style is relaxed and warm.

The song that evolved to accompany work is definitely an outgrowth of black culture. Songs sung *while* working (not songs *about* work) are not common in Western music, except in sea chanties. The text of some of these songs is not related directly to the job at hand; often the words supply only a pleasant accompaniment to labor.

As in Africa, instruments play an important role in Afro-American folk music. Some of the instruments are derived from Europe, while others are intended to duplicate sound effects. Included in the latter category are washboards, pans, cowbells, bottles, various clappers, and the gutbucket (an inverted washtub with a rope pulled through it and connected to a stick; the pitch is varied according to the tension of the rope).

The greatest contribution of blacks to American music is jazz. It is so significant that half of a chapter of this book is devoted to it.

Folk and ethnic music is important partly because there is so much of it and so many people find it appealing. It has influenced the development and content of art music. In some cases folk melodies have been incorporated into operas or symphonies, but more often composers have been influenced by a rhythmic pattern or style of melody that they heard in folk music.

Folk music can stand quite well on its own merits. It has a simple charm and a basic expressiveness that are fascinating.

Seventeen

Music of the Ancients and the Not-So-Ancients

No one knows how or where music began, but it seems to be a part of life in every age and place. Pictures on the walls of pyramids and on Mesopotamian vases show people making music. In early Greek civilization poets like Homer sang their tales as they accompanied themselves on simple stringed instruments. In ancient Israel David soothed King Saul with harp music.

The intellectual Greeks considered music an important part of a citizen's education. Their dramas included a chorus that chanted and sang its lines. The Greeks developed several instruments, including the harplike lyre, which is seen on many music emblems today. Most impressive, however, were Pythagoras' discoveries about the physical laws of sound. Pythagoras (or some of his assistants) discovered that intervals are determined by mathematical ratios, and that there is a correlation between these ratios and the degree of consonance or dissonance suggested by any particular interval.

Our understanding of Greek music is as limited as our knowledge of almost all music until about the twelfth century: We cannot determine how the music sounded. No recogniz-

able system had been devised for writing music; or if one existed, it has been lost. Only a few scraps of music notation have been found, and attempts to reconstruct these fragments have been mostly guesswork.

The Romans had music, too. Probably most of it, along with much of Roman culture, was taken over from Hellenic (Greek) civilization. The Romans emphasized military music more than did the Greeks.

With the fall of the Roman empire, the Christian church deliberately attempted to root out of society everything that had been associated with pagan Rome. One object of this reform was Roman music, which had often enlivened festivals and orgies. Almost all remnants of Roman music have been lost or destroyed.

Early Christian music assumed much of the heritage of the Jewish temple. Daily prayer hours were adopted, along with the responsive singing of psalms between a soloist and congregation. As the church spread through Asia Minor into Europe and Africa, it accumulated other musical elements. The fact that the early church incorporated singing into its worship activities is recorded in Matthew 26:30

and Mark 14:26 and in non-Biblical writings. It's probable that during the first three centuries of the Christian church, there were no uniform musical customs.

From the fourth to the sixth centuries A.D., music in the church became more uniform and evolved along Western lines. Trained singers were given more responsibility for the music. Late in the sixth century Pope Gregory I, with the help of many assistants, began a recodification and compilation of chants. He assigned particular chants to certain services throughout the year. Gregory's work was so highly esteemed that even today this entire body of church music is called *Gregorian chant*. (It is also known as *plainsong* or *plainchant*.) When Gregory's work was done, the church had a *liturgy*—a body of rites prescribed for public worship.

Gregorian chant is different from most music heard in America. In chant only one line of music is heard, without the enriching sounds of harmony. And even the melodic line is different. For one thing, in place of beats and regular rhythmic patterns, there is a flexible rhythm. Furthermore, the familiar major-minor scale system is lacking. No attempt is made to appeal to the senses or to involve the listener's emotions. Only men's voices are used, and they sing in a restrained, nonemotional way.

Gregorian chant is very much interwoven with religious practice. It was created for one purpose only: to contribute to the spirit of worship. Heard as concert music, Gregorian chant seems rather dull. When sung by the religious in a seminary or monastery, however, it is strangely moving. Undoubtedly the impression is created partially by the setting and the obvious religious devotion of the participants, and by the knowledge that the music helps to put worshippers in the procession of the faithful stretching back nearly 2,000 years. But much of the effect is due to qualities of the music itself.

Traditionally, the Roman Catholic Church specified the order and content of every service, depending on the type of service and its place in the church year. Since Vatican Council II (1964–1967), much of the former practice has changed, and more freedom is permitted in the amount and type of music that can be incorporated into the service. The most significant change has been the acceptance of *vernacular* languages (non-Latin). Unfortunately, most chants lose much of their effectiveness when translated, so chant is being heard less widely now than in the past.

The liturgy of the Roman Catholic Church can be either spoken or sung. The services for which the liturgy is written fall into two categories. One is the *Offices*, or *Canonical Hours*. These services are celebrated at stated times in the day according to the Church calendar. The other service is the *Mass*, which celebrates the Eucharist or Holy Communion. Mass also consists of two categories: the *Ordinary*—those parts that are ordinarily present in every Mass; and the *Proper*—those parts that are proper to a particular day in the Church calendar.

The musical example on page 156 shows a Kyrie (*keer*-ee-ay), which is one of the parts of the Ordinary of the Mass. The words, which are Greek, are translated, "Lord have mercy upon us; Christ have mercy upon us." The first part of the example is the Kyrie in the traditional Roman notation with its four-line staff. Following it is the same music in modern notation.

Even in modern notation the music looks unusual. It has no meter signature. Almost all the notes have the same rhythmic value, but the last note of each phrase is consistently longer. The grouping of notes is irregular; sometimes there are two in a group, sometimes three or more. Except for the places at which the double vertical lines occur, the melody does not move very far from one note to another; its contour is smooth. The entire melody covers a range of only seven notes, and most of its phrases begin and end on the same note. The piece is quite short.

As you listen to a recording of the *Kyrie* or other examples of Gregorian chant, remind yourself that this is not concert-hall music. It's not going to command your attention through mighty sounds or dramatic changes. Rather, it seeks to convey a spirit, an attitude. The music strives for a purity and reverence worthy of acceptance by God. Although such an ideal may seem remote from the busy pace of present-day American life, seldom has an ideal come closer to fulfillment in an artistic medium.

Unlike other early music, Gregorian chant was carefully preserved in the monasteries by oral tradition and written manuscripts. This music has been painstakingly researched by musicologists both within the Church and outside it.

Secular Music

Although Gregorian chant dominated the musical world for many centuries, there also existed music of a *secular* (worldly or nonsacred) nature. Most nonreligious music was not preserved, so less is known about it. Secular music was in the language of a particular country—French, German, English, Italian, Spanish—rather than in the ecclesiastical or church Latin that was prescribed for worship.

At first, secular music was largely the contribution of wandering musicians who traveled from place to place singing songs, reciting poems, and even exhibiting trained animals. They were the entertainers of that time. Later, about the twelfth and thirteenth centuries, troubadours and trouvères dominated secular music in France. They were noblemen who were poets and composers but not performers; they hired minstrels to sing their songs. The music was for solo voice and was often sung with instrumental accompaniment. Most of the poems and songs were about an idealized type of love, not bawdy or physically passionate. Several thousand such poems and songs have been preserved. Unlike Gregorian chant, they display regular rhythmic patterns.

During this time a close relationship existed between secular vocal music and instrumental music. A song could be played or sung, or both. Many of the songs appeared in conjunction with dancing. The rhythm for the dances and for other secular pieces followed any of six *rhythmic modes*—patterns that are similar to those by which poetry meters are classified today. The short-long pattern corresponds to today's iambic meter, while the long-short pattern corresponds to the trochaic. *Rhythmic mode* is unrelated to the word *mode* as it is applied to scale patterns.

Until about 1000 A.D., music consisted largely of single melodic lines. Although examples of the simultaneous sounding of tones are found in early Western music, as well as in the music of other civilizations, these examples account for only a small part of the total body of music. In the eleventh century Western music began to change. It began to feature the sounding of musical tones at the same time. Medieval composers, many of whom were anonymous monks, accomplished the simultaneous sounding of pitches in the simplest possible way. They merely added another layer of sound to the existing lines of Gregorian chant, something like adding a second layer to a cake. At first the added line ran exactly parallel to the original line, but four or five notes below it. Since this did not allow much musical freedom, the added line was permitted to break out of its strictly parallel

pattern, and little by little it assumed a more independent character. When independent lines of melody were written to be performed at the same time, *polyphony* was accomplished.

Polyphony (pronounced po-*lif*-o-nee) is an important concept in music. It is the combining of lines of nearly equal melodic interest; no particular line is superior. Listening to polyphony might be compared to watching a three-ring circus. Each act is equally interesting. Although it is not easy to look at all the acts at once, there are no lapses of action.

An interesting aspect of this early polyphony was that notes of the same pitch, those an octave apart, and those four and five tones apart were considered to be consonant. These are the same intervals Pythagoras had regarded as most consonant. In other words, the interval of a third—the interval upon which our present system of chords is based—was regarded as a dissonance. It would be nearly 500 years before chords containing thirds would be considered consonant enough to appear as the important final chord of a piece.

The Gothic Period and the Motet

The late medieval period from about 1100 to 1450 has come to be known as the *Gothic* period. This was the era during which great cathedrals were built, universities were founded, and the Magna Carta was formulated. It was also the period of the Crusades and the Hundred Years War.

The music that developed during this time is termed Gothic, and it was characterized by a sophisticated, intellectual type of polyphony. One type had the chant melody sung or played in long notes, while the added part sounded several shorter notes within the same duration. Later the chant melody and extra part were designed to match the specified patterns of the rhythmic modes. Sometimes as many as four lines were combined in the music. When words were added, the piece became known as a *motet*, from the French *mot*, meaning word.

The motet was a curious musical animal. First of all, it combined various languages as well as sacred and secular texts. One line might be a French love song, another might be a Latin song praising the Virgin Mary, and still another might be a phrase of Gregorian chant. Second, the composers tended to concentrate on working out each line, and they were relatively unconcerned about how it sounded with the other lines. Some strong dissonances were the result. Third, composers became fascinated, especially in the fourteenth century, by mystical relationships and concealed meanings in the music. They took delight in concealing a chant phrase in the upper lines. Or they set up a complicated scheme of rhythmic and melodic patterns, so that a rhythmic pattern might appear three times for every two times the melodic pattern was repeated. Such intellectual complexities pleased the medieval musician, but they were generally lost on the listeners, since they could be comprehended only by looking at the music and not by hearing it. Such music was a form of intellectual puzzle rather than an art form to be heard.

As the 1450s approached, the Gothic motet rapidly disappeared, although traces of its compositional techniques can be found even today. Gregorian chant was continuing to influence other musical forms. The long stretch of human history called the Middle Ages was drawing to a close. This period had not been dark, as it is sometimes described. Developments had taken place in music and other fields. In fact, the years leading up to 1450 had laid the foundation for a new era—the Renaissance.

Sculptured figure of Christ on the cathedral at Chartres. Courtesy of Marburg—Art Reference Bureau.

The Renaissance Era

The word *renaissance* literally means rebirth. Historically it meant a revival of interest in the philosophy and arts of ancient Greece and Rome. Music, however, had no ancient Greek roots to return to, so the concept of rebirth in regard to music has little direct significance. The term *Renaissance* as applied to this field simply refers to the style of music that predominated from about 1450 until 1600.

The Renaissance reflected an intense interest in ancient Greek civilization. This interest led to a curious union of Greek and Christian belief. Michelangelo combined pagan and Christian elements by decorating the ceiling of

David *by Michelangelo.*

Closely allied with the renewal of interest in ancient Greek ideals was the "humanistic" view of mankind. This ideal, still very much alive today, affirmed that human dignity consists of moral and intellectual freedom. Rabelais expressed it in *Gargantua* with the words "fais çe que voudras" ("do what you will"), and Leone Battista Alberti phrased the spirit of the time by writing "men can do all things if they will." As a result of such thinking a new emphasis was placed on people and their lives on earth. People began to delight in the natural world and their place in it.

Leonardo da Vinci was one of the few persons who actually could do all things well. He was a painter, sculptor, mathematician, musician, inventor, writer, anatomist, and athlete. Many people, however, had interests and knowledge in a variety of areas of life.

The results of humanism are well illustrated by the two treatments of the human body shown here. One is a piece of Gothic sculpture found on the cathedral at Chartres, France. Notice that this figure has a spiritual, other-worldly quality. The attitude of the head is serene, and the position of the body is formal. The proportions of the figure are distorted through exaggerated length, thus giving the body an emaciated look. The feet seem to dangle from the robes as though they were merely attached. Michelangelo's *David*, on the other hand, looks like a magnificent Greek god. (The figure of David stands over thirteen and a half feet in height.) The impression is one of confidence in and admiration of man. David looks natural, almost casual, and free. The human body emerges from the withered state given it by medieval beliefs to the idealized status accorded it by Renaissance attitudes.

With the increasing interest in the value of human existence, there was a corresponding interest in the fine arts. A beautiful painting or piece of music began to have value for its own sake and not merely as a means to religious devotion. As a result of this fortunate change of outlook, the list of great Renaissance sculptors and painters is long—Botticelli, Leonardo, Michelangelo, Dürer, Raphael, Titian, Breughel, Tintoretto. Botticelli's "The

the Sistine Chapel with alternating figures of prophets and sibyls. Erasmus, the great philosopher, regarded Socrates as a pre-Christian saint and once wrote, "St. Socrates, pray for us."

Adoration of the Magi" (colorplate I) shows the Renaissance fondness for order and balance. A group of figures at the left of the painting is balanced by a group on the right. The infant Jesus is in the center. The converging lines of the Greek and Roman ruins add perspective to the painting and show the renewed interest in these ancient civilizations.

Not only were works of art being enjoyed in a new climate of acceptance. The increasing level of the economy, especially in the cities of northern Italy and the Netherlands, meant that money to hire artists and musicians was available. The Church sought rich adornment for its buildings—one of several practices that led to the reform movement started by Martin Luther in 1517. The effect of the Reformation on the world of music did not show its full impact until after 1600, but the seeds of change had been planted.

An event that reached into every area of human endeavor—education, religion, commerce—was Gutenberg's invention of printing from movable type. Printing made possible the wide dissemination of music, beginning with the appearance of the first printed music book in 1501.

The spirit of the times was one of optimism and discovery. The voyages of Columbus, Cabot, Balboa, and Magellan took place during the Renaissance. Science advanced, too, but not without opposition from the Church. In anatomy Andreas Vesalius made the main contributions, and in astronomy Copernicus set forth the heliocentric theory of the universe. Francis Bacon cheered on the new discoveries with the words, "We are not to imagine or suppose, but to discover, what nature does or may be made to do." Rabelais, Machiavelli, Boccaccio, Montaigne, Thomas More, and Erasmus were exploring new ideas in literature and philosophy.

and parts of France. Composers of the area had reached a level of proficiency that was the envy of Europe. They were lured away from their homeland to better-paying jobs in Spain, Bohemia, Austria, Germany, and especially the cities of northern Italy. The style and technique of the Netherlands became internationally known and imitated. So cosmopolitan did composers become that they thought of themselves as musicians first and as citizens of a particular country second. This outlook is well illustrated by Orlando di Lasso (the name he used in Italy), alias Roland de Lassus (the name he used in Germany), who wrote music in the German, French, and Italian idioms, as well as in the Netherlands style. Versatility was further evidenced by the scope of a musician's duties. A musician was employed not just to compose, but also to perform, to train a choir, and to teach.

The two main employers during the Renaissance were the Church and wealthy nobility. Logically, the music tends to divide itself into two types, secular and sacred. Sacred music was often based on chant, although themes from other compositions and secular tunes were woven in. The vocal lines often imitate each other, especially at the beginning of a new phrase of text. By having one voice enter after another, the composer can draw attention to each successive voice part, and the words can be more easily understood.

Secular music was less imitative. It was influenced by dance styles and forms and was intended to be entertaining.

During the Gothic period the chant phrase had been in the middle voice, with other parts added on either side; together they encompassed a rather narrow pitch range. About 1450 the voice parts were spread over a greater range with the addition of a bass part, and this change established the soprano, alto, tenor, and bass structure still used today. All parts were given equal importance.

Renaissance Music

The musical Renaissance started in the Netherlands, which then included Holland, Belgium,

The Renaissance Motet

As was said earlier, during the Gothic period a motet was a composition based on a line of

Gregorian chant to which were added other melodies containing other words, often in various languages. The motet of the Renaissance is quite different. It is a unified piece with all voices singing the same text. The Gothic motet was always based on Gregorian chant. The Renaissance motet, on the other hand, did not always borrow from chant, but it conveyed that spirit and was suitable for inclusion in worship.

Palestrina's "Sanctus" from the Mass *Aeterna Christi Munera* (a portion of it appears on page 162) shows many characteristics of his writing style. The title of the Mass comes not from its words but from the phrase of chant on which portions of this particular mass are based.

What are the significant features of "Sanctus" and other Renaissance motets?

1. The text is in ecclesiastical Latin. It is:

> *Sanctus, Sanctus, Sanctus,*
> *Dominus Deus Sabaoth.*
> *Pleni sunt coeli et terra*
>   *gloria tua.*
> *Hosanna in Excelsis.*

> Holy, Holy, Holy,
> Lord God of hosts.
> Heaven and earth are full
>   of thy glory.
> Hosanna in the highest.

2. The music is polyphonic. All of the lines are given equal attention, and each has distinct melodic character.

3. Each voice usually enters in imitation of another. Look closely at the notes for the words "Sanctus." First the soprano starts, followed by the alto two beats later, the tenor halfway through measure 3, and finally the bass in measure 7. All voices sing the first eight or nine notes in imitation. But as the music progresses, the voices tend to move on to melodies of their own. At each addition of a new phrase of the text, the process of imitation is repeated. It is through the use of such imitative entrances, sometimes called *staggered entrances* or *points of imitation*, that Palestrina makes the words of the text easier to hear.

4. It does not have a strong feeling of harmonic movement. The sound is pleasing and smooth, but the chords lack the harmonic "drive" found in later styles. This is due partly to the polyphonic nature of the music, with its emphasis on the horizontal line, and to the fact that systematic harmony had not yet been developed.

5. The music lacks a strong feeling of meter or beat. Again, this is similar to Gregorian chant, which has no meter. Although present-day notation for "Sanctus" includes measure bar lines, the original probably had none. The bar lines have been added by editors for the convenience of modern-day singers so that they can more easily keep their place. Most of the chord changes in Palestrina's music occur at moments of subtle stress, giving the music a gentle rhythmic regularity. Absent, however, is a feeling of definite rhythmic patterns.

6. The motet has no written accompaniment. Most motets are performed today *a cappella* (literally, for the chapel, meaning without accompaniment), although during the sixteenth century instruments often doubled the voice parts.

7. A small choir is most appropriate for performing the motet. During the Renaissance probably not more than two singers were assigned to each part. Boys, or men singing in falsetto voice, sang the high voice parts since women were not allowed to participate in the Mass.

8. The melodies are very singable. The range of notes in any one part generally does not exceed an octave. Furthermore, the singers do not have to move far from one pitch to the next, although the bass part usually contains more leaps than do the other lines.

9. The form of this motet is derived from the structure of the text. Each verse is treated to its own polyphonic setting. The form, then, is a succession of verses, each with music that is not repeated in other verses. The fact that the opening melodic line reappears in this motet is quite unusual.

10. The music has a restrained, unemotional quality. Bombast and emotionalism were considered insincere and not in keeping with

SANCTUS

the attitude of respect and awe that should prevail in the worship of God. Even though the text speaks of "Hosanna in the highest," the music does not suggest a triumphal procession or a fanfare. When Palestrina does emphasize particular words, he does it so subtly that the modern listener may not notice the emphasis.

11. The melodic lines are fitted together with unexcelled craftsmanship. It's hard to appreciate this unless you are familiar with Renaissance choral music, but this is why Palestrina stands out among composers of his time.

The Madrigal

The main type of secular music was the *madrigal*. It has sometimes been described as a secular version of the motet, but there are significant differences between the two forms. The madrigal was in vernacular language rather than Latin. Its text dealt with sentimental and sometimes erotic love. The texts of madrigals written early in the Renaissance generally had little literary merit, but later better texts were selected. Madrigals were sung at courtly social gatherings and at meetings of learned and artistic societies. Madrigals were very popular, and an enormous number were composed. In England, madrigal singing—with its requirement of music reading—was expected of an educated person.

A lute or harpsichord was often used to accompany the singing of a madrigal. The instrumentalist simplified the written parts, reducing the complicated polyphony to chords.

The madrigal was largely an Italian development, associated with composers such as da Rore and Marenzio. By the mid-1500s madrigals had spread to other countries, reaching England late in the century. When the first madrigals with English translation were printed in 1588, the response was a brief but brilliant period of original English secular music. The English madrigal is especially enjoyable for three reasons: (1) Its text is in English, so no translation is necessary; (2) its composers had a knack for making the lines of music tuneful and singable; and (3) the English had the delightful trait of not taking themselves too seriously. No matter how sad the song may be, the listener senses a tongue-in-cheek quality.

One well-known English madrigal is "April Is in My Mistress' Face" by Thomas Morley. About half of the music appears on pages 164 and 165. The text is a wistful comment on life. In this work *Mistress* does not mean paramour, as it does today; fiancée is closer to the original intent.

The madrigal is similar to the motet in several respects. There are imitative entrances at the beginning of word phrases, and the texture is basically polyphonic. The vocal lines are smooth and singable. The harmony is not firmly established in one particular key. The use of instruments was optional during the Renaissance, but today both madrigal and motet are sung without accompaniment. The form is a phrase-by-phrase setting of the text.

There are significant differences between the two forms, however. The madrigal's rhythm is more metrical, causing the moments of rhythmic stress to fall in a more regular pattern. The tempo is faster. There is a tendency to set the women's parts in contrast to the men's, which may or may not be an attempt to relate to the text. The language is English not Latin. And in overall spirit Morley's madrigal is vastly different from Palestrina's motet.

Other Renaissance Music

Vocal music was not the only type of music composed in the Renaissance, although it predominated. Keyboard instruments included the delicate virginal and the organ. There were string instruments called viols, which came in a variety of sizes.

The lute was the most popular instrument of the Renaissance. It had a pear-shaped body and varying numbers of strings. Its pegbox was slanted back sharply away from the rest of the instrument. The fingerboard had frets—upraised strips placed across the neck, as on a guitar. The lute was played by strumming, and rather intricate music could be executed on it.

Wind instruments included the sackbut,

which was a medieval trombone, and the krummhorn, which was similar to an oboe. The trumpet, recorder (a type of flute), and drums were found during that time, too. Composers did not specify what instruments were to play a part unless the piece was clearly for a keyboard instrument.

Renaissance music is not concert music in the usual sense of the term. Madrigals and virginal music were written to be performed at

April Is in My Mistress' Face

Thomas Morley (1557-1603)

social gatherings in large houses by trained amateurs—usually the educated elite of a society. Motets were written for worship services. Because Renaissance music is not particularly suitable for a concert hall, it's not heard frequently today. Recordings and college concerts are its chief promoters, and many high school choral groups perform a few Renaissance works during the school year.

Giovanni Palestrina

Giovanni Pierluigi da Palestrina was born in 1525 in the town of Palestrina near Rome. His music education began at Rome's Saint Mary Major, where he was a choir boy. From that time on, Rome was the center of his life. He studied music with two Frenchmen who lived in Rome, and for a short while he studied with a famous Netherlands composer named Jacob Arcadelt. Within five years after the bishop of Palestrina became Pope Julius III, he installed Palestrina as choirmaster at St. Peter's.

The Council of Trent was held intermittently between 1545 and 1563. The Church felt threatened by the impact of the Reformation, so the Council met to respond to the situation and to acknowledge the need for some reform within the Church. One phase of the Church's life that came under attack was the music for the Mass. Over the centuries it had acquired a complicated polyphony that made the words unintelligible, and the church fathers did not like the use of noisy instruments and the careless and irreverent attitude of many of the church singers. So Palestrina composed for a Church that wanted to return to the simplicity and purity of its earlier music. To his credit he achieved this ideal *without* discarding the highly developed style of his predecessors. His music is the embodiment of the worshipful ideal of Gregorian chant.

With the election of Paul IV there was a general tightening of rules, and Palestrina was dismissed because he was married. For five years he directed the music at St. John Lateran, and then he was called back to Saint Mary Major. As he grew older, his fame and fortune increased, and included responsibilities such as serving as advisor to a society of professional musicians. At his funeral in 1594 his coffin bore the words *Musicae Princeps*. He was truly the prince of Roman music during the Renaissance.

Thomas Morley

Little is known about Thomas Morley's early life, and there is some doubt about the year of his birth, which was either 1557 or 1558. For a while he was a student of William Byrd, the greatest English composer of his time. Morley held several appointments as a church musician, eventually leading to his appointment as organist at St. Paul's in London. It's likely that he knew Shakespeare and wrote music for some of his plays. In 1591 he undertook some espionage work among the English Catholics living in the Netherlands (these were the times of religious wars), and the assignment nearly cost him his life. Soon after this venture he was sworn in as gentleman of the Chapel Royal.

In addition to writing much church music and some instrumental works, he took advantage of the popularity among the English in the 1590s for Italian madrigals fitted with English texts. He published a number of madrigal collections, and in 1598 Queen Elizabeth's government gave him a monopoly to publish music books. Some of his madrigals are original, while others are plagiarized without acknowledgement, not uncommon in his time. His most famous publication was a textbook, *A Plaine and Easie Introduction to Practicall Musicke*, which was widely read for 200 years.

Morley was in ill health during the last years of his life, and the information available today indicates that he died about 1603.

Other Renaissance Composers

English Composers

William Byrd	(1543–1623)	probably the best English composer of the Renaissance; madrigals, church music, and keyboard music
William Cornyshe	(c. 1465–1523)	songs
John Dowland	(1562–1626)	madrigals
Robert Fayrfax	(1464–1521)	church music
Thomas Tallis	(c. 1505–1585)	church music
John Taverner	(c. 1495–1545)	church music
Thomas Weelkes	(c. 1575–1623)	madrigals
John Wilbye	(1574–1638)	madrigals

Netherlands Composers

Jacob Arcadelt	(c. 1505–c. 1567)	*chansons* (songs), madrigals; influential teacher in Rome
Jacobus Clemens	(c. 1510–c. 1556)	church music
Heinrich Issac	(c. 1450–1517)	church and secular music; international in use of texts
Jacob Obrecht	(c. 1452–1505)	church music; introduced new technical devices
Johannes Ockeghem	(c. 1430–1495)	church music; introduced new technical devices
Jan Sweelinck	(1562–1621)	*chansons* in old style
Adrian Willaert	(c. 1480–1562)	influential composer and teacher at St. Mark's in Venice

French Composers

Clément Jannequin	(c. 1475–1560)	*chansons*; fond of imitative sounds in music
Claude Le Jeune	(1528–1600)	madrigals, *chansons*
Claudin de Sermisy	(c. 1490–1562)	*chansons*

German Composers

Hans Leo Hassler	(1561–1612)	*lieder* (a *lied* is a German version of the *chanson*), church music
Orlando di Lasso (Roland de Lassus)	(1532–1594)	*lieder* (also wrote in French and Italian styles)

Italian Composers

Costanzo Festa	(c. 1490–1545)	early madrigals
Carlo Gesualdo	(c. 1560–1613)	madrigals with experimental harmonies
Luca Marenzio	(1553–1599)	madrigals
Philippe de Monte	(1521–1603)	madrigals
Claudio Monteverdi	(1567–1643)	madrigals written when a young man; important Baroque composer later
Giovanni Mario Nanino	(c. 1545–1607)	Palestrina's successor at Papal Chapel
Cipriano da Rore	(1516–1565)	probably the best composer of madrigals

Spanish Composers

Antonio de Cabezón	(1510–1566)	keyboard music
Francisco Guerrero	(1527–1599)	church music
Cristóbal de Morales	(c. 1500–1553)	church music
Tomás Luis de Victoria	(c. 1549–1611)	church music in style of Palestrina

Eighteen

The Baroque and Baroque Music

Even before 1600, the approximate beginning of the Baroque period (Ba-*roke*), a new style and spirit were emerging. The Renaissance was being replaced, not necessarily by better artistic works but by creations in a different style. The result was a vast enrichment of the art of music.

Sometimes in everyday usage *baroque* means extravagant, grotesque, and in bad taste. In discussions of the fine arts, however, *baroque* refers only to the style of artistic expression prevalent roughly from 1600 to 1750. And this expression was by no means grotesque or in bad taste.

The years from 1600 to 1750 saw such turbulence and change that it is impossible to characterize the period fully in a few lines. The following comments, however, may provide at least some indication of the times.

Characteristics of the Baroque Style

One of the most striking features of the Baroque was its fondness for the large and grandiose. An architectural example is seen in Lorenzo Bernini's monumental colonnades enclosing the vast piazza in front of St. Peter's Basilica in Rome. The huge columns reach out before St. Peter's like giant pincers seeking to draw everyone into the building. There are four rows of columns running parallel to one another. Measured across, the piazza exceeds the length of two football fields; the colonnades are made up of 284 different columns. Statues of 140 saints sit on top of the columns. Baroque painters, architects, and composers seemed at times to want to overwhelm the viewer or listener.

A second notable characteristic of the Baroque was its interest in the dramatic. In music three major dramatic forms were developed: opera, oratorio, and cantata. Drama can also be seen in the twisted lines and struggling subjects in art works. Rembrandt van Rijn's "The Descent from the Cross" (page 14), painted about 1650, features the play of light on the faces of the people to achieve a sense of drama. The light actually seems to be coming from the candle shielded by a man's hand, and it gives the scene an eerie pall. The cross is not in the center; it is to the side. Jesus' body is twisted, another popular Baroque effect. The emotions of tenderness and grief are evident in the faces.

A third significant trait of the Baroque was the intensity of religious feeling, which tended to take two forms: Protestant and Catholic. The Protestant churches established themselves generally in northern Europe and on the

View of the piazza in front of St. Peter's in Rome from the roof of the Basilica. In the picture can be seen the huge colonnades designed by Lorenzo Bernini. The statues of Christ and the Apostles in the foreground are 19 feet high.

British Isles. Protestant worship was devout, unvarnished, and very serious. John Milton's *Paradise Lost* and John Bunyan's *Pilgrim's Progress* were two monumental writings that expressed the Protestant spirit.

The other form of religious intensity was Catholic and was generally found in southern Europe. The Catholic Counter-Reformation developed in response to the Protestant Reformation, and a series of tragic religious wars between Protestants and Catholics ensued. A happier result, however, was the encouragement of some outstanding religious art.

Although it was marked by religious fervor, the Baroque era was also a time of sig-

nificant advance in science. Among the famous scientists of the period were Sir Isaac Newton, who developed the theory of gravity; Kepler and Galileo, who developed Copernicus' theories about the movement of planets; William Gilbert, who introduced the word *electricity* into the language; Robert Boyle, who helped make chemistry a pure science; Robert Hooke, who first described the cellular structure of plants; Sir William Harvey, who described the circulation of the blood; Gottfried Wilhelm von Leibniz, who with Newton developed infinitesimal calculus; and René Descartes, who founded analytical geometry.

The Baroque saw the rise ot a sizable middle class that was breaking away from the traditional society based on inherited land, title, and wealth. One result of this change was the inclusion of some everyday scenes in paintings, prose novels, and comic operas.

Governmentally the Baroque was a mixture of petty principalities and absolute monarchies that were continually quarreling with one another. The church still patronized the arts, but its role was less important than it had been in the Renaissance. The middle class, made up of merchants and financiers, ran the cities of northern Europe, while the Hapsburg and Bourbon dynasties ruled to the south.

In short, the Baroque era was a time of contrasts. Religious fervor existed side by side with scientific advances, drama, and grandeur. This quality of dualism, at times bordering on cultural schizophrenia, is also evident in Baroque music.

Features of Baroque Music

The Baroque period covers about 150 years. Some scholars have divided the period into three sections: early, middle, and mature. Music in the early years tended to be experimental, while the middle and mature periods represent the style usually associated with the term *Baroque*. The mature Baroque brought forth more sophisticated works, which culminated in the music of Bach and Handel.

Homophony

Homophony (pronounced ho-*mof*-o-nee) is the type of music that is most familiar to us today. Most pieces we know have melodies that we can whistle or sing. Usually they are accompanied, but we seldom pay much attention to the accompaniment. The main thing is the melody. It may seem illogical that homophony developed after polyphony (music with several equal voice parts). Apparently medieval musicians found it easier to combine melodies than to analyze and rearrange the simultaneous sounds that produce chords.

Homophony existed long before the Baroque, but composers had given it little attention in serious musical works, so it had not developed very far. By 1600 the polyphonic style of Palestrina had reached its fullest potential. Composers began to feel that something new and fresh was needed. The process of change is clearly evident in the books of madrigals by the outstanding innovative composer Claudio Monteverdi (1567–1643). Between 1587 and 1603 Monteverdi published four books of madrigals in Renaissance style. In 1605 he published a book of pieces that were homophonic. They were no longer madrigals but rather songs—solos, duets, trios—with accompaniment. By the eighth book (1638), Monteverdi's music called for chorus, soloists, and/or orchestra.

Actually, Baroque musicians did not throw away polyphony. They wrote and performed in both the homophonic and polyphonic styles. They called the homophonic the "new style" and the polyphonic the "old style," and they maintained a rather good balance between the two.

Major-Minor System

The Baroque saw the culmination of a process that had been developing slowly for a hundred years or more: the abandonment of all modes except the two that today are called major and minor. This change opened up two possibilities that composers had not explored: (1) A more solid tonal center could be established, and (2) the tonal center could be moved to different pitches during a musical work.

The establishment of a tonal center means that at almost any point in the music the composer can create a feeling of motion or of rest, depending on the harmonies chosen. The effectiveness of a harmonic progression depends in part on the convincing presence of the tonic or key center. Without an established key center there is nothing for the chords to go out from or return to. The "magnetic pull" of the tonic is necessary.

Baroque composers discovered that if it

was possible to establish a key, then it was also possible to move that key center—to modulate. It was simply a matter of transposing the chord patterns to a different key center at a later point in the music.

Tuning

The opportunity to modulate was helped when musicians finally overcame the 2,000-year-old problem of how to tune instruments. Acoustics is a complex topic, and it would take too much space to explain it here. Briefly, nature made a mistake. If some intervals are adjusted so that they are perfectly in tune, other intervals will be out of tune. If keys with one or two sharps are tuned perfectly, keys with many sharps or flats will sound terrible. The solution, which was finally adopted in the Baroque, was to tune all intervals slightly but equally out of tune, by a standard known as *equal temperament.* It was to promote such tuning that J. S. Bach wrote his *Well-Tempered Clavier,* which included a piece in each of the 12 major and 12 minor keys.

Figured Bass

The harmonies in Baroque music became so well standardized that musicians devised a system of shorthand called *figured bass* to notate chords. The composer was responsible for writing out in full the bass and soprano (bottom and top) parts, but he needed to provide only cues in the form of numbers and an occasional sharp, flat, or natural for the inner (alto and tenor) parts. The outer voices became the two important lines in Baroque music, with the melody being the most important. The bass part provided a foundation to the music. Because it sounded nearly all the time, it came to be known as *basso continuo* (continuous bass), for convenience usually shortened to *continuo.*

Metrical Rhythm

Although Renaissance music had a steady pulse, this pulse was not organized into patterns. Metrical rhythm with its bar lines and meter signatures was a product of the Baroque period, and Baroque musicians adhered to metrical rhythm slavishly, with the one exception of the performance of recitatives. The patterns came to rule the music to such an extent that later composers complained about "the tyranny of the bar line." Tempos were steady except for a slight slowing down at the end of a piece. The rhythm of Baroque music was so regular that Baroque orchestras, which were small by today's standards, could perform the music without a conductor. All they needed was a nod from the keyboard player to start.

Terraced Dynamics

The gradual increase or decrease of volume, which is so familiar today, was not common in music of the Baroque period. Renaissance composers had written no dynamic markings at all in the music, and Baroque composers wrote very few. Often composers rehearsed and performed their own music, so extensive markings were not necessary. The few dynamic markings that are present, however, call for abrupt changes of dynamic level. A *forte,* or loud level, is likely to change suddenly to a *piano,* or soft level. Logically, these changes are called *terraced dynamics.* One can only speculate on the reasons for the abrupt changes. Artists and musicians in the Baroque were interested in dramatic contrast, both visual and aural. Also, the keyboard instruments of the time could not make gradual changes, so variety in dynamic level had to be achieved abruptly or not at all.

Doctrine of Affections

The word *affections,* as used in the term *doctrine of affections,* has little to do with love. Instead, it is related to the mental state projected by the music, and often with the union of words and music. For example, if the text says "leap up," the composer might make the pitches "leap up" at that point. Another result of this doctrine was the repeating of words or fragments of the music to allow time for expression. Sometimes long runs were written for particular words or syllables. In instrumental music the doctrine of affections dictated that the composer establish a mood or "affection" at the outset of a piece, and then stay with that mood until the end of the movement. The doctrine of affections was of considerable importance during the Baroque, but it's of little concern to the listener today.

Instruments

Two keyboard instruments were important in the Baroque period: the organ and the harpsichord. Both were described in Chapter 7. The organ had existed in rudimentary form for 1,500 years, but it reached its highest development during the Baroque. In fact, many organs built in the twentieth century represent attempts to copy the organs of the eighteenth century. During the late nineteenth and early twentieth centuries several ranks of pipes were added to organs to imitate the sound of trombones and other instruments. These synthetic efforts were nearly always unsuccessful parodies.

The harpsichord was frequently played in the Renaissance, but it became more important in the Baroque period. At about the time the Baroque period ended, the harpsichord faded in prominence and was not heard much again until the twentieth century. In the last several decades there has been a revival of interest in the harpsichord, and new instruments are being manufactured. The harpsichord has even enjoyed some vogue in popular music in recent years.

Several orchestral instruments are featured in Baroque music. One is the flute, which during that time was usually constructed to be held straight out from the player's mouth, rather than to the side as it is today. The flute was made of wood and had a lighter, less penetrating tone quality. The trumpet was given important solo roles during the Baroque period. It had no valves, and therefore the pitches had to be controlled entirely by the player's lips. Many of the Baroque trumpets were small, which made it easier for the player to reach the very high notes heard in some Baroque compositions. The violin achieved a major role in Baroque music. It did not look quite the same as it does today. The fingerboard was shorter because players were not required to play very high notes. The bow stick curved slightly away from the hair, with a shape resembling an archer's bow, for which it was named. The hair tension was rather loose, and the strings of the instrument were set on a flatter plane, making it easier for the violinist to play on more than one string at a time.

The quality of performance on orchestral instruments was probably not impressive by today's standards. Most players held other jobs, usually not associated with music, and the technical development of their instruments was not advanced. The exceptions to this general situation were the trumpeters of the time, who were extremely competitive; it's probable that they performed impressively. The level of playing on the organ and probably the harpsichord was also quite good.

Performance of Baroque Music

There were no professional orchestras during the Baroque period. The orchestras that did exist were associated with the court, and often involved only part-time musicians. The orchestra was small—about 20 to 25 players. There was no conductor who stood before the group. Usually the leader was the harpsichord player, who began the music by giving the other musicians a nod.

There were no public concerts as we know them. Performances of music were held in churches or in the courts of the nobility.

The choirs were also small by today's standards. For instance, Bach's choir at Leipzig sometimes numbered fewer than 30 singers. At one time he was down to three altos, and he wrote a letter to the town fathers asking for funds to employ a fourth alto. (The request was refused.)

Improvisation was an important aspect of Baroque musical performance. The fact that the figured bass had to be partly filled in by each player has been mentioned. A church organist was expected to improvise intricate and complex music. The improvisational ability of some Baroque composers, including organists Bach and Handel, made them legends in their time. A singer or instrumentalist would frequently add little ornaments and embellishments to the line of music in an improvising manner. What we see notated in Baroque music is in some cases only a skeleton of what was actually performed.

Forms

The significant types of Baroque music have been presented earlier in this book. At this point it would be wise to summarize them and associate them with the characteristics of Baroque writing and performance practices.

Instrumental music.   The suite is one of the Baroque's primary contributions to instrumental music. It was discussed in some detail in Chapter 13 in conjunction with keyboard music.

Another prominent instrumental form of the Baroque is the fugue. It was also discussed in Chapter 13. It is a contrapuntal form that is especially well suited to keyboard instruments such as the harpsichord and organ, which have different manuals and stops for producing varied tone qualities for each entering voice in the fugue.

A third important instrumental form of the Baroque is the concerto grosso, discussed in Chapter 11. Corelli's *Christmas Concerto* is an example of this form, which illustrates the Baroque fondness for contrast—in this case, between small and large groups. Several solo sonatas were also written during the Baroque period.

Vocal music.   A most important contribution to the Baroque period was opera, which was discussed in Chapter 14. Despite their historical importance, Baroque operas are seldom performed today. Early in the Baroque period opera sank into mere virtuoso display by the

singers, to the detriment of the musical quality. The recitative style has remained, however, not only in opera but also in the oratorio and cantata. The aria is another feature of opera that has carried over into other musical forms.

Baroque oratorios and cantatas are still performed widely today. The oratorio was presented in Chapter 9. The cantata is strongly associated with the Baroque period and contains many of the features of Baroque music that have just been presented.

Bach's Cantata No. 140

In many ways a cantata is a "mini" oratorio. It is for soloists, chorus, and orchestra and contains recitatives, arias, and choruses. There are no costumes, scenery, or acting. There are some differences, however. The cantata is shorter, smaller in scope, and less of a drama. For example, Handel's *Messiah,* which was discussed in Chapter 9, has 53 parts and covers the entire mission of Jesus. Bach's Cantata No. 140, *"Wachet auf, ruft uns die Stimme"* ("Wake Up, Call the Voices") tells the parable of the five wise and five foolish maidens and contains only seven parts. Another difference is the presence in Baroque cantatas of a *chorale* (cohrahl) melody as a theme for several sections of the work. A chorale is a type of hymn closely associated with Martin Luther and the Reformation. Its melody is solid, stately, and uncomplicated. Luther's "A Mighty Fortress Is Our God" is a good example of a chorale. Chorales were designed for singing by the congregation during worship services, and so the "theme" for the cantata was familiar to the listeners in the Lutheran church service, for which this cantata was composed.

The first half of the chorale melody for this cantata is shown on the next page. (The type of note ♩, called a half note, receives one slow, steady beat in the preceding example.) Because it is not a short melody, attention will be focused only on the first three phrases. Notice that the first three notes outline a chord. Notice also the symmetrical quality; it begins low, then moves up, and then finishes on the same note on which it began.

The chorale melody appears in Sections I, IV, and VII of the seven sections in the cantata.

The first section is a chorus consisting of variations on the chorale. Its text is:

Wachet auf, ruft uns die Stimme
Der Wächter sehr hoch auf der Zinne,
Wach' auf, du Stadt Jerusalem!
Mitternacht heisst diese Stunde;
Sie rufen uns mit hellem Munde:
Wo seid ihr klugen Jungfrauen?
Wohl auf, der Bräutgam kommt,
Steht auf, die Lampen nehmt! Alleluja!
Macht euch bereit zu die Hochzeit,
Ihr müsset ihm ensprungen gehn.

Wake up, call to us the voices
Of watchmen high up on the tower,
Wake up, thou town Jerusalem!
It is now the hour of midnight;
They call to us with shining faces:
Where are you now, clever maidens?
Cheer up, the Bridegroom comes,*
Get up, and take your lamps! Alleluia!
Prepare yourselves, the wedding nears,
You must go forth to welcome Him.

This chorus (the music is shown on pages 176–177) is the longest and most complex portion of the cantata. There is a driving, uneven rhythmic figure (found in many Baroque overtures) contrasted with a countermelody played by the violins. The chorale melody itself appears in long notes in the soprano. As these notes are sung, the alto, tenor, and bass sing contrasting musical lines in contrapuntal style. The orchestra plays a significant part.

This chorus illustrates the Baroque doctrine of affections in several places. To begin with, the entire chorus maintains the same mood and feeling throughout. In addition, the notes leap up on the words "wach' auf" (wake up), "wohl auf" (cheer up), "steht auf" (get up).

The second part of the cantata is a recitative for tenor. It sets forth the image of Christ as the Heavenly Bridegroom and tells about His coming. The third section is a duet for soprano and bass. It is in dialogue form with an important part for violin solo.

The fourth section is also a contrapuntal section. It features only the tenor section of the chorus and the orchestra, each sounding different melodies. A simplified score of the section appears in the *Study Guide and Scores* book.

As is true of the first section of Cantata No. 140, the fourth section is typically Baroque in its use of metrical rhythm and the major-minor system of harmony. Both use a continuo of low strings and probably organ since the cantata is church music.

The fifth section is a recitative for the bass soloist. The sixth part is another duet, which is an aria for two singers. The oboe has important solos in this duet.

The seventh and concluding section (page 178) presents a harmonized version of the

---

*In many cantatas Jesus is referred to symbolically as the bridegroom and the church as His bride.

Cantata no. 140

Seventh Section

chorale melody. That is, Bach wrote a chordal part to enrich the melody. In the music shown here the melody is in the soprano or top notes. The chords are formed by the notes in the alto, tenor, and bass parts. It was customary for the congregation to join in the singing of this section. It is an example of Baroque homophony. The harmonization shows the emphasis on the outer (highest and lowest) parts. The alto and tenor parts largely fill in the chords.

Giovanni Gabrieli

Giovanni Gabrieli (c. 1557–1612) was the nephew and pupil of Andrea Gabrieli (1520–1586), an outstanding Renaissance composer. Giovanni's fame later eclipsed that of his uncle. The church music of Venice, where the Gabrielis spent most of their lives, was written for St. Mark's cathedral, which featured two choirs facing each other from opposite sides of the room. In addition to the choirs Giovanni Gabrieli placed instrumental groups in the galleries. The effect was a sixteenth-century version of stereophonic sound. In its rich sounds and powerful qualities, G. Gabrieli's music is more a forecast of the Baroque style than it is typical of the Renaissance style. He was one of the first composers to indicate dynamic levels in the music and to designate specific instruments for certain parts.

Claudio Monteverdi

Claudio Monteverdi lived from 1567 to 1643. His life seems to parallel the change from the Renaissance to Baroque styles in music. He was schooled in the Renaissance tradition and wrote well in the Palestrina idiom. His books of motets and madrigals, however, paved the way for the coming of the Baroque style and homophonic music.

Monteverdi held two important positions during his lifetime. One was in the court of the Duke of Mantua. Then in 1613 he was appointed choirmaster of St. Mark's in Venice, a post he held until his death 30 years later. Not only did he compose many religious works and madrigals, but he was also the most successful opera composer of his time. More than anyone else he promoted the ideals of opera and transformed it into a successful public medium. His contributions to opera include a reduction in the amount of recitative, which had predominated in early opera, and the addition of more beautiful melodic lines. He also infused his operas with more musical expression and encouraged instrumentalists to try effects such as tremolo (an agitated, back-and-forth movement of the bow on the string) to create more drama.

Heinrich Schütz

The life of Heinrich Schütz (1585–1672) spanned the transition from the Renaissance to the Baroque. His music seems to combine the cultures of Germany and Italy. His early life was spent in the service of a prince at Hesse-Cassel. Later he went to study in Venice with Giovanni Gabrieli. He adopted from him the idea of using two choirs in contrast to each other. Schütz had an interest in drama and became the first German composer to write an opera. His best works are in the area of church music. He composed several cantatas and Passions, a number of which are still performed today.

Jean-Baptiste Lully

Jean-Baptiste Lully lived from 1632 until 1687. He was a dominating and sometimes exasperating personality. Though he was Italian by birth, he made his way into the court of the French kings by wit and luck. There he changed his name from Italian to the French version by which he has been known throughout history. Lully was a supreme entertainer in what at the time was the most sumptuous court in Europe. He staged dance spectaculars that were the favorites of the king of France. His major musical contribution was the development of the French overture, an instrumental form in which the three sections are arranged in a slow-fast-slow pattern. The story of Lully's death is apparently true. To keep the performers together, he would beat time by pounding a stick on the floor. One day he happened to hit his toe with the stick, his foot became infected, and he died.

Henry Purcell

Henry Purcell lived from 1659 to 1695 and holds a special place in the hearts of Englishmen. He was the foremost composer of his time, and much of his music is still heard today. His brief career as a composer began in the court of Charles II and extended through the rather turbulent reign of James II into the period of William and Mary. Purcell was a successful composer in all forms, including opera, anthems, and instrumental music.

Antonio Vivaldi

Vivaldi (about 1675 to 1741) is much admired by musicians but is not so well known by the general public. He was an amazingly prolific composer who turned out an enormous amount of music of practically every type. He was born in Venice and was the son of a violinist. As a young man he was ordained a priest, but a few years later he decided on a musical career. The job he held for most of his life was as a teacher in a girls' music school.

He wrote many works for the girls to play or sing, including concertos for violin, flute, bassoon, guitar, mandolin, and piccolo. One of his most famous works is *The Four Seasons*, which is a series of four concerti grossi with a solo violin part; each one depicts a different season of the year. In it one can almost hear the people's teeth chattering in winter and feel the warm breezes of spring.

Georg Phillipp Telemann

Telemann was born in 1685 and lived until 1767. He was the most famous composer of the first half of the eighteenth century. Most of his life was spent around Hamburg. He left behind an enormous amount of music—40 operas, 44 Passions, 12 Lutheran services, and well over 3,000 works of other types. He was adept at composing instrumental music, including a number of well-known flute works.

Baroque Composers Presented Earlier

Nineteen

Classicism and Classical Music

By the time of Bach's death in 1750, the elements of Baroque style in art and music had largely fallen into disuse. In fact, Bach's own sons thought of their father as an out-of-date old man—not an unusual attitude of sons toward their fathers. The world *was* changing. The intensity of religious feeling and the domination of the churches were passing. Gone was the love of the dramatic and grandiose. A new age had arrived—one that would see significant changes in the style of art and music.

The Rococo Subperiod

As with all stylistic periods in music, the Classical period didn't have a clearly marked beginning. Evidence of the gradual departure from the heavy, complex Baroque style was the *Rococo* or *galant style,* which began early in the eighteenth century in the courts of Europe, especially France. It was the art of the nobility, of the lavish courts of Versailles and similar places. Like the aristocracy they served, Rococo music and art were light, elegant, and frivolous. In painting the Rococo was represented by Fragonard, Watteau, and Boucher. Their subject matter was often amoral love, and their pictures were laced with figures of cupids and thinly clad nymphs. Boucher's "Venus Consoling Love" (page 183) is typical. Rococo furniture and clothing were highly decorated; the lace cuff and the powdered wig were in vogue. Elegant manners were cultivated.

François Couperin (1668–1733) is probably most representative of Rococo composers. He wrote a large amount of music, mostly suites, for the clavecin, the French version of the harpsichord. The titles of some of his pieces include "The Prude," "Tender Nanette," and "The Seductress." Bach later used some of Couperin's music as models when he wrote his *French* and *English Suites.* Couperin's music is highly embellished, with many ornaments added to the happy, short melodies.

Another Rococo composer was Jean Phillippe Rameau (1683–1764). He is as much remembered for his writings on music theory as for the music he composed. Some of Bach's sons also contributed to the Rococo style. Carl Phillip Emanuel Bach (1714–1788) was the best known of them. Domenico Scarlatti (1685–1757), who was mentioned in Chapter 13, and Giovanni Battista Pergolesi (1710–1736) also write Rococo works.

Although music and art in the Rococo style were not profound, they served as a pleasant diversion for the aristocracy during much of the eighteenth century. More important, the Rococo represented a break away from the complex counterpoint of the Baroque, and it ushered in a new type of music.

The Classical Attitude

The words *classic* and *classical* have several meanings. They can describe something of high quality that has achieved a degree of permanence, such as a novel that has become "an American classic." They can indicate that something conforms in every way to the standard. The terms are often used to distinguish music of the nonpopular type from the popular. But designating music as "popular" and "classical" is an overworked and inaccurate way of classifying it.

What does the word mean to a student of the fine arts? In the arts and literature, *classical* refers to the works of the ancient Greeks and Romans. At a university the Department of Classical Studies explores the writings, languages, and other cultural contributions of ancient Athens and Rome.

A return to the style of ancient Greece and Rome presents the musician with an impossible task. No one knows how Greek and Roman music sounded because recordings were 2,000 years in the future, and no systems of early notation remain today. For these reasons, the word *classical* when used in music means an attempt to capture the ancient Greek *attitude* toward works of art.

In music the classical outlook was predominant from about 1750 to 1825. These years are called the Classical period. They are also known as the Age of Reason or the Age of Enlightenment. The thinkers of that time believed that truth can be realized only by the process of reason, so there was an emphasis on intellectual activity and learning. They also believed that the universe is a machine governed by inflexible laws that people cannot override. So whatever is true is true throughout the world; it is universal. In addition, people's emotions as a guide to truth were considered false, so rational intellect should control behavior. Classical thinkers were not impressed by

the unknown because they believed that in time they would come to know it through thought and study. They rejected the mysticism of the Middle Ages because they felt that it had stifled natural capacities. Reason, not faith, was to be mankind's new beacon.

Look at a nickel. Thomas Jefferson is on one side, and Monticello, his home, is on the other. Jefferson designed Monticello himself. Notice that it has pillars and a dome; Jefferson adapted his design from Greek and Roman architecture. In his intellectual curiosity and delight in reasoning, Jefferson personifies the Classical man. He was gifted in the arts, he appreciated order, and he sought truth through logic.

Another man of the Enlightenment was François Arouet (1694–1778), who called himself Voltaire. His brilliance, energy, passion for justice, wit, and hatred of superstition and intolerance made him a feared and respected thinker. Yet Voltaire personified the inconsistencies of the age. His writings shook the established government and religion, and his diatribes led to a year in prison; but several of his most searing writings were published anonymously, and when their authorship was attributed to him he violently denied them. He reflected the spirit of his age by demonstrating a general optimism about mankind; but this view did not keep him from believing in rule by the elite. Again and again he campaigned against the Church, proclaiming *"Ecrasez l'infame"* ("Crush the infamous thing"); but he also believed in God and wanted "a wise and simple cult with one God." One of his books is even dedicated to Pope Benedict XIV. Voltaire lived comfortably and was a shrewd businessman. "This profane time," he wrote, "is just right for my ways. I love luxury, even a soft life, all the pleaures, the arts and their variety, cleanliness, taste, and ornaments."

Patronage

Although it was beginning to wane, patronage was still a part of the Classical era. Briefly, the patronage system was one in which a composer accepted exclusive employment under

Venus Consoling Love *by Boucher. Courtesy of the National Gallery of Art, Washington, D.C. (Chester Dale Collection)*

the auspices of a patron. Patrons were from either the aristocracy or the Church. The more frivolous taste of the aristocracy gave impetus to the movement away from the heaviness of Baroque style toward the more fanciful style of the Classical period.

When a composer found a good patron, he was assured a comfortable life and a cultured audience for his compositions. The writing of new works was expected. At its best, patronage was a good incubator for creative talent.

There were liabilities, however. Most serious among these was the fact that the composer had to please the patron, or else perhaps end up helping in the stables or looking for a new patron. The result was much trivial music written according to standard formulas. Too, the patronage system regarded the composer not as a unique creative artist but as the source of a product for the privileged classes to exploit and enjoy. Since the relationship between a composer and his work was taken lightly, it was common practice for composers to borrow themes and ideas from one another. In fact, plagiarism was understood to be a form of flattery and commendation. Legal niceties such as copyrights and royalties were unheard of. Not until the arrival of the Romantic philosophy of the nineteenth century did composers feel compelled to create in a way that was uniquely individual.

Music of the Classical Period

It is hard to realize that Mozart and Haydn were only two generations later than Handel and Bach. Their music is so different. What were the changes that occurred from Bach's generation to Mozart's?

One Baroque feature that was abandoned was the continuo and its figured bass. Classical composers wrote out every note, with the exception of cadenzas. Also dropped was the idea that a single mood or feeling should prevail throughout a movement. Classical composers wanted to achieve a difference between themes.

Homophony

The Classical period saw the balance shift more heavily in favor of homophonic music. Some counterpoint is still heard in Classical music, of course, but it's more as contrast with the prevailing homophonic texture than as an equally prominent style. Symphonies, rondos, and sonatas have themes—predominant melodies that are best shown off when treated singly rather than in combination with other melodies as in polyphony.

Instrumental Music

The balance shifted somewhat more to instrumental music during the Classical era, but vocal music was still important. Mozart, for example, earned most of his income from composition of his operas not his symphonies.

Absolute Music

The main output of the Classical period consisted of abstract or *absolute music*—music with no nonmusical associations. Much of the instrumental music of the time is known only by number or by key: Symphony No. 40 in G Minor. In some cases, publishers added a title because titles are easier to remember. It may or may not have much to do with the content of the music. Haydn's *Sunrise* Quartet was so named because the first edition carried a design that looked like the sun on the front of the music. Absolute music must stand or fall on its ability to be interesting in and of itself.

Dynamic Changes

To make their music more interesting, composers in the Classical period developed the crescendo and decrescendo. Musical performance during the Baroque probably included some gradual changes in dynamic level, in addition to the abrupt changes of terraced dynamics. Performers probably added some dynamic changes that were not written out in the music. But during the Classical period the gradual change of dynamic level was notated and carefully rehearsed.

Key Arrangements

Classical composers were also conscious of keys. Most of the forms mentioned earlier—sonata form, minuet and trio, and others—call for a pattern of keys as well as a pattern of themes. The composer's careful attention to key may have had an effect on the eighteenth-century listener; it is hard to say how people heard things almost 200 years ago. Today we are accustomed to music that modulates frequently or has no key at all, so the impact of key change in Classical music is reduced for us.

Melodic Style

Many Baroque melodies are broad and overarching, but Classical melodies often seem to be made up of short fragments that have been strung together. The Classical type of melody helped produce clear formal designs. The melody composed of short musical ideas is especially suitable for development—an important feature of sonata form.

Musical Performance

Symphony orchestra. The most important development of the time was the orchestra. Prior to the Classical period there was no clear-cut distinction in music for large and small groups. The music was much the same, and the composer often did not specify what instruments should play the work. But Classical composers realized that music can be composed to exploit the advantages of either a small or a large group. Containing 30 to 40 players, the Classical orchestra was small by today's standard. Its backbone was strings, and the rest of the orchestra consisted of one or two flutes, two oboes, two bassoons, two French horns, two trumpets, and timpani. Clarinets were added

before the Classical period ended. This orchestra was not intended for the concert hall. Rather, it played in large rooms, such as in the Schönbrun Palace in Vienna, before private audiences. And the few concerts that were held took place in theaters not in large halls. There were no permanent orchestras such as the London Philharmonic; those would be organized in the next century.

Chamber groups. Just as the symphony orchestra became somewhat standardized, so did several chamber music combinations. The most important types of chamber groups were the string quartet and the sonata combination of piano and another instrument.

New Large Forms

Sonata. The sonata became somewhat standardized in the Classical period. Usually it is a work in three or four movements for piano plus another instrument or just for piano alone. The first movement (often the longest) is moderately fast and employs sonata form. The second is melodious and generally utilizes a theme-and-variation form or an *A B A* scheme. The final movement is a lively rondo, or sometimes a theme-and-variation or sonata form. If four movements are used, the third is a dancelike movement. Two sonatas have been discussed in this book: Beethoven's *Pathétique* Sonata, which is for solo piano, and Franck's Violin Sonata.

Trios, quartets, quintets. Many of the chamber music works of the Classical period adhere to the same forms and follow the same pattern of movements as the sonata. Mozart's Clarinet Quintet discussed in Chapter 12 is a good example of this type of ensemble.

Solo concerto. In a sense the solo concerto, which in the Classical period displaced the concerto grosso, is a sonata for solo instrument and orchestra. There are some differences, however. The concerto has two expositions in sonata form, one for the orchestra and another featuring the solo instrument. Then there is the element of virtuosity in the soloist's part. The solo music is more difficult and showy than that given the orchestra. The contrast of the concerto grosso is still there, but it now includes a contrast in the technical proficiency demanded as well as a contrast in the size of sound. In all these characteristics Haydn's Trumpet Concerto is typical.

Symphony. The symphony was a most significant contribution of the Classical period. This sonata for full orchestra contains four movements; a minuet or scherzo is generally inserted after the second movement. As are most instrumental pieces of the period, symphonies are known by number, and the key is traditionally given along with the title. Chapter 10 presented two examples of Classical symphonies: Mozart's Symphony No. 40 and Beethoven's monumental Symphony No. 5. The "synthesis" example in this book for the Classical period is Haydn's Symphony No. 101 in D Major. It will be presented shortly.

New Musical Forms

The Classical period probably surpassed all others in its promotion of new formal schemes, a not surprising fact in view of the interest in rational thought that characterized the time. It would be inaccurate to say that there were no forms prior to the Classical period, because there certainly were. But the Classical period introduced a number of new designs and clarified and standardized other forms.

The most important forms are:

Sonata form. The sonata plan presents two contrasting themes in different keys, provides for the developing of those themes, and then presents the themes again. Sonata form is found in the first movement of almost all instrumental works containing more than one movement. It appears in other movements as well. Mozart's Fortieth Symphony has three movements in sonata form.

Rondo. The basic idea of rondo is a theme that recurs, with contrasting material sandwiched between appearances. The idea dates back to medieval times. Composers of the Classical period refined it and placed it as the closing form in multimovement works. The last movement of Haydn's Trumpet Concerto is a good example of a rondo, as is the last movement of Beethoven's *Pathétique* Sonata.

Theme and variation. Writing a set of variations on a theme was not a new idea, but Classical composers gave it more attention than it had received earlier. The theme-and-variation format is sometimes found as a second movement, and often it's the basis for an entire piece. The fourth movement of Mozart's Clarinet Quintet is a typical adaptation of this principle in a chamber work. The second movement of Beethoven's Symphony No. 5 is a more complex example.

Minuet and trio. The minuet was not a new musical form during the Classical period, but Haydn and Mozart made it more sophisticated and more appropriate for inclusion in a symphony. The movement as a large three-part form is found in Mozart's Symphony No. 40 and Haydn's Symphony No. 101 (which has a second trio, giving it five parts).

Scherzo. The scherzo is a contribution of Beethoven. He retained the pattern of the minuet but accelerated the tempo, added accents, and in other ways made it more rollicking. His Fifth Symphony contains a scherzo as its third movement.

Classical Vocal Music

The chief vehicle for vocal music activity in the Classical period was opera. Indeed, opera was the most important musical entertainment of the time. Classical operas contain clearly delineated choruses, arias, and recitatives. The singer's part is most important, but the orchestra has some interesting music of its own.

Mozart's *Don Giovanni*, which was discussed in Chapter 14, is typical in its Classical outlook and style.

Because the center of music making had moved from Protestant north Germany to Catholic Bavaria and Austria, Classical composers wrote primarily for Catholic services. Mozart, Haydn, and Beethoven produced church music such as Masses, vespers, and Requiems in the best conservative tradition of the Classical period. Their sacred music represents a rational approach to the faith of the time.

Haydn's Symphony No. 101 ("The Clock")

Haydn's Symphony No. 101 (nicknamed "The Clock") is a good example of music of the Classical era. It certainly represents the Classical outlook in its well-thought-out, tasteful writing. It seems to contain the "variety, cleanliness, taste, and ornaments" that Voltaire said he liked. It is also "happy" music; its sounds seem to bubble along.

The Symphony is homophonic music, with only hints of counterpoint, except in the fourth movement, where there is a brief fugal section. It contains gradual dynamic changes and the expected key arrangements. The melodies are made up of short phrases, which is characteristic of the style. And several of the forms developed in the Classical period are used.

First movement. The first movement is in sonata form; it is preceded by an introduction. Many Classical symphonies include an introduction to the first movement, which usually is not related to the remainder of the symphony except by key. The introduction to the "Clock" Symphony is in D minor, while the Symphony is basically in D major.

The first theme is:

The second theme is:

The development section uses mostly the second theme and a fragment from the first theme. The coda is somewhat longer than usual, a pattern that Beethoven would follow more extensively a few years later.

Second movement. The name *Clock* probably was the result of the tick-tock pattern heard at the beginning of the movement. It is basically a large three-part form. The movement is presented in a Listening Guide on pages 188–189. Of all the movements in the Symphony, the second seems to present best the ideal of clear, logical beauty that is a mark of the music and art of that time.

_____ *Listening Guide* _____

Haydn: Symphony No. 101 in D Major, "Clock"

Second Movement

Three-Part Form

A Section

0:03   Principal theme, first part *(a)*, consisting of a four-measure and a five-measure phrase, is played by the first violins; accompaniment is a steady "tick-tock" pattern played by low strings and bassoon:

0:33   Principal theme, first part, repeated exactly.

1:00   Second part of principal theme begins *(b)*; "tick-tock" accompaniment continues, with beats alternating between loud and soft; violins play figure from first part of theme:

1:16   New melodic idea played by violins; long tone held by oboe:

1:39   Principal theme, first part *(a')*, returns, with second phrase somewhat changed; soft dynamic level.

B Section

2:09   Music becomes suddenly loud, with full orchestra playing the figure from the principal theme:

New major key arrived at abruptly.

2:26   Short melodic figure introduced by violins; figure played several more times by upper strings:

2:55   Another melodic figure introduced by violins; is played another five times over an accompaniment that includes the running notes from the earlier melodic figure and from the principal theme:

A Section

3:32   "Tick-tock" accompaniment begins in flute and bassoon; soft.

3:35   Principal theme, first part, played softly by violins.

4:03   Principal theme, second part, played by flute.

4:46   Principal theme, first part, played by violins.

5:16   (Pause)

5:20   Principal theme, first part, in a new key, starts up played by violins, but continues only a couple of measures.

5:33   "Bridge" passage using fragments from the principal theme played in violins, with some counter material played by the flute.

6:03   Principal theme, first part, begins again, but continues in varied form with running passages of six notes per beat.

6:32   Principal theme, second part, played by flute, violas, and bassoons; violins continue variation material with six notes per beat.

7:10   Coda begins; suddenly music becomes loud, with full orchestra playing; variation of principal theme continues in violins and flute.

7:37   Music quiets down; six-note-per-beat pattern heard in cello, then violas, violins, flute, and cellos again.

7:56   Closes with three soft chords.

Third and fourth movements. The third movement is a minuet and trio with an unusual feature—an extra trio.

The fourth movement is a rondo that is filled with rapidly moving notes. Its main theme is:

It exudes energy, clarity, and good cheer. It is these qualities that perhaps best summarize the Classical period.

Classical Composers Presented Earlier

Franz Joseph Haydn, pages 92–93   Wolfgang Amadeus Mozart, page 79

Twenty

The Romantic Outlook and Romantic Music

To most people, the word *romantic* pertains to the emotion of love. To the scholar, however, romanticism means much more. The word *romantic* comes from *romance,* which originally referred to a medieval poem written in one of the Romance languages and dealing with a heroic person or event. Later the word took on the connotation of something far away and strange or something imaginative and full of wonder. Yes, it also included the idea of romantic love.

Characteristics of Romanticism

Romanticists were fascinated by the unknown and stood in awe of the world. They were impressed by the mystery, not the clarity, of the world and its inhabitants. At times they were almost mystic. Such a quality is revealed in this passage from Wordsworth's *Lines Composed a Few Miles above Tintern Abbey:*

> . . . that blessed mood,
> In which the burthen of the mystery,
> In which the heavy and the weary weight
> Of all this unintelligible world

> Is lightened:—that serene and blessed mood,
> In which the affections gently lead us on,—
> Until, the breath of this corporeal frame
> And even the motion of our human blood
> Almost suspended, we are laid asleep
> In body, and become a living soul:
> While with an eye made quiet by the power
> Of harmony, and the deep power of joy,
> We see into the life of things.

Romanticists tended to rely on emotion rather than on the intellect that had been central to the Classical outlook. Feelings replaced reason. Truth became what one *felt* to be true, and it was wrong to deny one's feelings. Keats said in one of his letters: "I am certain of nothing but the holiness of the heart's affections, and the truth of the imagination. What the imagination seizes as beauty must be truth." Inevitably, Romanticism became distrustful of reason and science (sometimes called philosophy). To quote Keats again, this time from *Lamia:*

> Do not all charms fly
> At the mere touch of cold philosophy?

The Romanticists were intrigued by the long ago and far away. During the Classical period intellectuals had thought of medieval times as the "dark ages"; the Romanticists thought of them as heroic. Literature contains many examples of this attitude, as in Tennyson's *Idylls of the King,* Keats' *Eve of St. Agnes,* Coleridge's *Christabel,* and Scott's *Ivanhoe.* Eugene Delacroix chose Dante's *Inferno,* a writing from early in the fourteenth century, as the subject matter for his painting "The Bark of Dante" (colorplate II). It shows the struggling souls of the wicked Florentines trying to escape from Hell by climbing into the boat with Virgil and Dante. Also evident in the painting is the Romantic artist's fondness for the far away and exotic. In music this trait can be found in works such as Rimsky-Korsakov's tone poem *Scheherazade* and Act II of the opera *Parsifal* by Wagner.

Not only were the Romanticists impressed by the unknown forces of the world; they reveled in the struggle against them. Coleridge's ancient mariner was "alone on a wide, wide sea." Delacroix's Florentines struggle helplessly against their fate. In this Romantic painting, the water and clouds swirl in a terrifying way. The twisted, pained bodies are very much involved in the scene. Gone are the even planes and the formal balance that typified Classicism. Dante (in the cloak and hat) stands about two-thirds of the way to the left of the picture. The bodies of the sinners writhe throughout the scene.

The Romanticists resented rules and restraints. They regarded the Classical period as cold and formal, and they were unimpressed by its rational deductions and universal laws. They felt perfectly capable of making their own rules, and they proceeded to do so in their artistic works. They cherished freedom, limitless expression, passion, and the pursuit of the unattainable. After all, what more glorious struggle could there be than the yearning and seeking after the impossible? This search is perhaps best epitomized in the legend of the Holy Grail, which was a favored theme in Romantic literature and operas (particularly Wagner's *Parsifal*).

The Romanticists had a rural orientation instead of the urban outlook of the Classical period. They were attracted by nature because it represented a world untainted by people. Sometimes nature was extolled to the point of pantheism—the belief that God and nature are one. The rural interest of the time led to landscape painting and poems on natural phenomena. Beginning with Jean Jacques Rousseau and the Earl of Shaftesbury, and continuing through the American Henry David Thoreau to the present time, a group of philosophers have expounded the idea of natural goodness, in which the "artificialities" of civilization are rejected because they corrupt human beings. Wordsworth summed up the Romanticists' thinking on nature when he wrote, in *The Tables Turned:*

> *One impulse from a vernal* wood*
> *May teach you more of man,*
> *Of moral evil and of good,*
> *Than all the sages** can.*

Because the Romanticists were highly subjective and individualistic, it was almost inevitable that they would become self-centered. Works of art were no longer objective examples of a person's craftsmanship; they were considered instead to be a projection of the person who created them. Romantic artists felt that a bit of their psyche had been given to the world in their poems or preludes. And this personal work was no longer done for a patron. It was now for posterity, for an audience that someday, somewhere would appreciate its true stature. Some Romanticists were nonsocial, if not antisocial. They withdrew into a world of their own, surrounded by a close circle of friends and admirers. And yet the Romantic era saw the establishment of the concert hall with its large audiences, and some Romanticists thoroughly enjoyed the adulation of the public. In any case, the attitude toward musical creativity changed, and with it came the altered position of the musician and composer in society.

---

*spring

**wise men

Romantic Music

A number of significant changes occurred in music during the nineteenth century. Some of them had a permanent impact on music, while others had a less lasting influence.

Aspects of Performance

Public concerts. One important change was the end of the patronage system and the increasing popularity of the public concert. No longer was music designed to be played in a room for a small audience of rich, well-born people. Now the music had to be louder, so that the sound would project in a large hall. And it catered to the new merchant class that had become significant in society. These changes encouraged a different way of thinking about music.

Virtuoso performers. The demands of the concert hall led to the development of the "personality" performer. People went to hear a certain person play the piano or violin, rather than just to hear some music. Often it was the personality of the performer that sold the tickets. He or she was expected to dazzle the audience with skill, and even the performer's appearance contributed to the desired aura. One famous concert artist of the time enhanced his image by carefully removing his white gloves as he sat down at the piano. These gloves were left on the piano at the conclusion of the program to give the ladies in the audience something to fight over.

The nineteenth century also saw the rise of the conductor and the permanent orchestra. Prior to the Romantic era, a group of musicians had usually been started by the first violinist or by the player seated at the keyboard. In some cases a conductor tapped out a few measures, and the orchestra continued the music by itself. Now the conductor had a more important role to fill. As music became longer and more complex, conducting technique made a greater difference in the quality of the orchestral sound. The conductor's role is to keep the performance together by starting the group precisely, maintaining the tempo, indicating levels of loudness and softness, and giving cues—visual indications that an important passage is to begin at that moment. The conductor also gives the musicians an idea about the interpretation of the music and its style.

Piano. As Chapter 13 pointed out, the nineteenth century was the "Golden Age" of the piano. Both the playing techniques for the instrument and the amount of music written for it expanded greatly. Showy virtuoso works, character pieces, and mighty concertos were composed for the piano by almost all of the great composers of the time—Beethoven, Brahms, Chopin, Schumann, Liszt, Mendelssohn, Schubert, and others.

Musical Forms

The character piece. During the Romantic period composers were especially interested in short works containing one predominant mood. These instrumental "character pieces" carry a variety of names: ballade, impromptu, fantasie, étude, prelude, berceuse, scherzo, and nocturne. The *ballade* and *berceuse* are songlike. An *étude* is a piece that illustrates a particular technical problem. Its name is French for study. In the hands of a composer such as Chopin, an étude is far from being a dull exercise, however. It is an attractive melodic study suitable for concert performance. An *impromptu* is supposed to convey the spontaneity its name implies. A *fantasie* is a completely free and imaginative work. Chopin's *Fantasie-Impromptu*, discussed in Chapter 13, contains both of these characteristics. The *scherzos* by Chopin are not the playful works that Beethoven's are. Instead they are longer and more serious. A *nocturne* (meaning night song) usually has a flowing melodic line; Chopin wrote quite a few works under the designation. Other short compositions were derived from dance forms—mazurka, polonaise, and waltz.

Program music. Because of its brevity the short character piece presented no problems of form. But when they wrote longer pieces, Romantic composers were forced to find something to replace the disliked formal schemes of the Classical period. One answer was program music, instrumental music in which the composer specifically intends the sounds to be associated with nonmusical ideas or objects.

The idea of relating nonmusical subjects to music was not new with composers of the nineteenth century. It had been done before, but the Romantic era saw an unprecedented interest in this type of composition. Program music was for Liszt and Berlioz what sonata form had been for Mozart and Haydn. It provided ideas and guidelines for sizable musical compositions. The next chapter is devoted to a more complete discussion of this type of music, which is so closely associated with the Romantic period.

Nationalism. Nationalism, when associated with works of art, refers to a deliberate, conscious attempt to develop a mode of artistic expression that is characteristic of a particular country, region, or ethnic group. Often it involves subject matter that is unique to one country or people, such as a painting of a national event or an opera about a historical character. During the nineteenth century this attempt at native expression reflected a desire to break away from the prevailing German-Austrian style. Bach, Mozart, Beethoven, Schubert, Liszt, Schumann, Brahms, and Wagner had long ruled the musical world. To composers from other areas, it was time for a change. They knew that Russians, French, and Norwegians were as capable of producing good compositions as were Germans, and they set about proving it. Specific examples of nationalistic music are presented in Chapter 22.

Virtuoso music. The rise of virtuoso performers encouraged the writing of technically demanding music for them to perform. Some stunning works were composed for pianists and violinists during the nineteenth century. Many notes were to be played at a dazzling speed over the full range of the instrument.

Liszt's *Mephisto Waltz* is an example of virtuoso music.

Art song. The Romantic era witnessed the development of the art song to its highest level. An art song is the musical setting of a poem, with the music specifically designed to enhance and give expression to the words. In Schubert's "The Erl King," which was presented in Chapter 8, the quality of the lines is fitted to the emotions and words of each of the characters in the text. The piano part contributes much to the artistic impact of the art song.

Romantic opera and choral music. Because of the many outstanding instrumental works by Romantic composers, it is easy to overlook their success in vocal music. The art song has already been mentioned. The power and sumptuousness of Romantic music are also evident in Romantic operas. Everything from the tenderness and passion of Bizet's *Carmen* to the nearly overwhelming sounds and dimensions of Wagner's music dramas is found. The characteristics of the nineteenth century cited at the beginning of this chapter are apparent in operas of that time: a fondness for the exotic and far away (the gypsy life and loves in *Carmen*); an interest in the long ago (Wagner's primeval German gods); an obsession with mystery (the cards foretelling death in *Carmen* and the curse on Wagner's Rhine gold); and a preoccupation with the struggle against fate (in both *Carmen* and Wagner's *Ring*).

In addition to art songs and operas, some great choral works were written in the Romantic era. Beethoven wrote several religious choral works, and Felix Mendelssohn (1809–1847) composed successful oratorios. Hector Berlioz (1803–1869) wrote a tremendous *Requiem* calling for many tubas, timpani, and a huge chorus. Liszt created some fine choral works, although they are not often heard today. Brahms' *Ein Deutsches Requiem (A German Requiem)* is one of the great masterpieces of Western music, and he also composed several other highly successful choral works. Verdi also wrote a *Requiem*, as did Gabriel Fauré (1845–1924).

Musical Characteristics

Homophony. Because nineteenth-century composers were interested in the expressiveness of music, they avoided intricate counterpoint. They generally wrote a flowing melodic line accompanied by rich harmonies. There are instances of counterpoint here and there in Romantic music, and Brahms was skilled in its use, but homophony predominated.

Rich harmonies. Romantic music has a luscious, sensuous quality found in no other style. When compared with earlier styles, its harmonies contain chords with more notes, its pitches are altered to give richer quality, and a greater percentage of its chords seem to move outside the "gravitational pull" of the traditional tonic and dominant. Romantic composers broke away from the strict adherence to key that had been established in the Classical era. Their harmonies are often highly chromatic, and as a result the feeling of key center is considerably weakened, as is evident in Wagner's music. But their harmonies are very rich and beautiful. The first movement of Franck's Violin Sonata is a good example of Romantic harmony.

Use of instruments. New instruments were added to the orchestra during the nineteenth century: English horn, bass clarinet, bass trombone, and harp. The size of most sections was increased, and instruments such as the viola were given more prominent parts. The result was a more powerful and colorful sound. Instrumental techniques were more advanced than in the preceding century. Brahms' Second Piano Concerto is a good example of the way Romantic composers drew the maximum of musical passion and brilliance from an instrument.

The increase in the variety of instruments in the orchestra and the desire for a larger, warmer sound caused an increase in the size of the orchestra. The orchestra of 30 or 40 players in Mozart's day grew to 90 to 100 players in the Romantic period.

Length of works. If the nineteenth century had a failing, it was a tendency to be longwinded. The length of concertos, symphonies, and other pieces of music tripled in some cases during the hundred years from Mozart to the end of the nineteenth century. Romantic operas are especially long. The high point (or low point, depending on how you look at it) is Wagner's *Ring* cycle of four operas, totaling over 12 hours of music.

Romantic composers were able to develop some magnificent and monumental pieces of music. One of their means for tying together long movements was the use of cyclical writing—the appearance of a theme in more than one movement. Also, Romantic composers wove their compositions in an almost seamless way. Gone are the clear-cut transitions and theme endings that marked the Classical period. Their music seems to roll on in a continuous stream.

Rubato. Rubato (roo-*bah*-toh) is not something that can be seen in the printed score. It exists in the style of performance. The player deviates slightly from the exact execution of the rhythm; a fraction of time is "borrowed" from one note in order to lengthen another. In fact, the word means robbed in Italian. Rubato gives the performer more opportunity to express feelings.

Undulating dynamics. The Baroque period featured terraced dynamics—abrupt changes from one dynamic level to another. The Romantic period is different in this regard. Instead of level and consistent dynamic planes, Romantic music displays ever-changing nuances of loudness and softness. It reminds one very much of watching a tossing sea. And the extremes at either end of the dynamics spectrum are more pronounced, to exploit the expressive potential of softness and loudness. These extremes of dynamics contribute to the great sense of climax that is often achieved in Romantic music.

Expression. The interest in expressing ideas led Romantic composers to write in many clues about the mood of the music. Their notation includes tempo indications and such words as *espressivo* (expressively), *cantabile* (songlike), *dolce* (sweetly), *misterioso* (mysteriously), *maestoso* (majestically), *con fuoco* (with fire), and many more. Also frequent are expressive signs such as accents, sforzandi, and holds or tenuto marks.

Wagner's Siegfried's Rhine Journey

The story of Wagner's massive four-opera cycle *Der Ring des Nibelungen* (The Ring of the Nibelung) was briefly described on pages 127–128.

In the Prologue to *Götterdämmerung*, the fourth opera of *The Ring*, the three Fates or Norns (weavers of destiny) are spinning. When their thread breaks, a terrible catastrophe is predicted. The Fates vanish. At this point, a section of the opera called "Siegfried's Rhine Journey" begins. It is often performed as a concert orchestral number without singers. A **Listening Guide** for *Siegfried's Rhine Journey* begins on this page.

Listening Guide

Wagner: *Siegfried's Rhine Journey*

Dawn

0:00 Timpani roll played very softly.

0:04 Fate motive played by trombones, soft and slow; followed by cellos playing a melodic line:

0:42 Siegfried motive played by horns softly; cellos again answer with melodic line at higher pitch than first time:

1:43 Siegfried motive played by French horns more strongly.

1:54 Brünnhilde motive played by clarinet; answered by bass clarinet; music is still soft and slow:

Anton Bruckner

Anton Bruckner (1824–1896) was born in the small Austrian town of Ansfelden. By nature he was a shy, almost mystical man. He was employed as a church organist, and he did not compose his first major work until he was past 40. A few years later he joined the faculty of the Vienna Conservatory. He wrote Masses, a Requiem, and other religious choral music.

Like Beethoven, he composed nine symphonies, and all of them are mighty works. The last was completed just before his death. His body, according to his wishes, is buried under the organ at the monastery of St. Florian, where he had spent much time as a young man.

2:21   Violins take up Brünnhilde motive; answered by cellos; music begins to grow in power, and tempo slowly increases.

Parting of Siegfried and Brünnhilde

3:09   Siegfried motive played powerfully by trumpets and woodwinds; portion of Walküire's motive from earlier opera played by trombone.

3:28   Brünnhilde motive returns, played by violins; followed by clarinet and oboe.

3:47   "Desire to travel" motive played by violins:

4:11   Music slowly builds, using the travel motive.

4:42   Siegfried motive played more impetuously and loud by trumpets.

5:09   Brünnhilde motive played by violins; followed by French horns as music slowly becomes calmer.

5:55   "Adventure" motive (a transformed version of Siegfried motive) played by solo French horn:

(Continued on page 198)

Gustav Mahler

Gustav Mahler (1860–1911), a pupil of Bruckner, was a successful conductor as well as an excellent composer. He wrote many songs and conceived his instrumental music in a style that is more vocal than instrumental. He followed Beethoven's lead by combining voices and orchestra in several concert works. Mahler believed in the unity of the arts and often combined music, poetry, and philosophical ideas into his compositions. Like Sibelius, he abandoned traditional forms. Instead, his symphonies contain many songlike melodies that are woven together, often contrapuntally, in an intriguing manner. The music sounds so effortless that the listener can easily miss the expertise in his handling of musical ideas.

Listening Guide

(Continued from page 197)

6:10   Bass clarinet answers with Brünnhilde motive

6:25   Motive for Brünnhilde love played by strings:

6:42   Motive called "Love's resolve" from earlier opera *Siegfried* is played by strings and woodwinds.

6:56   Adventure motive played quietly by French horn; oboe takes up motive shortly.

Siegfried's Journey to the Rhine

7:16   French horns play a short extension of adventure motive; violins play a decorated version of that motive.

7:37   Orchestra takes up extension of adventure motive; many changes of note by half step are heard.

8:08   Rhine motive played strongly by brasses; later joined by woodwinds and French horns:

Sergei Rachmaninoff

Sergei Rachmaninoff (1873–1943) was famous as a composer and pianist during his lifetime. Like several post-Romantic composers, he tended to be in the shadow of someone else's musical style. In Rachmaninoff's case, it was Tchaikovsky. Rachmaninoff at times equalled his predecessor in the writing of lovely, sentimental melodies, although his composing techniques were perhaps not so imaginative.

His best works are for piano; the Second Piano Concerto is the most popular. Like Brahms and Liszt, he drew on a violin caprice by Paganini for his *Rhapsody on a Theme of Paganini*, which was written for piano and orchestra. His solo piano works include two frequently performed Preludes, one in C sharp minor and another in G minor.

9:12   Portion of Siegfried motive played rapidly by trombone; later by woodwinds.

9:36   Motive for Rhine maidens and Rhine gold:

10:24   Ring motive is clearly presented; gold motive is passed quietly among the brasses:

11:01   French horns and then trombones play the gold motive.

11:37   Brünnhilde motive and the first portion of Siegfried motive are heard.

12:00   Music closes with full-sounding chords.

Camille Saint-Saëns

Camille Saint-Saëns (1835–1921) was a gifted, intelligent man who could converse authoritatively on many subjects other than music. His outlook toward music was more in the Haydn-Mozart Classical tradition than in the Romantic spirit of his time. In this respect he was like Brahms. Unfortunately, in Saint-Saëns' case his attitude led to music that at times seems to lack conviction. He tried little that was unique or innovative.

He did write some interesting works, however. The well-known *Danse Macabre* is one of them. The program that inspired the music is a postmidnight dance of the skeletons and spirits in a graveyard; the event ends with the crow of a rooster. Other quality works are *Introduction and Rondo Capriccioso* for violin, the opera *Samson and Delilah*, and *Carnival of the Animals* for two pianos and orchestra.

Gabriel Fauré

Gabriel Fauré (For-ay; 1845–1924) was for many years not fully appreciated outside his native France. Like Franck, he was masterful in his handling of harmony, and his music is subtle and melodious. He wrote many songs and a *Requiem*, which is frequently performed. He also composed for piano, orchestra, and chamber ensembles, especially those including strings.

Hector Berlioz

Hector Berlioz (1803–1869) was born in a small town near Grenoble, France. His father was a well-to-do physician and expected his son to follow in his footsteps. Young Berlioz was even sent off to Paris to go to medical school, but he was much more interested in the musical life of the city, so he decided to give up medicine for music.

While in Paris, he became fascinated with the music of Beethoven and the dramas of Shakespeare. It was while observing one of these dramas in 1827 that he first saw Harriet Smithson and became obsessed with her. Harriet was much too famous an actress to bother with unknown French composers.

In 1830 Berlioz was awarded the coveted Prix de Rome, which gave him an allowance and an opportunity to work in Rome. It was in that year that he turned out his famous *Symphonie fantastique*. When he returned from Rome, after the breakup of an engagement to another woman, a hectic courtship of Harriet Smithson followed. They were finally married, but their marriage turned out to be a stormy one and ended in divorce some years later.

Like some other composers of the nineteenth century, Berlioz also wrote reviews and articles. His music achieved success in his lifetime, although some of his compositions have long since been dropped from the standard repertoire. He tried his hand at several operas and wrote a gigantic Requiem.

Jean Sibelius

Jean Sibelius (1865–1957) is noted for his nationalistic compositions, which will be mentioned in the next chapter. His reputation among musicians stems primarily from his symphonies and a violin concerto. He employed vibrant, motivelike themes that seem as sturdy and enduring as the rocks and trees of his native Finland. He treated those themes to extensive development. He was fond of ostinato—those persistent, continuous accompanying figures—and he exploited this device to help build toward climactic moments. He was also a master in writing for the brasses of the orchestra, achieving from them a maximum of brilliance and power.

Sibelius' symphonies are often cyclical. Usually they do not contain traditional forms. The music has a free sound, with many stops and starts and changes of tempo.

In 1914 Sibelius visited the United States, where he conducted some concerts and received an honorary doctorate from Yale University. Although he lived until 1957, almost all of his works were written before 1925. The last years of his life were spent teaching.

Felix Mendelssohn

Felix Mendelssohn (1809–1847) was born in Germany into a wealthy and cultured family. His grandfather, Moses Mendelssohn, was a famous philosopher and author; the composer's father, Abraham, was a successful banker who was well educated in the arts.

Felix Mendelssohn showed obvious musical talent at an early age and was given every chance to develop it with world travel and the finest education. He was skilled in sports as well as in several of the arts. When he was 17, he wrote the overture to Shakespeare's *Midsummer Night's Dream*, which is regarded as something of a masterpiece even today. (One section is the well-known "Wedding March," often played as the recessional at weddings.)

At the age of 20 Mendelssohn rediscovered Bach's *St. Matthew Passion*, which had been completely neglected since its first performance 100 years before. To promote Bach's forgotten music, Mendelssohn organized a chorus and orchestra and directed them in a public performance of the work.

He himself conducted the first performance of his oratorio *Elijah* in Birmingham, England, in 1846. He had accepted many invitations to visit England and was received with great acclaim each time, especially on this occasion. Mendelssohn died one year later, at the age of 38.

Robert Schumann

Robert Schumann (1810–1856) was born in a small town in Saxony, a part of Germany. His father was a bookseller, and Schumann learned a love of literature at an early age. He undertook the study of law, largely at his mother's urging, but his real interest was piano and literature. Finally he was able to win his parents over to the idea that he should continue in music. He went to study with Friedrich Wieck, one of the leading teachers of his day.

One of the more famous romances of the century occurred when Schumann fell in love with Wieck's daughter Clara. When he first met her, she was a nine-year-old prodigy. She was 16 when Robert realized his love for her.

Friedrich Wieck's opposition to the match was extreme. The marriage took place several years later, but only after the couple appealed to the courts against her father. Fortunately, the marriage was a happy one. Clara became the best interpreter and foremost promulgator of Robert's music. In 1844 Schumann suffered a severe nervous breakdown. He recovered from it, only to succumb to other illnesses and periods of depression. By 1850 Schumann could neither carry on a public life nor deal with people outside the family. He died at the age of 46.

Schumann's outstanding compositions are for piano, although he did write a number of symphonies, chamber works, and songs.

Romantic Composers Presented Elsewhere

Twenty-One

Program Music

Program music is instrumental music that the composer associates with some nonmusical idea. The particular associations are often indicated in the title, or in some cases by an explanatory note—the "program." It's the composer who supplies the information about these nonmusical associations. Works that have been named by publishers merely as a means of identification are not really program music. When there is no suggestion of a program, the music is called absolute.

Program music is a special feature of the nineteenth century. It provided composers of that time with a means of organizing a musical work without adhering to the forms that had been so frequently used in the eighteenth century. A nonmusical association provided a stimulus for musical ideas and a "form" of sorts for a musical composition. But the separation between absolute music and program music is not always a clear one. Some program works actually reveal an established form. In other cases music with an absolute title, such as Symphony No. 3, may have been stimulated by nonmusical associations that the composer doesn't care to identify or admit.

Music cannot "tell a story" in and of itself. Only a song with its words can provide a specific message. Music can convey an atmosphere or feeling and can give the listener a general idea. One may hear some massive chords and assume it's the coronation of a king, when in fact the composer had in mind the walking motion of a large animal. The idea of size is there, but a specific association through music alone is impossible. One can make up a story to accompany a program work—or any piece of music. But that story will often bear little resemblance to what the composer had in mind.

Good program music has substance in and of itself and can stand without being associated with a story. Its musical qualities, not its program, determine its success or failure. Sometimes, in fact, programmatic titles are added after the music is completed—certainly a most casual association.

Types of Program Music

Concert overture. An overture to an opera is an instrumental introduction that incorporates programmatic ideas from the story that follows it. A concert overture is similar, but it is not associated with an opera. It's an independent concert piece whose program is self-contained. Several overtures of this type were composed in the nineteenth century. Examples include Mendelssohn's seascape *Hebrides (Fingal's Cave)* and Tchaikovsky's *Festival Overture, "1812."*

Incidental music. Early in the nineteenth century composers were often asked to write music for a drama, not an opera. They would write an overture and five or six other pieces to be performed between acts of the play. Although strictly instrumental music, these works are associated with a particular drama at least by title. Beethoven wrote incidental music, including some of his better known overtures such as *Egmont* and *Coriolan*. Mendelssohn wrote incidental music for Shakespeare's *A Midsummer Night's Dream*. Georges Bizet composed his *L'Arlesienne* for a drama, as did Edvard Grieg for Ibsen's drama *Peer Gynt*.

Tone poem. The most important type of program music is the *tone poem*, also called a *symphonic poem*. The contrasting sections of these long orchestral works are developed along the lines suggested by the nonmusical program being followed. These works are lengthy and complex, almost like symphonies.

Liszt's Les Préludes

Les Préludes is undoubtedly Liszt's best known tone poem. It was written first as an overture to a choral work, and it was given a name and program after it had been completed. Liszt chose to associate the work with Alphonse de Lamartine's *Méditations Poétique*. The program that Liszt attached to the score contains this quotation from Lamartine's poem:

What is our life but a series of preludes to that unknown song whose first solemn note is tolled by Death? The enchanted dawn of every life is love. But where is the destiny on whose first delicious joys some storm does not break? . . . And what soul thus cruelly bruised, when the tempest rolls away, seeks not to rest its memories in the pleasant calm of pastoral life? Yet man does not long permit himself to taste the kindly quiet that first attracted him to Nature's lap. For when the trumpet sounds he hastens to danger's post, that in the struggle he may once more regain full knowledge of himself and his strength.

The lines of the poem are pure Romanticism, from the personification of death and its description as "that unknown song" to the exaltation of love and nature, which is also personified.

Les Préludes begins with a three-note germinal idea, one that seems to indicate impending trouble. It is marked with a bracket and X's in the example:

The full orchestra then takes up the idea and plays a longer melody and accompaniment, both of which expand on the original motive:

The "love" theme that follows also contains the opening motive:

As one would expect, Liszt writes the love music to sound as rich and warm as possible. A second theme is heard in the section depicting love. It too contains the pattern of the motive at the beginning of the measure:

The poem speaks next of a storm and a tempest, so the music suggests upheaval and turbulence. The strings scurry up and down the chromatic scale while the brasses bark out foreboding chords.

The calm of pastoral life is represented in a section embodying some of Liszt's best writing. The motive is now woven into an idyllic theme played by the horn and woodwinds:

A shepherdlike melody is then combined with the theme containing the original motive:

This music evolves into a robust closing section that depicts the final triumph of mankind.

Again the motive is incorporated into a theme that suggests a call to battle:

One of the features in *Les Préludes* is Liszt's considerable skill in *theme transformation,* the technique of taking a motive or theme and transforming it into an entirely new melody. The original motive in *Les Préludes* assumed several widely differing characters in the course of the tone poem. Theme transformation should not be confused with theme development or theme and variation, which was discussed in Chapter 12. Variation involves keeping the theme intact to some extent (perhaps only its harmony or rhythm) through a series of musical treatments. Transformation is a freer concept, in which only a few characteristic intervals are preserved, sometimes interspersed with new material.

Theme transformation provides music with some degree of unity, although the listener may not be aware of it. Since tone poems often lack traditional formal structure, the employment of elements of a theme in several guises helps provide a better sense of organization. Composers other than Liszt have exploited this technique; Brahms was a master in its use.

Richard Strauss' Don Juan

Strauss wrote *Don Juan* in 1888 when he was 24 years old. The literary work that inspired Strauss was a poem by Nikolaus Lenau. Don Juan is the legendary hero whose life has become a search for one momentary pleasure after another. He jumps from mistress to mistress. In Lenau's version of the story, Don Juan's escapades are part of his idealistic search for the perfect woman, an explanation that seems hardly credible in light of his conduct. Nevertheless, the harm he has brought to others begins to weigh upon him, and his concern for the pleasure of the moment leaves him increasingly dissatisfied and bored with life. Finally he is challenged to a duel by Don Pedro, the son of a nobleman whom Don Juan has killed. Don Juan battles gloriously and has Don Pedro at his mercy. At that moment he realizes that victory is worthless and that defeat would relieve him of the tedium of living. He allows Don Pedro to kill him.

Strauss included only three excerpts from Lenau's poem at the front of the score. Nothing else is indicated about the program, so listeners can fill out the details to suit themselves. This process may in fact make the music more enjoyable. Like all good program music, however, it can stand very well without literary association.

Despite the fact that *Don Juan* is a tone poem, it is in a rather loose sonata form. A simplified score is included in the *Study Guide and Scores* so that this rather complicated work can be comprehended more easily.

The most important theme, which might be called the Don Juan theme, is a composite of motives that are developed later in the work. The profusion of melodic ideas is in itself a commentary on Don Juan's nature—impatient for adventure, full of vitality and power, lusting for love and life:

Later:

The first amorous episode suggests light-hearted flirtation:

Soon comes the first true love scene. The winds sound a radiant chord, the solo violin plays sweetly, and this lovely theme appears:

It grows more passionate as the music progresses. The Don Juan theme is heard again as the hero awakens from the oblivion of this love and sets out for new adventures.

His next conquest is less willing. Don Juan pleads with her, and the gasping tones of the flute seem to indicate her halfhearted resistance. She soon weakens, and a second beautiful love theme is heard:

This theme has about it an air of sadness and regret, and there follows the inevitable feeling of boredom. The music reaches a soft, quiet climax, ending with a touch of hopelessness.

Here another Don Juan theme appears, played by the four horns:

Presently Don Juan runs to a carnival (in Lenau's version it is a masked ball). The section juggles a theme of its own with motives from the original Don Juan theme. After a while the music becomes increasingly solemn, reflecting Don Juan's feelings of depression. In this condition he sees the ghosts of his previous mistresses, and their melodies reappear briefly.

Then comes the challenge of the duel. Don Juan responds, and the music grows stronger, reinforced by the second Don Juan theme played again by the horns. The pitch level is three notes higher than it was in its first appearance, and this change adds to the exhilaration of the music. There is a short return of the opening music, which gains in driving force.

Suddenly there is a deathly halt—apparently the moment in which Don Juan decides to give up. The music shifts to minor, and the trumpet jabs out a dissonant note. In shuddering sounds Don Juan's life is ended.

Richard Strauss

Richard Strauss (*Ree*-kard Strouse; 1864–1949) was born of a musical family but was related neither to the Johann Strauss family of waltz fame nor to Oskar Straus, composer of operettas. Richard's father was a horn player in the orchestra at Munich, and his mother was the daughter of a wealthy brewer. His parents' aptitudes may explain his own love of music and good business sense.

From childhood Strauss displayed unusual musical talent. In his early twenties he was already writing his famous tone poems, and he soon established himself as an outstanding musician. In those days he was considered a radical. His works were in the general style of Wagner, who had been dead for five years when Strauss wrote *Don Juan,* his first successful tone poem. Probably it was the colorful quality of his writing, rather than any musical innovations, that earned him his early reputation. His best-known works composed before 1900 are tone poems. Six are standard orchestral fare today: *Don Juan, Death and Transfiguration, Till Eulenspiegel's Merry Pranks, Thus Spake Zarathustra, Don Quixote,* and *Ein Heldenleben (A Hero's Life).*

After 1900 Strauss turned to opera. His first successful opera, *Salome* (1906), was a German setting of Oscar Wilde's decadent version of the Biblical story. Strauss' next opera, *Elektra,* is based on a version of Sophocles' play. Since the opera dwells on the emotions of hatred and revenge, Strauss seized the opportunity to experiment with bold and innovative harmonic writing. In both *Elektra* and *Salome* the action involved such excesses of blood-letting that the public began to wonder if Strauss could surpass his reputation for producing the macabre. Evidently he couldn't, or he chose not to do so, because for his next opera, *Der Rosenkavalier (The Knight of the Rose),* he switched style completely. The story is humorous, centering on the decadent elegance of the powder-and-wig world of the eighteenth century. The music is romantic and sensuous rather than innovative.

By the end of the First World War, Strauss's creative career was largely behind him. He continued to live in his villa in the Bavarian Alps and write operas until his death in 1949.

Twenty-Two

Nationalism and Impressionism

Several factors in the nineteenth century encouraged nationalistic movements in music. One was the prevalence of Romanticism, which exalted individual feelings and the inherent goodness of mankind in the natural state. The eighteenth-century intellectual had considered common folk to be untutored and rough; Romanticists idealized them. They thought their way of life was good because it was uncorrupted by the vices of civilization. Furthermore, the life of the common people was a source of subject matter that composers and artists had seldom tapped in the past.

There was another reason for the growing tide of nationalistic art. The nineteenth century was a time of rising political nationalism. The countries of Italy and Germany were finally organized. Wars were pathetically frequent, and in such conflicts a nation's efforts involved the citizenry to a degree that was unknown in previous centuries.

To assert their independence from German influence, nationalistic composers often wrote tempo markings and other musical indications in their native language instead of the more internationally accepted Italian. So Debussy wrote *vif* instead of *vivace*, and some Americans even today write *lively* or *fast*. Such manuscript notation does not affect the sound of

the music, of course, but it provides some insight into the composer's thinking and the temper of the time.

The Russian Five

Until well into the nineteenth century, Russia had little musical tradition of its own. For entertainment the Czars imported French and Italian opera as well as French ballet. Mikhail Glinka (1804–1857) was the first native Russian composer to write an opera on a Russian theme. Today he is generally considered the father of Russian music.

More important to the emergence of Russian music was a group of five composers who lived in the latter half of the Romantic period. Their leader was Mily Balakirev (Bah-*lah*-ke-ref; 1837–1910). He himself was not a talented composer, but his contribution was significant. He persuaded the others—César Cui (1835–1918), Alexander Borodin (*Bor*-oh-deen; 1833–1887), Modest Mussorgsky (1839–1881), and Nikolai Rimsky-Korsakov (1844–1908)—that they needn't copy the German style in order to compose great music. He urged them to draw on the musical resources of their native Russia.

Generally the "Five" had little formal training. Balakirev was self-taught, and Cui, an engineer, was not a particularly successful composer. Rimsky-Korsakov was an officer in the navy and he sailed extensively; his travels included a trip to the United States. At the age of 27 he was appointed professor of composition and orchestration at the Conservatory of St. Petersburg. Like Berlioz, he wrote a widely acknowledged treatise on orchestration.

Rimsky-Korsakov represents a phase of Romanticism called *exoticism.* Like many other Romantic composers, he felt drawn by the mystery and splendor of Eastern cultures. For example, his best known work is *Scheherazade,* a tone poem based on the Persian legends in *A Thousand and One Nights.* His "Song of India" from the opera *Sadko,* and "Hymn to the Sun," from the opera *Le Coq d'Or* (The Golden Cockerel), are other familiar works that reveal his interest in the Orient. Rimsky-Korsakov also wrote nationalistic music and worked avidly to advance the cause of Russian music.

Of the "Five" the most original was Mussorgsky. He chose an army career and later became a clerk in the engineering department. He was perhaps the most technically inept of the five composers, but his music best represents the Russian character. His opera *Boris Godunov* (*Goh*-duh-noff) explores the intrigue and tragedy that shaped the reign of Czar Boris. The libretto is derived from a play by Pushkin.

Mussorgsky wrote in other mediums in addition to opera. He was an especially good art-song composer. His tone poem *A Night on Bald Mountain* is descriptive and somewhat eerie. *Pictures at an Exhibition,* originally for solo piano, was orchestrated by Maurice Ravel. It is an exciting work in either form—a musical description of a series of paintings created by Victor Hartmann, an artist friend of Mussorgsky's. The music ranges in mood from the twittering "Ballet of the Chickens in Their Shells" to the massive finale, "The Great Gate of Kiev."

Borodin was a celebrated chemist and an excellent composer. Had he been able to devote more time to composing, his name would be better known than it is today. His Second Symphony is still performed, as are *In the*

Steppes of Central Asia and *String Quartet No. 2.* His greatest work is an opera, *Prince Igor,* which was completed after his death by Rimsky-Korsakov and Alexander Glazounov (1865–1936). Excerpts from Borodin's works were once used for most of the music for a Broadway musical.

Borodin's Polovtzian Dances

Prince Igor is not so much a drama as it is a series of scenes or tableaus. In Act Two there appears a section called "Polovtzian Dances" (Poh-*loft*-zeon). These dances are available in two versions: One is for orchestra alone; the other, more nearly resembling the original, is for chorus and orchestra. The dances themselves are only distantly related to the story line. After a short introduction a wistful melody is heard in a section called "Dance of the Young Girls." (It is the melody for a popular song called "Stranger in Paradise.")

The haunting quality of this melody is precisely what marks Borodin's music as nationalistic and Russian. It is inconceivable that Liszt or Brahms would have written that melody—it just doesn't sound German. Nor is there anything Italian, Irish, or American about it—it *feels* Russian.

Without pause the music moves to the "Dance of the Men." It features a brilliant clarinet solo, which is soon taken up by other instruments. As the clarinet finishes its solo, the brasses come in strongly with a vigorous theme reminiscent of the music in the slow introduction:

The music has a primitive quality, which is another feature of Russian nationalistic music. To the cultured European musician of the day, this music sounded coarse and crude.

The "General Dance" that comes next is novel, even after a hundred years. The rhythm has a barbaric force that impels the music along. There are pedal tones and chords with their middle notes missing. The contrasting middle section of the dance is named "Dance of the Female Slaves." The three chromatic notes in the melody suggest the enticing movements of the girls as they dance for the Khan.

The "Dance of the Little Boys" is in a brilliant $\frac{6}{8}$ meter conducted with one beat per measure. Logically, the "Dance of the Little Boys" grows into a repeat of "Dance of the Men." The rapid notes of the boys' dance are combined with a sturdy melody sung by the men:

All the dances are then repeated and combined. First the young girls' music is heard, then it is enhanced with a flashy line of counterpoint in the violins and flutes. The dances of the boys and men are repeated before a second "General Dance" concludes the work. Even this final number is combined with an earlier dance—the first "Dance of the Men" —with long, sustained notes in the chorus. The music pushes forward to a dazzling conclusion.

Hungary-Bohemia

Franz Liszt was affected by the spirit of nationalism. His interest in such music is apparent in 20 *Hungarian Rhapsodies* and several shorter works.

Bohemia, which is today part of Czechoslovakia, produced two nationalistic composers in Antonin Dvořák and Bedřich Smetana (1824–1884). Throughout most of the nineteenth century, Bohemia was part of the Austrian empire. So the style of Dvořák and Smetana does not differ substantially from the prevailing Romantic style of the time. Bohemia was too steeped in the German-Austrian culture to create new styles. But Bohemian nationalism asserted itself in folk melodies and native subject matter. Music from Smetana's opera *The Bartered Bride* and his tone poem "The Moldau" are frequently performed today. Dvořák, whose String Quartet is discussed in Chapter 12, also arranged native dances and wrote several operas. His Symphony No. 8 makes skillful and charming use of folklike melodies.

Scandinavia

Edvard Grieg (1843–1907) of Norway was the leading proponent of Scandinavian music. Among his well-known works are the *Peer Gynt* Suites, which were originally written as incidental music for Ibsen's play. He also wrote a highly successful and melodious Piano Concerto, as well as many shorter piano pieces and chamber works.

Finland's Jean Sibelius also exhibited nationalistic tendencies, especially in the early part of his career. One of the themes from his *Finlandia* was made the national anthem of Finland. He also used native themes as the basis for program works such as *The Swan of Tuonela* and *Pohjola's Daughter.*

England

The music of Edward Elgar (1857–1934) enjoys perennial popularity among the English and the musical world at large. His music is not conspicuously different from that of other Romantic composers, nor is it particularly nationalistic, but it is melodious and varied. Elgar is the composer of *Pomp and Circumstance,* the stately march that has become standard fare at graduation exercises. More typical of his writing, and more worthy of attention, is his *"Enigma" Variations* for orchestra. On the score, before each variation, he has inscribed anagrams, initials, and other clues to indicate which family member or friend is being represented in each variation. Guessing the intended identities is the puzzle or "enigma" for which the work is named. This composition would be little more than a clever gimmick if the music were not so listenable and well constructed.

Italy

Nationalism in Italy was evident primarily in its operatic tradition. Italian nationalism in instrumental music did not come to the fore until the twentieth century, with the works of Ottorino Respighi (Res-*peeg*-ee; 1879–1936). His familiar *Pines of Rome* and *Fountains of Rome* are decidedly nationalistic, and his handling of coloristic effects is typically Romantic.

Spain

Nationalism in Spain was evidenced by composers such as Isaac Albéniz (Al-*bay*-neez; 1860–1909), Enrique Granados (1867–1916), and Manuel de Falla (de *Fy*-ya; 1876–1946), all of whom exploited the rhythm of Spanish dances. Although their careers extended into the twentieth century, their works are essentially Romantic in character.

Impressionism

The predominant style of French music at the end of the nineteenth century and the beginning of the twentieth was *impressionism.* In one sense it represented French nationalism, because it was a conscious attempt to break away from the influence of German music. French composers also wrote program works based on French stories. But impressionism made more of a mark in the musical world.

Impressionism is an artistic viewpoint. It is based on the belief that experiences in life are largely impressions or sensations rather than detailed observations of artificial experiences. For example, when we enter a room we do not note every imperfection or the placement of each small article. Under normal circumstances we are content to gain a general impression of the room and to disregard the unnecessary details within it.

Impressions are not stationary. A cloud may reveal an interesting and distinctive shape, but within a minute or two it has changed somewhat. People move about, too. They do not normally pose in the manner traditionally required by portrait painters. So impressionistic painters caught people at a particular moment in a casual, unposed situation.

Impressionist painters also experimented boldly in the treatment of light, since lighting conditions markedly affect the visual impression of a scene. Realizing that a view changes as the light conditions change, impressionist artists tried to capture a scene quickly. They would make several rough sketches of a landscape. Perhaps they would make one early in the morning, another at noon, and another at sunset, and then they would finish the scenes in the studio. Their most frequent subjects were landscapes and casual views of people. Claude Monet's "Rouen Cathedral, West Façade, Sunlight" (colorplate III) demonstrates the impressionistic style of painting.

Writers and poets worked along similar lines. Some, including Mallarmé and Verlaine, were known as symbolists because they were more interested in mystery and broad truths than in reality. Symbolism appealed to these writers because a symbol hints at a truth without actually stating it. Here again is the characteristic vagueness of impressionism. Lines in a poem were intended to convey an impression through the sounds and rhythms of the words. Definite meaning was avoided. According to Mallarmé, "To name an object is to destroy three-quarters of the pleasure in it."

The impressionistic movement was unusual in the extent to which writers, artists, and musicians were united by common attitudes. Many of them knew and admired one another's work. They exchanged ideas. Perhaps the impressionist view of the time was the common denominator among the arts: The painter wanted to capture a fleeting moment on canvas, the author in the printed and spoken word, and the composer in the transitory world of sound. And so they shared in common the subtle nuances of light and shadow, the vague contours, and the veiled thoughts that mark the impressionist. The compositions of Claude Debussy are the epitome of impressionism in music.

Debussy's Clair de Lune

"Clair de Lune" ("Moonlight") is one of Debussy's best-known compositions. It is a portion of the *Suite Bergamasque* for piano, but it's usually heard today as a separate piece, often transcribed for instruments other than piano. It is full of impressionistic writing. To help you study this work, a simple one-line score of this work is provided on pages 214–215.

First of all, notice that the opening melody consumes the first 14 measures of the piece. Many times the last note of a measure is tied to the first note of the next measure. (In music a *tie* is a curved line connecting two notes of the same pitch so that they sound as one long note.) The effect of this is to blur the metrical pattern of the music. In measures 3, 13, and 14, Debussy borrows the pattern of two subdivisions per beat, while during the rest of the piece he has established a pattern of three subdivisions per beat. This alteration also tends to blur the rhythm. Similar effects are evident throughout the piece. At measure 15 the music is marked *tempo rubato*, meaning that the music should be played with a flexible tempo. All of these techniques convey a feeling of rhythmic fluidity that is characteristic of impressionistic music.

The melody is exceedingly simple. Actually, it's nothing but the major scale of the piece: D flat major. To this simple melody Debussy merely adds a few alternating notes, more or less as ornamentation. In any case, the melody is not the kind of solid tune that one might find in a Bach chorale or an operatic aria. It's more delicate and decorative.

One characteristic that a line score does not show well is the general effect of the music. At measure 25 a wiggly line has been placed to the left of each chord. This indicates that the pianist should not strike all the notes simultaneously, but rather should roll out the chord, which gives the music a harplike effect. The harmonies, not shown here, add richness to the sound. Then there are frequent doublings and even triplings of various notes, so that the same note is repeated in one or more octave. The spacing of the chords and melodic notes creates a certain haunting effect that can soon be recognized as characteristic of impressionistic music.

The opening melody returns in measure 51, to give the piece a three-part form. Impressionistic writers, along with other Romantic composers, tended to reject the forms of the

Classical era, but there is something so basic about many of the structures that composers found themselves using them whether they favored them or not.

Clair de Lune
(Moonlight) 1890

Claude Debussy

Claude Debussy (Deb-you-see; 1862–1918) was born in a small town near Paris, and at the age of eleven he entered the Paris Conservatory. He often revolted against the rules of composition his professors tried to teach him—a trait that lasted throughout his life. When he was 22 he won the Prix de Rome, a coveted award that included a period of study in Rome.

Debussy loved the gaiety and bustle of Paris, and he also valued the company of painters and writers such as Mallarmé, in whose home they often gathered. His early admiration for Wagner faded after a second visit to Bayreuth in 1889, and he developed a strong dislike for German Romantic music and philosophy. He was a writer of articles on music, and he articulated his sentiments well. He regarded sonata form as "a legacy of clumsy, falsely imposed traditions," and he considered thematic development to be a type of dull "musical mathematics." He offered another observation to the French who were tempted to imitate Wagner: "The French forget too easily the qualities of clarity and elegance peculiar to themselves and allow themselves to be influenced by the tedious and ponderous Teuton."

Predictably, Debussy cast his own opera, *Pelléas et Mélisande*, from a completely different mold. Built on a story by Maeterlinck, it is dreamlike and restrained. In one scene with her lover Pelléas, Mélisande unbinds her hair while doves fly about. The text is elusive; nothing is stated clearly. Mélisande's words exemplify the effect: "Neither do I understand each thing that I say, do you see. . . . I do not know what I have said. . . . I do not know what I know. . . . I say no longer what I want to." This opera is not a favorite of the opera-going public, but many critics consider it a masterpiece, and it did establish Debussy as a first-rate composer during his lifetime.

World War I profoundly affected Debussy. For a while it caused him to lose all interest in music. The war was not his only torment, however, for he was slowly dying of cancer. In

Claude Debussy

March 1918, during the bombardment of Paris, he died.

Debussy was a careful workman, and his piano works are held in high regard, perhaps because they reveal a free and sensitive style that is reminiscent of Chopin. Debussy added much that was his own, however: parallel chord movement (forbidden in conventional harmonic writing), chords with added notes, and new colors. He wanted the sound of his piano works to suggest a "sonorous halo"—an apt description of impressionism. Representative of his piano works are *La Cathédrale Engloutie* (The Sunken Cathedral), *Reflects dans l'Eau* (Reflections in the Water), and several preludes in addition to "Clair de Lune."

His orchestral works, too, are typically impressionistic. There are three Nocturnes, each conveying a distinctive mood: *Nuages* (Clouds), *Fêtes* (Festivals), and *Sirènes* (Sirens). In *La Mer* (The Sea), Debussy writes his impressions of the sea as it might be observed on three different occasions. Also frequently performed are *Ibéria* and the perennial favorite *Prélude à l'après-midi d'un Faune* (Prelude to the Afternoon of a Faun).

Maurice Ravel

The fact that Maurice Ravel (1875–1937) followed Debussy both chronologically and stylistically has tended to place him in the background despite his many fine compositions. He did have the good fortune to be born into the family of a mining engineer who had once aspired to be a musician himself, so the father encouraged his talented son's musical education. Like Debussy, Ravel studied at the Paris Conservatory. Although he was a composer of some merit, the professors at the Conservatory four times denied him the coveted Prix de Rome, an award for which he was highly qualified. The arbitrary nature of these decisions caused a public furor that eventually led to the resignation of the Conservatory's director.

A French patriot, Ravel drove an ambulance along the front lines during the First World War. After the war he was recognized as France's leading composer, and he toured the United States in 1928. Eventually his polished postimpressionistic compositions became dated in a world whose tastes had changed. As he grew older, he became more despondent and depressed. At about the age of 60 he developed a rare disease of the brain and slowly lost his speech and motor coordination. In desperation he agreed to a dangerous operation, from which he never regained consciousness.

One of Ravel's best known orchestral works is *Bolero*, which draws its rhythm and spirit from the Spanish dance of the same name. He wrote it in 1928, and its fame derives from its hypnotic melody, its gradual crescendo that proceeds uninterrupted from beginning to end, and its two-measure rhythmic pattern that is reiterated without pause throughout the entire 17-minute work. Other compositions include the Concerto in G Major for Piano and *Concerto for the Left Hand,* as well as works for orchestra: *Daphnis et Chloé, La Valse, Rapsodie Espagnole* (Spanish Rhapsody), and *Ma Mère l'Oye* (Mother Goose)—a ballet from which he compiled music for a suite.

Originally created for Diaghilev's Ballet Russe, *Daphnis et Chloé* was rewritten by Ravel into two suites. The second of these is an enormously exciting work that presents music from three scenes in the ballet. "Daybreak" offers a musical impression of rippling brooks, bird songs, and shepherd's tunes. "Pantomime" portrays a mythical meeting of a shepherd with Pan and the nymph Syrinx. The invention of a simple musical instrument, the Pan's pipe, is represented by a long flute solo. The final scene of the Suite is the "General Dance," which suggests a fiery pagan ritual and features the unusual meter of $\frac{5}{4}$.

23

Twenty-Three

What's Different about Twentieth-Century Music

Living in the twentieth century, we are so close to the events going on around us that it's hard to see them in perspective. Furthermore, most of us seldom consider how the changes in society affect the creative artist. For these reasons, it is wise to take a closer look at the character of our time and assess the ways in which it is influencing the fine arts.

Modern Society and the Creative Artist

The modern world is increasingly shaped by technology and machines. Just about every civilized human activity is involved in some way with technology. Not only does this fact have vast economic implications, it affects people's values and thinking as well. The vast array of goods made possible by technology and mass production in an affluent society has encouraged an attitude termed *materialism*— the placing of primary value on material goods. As someone has said of the average American: "He buys things he doesn't need, with money he doesn't have, to impress people he doesn't like." Whether this is true or not, the description indicates that nonmaterial

items such as learning, truth, and beauty usually come out second to a Florida vacation and an imported sports car.

Twentieth-century society is becoming increasingly urban in its orientation. More and more people live in metropolitan areas, and the urban way of life is being imitated by those living in the country. Nature no longer seems central to existence or to the enjoyment of that existence. Rather, nature is manipulated to achieve other ends, most of which are beneficial to society, as when rivers are dammed to produce electric power and water for irrigation.

Technology has made any place in the world accessible in a few hours by jet, and instant communication via radio and television has been a reality for years. These advances have made human beings think and act in international terms. Except in newly emerging nations, the ardor of nationalism has decreased somewhat. The nations of Europe, which were at war with one another so frequently during the nineteenth century, have now joined into the European Common Market.

Despite the many factors that might be expected to draw the peoples of the world together, international relations have been chaotic in the twentieth century, erupting into two world wars and numerous lesser conflicts. Society has been further shaken by the changes and problems arising from the vast increases in population, the pollution of water and air, the burgeoning and decay of large cities, technology, the new status of women—and the list could be lengthened considerably.

The intellectual climate of the twentieth century differs from that of the nineteenth. Generally, contemporary thought is far more objective and concerned with scientific inquiry. Sometimes, in fact, it is charged that the modern outlook is objective to the point of being cold and calculating, like a machine. Many intellectuals feel that they have outgrown the slushy sentimentality of the Romantic period. They no longer stand in awe of mystery and the unknown. On the contrary, they are exploring the outermost reaches of space and the innermost realms of the mind.

In spite of their material comforts and intellectual achievements, people today seem to be less clear about the meaning of life than were their predecessors; consequently they seem no happier. Many old beliefs have been rejected, but new understandings and beliefs have not appeared. The result is a feeling of confusion, a desire to escape from reality, or a sense of being hopelessly trapped in the tangle of life. Modern drama illustrates these points well. In Jean-Paul Sartre's *No Exit* the three characters are trapped in their private hell, which is largely of their own making. In Samuel Beckett's *Waiting for Godot*, two characters symbolizing mankind wait for Godot, who will take care of their problems. Godot never shows up.

There is a fear that people are becoming dehumanized and depersonalized; people and feelings seem to be lost in the hectic activity of life. This fact has encouraged several counterintellectual movements—faddish interests in oriental philosophies and religions, astrology, and quasi-psychological theories of self-fulfillment, for example.

Coupled with the difficulty of finding

meaning in life is the constant change that people see all about them. But change to what, and for what reason? Sometimes change seems to be valued for its own sake. Yet a few of the older values persist. Certainly some nineteenth-century ideas, specifically those of Thoreau (who in turn drew upon the ideas of Jean Jacques Rousseau), have received renewed attention in recent years.

Creative artists are especially sensitive to what they see about them. They often mirror the feelings of the times in which they live. They react to circumstances and give expression to prevailing attitudes. Creative artists do not, of course, all react alike. Some become cynical and discouraged; others withdraw along an escapist route that ignores society. Still others become "commercial," bowing to mass taste in order to get a fair share of society's material comforts.

With advances in transportation and communication, creative artists are usually internationally minded. They know the work of other writers, painters, and composers, and this exchange encourages international styles in architecture, art, and music.

Twentieth-Century Musical Characteristics

Virtually every aspect of music has been altered in the twentieth century, but not by everyone and not in a unified manner. One characteristic of twentieth-century music is its diversity, its pluralism. (Subsequent chapters in the book look at the more significant types of music this century has brought forth.) There is, however, a sizable carry-over into the twentieth century from the music of preceding centuries. Although there are some composers who have created music that bears little relationship to previous music, most composers have been evolutionaries not revolutionaries. The twentieth century has retained some of the old, while adding much that is new to music.

Rhythm

The twentieth century has seen a move away from metrical patterns based on the regular recurrence of an accented beat. Composers in this century have preferred freer concepts of rhythm. One of these concepts is the use of mixed meters. The composer shifts the metrical pattern to suit the music, rather than making the music conform to a regular meter. For example, the frequent meter changes in Stravinsky's *The Rite of Spring* were pointed out in Chapter 4. The effect, when done with the right type of music, can be quite exhilarating.

Another feature of rhythm in this century is the presence of polyrhythm and polymeter, which were also discussed in Chapter 4. These words imply the use of more than one rhythmic pattern or metric pattern simultaneously. As you may recall from the discussion of ethnic music (Chapter 16), polyrhythms are frequent in African and Latin-American music. Small amounts of polyrhythm can also be found in compositions of Western composers in the nineteenth century, but the twentieth century has exploited these devices as never before in art music. A similar feature of contemporary music is the rhythmic ostinato—the persistent repetition of a rhythmic pattern. When used properly, the effect of rhythmic ostinato is almost hypnotic.

Rhythm itself has become more prominent in twentieth-century music. Although melody and harmony are certainly significant in this century's music, they are less important than they were in the nineteenth century. Composers have become much more interested in rhythmic effects.

The percussion section is featured more prominently. In music of previous centuries, timpani rolls and an occasional cymbal crash are heard, but not the variety of sounds that characterize the music of more recent years.

Melody

The twentieth century has witnessed a return to the medieval modes that flourished before 1600. Modal scales reappeared in art music early in the century and began to surpass major and minor keys in popular music in the 1960s.

Composers in the twentieth century have broken away from the idea of balanced phrase design. In the Baroque and Classical eras phrases seemed to run in multiples of four. Four measures were answered by another four measures, and these eight measures added up to a logical unit of musical thought. It was all very symmetrical. But with increasing frequency composers in the nineteenth century began to favor phrases of irregular length, and this trend continued extensively into the twentieth century. Gone is the idea of statement and answer, the symmetrical design that is so basic in music of previous centuries.

Many twentieth-century melodies have moved away from the idea of the song melody—a beautiful, singable series of tones. Instead, melodies have become far more angular and instrumental in concept. Their range is wider, their intervals are greater and more awkward to sing, and some of the patterns must be executed too rapidly to be singable.

Harmony

By the end of the nineteenth century, composers had "stacked" more pitches onto the triad and the seventh chord. Such procedures weaken the feeling of a root or fundamental tone in the chord because the total sound contains the notes of two or more triads:

In the example the ninth chord contains three complete triads: C E G, E G B♭, and G B♭ D. Depending on how the composer treats this chord and how the listener hears it, the sound can be interpreted in several different ways. The logical consequence of an increase in chord size is *polychordal* and *polytonal* music, in which two or more key centers occur simultaneously. The effect is almost always more dissonant, but it can also be quite interesting.

Some twentieth-century composers, beginning with Arnold Schoenberg (see Chapter 26), felt that the tonal system of the eighteenth and nineteenth centuries had been pumped dry of its possibilities. So they discarded it entirely, including the idea of a tonal center, and replaced it with a type of music that is called *atonal*—music with no feeling of key. Such music still contains harmony, but it is not related to any tonal system.

A third development of the twentieth century harmony is the practice of *pandiatonicism*. Instead of adhering to a particular tonal system, with its implication of a key and particular chords to go with that key, the composer is free to harmonize according to intuitive instincts. Tones appear in a chord merely because the composer likes the particular sound at that point in the music.

A fourth development affecting harmony in the twentieth century is the exploration of different chord structures as an alternative to the "every-other" pattern of thirds that prevailed from about 1650 to at least 1900. Composers are experimenting with chords built in fourths (C F B♭), in fifths (C G D), and in seconds (C D E F). Seldom do composers rely on an unusual chord structure for an entire piece, but they do intersperse the new chords among the more traditional chords that are based on the every-other pattern.

A fifth influence on contemporary harmony is the return of modes. If two similar chord progressions are played, one major and one modal, the listener hears two different musical effects.

Sixth, composers began more and more to use progressions that differed from what was common in the eighteenth and nineteenth centuries.

Dissonance

The history of music shows a steady trend toward increasing dissonance. It's as though the temperature were creeping up from 0 degrees to 100 degrees on the thermometer. Of course,

the amount of dissonance is a relative matter. There is little that is purely dissonant, except perhaps a chord in which every note on the keyboard is sounding, and little that is purely consonant, except possibly the octave. In any case, the twentieth century has moved about as close to complete dissonance as is possible. One composer calls for the pianist to take a stick that is 14⅔ inches long and push it down on the keyboard. Obviously all notes under the stick will sound. Another composer asks the performer to push an elbow down on the keyboard. Although most composers do not go to this extreme, it is clear that dissonance is a more important factor in twentieth-century music than it has been in any other century.

Some current dissonances do not create tension, which was their usual purpose in previous centuries, but rather offer a certain color or tonal effect. Whether the dissonant chord is perceived as tension or as a coloristic effect depends on the listener's inclination and the structure of the music.

Counterpoint

After the Baroque period counterpoint was less common than homophony. This situation has changed in the twentieth century. The line-against-line writing of the Renaissance and the Baroque has interested composers again, and today counterpoint and homophony exist as equals. Contemporary counterpoint differs, of course, from the counterpoint of the sixteenth century. Now the notes and intervals can be as free as any found in lines of melody, so counterpoint is often quite dissonant.

Orchestration

The orchestra reached its maximum size at the beginning of the twentieth century. A few post-Romantic composers wrote gigantic works. (One calls for a thousand performers. Most of them are singers, but the orchestra does include such uncommon instruments as chains and euphoniums.) Stravinsky's *Rite of Spring* requires a large orchestra. Around 1920, however, there was a swing away from the large orchestra and the monumental composition, with a renewed interest in the smaller orchestra and chamber music. Composers, instead of striving for an impressive mass of sound, tried to achieve greater clarity in their writing. Even when a full-sized orchestra is present, many of the players do not play much of the time. Gone are the rich sounds of the nineteenth century. There is new interest in the concerted style that characterized the concerto grosso, and new effects are achieved by balancing different timbres and sections of the orchestra.

Timbre

A most significant development in twentieth-century music is the interest musicians have taken in sounds and tonal effects. Every conceivable sound has been milked from conventional instruments and the human voice—shrieks, babbling, teeth-clicking, tongue-clacking, banging, rasping, squeaking, buzzing, and noises of every type. In addition, composers have moved on to unconventional sounds created by synthesizers and recorded on tape. The timbres heard in the twentieth century are more varied than those occurring in any other century.

Cosmopolitanism

Twentieth-century musicians have been influenced by music from every geographical and historical source. Although nationalism is still alive, with evidences of ethnocentrism (the belief in the superiority of one's own culture), composers display a wide-ranging musical interest. Twentieth-century music is pancultural and panhistorical as no other music has been.

Composers also feel free to change styles, as Stravinsky did, and to seek out new directions for their compositions. For example, Karlheinz Stockhausen changed his orientation from highly controlled, intellectual electronic music to a farcical stage work in which the performers do partly what they want to.

In fact, styles in the twentieth century seem to "burn themselves out" much more rapidly than in the past. The throbbing style associated with Primitivism was favored for about a dozen years. It was replaced by Neo-Classicism, which lasted for about 20 years. During these same 30 years works in other styles were also being composed.

The music of this century has undergone enormous changes and has moved in several different directions at the same time. That fact, among many others, makes this a fascinating century.

Twenty-Four

Twentieth-Century Music:
The Mainstream

As the preceding chapter pointed out, twentieth-century music is highly diversified. Some of it is new and experimental, deliberately rejecting the influence of other times and places. Some of it is subjective, or what is called *expressionistic*; this type of music is presented in Chapter 25. Some twentieth-century music is cerebral, intellectual, and academic; it is covered in Chapter 26. If the experimental, expressionistic, and intellectual music were somehow to be removed from the body of music composed in this century, probably more than half of all twentieth-century music would still be left. Much of it is a logical evolution of trends observable in the nineteenth century. Some of it utilizes ideas and practices from folk-ethnic music.

It's hard to know what to call this body of "conventional" music. Some writers have coined the word *folkloric* because the music is partly derived from folk or ethnic sources. But folk influences are found in only a portion of this music, so folkloric is not an adequate term. *Traditional* is not an accurate word because most twentieth-century composers broke with nineteenth-century traditions to some extent. *Cosmopolitan* or *eclectic* are not ideal de-

scriptions because many composers did not attempt to integrate a variety of musical styles in their music. *Mainstream* seems to say it best; it refers to music that is neither experimental nor committed to a particular compositional outlook.

One feature of twentieth-century music is its lack of a clearly dominant style. Although the music of the past 75 years is quite pluralistic, these works exhibit enough similarities so that they can be grouped logically in the same chapter.

Bartók's Concerto for Orchestra

No single work can adequately display all the traits of "mainstream" twentieth-century music. Béla Bartók's Concerto for Orchestra is as representative an example as any. It contains most of the twentieth-century features described in Chapter 23: polymeters, disjointed melodies, dissonance, counterpoint, coloristic writing, an interest in timbres, and aspects of folk music and eighteenth-century art music.

Bartók wrote his Concerto for Orchestra in

the summer of 1943 for a $1,000 commission from the Boston Symphony Orchestra. "The general mood of the work," he wrote, "represents, apart from the jesting second movement, a gradual transition from the sternness of the first movement and the lugubrious death-song of the third to the life-assertion of the last." The work is called a concerto because single instruments and sections are treated in a concerted manner, as in the Baroque. There is also an element of virtuoso musicianship in the concerto.

First movement. The first movement opens with a spacious and quiet introduction. The theme is based on the interval of a fourth (indicated by brackets):

The phrases of this theme are separated by shimmering chords played by muted strings —an indication of Bartók's interest in tonal effects.

The first theme of the main part of the movement, which moves at a rapid tempo, consists of a syncopated figure that ascends and descends rapidly. The second half is a nearly exact inversion of the first half:

Again the interval of a fourth is prominent. There is a contrasting idea that is somewhat folklike in style. The development section of the movement is highly imitative, and there is a shortened recapitulation. The movement contains many elements of sonata form.

Second movement. This movement is entitled "Games of Pairs" because the wind instruments are paired off at specific pitch intervals: the bassoons in sixths, the oboes in thirds, the clarinets in sevenths, the flutes in fifths, and the muted trumpets in seconds. This is the "jesting" movement that Bartók mentioned in his synopsis. The whole thing seems to be a tease.

After five short sections in which each pair of instruments is featured, there is a chorale for the brass, accompanied by a snare drum with the snares disengaged. Following this there is a restatement with more elaborate instrumentation, giving the movement a large three-part form.

Third movement. This movement is the "lugubrious death-song." It features a long oboe solo. The music is rhapsodic, and seems to rise to a peak moment of tragedy.

Fourth movement. Bartók calls this movement "Interrupted Intermezzo." The melody is folklike; it is introduced by the oboe and continued by the flute. Notice that the first six complete measures all begin on the same note, A#:

The melody that follows sounds almost like a waltz, but not quite. Its meter changes repeatedly, usually adding or subtracting half a beat.

Fifth movement. The final movement of this monument of twentieth-century music is presented in the Listening Guide, which begins on pages 226–227. In the movement Bartók engages in a great deal of contrapuntal writing. He also employs a theme of continuously running notes, much like the "perpetual motion" pieces by Paganini and others.

England

The twentieth century has produced several first-rate English composers. The foremost is Ralph Vaughan Williams (1872–1958). Vaughan Williams helped revive interest in English folk music and contributed to the improvement of music in the Church of England. For vocal texts he drew on the works of England's finest poets. He also incorporated themes from Elizabethan composers into such works as *Fantasia on a Theme by Thomas Tallis,* for double string orchestra. As he grew older—he composed until he was eighty—his music became more modern and complex. His Sixth Symphony, an important work, is far different in style from his early folklike compositions, such as *Fantasia on "Greensleeves."*

Another outstanding contemporary English composer is a man with the wonderfully appropriate name of Benjamin Britten (1913–1976). His natural musical ability has been compared to Mozart's. Britten began composing at an early age and was remarkably facile at working out music in his mind. He wrote for every medium and for varied levels of musical sophistication. His *The Young Person's Guide to the Orchestra* was presented in Chapter 7. Britten toured the United States frequently and at one time considered living here.

Britten's forte was the composition of vocal works, especially operas. Among his successful operas are *Peter Grimes* (1945), *The Rape of Lucretia* (1946), *Let's Make an Opera* (1948), *Billy Budd* (1951), *The Turn of the Screw* (1954), *Noye's Fludde* (Noah's Flood, 1957), and *A Midsummer Night's Dream* (1960). He also wrote for voices and instruments: *Serenade for Tenor, Horn, and Strings* (1943); *Nocturne,* for tenor and small orchestra (1958); *The Ceremony of Carols,* for boys' voices and harp (1942); and the *War Requiem* (1962).

William Walton (b. 1902) seems to have inherited the great choral tradition of his English predecessors. Perhaps his most famous work is the oratorio *Belshazzar's Feast,* which was presented in Chapter 9. Since then he has composed several film scores, including the music for Sir Laurence Olivier's *Henry V* (1944) and *Hamlet* (1947).

France

Following World War I, France went through a violently anti-Romantic reaction. The informal spokesmen for the new music were a poet, Jean Cocteau, and an eccentric musician, Erik Satie (1866–1925). Satie reacted to past music in his own inimitable way by writing little compositions entitled *Three Pieces in the Shape of a Pear, Three Flabby Preludes for a Dog,* and *Dried Embryos.* He filled his scores with sly directions: "Play like a nightingale with a toothache" and "With astonishment." The purpose of such titles and directions was to ridicule the seriousness with which Romantic and impressionistic composers had approached their craft.

From this stream of irreverent thought came a group of French composers known as "The Six," so named by a critic who likened them to the Russian Five. The most important of these composers were Darius Milhaud (Mee-yo; 1892–1974), Arthur Honegger (Oneh-gair; 1892–1955), and Francis Poulenc (Poo-lank; 1899–1963). These men progressed beyond the Cocteau-Satie phase into mature composers in their own right.

In 1914 Milhaud went to Brazil to serve as

secretary to the French ambassador. Latin-American music made a lasting impression on him, as did the jazz he heard in the United States. Although hindered by arthritis, he toured extensively. During World War II he fled France for the United States, where he taught for several years at Mills College in California.

Listening Guide

Bartók: Concerto for Orchestra

Fifth Movement

Three-Part Form

A

0:00   Introductory theme played forcefully by French horns:

0:05   Tempo becomes very fast and dynamic levels very soft; violins play "perpetual motion" type of theme of continuous fast notes; basses and timpani add interesting rhythmic pattern:

0:34   Fast notes break off; orchestra plays several times a figure with two faster notes and a longer note:

0:46   Fast notes and "perpetual motion" idea begin again; rhythmic interest added by chords played by French horns.

0:57   Pattern with two fast notes and longer note appears again.

1:14   Woodwinds take up "perpetual motion" theme.

Milhaud was a prolific composer. He wrote in every medium. Most of his music is characterized by a French lightness and charm. He is fond of bitonality. Some of his works show the influence of the jazz he heard in Harlem, especially his ballet *La Création du Monde* (The Creation of the World), written in 1923. Its plot is similar to Stravinsky's *The Rite of Spring*. The

---

1:27   Strings answer woodwinds; syncopated chords are played in contrast to rapidly moving notes.

1:53   Bassoon plays theme from opening measures of movement; is followed by other woodwinds, sometimes playing theme in inversion (upside down).

2:05   Tranquil section featuring woodwinds; is based on opening theme.

2:20   Strings answer quietly with notes moving only a half step apart.

B

2:35   Violins begin continuous fast notes again; syncopated rhythmic patterns in low strings in a pedal-note effect.

2:46   Trumpet plays new theme at loud dynamic level:

2:55   Theme played in inversion by another trumpet.

3:03   Theme played by French horn; followed one measure later by trumpet playing theme in inversion; pedal note in low strings changes.

3:11   Trumpet begins developing theme; pedal note changes; music leads to short timpani solo.

3:32   Harp and violins quietly play very high notes as introduction to strings playing a short fugue based on theme; music has an oriental quality.

3:42   Theme played by second violins.

3:53   Theme played by first violins; second violins begin counterpoint.

4:08   Cellos play theme.

4:30   Theme enters quickly in basses, cellos, violas, and violins as woodwinds continue moving notes and then play portion of theme containing repeated notes.

4:38   Same entrance procedure for theme repeated, with theme in inversion.

(Continued on page 228)

similarities stop there, however. Milhaud specifies a 17-piece jazz band instead of a huge orchestra.

Honegger was more conservative than Milhaud. While Milhaud was writing his early irreverent works, Honegger was writing the tone poem *Pacific 231*, a description of a steam-powered train. By that time, 1922, tone poems had become strictly passé. Throughout his life he proceeded to write as he wished,

---

Listening Guide

(Continued from page 227)

4:53 Woodwinds play slightly varied version of theme in rapid order—first flute, second flute, first oboe, second oboe, clarinet, French horn.

5:04 Rapid entrances of varied and inverted theme—second bassoon, bass clarinet, first bassoon, clarinets; fragments of theme passed among strings.

5:19 Repeated notes giving "chattering" effect played by strings; lead to timpani solo.

A'

5:27 Strings begin "perpetual motion" idea; soft dynamic level; timpani also has important part; syncopated pattern played by French horn and low strings.

5:46 Loud pairs of chords by orchestra alternated with runs by strings.

5:54 Two fast notes and longer note pattern featured; very loud and complex.

6:02 Repeated notes from fugue theme played by woodwinds.

6:18 Tranquil section; slower and softer; violins play melodic line similar to tranquil portion found in *A* portion of movement.

6:38 Many changes of notes by half step played by woodwinds.

6:53 "Perpetual motion" theme starts very quietly again in strings; opening theme played in imitation by bassoons, bass clarinet; the opening interval and other fragments of theme played by other woodwinds; music builds slowly in loudness and intensity.

7:33 Opening notes of fugue theme played by muted trumpet, then trombone; music continues to increase in loudness as more instruments enter.

7:43 Coda begins as brasses play fugue theme in long notes, similar to chorale; woodwinds and strings play continuous running notes; very loud.

8:00 Strings play portion of opening theme very loudly in repeated pattern; woodwinds continue rapidly moving notes in contrary direction to strings.

8:20 Music slows down and speeds up again over snare drum roll; woodwinds and strings exchange measures of rapidly moving notes.

8:27 Brasses play portion of fugue theme in long notes.

8:38 Closes with kaleidoscopic rush of sound.

without being unduly influenced by changing compositional fashions. His most successful works are of large scope, involving chorus, soloists, and orchestra. *Le Roi David* (King David, 1921) is the best known of these. Later he wrote more purely instrumental numbers, including symphonies and chamber works.

Poulenc's music most nearly expresses the Cocteau-Satie attitude. Most of his works are intended to be charming and pleasant, even gauche in a well-mannered way. He wrote nothing for full orchestra, preferring instead to write songs, vocal works, and some chamber music. He also wrote two operas: *Mamelles de Tirésias* (1947) and *Les Dialogues des Carmélites* (1953). The two operas are entirely different. *Mamelles* is a surrealistic farce in which people change sex, and babies are born in incubators. It also spoofs some well-known composers and old-fashioned music. *Les Dialogues* is serious and devout—the story of a Carmelite nun who chooses death rather than return to the outside world.

Germany

Carl Orff was born in Munich in 1895, and is best known for the dramatic cantata *Carmina Burana*, which he wrote in 1936. It is based on a famous thirteenth-century collection of student songs and poems that were discovered in an old Bavarian monastery. Orff inserts spoken lines of Latin into the work and makes extensive use of ostinati. The music has a driving rhythm and a primitive feel.

Hebrew

Ernest Bloch (1880–1959) is international in his musical outlook. He is Jewish, and his music shows the strong influence of that culture. He wrote a number of works, such as the Hebrew rhapsody *Schelomo* (Solomon) for cello and orchestra, *Baal Shem* for violin, and *Avodath Hakodesh* (Sacred Service) for baritone, chorus, and orchestra. Born in Geneva, Bloch lived in Switzerland and France before settling in the United States.

Italy

Ottorino Respighi (1879–1936) wrote in the romantic tradition and is one of the few Italian composers to be known for his symphonic music rather than his operas. His most famous works are three nationalistic symphonic poems: the *Fountains of Rome*, the *Pines of Rome*, and *Roman Festivals*. *Fountains* recalls historic sites, *Pines* is impressions of nature, and *Festivals* describes various moods of the Roman people. *Pines* includes the song of a nightingale played from a recording.

Central Europe

Zoltán Kodály (Ko-*die*-ee; 1882–1967) was a Hungarian composer, a collaborator and friend of Béla Bartók. Both men spent years collecting and editing Hungarian folk music. Kodály was not an experimental composer, but rather chose to update idioms that would be understandable and appreciated by the people. At times his style is strongly romantic. He is well known among music teachers in America for his contributions to teaching children to sing accurately and listen carefully.

Leoš Janáček (*Ya*-na-check; 1854–1928) is a Czechoslovakian composer who has been compared to the nationalistic Russian Mussorgsky because of his rather untrained, roughhewn style. He never lost his love of folk music and its style. Many scholars consider him an underrated composer, and his music is much better known in Europe than in America. His most famous work is an opera, *Jenufa*. He also composed a *Slavonic Mass, Sinfonietta* (for orchestra, with heavy brass scoring), and a number of chamber works.

Latin America

The Brazilian Heitor Villa-Lobos (1887–1959) was encouraged by Milhaud in 1915 while the latter composer was with the embassy. Villa-Lobos was a man of tremendous energy who adopted ideas from many sources. His greatest inspiration was the music of the Brazilian people. Although his 2,000 works are of uneven quality, many are fascinating and unique. His *Bachianas Brasileiras* and *Choros* are filled with rich sound that alternates between being romantic and blatant.

Villa-Lobos composed nine *Bachianas Brasileiras,* in which he tried to combine Bach with Brazilian music. Villa-Lobos wrote: "This is a special kind of musical composition based on an intimate knowledge of J. S. Bach and also on the composer's affinity with the harmonic, contrapuntal, and melodic atmosphere of the folklore of the northern region of Brazil." The "Aria" of *Bachianas Brasileiras No. 5* was composed in 1938. In 1945 a second movement was added.

The "Aria" is for soprano and eight cellos—hardly a typical scoring. The music is not typical either. During much of the work the singer just vocalizes on *ah.* The melody is luscious:

The middle section is somewhat like a Brazilian popular song, with syncopation and frequent changes of tempo. The soloist's line sounds improvised. The text is a poem praising the beauties of nature. When the opening theme returns, the singer hums it.

Carlos Chávez (1899–1978) is Mexico's leading composer. His *Symphonie Indea* is based on genuine Inca music, and his *Toccata for Percussion* is an exciting, rhythmic work.

Alberto Ginastera (Hee-nah-*stair*-ah; b. 1916) is an Argentinian composer who has achieved fame for his instrumental and vocal works. His music sparkles with Latin-American color. Two of his operas are *Bomarzo* and *Don Rodrigo.*

Russia

Since the revolution in 1918, the philosophy of Social Realism has dominated in Russia. It demands that composers write music that is useful and understandable to the general public, so composers in communist countries are required to be acutely aware of the musical traditions of the people. *Avant garde* compositions are frowned upon by the government because of its desire to prevent cultural elitism.

One of the most important Russian composers of this century, Dimitri Shostakovich, is discussed in Chapter 10. Another important composer is Sergei Prokofiev (Pro-*ko*-fee-eff; 1891–1953). His Second Violin Concerto serves as the concluding work in this discussion of mainstream twentieth-century music.

Prokofiev's Second Violin Concerto

Prokofiev composed his Second Violin Concerto in 1935 for the French violinist Soëtans. The work, like much of Prokofiev's music, seems to be a mixture of nineteenth-century lyricism and twentieth-century dissonance and hardness. The result is some truly beautiful and interesting music.

First movement. The first movement is in traditional sonata form, except without the double exposition. A *Listening Guide* for the movement appears on pages 232–233.

Second movement. The slow movement is testimony to the romantic side of Prokofiev's writing. As the strings delicately pluck out accompanying chords, the solo violin plays this expressive melody:

Later a second theme appears; it contrasts with the earlier lyric melody. The first theme, somewhat varied, returns to close out the movement.

Third movement. In contrast to the second movement, the third is aggressive, rhythmic, and dissonant, thereby showing the other side of Prokofiev's musical personality. The movement has several themes; the main one is:

Although the movement contains some moments of lyrical melody, the overall quality is one of brashness.

Sergei Prokofiev

Sergei Prokofiev (1891–1953) was born in a village in southern Russia. His mother taught him to play the piano and encouraged him to compose. By the age of nine he had written a three-act opera. After his family moved to Moscow, Prokofiev studied with outstanding teacher-composers, including Rimsky-Korsakov, there and at the Conservatory in St. Petersburg. In his early years his music was more dissonant and the melodies unpredictable; his teacher considered him somewhat of a musical revolutionary. Before the revolution in 1917 he had composed his First Piano Concerto and his well-known *Classical Symphony.*

After the revolution he left his native country and lived in Paris. He continued to compose and give concerts. In 1933 he decided to return to the Soviet Union, where he was greeted warmly by both the public and the government. As he grew older, his music became more mellow. During these years he composed the popular *Peter and the Wolf, Lieutenant Kijé, Alexander Nevsky,* and other works. Following World War II he, along with Shostakovich, was accused of being "formalistic," but he did not allow the pressure from the government to interfere with his work or musical style. By the time he died Prokofiev had composed eight operas, seven ballets, seven symphonies, five piano concertos, two violin concertos, two cello concertos, music for films and chamber groups, ten piano sonatas, and many songs. Prokofiev is one of the giants of twentieth-century music in terms of both quantity and quality of composition.

Listening Guide

Prokofiev: Violin Concerto No. 2

First Movement

Sonata Form

Exposition

0:00   First theme, outlining minor triad, played softly by solo violin:

0:24   First theme in violas and cellos; free material (not related to any theme) in solo violin.

0:46   First theme in imitation between low strings and solo violin; rather soft.

1:21   Transition theme, marchlike, played in little faster by woodwinds; free material for solo violin:

1:40   Descending pairs of chords played somewhat softly by woodwinds, with solo violin playing free material.

2:03   Second theme, in major key, played by solo violin; slower tempo:

2:29   Horn plays part of second theme, followed by solo violin.

2:44   Oboe plays part of second theme in high notes.

2:55   Descending pairs of chords again; free material in solo violin.

3:02   Tempo increases.

3:12   Codetta, in rapid tempo and louder dynamic level; solo violin outlines chords; music grows louder.

3:33   Music becomes calmer, with solo violin playing figures outlining chords.

3:43   Pause.

Development

3:45   Solo violin and strings outline chords, quietly and slowly, linking exposition and development.

4:12   First theme plucked in low strings; decorated first theme played by solo violin; off-beat chords plucked by upper strings.

4:33   First theme appears in the first note of the pairs of eighth notes played by solo violin; faster tempo:

4:49   First theme plucked by low strings; solo violin plays decorative material in triplets based on the first theme; afterbeats in strings.

5:01   Second theme in long note values played by winds at rather full dynamic level.

5:15   Second theme in long note values played by violins; free material for the solo violin; music is quieter and slower.

6:01   First theme plucked by low strings; afterbeat chords plucked by violins; free material for solo violin.

6:18   First theme fragment passed among woodwinds, with solo violin and low strings playing material based on scales.

6:37   Loud chords in descending patterns; three consecutive sets of four chords in pulsating manner.

Recapitulation

6:47   First theme in low strings; soft dynamic level.

7:26   Transition theme in woodwinds; free material in solo violin; faster tempo.

7:53   Chords in woodwinds in long note values; solo violin outlines chords.

8:11   Second theme played in high notes by solo violin; slower tempo.

8:41   Second theme, with rhythmic changes, played in imitation by solo violin and strings.

9:12   Coda begins softly at a fast tempo, with chords outlined by solo violin; chords in long note values in woodwinds.

9:43   Fragment of first theme in low strings and horn and violin in imitation; rather soft dynamic level.

10:23   Closes quietly with plucked chords by strings and solo violin.

Béla Bartók

Béla Bartók (1881–1945) was born in a small town in Hungary. His father was director of an agricultural school, and his mother was his first music teacher.. After she was widowed, she became a schoolteacher, and they moved frequently. Finally they settled in Pressburg, where Bartók began serious study of piano and composition. In 1899 he enrolled in the Royal Conservatory in Budapest. He became an excellent pianist and gave concerts throughout Europe. During much of his life, piano teaching was Bartók's main source of income.

Bartók first became noted, however, not as a pianist or composer but as a collector of Hungarian folk songs. He made a significant contribution to scholarship in this area.

In 1907 he became a professor of piano at the Royal Conservatory and spent most of the next 30 years in Budapest. He received little recognition until the late 1920s, when his works began to earn attention outside of Hungary.

After the rise of Hitler and the subsequent collaboration of Hungary with Nazi Germany, Bartók felt impelled to leave his homeland. In 1940 he came to the United States. He had to leave most of his worldly goods behind, and his health was failing. He was appointed to a position at Columbia University, primarily to continue his folk music research. He received a few commissions for compositions. ASCAP (the American Society of Composers, Authors, and Publishers) provided him with medical care, and jazz musician Benny Goodman also aided him. In 1945 he died of leukemia, with his true stature as a composer still not appreciated.

Béla Bartók

Bartók's early works display an admiration for Richard Strauss and Debussy, but in 1911 he changed to more barbaric, heavily dissonant works. He is best remembered for his six string quartets, *Music for Strings, Percussion, and Celesta*, three piano concertos, and the Concerto for Orchestra. His *Mikrokosmos* is a set of 153 piano pieces in six volumes, arranged so that the music progresses from simple pieces for the beginner to works of awesome difficulty. His later works are more consonant and mellow.

25

Twenty-Five

Expressionism and Primitivism

Although dissatisfaction with Romanticism began to appear late in the nineteenth century—in music of the Russian Five and Debussy, for example—the real break came just before World War I. Two somewhat similar courses were taken: *expressionism* and *primitivism*. The two movements largely spent themselves by the end of the first quarter of this century.

Expressionism

One writer has described expressionism as "a particular attitude of hedonistic pessimism, joyful scepticism touching on morbid sophistication." Its center was Vienna, the home of Sigmund Freud—a circumstance that may or may not be related. Vienna was also the home of the painters Wassily Kandinsky (1866–1944), Paul Klee (1879–1940), Oskar Kokoschka (b. 1886) and Franz Marc (1880–1916). These painters distorted images on their canvases and probed into the realm of the subconscious. They depicted hallucinations that defied conventional ideas of beauty in an effort to

achieve maximum expression. Their colors are often blatant and unreal, with emphasis on intensity of experience and grotesque subjects. Expressionism takes special interest in the demonic forces hidden within the human personality. "The Cry," the painting by Edvard Munch on page 237, indicates the nature of art during this time. Many paintings are completely abstract, especially those by Kandinsky. Elements of expressionism found their way to America in the writings of Franz Kafka (1883–1924). In a sense, the writers James Joyce, William Faulkner, and Tennessee Williams are descendants of this tradition.

The musical leader of expressionism was Arnold Schoenberg. Beginning with his Op. 11 (*Three Pieces for Piano*) written in 1909, he began composing atonal music—music with no tonal center. To musicians of the time, eliminating the tonal center was almost as traumatic as eliminating gravity from our universe would be to us. It was just that unimaginable. To fill the void left by the lack of tonality, Schoenberg concentrated on changes in orchestral color. Instead of changing key center, he alters the timbre. This interest in sounds is characteristic of twentieth-century composers.

Schoenberg's one-character opera *Erwartung* is typical of the expressionists' preoccupation with the macabre. The opera portrays the actions and thoughts of a woman who goes at night in search of her lover in the forest. In her overemotional state, her moods range from joy to fear to anguish and hysteria. She can't find him. Exhausted, she sits down on a bench. She feels something at her foot, and discovers that it is the body of her lover. She lies down beside it and kisses it. Her mood changes as she reviles her dead lover for having been unfaithful to her (Death being the "other woman"). She kicks the body. Later she caresses it again, and as the sun rises, she sings her irrational goodbyes.

In 1912 Schoenberg wrote *Pierrot Lunaire*, a setting of 21 short poems by Albert Giraud. The poems are sophisticated and expressionistic. One verse of the poem "The Sick Moon" is:

You die of unappeasable sorrow,
Of longing, deep within,
You nocturnal, deathly-sick moon,
There on the dark pillow of the sky.

To add to the expression of the music, Schoenberg calls for a sing-song vocal style called *sprechstimme*, which is a combination of speaking and singing. Audiences found the work eerie. One critic said, "If this is the music of the future, I pray that my creator may spare me from it."

Closely associated with Schoenberg were Alban Berg and Anton Webern. Although both men moved on in their mature years to individual styles, they followed the expressionistic tendency to some extent. Berg's opera *Wozzeck* (*Vot*-zek) is an important work of the twentieth century. The plot is about a soldier, Wozzeck, who offers himself to a doctor for medical experiments in an effort to support his mistress and her child. She is unfaithful despite Wozzeck's devotion, and he slits her throat. He throws the knife into a pond, then, afraid that it might be found, he wades into the water after it and drowns.

Primitivism

A second main trend in the early twentieth century was an interest in the art and music of non-Western civilization. African sculpture and masks began to interest the artistic world, as did Gauguin's paintings of Polynesian culture. Although it was written in the nineteenth century, James Fenimore Cooper's phrase "the magnificent savage" didn't catch on until the twentieth century.

The high point of primitivism was probably reached in 1913 with the premiere of Igor Stravinsky's ballet *Le Sacre du Printemps* (*The Rite of Spring*). The music was written for a production conceived by Sergei Diaghilev, impresario of the Ballet Russe. Each year he brought a new and stunning ballet production to Paris. With keen artistic judgment and calculated showmanship, he decided to capitalize on the Parisians' interest in primitive art. He chose to depict prehistoric rites culminating in the sacrifice of a human being—hardly typical of the stories usually associated with classical ballet.

On opening night the ballet and its music literally caused a riot. The audience was split between those who cheered and those who jeered at the new production. Objects were hurled into the orchestra pit and onto the stage. Pandemonium reigned. No one, not even the dancers, could hear the music. The choreographer stood in the wings yelling out the rhythmic pattern so that the dancers could stay together.

How could any serious work, written in good faith, cause such violence among a fashionable audience? Probably no one on that famous evening in 1913 thought about it at the time, but the disagreement involved the purpose of the fine arts. The audience was accustomed to ballets that presented pleasant music amid beautiful scenery. Their main expectation of art, music, or ballet was that it be lovely. In *The Rite of Spring*, the dancers were clothed in dark brown burlap; their gestures were rough and angular, lacking the grace and charm of classical ballet movements. The music seemed brutal to the point of vulgarity. The very basis of artistic belief was being assaulted.

The Cry *by Munch. Courtesy of Vaerihg—Art Reference Bureau.*

A simplified score for the First Act of *The Rite of Spring* is included in the *Study Guide and Scores;* the use of the score greatly improves the understanding of the music. Act I opens with an orchestral "Introduction." The scene is a primitive forest in which strange and eerie sounds are heard, buzzing and bubbling. The bassoon begins in its highest range with a haunting, hooting quality. Its melody is not very tuneful. The pitches are confined to a narrow range and the rhythmic pattern is irregular, with frequent stops and starts.

Lento, tempo rubato

Bassoon

In the "Dance of the Adolescents" that follows, Stravinsky unleashes the potent power of rhythm. The effect resembles the wild beating of savage drums. The strings achieve this by playing a dissonant chord with short bow strokes, each punctuated by a rest. Suddenly eight horns (four more than are normally used) enter to add to the barbaric sound. This sensational new effect is produced by an irregular pattern of accents:

Strings

Between the accented chords there is sometimes one chord, sometimes two, three, four, or five. Gone is the underlying regular beat that had prevailed for 300 years. In its place are irregular rhythms that have their roots in nonliterate cultures.

As the chords bump along in their irregular way, several short primitive-sounding tunes are heard:

The tunes encompass only a few pitches and sound as though they were being played on a crude flute or pipe with a limited number of pitches.

The "Dance of Abduction" is even wilder. A scampering tune is played by the woodwinds and answered by a horn call. The timpani have a prominent part that contributes to the violent mood. The meter signatures change with dizzying frequency. At one point they occur in this order: $\frac{7}{8}, \frac{3}{4}, \frac{6}{8}, \frac{2}{4}, \frac{6}{8}, \frac{3}{4}$. Polyrhythm—the superimposing of two or more rhythms—is also evident.

"Round Dances of Spring" brings some relief from the frenzy that precedes it. The tempo is slower and the flutes and other woodwinds play a clearer, sweeter melody that resembles an American Indian tune in its simplicity:

Flutes, Violas

Later the orchestra takes up the melody.

The music becomes energetic again in the scene entitled "Games of the Rival Tribes." Stravinsky expresses the idea of competition musically by pitting one section of the orchestra against another, each with its own distinctive music. Then, in the manner of a contest or debate, the "tribes" answer each other. The music is often *bitonal*—occurring in two keys at once.

The "Entrance of the Sage" brings back the main thematic material with a thick orchestration.

Act 1 ends with "Dance of the Earth." It, too, suggests violence and upheaval. The low-pitched instruments play an ostinato line, but, because of the dense quality of the music, the individual lines tend to become lost. The ballet must be seen with this portion of the music if the music is to be fully appreciated.

The second and final act of the ballet depicts the sacrifice of a young maiden to the Chosen One so that the God of Spring may be satisfied. It is similar in style to the first act.

To the listener hearing it for the first time,

The Rite of Spring may sound like a jumble of random notes. It may even seem that the instrumentalists can play anything they want, and no one will know the difference. Such an idea is, of course, incorrect. Stravinsky carefully planned everything in the score, and he writes detailed directions for the playing of each part. He even goes so far as to tell the timpani player when to change from hard to soft sticks, the French horn players when to tilt the bells of their instruments in an upward direction, and the cellists when to retune a string so that a chord can be played on open strings to achieve a more raucous effect.

Primitivism appealed to other composers during this time. Béla Bartók wrote *Allegro Barbaro* in 1911, and several of his other works are wild and rhapsodic. Some of Sergei Prokofiev's early works have driving rhythms and blatant melodies. Ernest Bloch's Violin Sonata, written in the 1920s, has a violent character.

Alban Berg

Alban Berg, the son of a shopkeeper, was born in 1885 in Vienna. At the age of 14 he took up composing, an interest that kept him occupied when he was confined by asthma and poor health. After graduation from school he took a position as an accountant for the government. He met Schoenberg when he answered Schoenberg's newspaper advertisement for composition students. He was Schoenberg's student for about seven years.

Berg's early compositions were in the Wagnerian, nineteenth-century tradition. But by 1911, the last year he studied with Schoenberg, Berg had changed to atonal, expressionistic works. Most of his instrumental music

is for chamber-music groups, except for *Three Orchestral Pieces*. Later works in the tone-row idiom (see Chapter 26) include a *Chamber Concerto* and his esteemed Violin Concerto.

Berg's place in music history is largely the result of his opera *Wozzeck*, which he composed in 1921. The plot, described on page 236, is pure expressionistic theater. The opera is carefully planned in terms of its musical forms. Its three acts each contain five scenes, and each scene uses a form: passacaglia, fugue, suite, sonata, scherzo, and so on.

He died in 1935 of blood poisoning that resulted from a bee sting and a subsequent infection.

Igor Stravinsky

Igor Stravinsky was born in 1882. His father was the leading bass at the Imperial Opera in St. Petersburg (Leningrad). The boy studied piano, but not intensively, because his parents wanted him to become a lawyer. He studied law at the University of St. Petersburg and simultaneously studied music with Rimsky-Korsakov.

Stravinsky soon became associated with Sergei Diaghilev, manager of the Ballet Russe. Once a year for several years, Diaghilev brought Russian music and ballet to Paris with great financial and artistic success. In 1910, after hearing only one of Stravinsky's compositions, he assigned the 25-year-old composer to write a new ballet. It was *The Firebird*, which is usually heard today in a suite that Stravinsky himself arranged. *The Firebird* was so successful that it earned for the young composer the chance to write a second new ballet, *Petrouchka*, for the next season. Like *The Firebird*, *Petrouchka* is based on a Russian legend. Stravinsky was given another commission, and this time his creation was the startling *The Rite of Spring*.

The year 1913 was the last before World War I, which seriously curtailed artistic activity in Europe. During the war Stravinsky moved to neutral Switzerland. The revolution in Russia cut off his income, and the ballet company had disbanded. He lived quietly in Switzerland for five years, recovering from a serious illness.

After the armistice, he settled in France. At that time Paris was rich with artists and writers—Picasso, Valéry, Gide—who expressed Neo-Classical sentiments in their works. Stravinsky became a French citizen and traveled widely as a conductor and pianist. In 1931 he came to the United States to lecture at Harvard University. When World War II prevented his return to Europe, he settled in Hollywood; he became an American citizen in 1945. Although none of Stravinsky's later

Igor Stravinsky at the age of 84. Courtesy of Louis Ouzer, Rochester, N.Y.

compositions caused riotous premieres, he is considered one of the greatest composers of this century. On his eightieth birthday he was the honored guest of President Kennedy at the White House, and on another occasion he was the subject of a special one-hour program presented on a national television network. He died in 1971.

Despite superficial changes of style, Stravinsky remained true to his objective conception of music: Since a piece of music is something a composer makes, it is essentially an object rather than a representation of his soul. Therefore a person's compositions need not be in a consistent personal style. The skill of composition is paramount; the composer's personality irrelevant.

Twenty-Six

Intellectualism: Mind over Music

Musical styles seem to move in either of two directions: toward emotional and subjective expression or toward intellectual objectivity. The Baroque period was more emotional than the Renaissance, and it was followed by the objectivity of the Classical period. Then came the most subjective style of all, the Romantic. The inevitable direction of music after Wagner and Debussy was toward more objectivity. And so there evolved an attitude called *Neo-Classicism*. It sought to duplicate the restraint of the Classical period and viewed artistic endeavor in a less passionate light. Neo-Classicism is exemplified in the sensitive painting "The Lovers" by Picasso (page 142). In some respects Mondrian's "Broadway Boogie Woogie" (colorplate IV) also represents an intellectual approach to painting.

On this matter Igor Stravinsky's position was straightforward and consistent: "What is important for the clear ordering of the work, for its crystallization, is that all the . . . elements . . . should be properly subjugated and finally subjected to the rule of law before they intoxicate us." For him, writing a musical composition was like solving a problem; it was a task to be done by applying the intellect. Therefore, music is meant to express nothing except the composer's ability to contrive interesting tonal and rhythmic patterns.

This Neo-Classical position earned Stravinsky a reputation as leader of a trend euphoniously named the Back-to-Bach movement. Baroque forms such as the concerto grosso were revived during this time, and there was a renewed emphasis on counterpoint and the linear aspect of music.

Stravinsky's Symphony of Psalms

The Neo-Classical, intellectual frame of mind was dominant throughout much of Stravinsky's life. He wrote stage works on such Classical subjects as *Oedipus Rex, Orpheus,* and *Apollon Musagete,* in addition to Neo-Classical instrumental works. His *Symphony of Psalms* was commissioned by the Boston Symphony Orchestra and completed in 1930. According to his *Autobiography,* Stravinsky went about the assignment very rationally. He decided to write a work of "great contrapuntal development" and chose a choral and instrumental ensemble in which "the two elements should be on an equal footing." He then decided on verses from the Psalms. The orchestra is unique: no violins, violas, or clarinets; twice the number of oboes and flutes, two extra trumpets, and two pianos. A choir of only men and boys is preferred.

First movement. The text for the first movement is taken from Psalm 39, Verses 12–13. It is, "Hear my prayer, O Lord, and give ear to my cry." This movement can best be studied while following the Listening Guide that appears below.

Listening Guide

Stravinsky: *Symphony of Psalms*

First Movement

0:00   Begins with short, accented chord, followed by oboes and bassoons outlining chords in free-sounding manner; same idea repeated two more times.

0:23   French horn and cellos play opening portion of first theme *(A)*:

0:34   Altos enter singing first theme *(A)*; accompanying woodwinds change to outlining chords at half the speed of previous outlining; some persistently repeated figures also heard.

0:53   Chorus enters; oboes soon change to descending line of alternating notes.

1:10   *A* theme performed again by altos and oboes; cellos and string basses play a steady pattern of very short notes.

1:30   Short, accented chords followed by chord outlines, as in opening of movement; tenors sing a line containing only one pitch.

1:41   Second theme *(B)* sung by altos and basses; trombones and bassoons play steady line of very short notes:

2:25   Music reaches climactic point; chord outlining played again by orchestra; chorus all in same rhythmic pattern.

2:33   *A* theme sung by tenors; very short "dry" notes played by low strings and oboes.

2:51   Sopranos sing first theme *(A)*; descending line of alternating notes played again by oboes and piano; music increases in intensity.

3:02   Brasses enter as music moves gradually to final climactic chord.

3:20   Closes at loud dynamic level.

Second movement. The text of the second movement is an affirmation of the power of God: "I waited patiently for the Lord: and He inclined to me, and heard my cry." The form of the movement is a double fugue. The opening subject is played by the oboes and is another angular melody:

After the first subject is played by the cellos and basses, the second subject is sung by the choral group. This melody is less angular than the instrumental subject.

The orchestra and chorus develop their subjects. The first four notes of the orchestral subject are repeated in an ostinato manner as the chorus reaches a climax of sound. The movement ends with a sudden hush.

Third movement. The third movement is a song of praise, beginning with the word "Alleluia," followed by "Laudate Dominum" (Praise ye the Lord). These words are heard frequently during the movement.

The movement is divided into three clearly defined sections. The first and last are slow, while the middle section is rhythmic and faster. The first section is built on the Alleluia figure sung by the choir (shown in the previous musical example), which is developed later against an ostinato in the orchestra. The second section features rapidly repeated chords in the brasses played against an ostinato in the piano and low strings:

In the third section the original tempo returns, and the chorus sings a melodic figure against a sustained background. A canon is heard, and the music works toward a mighty climax of sound, which subsides with a repetition of the words "Alleluia, laudate Dominum."

Hindemith's Kleine Kammermusik für fünf Bläser, Op. 24, No. 2

Paul Hindemith was a German composer who lived from 1895 to 1963. He was strongly Neo-Classical in his approach to composing. Much of his music sounds like an updated version of the eighteenth-century counterpoint of Bach. Translated, the title of this piece means "Little chamber music for five winds." The work is for woodwind quintet: oboe, flute, clarinet, bassoon, and French horn. It was composed in 1922 and represents Hindemith at his exuberant best. Like Stravinsky's mature works, it shows strong Neo-Classical tendencies in its sparse scoring and the short, concise format of its movements. There is no attempt to impress the listener with lush sonorities.

The first movement is marked *Lustig* (cheerful). Its chromatic first theme is clearly presented by the clarinet and then the oboe:

The accompanying rhythmic figure is taken from the first four notes of the theme. The second theme in the movement is more songlike and is first played by the oboe.

The second movement is a waltz. The sections are rather short, and their pattern is *A A B C B A*.

The third movement is marked *Ruhig und einfach* (Quiet and simple). It's an elegant slow movement with long melodic lines. There are several ostinato accompanying patterns. One feature of the movement is the imaginative manner in which Hindemith writes for the instruments. In one place the flute plays notes lower than those of the clarinet and horn, an unusual arrangement that gives an interesting tonal effect.

The fourth movement is quite fast. It's built around a short pounding theme that alternates periodically with short solos for each instrument:

The fifth movement is very fast, with an "arch" form that is *A B C B A*. The differences among the themes are as much rhythmic as melodic. The first theme has accents falling logically on the beat:

In the second theme the accents occur off the beat, while a regular bass line is sounded in contrary motion (its pitches descend when the upper notes ascend, and vice versa):

There is a contrasting center section, then the first two themes are heard again—the second one before the first. The movement concludes with a coda containing fragments of both themes.

Tone-Row Music

Arnold Schoenberg (whose expressionistic compositions were mentioned in Chapter 25) experimented with different principles of composition until 1923, when he settled on a type of atonality variously called *twelve-tone, tone-row, dodecaphonic,* or *serial* music. The principle is relatively simple. The composer arranges the 12 tones of the chromatic scale in any order. This is the "row"—a series of intervals that form a unique melody. It's not a chromatic scale, because the notes do not progress by half steps. The pitches in the row need not all appear within the range of a single octave, either, so wide interval leaps are sometimes encountered. No tone in the row can be repeated until all 12 tones have been heard, because such repetition would emphasize one particular note. No special importance is attached to any tone in the row; all are equally significant. So there can be no tonic or tonal center.

While the tone-row technique may appear limited at first glance, it has been calculated that there are 479,001,600 different tone rows available. And each row can be treated in countless ways. It can appear in chords as well as in melodies. The row can be transposed, or it can be moved to a different octave. It can be subdivided into phrases of different lengths.

Tone-row music is *not* a set of variations on a theme. Schoenberg saw it as an entirely new approach to music, not a vehicle for more examples of theme and variations. In some works the row can seldom be detected by ear. It is more of a springboard for musical ideas than a recognizable theme.

Schoenberg's "Unentrinnbar"

In the late 1920s Schoenberg wrote several choral works, including *Four Pieces for Mixed Chorus*. One of these is "Unentrinnbar" ("Inevitable"). In this work the sopranos begin the row, which is easily recognizable in its various forms as the piece progresses:

The tenor part enters exactly four measures later, in strict imitation. The alto part starts in measure 3 and presents the inversion, or upside-down version, of the row. The example includes the original row for purposes of comparison:

The bass then enters in strict imitation of the alto.

The soprano part begins something different after it has completed the row. The two versions are:

The second line is the reverse of the first. The musical term for this relationship is *retrograde*. In this piece the rhythm of the retrograde differs from the rhythm of the original row.

Finally the fourth version of the row is heard, the *retrograde-inversion*:

The four versions of the row—the original row, the inversion, the retrograde, and the retrograde-inversion—represent the basic techniques of the tone-row system. Here is the scheme for the entire 31 measures of Schoenberg's "Inevitable":

The rules of tone-row composition as applied in pieces of music display some flexibility. "Inevitable" adheres to the rules closely, probably because it's a short piece. But the tone-row composer can move notes from one octave to another in a technique called *octave displacement*. The composer can also spell a note differently, as long as it sounds the same.

The notes F$^\sharp$ and G$^\flat$, for example, are the same pitch and can be seen in the excerpt showing the original and the retrograde. Notice the first note of the original and the last note of the retrograde. Some repetition of notes is allowed in the row, as long as it does not give dominance to a particular tone. A few short interruptions of the row are permissible.

Serialism

Since 1950 a number of composers have turned to the tone-row principles developed by Schoenberg. This trend can be attributed primarily to the influence of a quiet student of his: Anton Webern (*Vay*-burn; 1883–1945). He wrote in the same compositional idiom as Schoenberg, but his music is even more austere and economical. Of his 31 compositions the longest is ten minutes, and his complete works can be performed in less than three hours. His dynamics are usually the softest imaginable, and his frail tone-row melodies are passed note by note from one instrument to another in the subtlest kind of interplay. The principle of economy in composing was carried to its limit by Webern. If he had written more sparsely, one feels, the music would disappear.

A parallel to Webern's music can be found in the art of a twentieth-century Russian painter named Kasimir Malevich. In 1918 he painted "White on White," which appears on page 248. Malevich's painting may be an idea carried to an extreme point, but the principle of a calm, objective, abstract art form holds some artistic appeal.

On first hearing, Webern's music sounds like muted chaos. Little blobs of sound appear and disappear at apparent random between gaps of silence. But intensive listening discloses that what at first seems disorganized is actually organization of an intense and compact nature. The musical ideas are trimmed mercilessly to exclude every bit of waste or decoration. Only the absolute essentials remain.

Webern's Concerto for Nine Instruments

Among Webern's most interesting works is a composition that is only nine minutes long: Concerto for Nine Instruments. It carries the idea of tone-row to a further level of development. The Concerto is based on this row:

The brackets over the row indicate that it can be divided into three-note segments, each consisting of two adjacent notes and one that is either a line or space further away. The first three notes can be considered a miniature row, followed by its retrograde-inversion, retrograde, and inversion. So the row itself is highly organized.

The composition starts:

If you analyze the example, you can see that the groups of three notes are retained, although with octave displacement. The first group is played by the oboe, the second by the flute, the third by the trumpet, and the fourth by the clarinet. Notice also that a different rhythm is associated with each three-note group, and that different articulations (slurring and tonguing) are specified.

The original three-note groups appear again in the Concerto, but the order of their appearance is varied, as are the time values and timbres. In the following excerpt notice that the three-note figures have the interval sequence varied, the time values and articulations reversed, and the timbre changed.

Webern's composition has no actual themes. It is held together by the row and the three-note motives. The composition is generated from a principle of composing that presents the same ingredients continuously but in

"White on White" (1918) by Kasimir Malevich. Collection the Museum of Modern Art, New York.

ever-changing ways. "It is always something different and yet always the same," Webern said of his music. In any case, his intellectual control over the music seems to be complete.

Anti-Intellectualism

Following World War I French artists, musicians, and writers grew increasingly anti-

Romantic in their reaction against the seriousness of recent styles in art and music. The informal spokesmen for the new music were the poet Jean Cocteau, and the musician Erik Satie, both of whom are mentioned in Chapter 24. On one occasion Satie created some music that he asked the audience *not* to notice. He instructed them to talk or wander about the room as it was being played. When the audience did not follow his suggestion, he became extremely irritated and walked around urging individuals to talk and otherwise ignore his music.

Elements of this irreverent approach found their way into the music of other composers, especially Francis Poulenc and Darius Milhaud. When balanced with a skilled composing technique, anti-intellectualism was in some ways a refreshing change from the heaviness of nineteenth-century music.

Aleatory Music: The "Uncomposition"

While Satie and Cocteau were anti-intellectual, the American John Cage (b. 1912) is purposely nonintellectual. He has been a prime promoter of chance or *aleatory* music. In such music the sounds are determined partly by chance and are therefore unpredictable. A clarinet player, for example, may be instructed to play anything he or she wishes for six beats, or to rest during that time. Or the selection of notes may depend on throwing dice. One of Cage's piano pieces is written on several disconnected sheets of paper. The player is told to drop the sheets, pick them up at random, and then play the pages in the new order. Cage has also written a composition for 24 radios and 12 "performers." The performers switch stations according to directions involving the use of a stopwatch. The resulting sounds are clearly a product of chance.

To understand what Cage is trying to achieve, you need to know his underlying philosophy, even if you don't agree with it. For centuries Western civilization held to the idea of progress, the idea of working toward goals. Through increases in knowledge, which in turn led to such practical outcomes as improved medical care, more food, a shorter work week, etc., it was held that the human race was progressing. But the idea of progress has come under attack in the twentieth century from existential philosophy and from advocates of oriental religious beliefs. The idea of progress is false, they claim; there is only change, not progress. The implications of the only-change, no-goal-toward-which-to-progress position are enormous. It's a little like removing the goal lines and uprights on the football field and ceasing to keep score or time; the game just happens. About the only assumption that one can make is that the players will eventually tire and stop playing.

This view rejects the idea that art must have meaning. As the poet Archibald MacLeish says:

A poem should not mean
But be.

Depicting a Campbell's soup can or comic strip character in a painting is not, as some people believe, a comment on the vulgarity of modern civilization. The content of such works is so blatant that it no longer invites interpretation, which is the way the artist wants it. A picture is a picture, and that's all. In his book *Silence* Cage urges the composer to "give up the desire to control sound, clear his mind of music [in the usual sense] and set about discovering means to let sounds be themselves rather than vehicles for man-made theories or expression of human sentiments." Relying on chance devices is one way in which Cage and others encourage the listener to listen to sound rather than to seek relationships in the sounds. While at first glance it may seem foolish to determine musical sequence by dropping pages on the floor, such a procedure comes from the consistent application of a philosophical position.

Cage's musical practices and philosophy have been adopted and adapted by composers such as Karlheinz Stockhausen. In a complete switch from his electronic works of the 1950s, Stockhausen's *Originale* (written in 1961) is based on a scheme of simultaneous, incoherent "happenings." The whole effect is something like the clowns taking over the circus. In one scene the directions are:

> *Pianist and percussionist put on clothes brought in by cloakroom attendant. The pianist takes off his cultic robes and puts on Oriental female costume. . . . When he is ready, he begins to brew up tea at the piano.*

It is difficult to predict much of a future for chance music. Although any object can be contemplated for what it is, the trouble with Pop art and chance music is that they lack the evidence of skillful invention and elegance necessary to make the works artistically interesting. Very little talent or devotion is usually exhibited in a painting of a soup can or in a musical work calling on the performer to manipulate a dial on a radio. As was pointed out in Chapter 1, things that nearly everyone can do are not valued highly.

Paul Hindemith

Paul Hindemith was born in Hanau, Germany in 1895. When he was 11 and his father objected to a musical career for him, he ran away from home. He earned his living by playing violin in dance orchestras and movie theaters. (Those were the days of silent pictures.) He later enrolled in the Conservatory at Frankfurt. There he won a prize for one of his compositions, a string quartet. After another successful string quartet he became interested in jazz, and this interest resulted in his Concerto for Piano and Twelve Instruments.

In 1927 Hindemith was appointed professor at the Hochschule in Berlin. He encouraged his students to learn several different instruments and to participate in a variety of musical activities. At that time he was much interested in practical, "usable" music; the term *Gebrauchsmusik*, which means literally use-music, was applied to it. This music was not technically difficult and was meant for everyday use. Between 1936 and 1955 he composed a sonata for almost every orchestral instrument, including the tuba.

When the Nazis came to power, German culture was purged of anything more modern than the music of Wagner. Shortly before the outbreak of World War II, Hindemith escaped and emigrated to the United States, where he later became a citizen. He accepted an appointment to the faculty at Yale University and continued to teach there until 1953. He retired to live in Zurich, Switzerland, although he did make many trips back to the United States. He died in 1963.

Hindemith's best known works are two operas: *Mathis der Maler* (Matthias the Painter), which is based on the life of Matthias Grünewald, and *Die Harmonie der Welt* (The Harmony of the World), which was based on the life of the sixteenth-century astronomer Johannes Kepler. Hindemith arranged symphonic poems that bear the same names as the operas.

Hindemith was influential not only for his compositions, but also for his writings on music theory and harmony. Several of his books have become standards for many students in music. He was a leader in the "Back-to-Bach" movement.

Anton Webern

Webern was born Anton von Webern, but he dropped the royal *von* from his name after the 1918 revolution in Austria. He was born in 1883, the son of a mining engineer in southern Austria. While in school young Webern took lessons in cello, piano, and music theory. When he completed school at the age of 18, his family gave him a trip to the Wagner Festival at Bayreuth as a graduation present. This trip inspired a youthful effort at a large-scale work entitled *Young Siegfried*. Webern's style soon began to change after he met Arnold Schoenberg in 1904. He studied with him for a little over two years, but they maintained a lifelong friendship even after Schoenberg had moved to Berlin and then on to the United States.

Webern began his professional career in 1908 as a conductor. Except for a tour of military service during World War I, he conducted orchestras in various Austrian cities. In 1920 his attention shifted to private music teaching. He also came in contact with the activities of the Social Democratic Party and took up duties as conductor of a workers' chorus. He was very active in the Socialist movement.

Webern's atonal style began to emerge shortly before World War I, but his better known works were written after that time, especially during the 1920s. In 1927 he was appointed conductor and advisor for Radio Austria, a job he held until his political party went out of power. He continued to compose throughout World War II, during which his son was killed in battle and his home was destroyed by bombing. As the last days of the war approached, his future looked brighter. He had received official letters from Vienna asking him to play a leadership role in reconstructing the cultural life of his country. He was shot in 1945 in an unfortunate accident as he lit a cigarette during a time of strict curfew. He died widely esteemed by a few other composers, including Stravinsky, but largely unknown to the general public.

Arnold Schoenberg

Arnold Schoenberg (*Shu(r)n*-bairg; 1874–1951) was born in Vienna. He began studying violin at the age of eight and was an avid participant in amateur chamber music performances. He also attended concerts frequently. After his father's early death he went to work as a bank clerk. He had little formal music training at an advanced level, but had for many years exhibited an interest in composing. This interest became increasingly stronger, and so he decided to make music his lifework. First he spent two years in Berlin as a music director in a cabaret; then he returned to Vienna as a teacher, theorist, and composer. His career was interrupted for two years while he served in the Austrian army in World War I.

In 1925 he was appointed professor of composition at the Berlin Academy of Arts. His stay in Berlin ended when Hitler came to power. Although Schoenberg had been converted from Judaism to Catholicism, he left Germany and came to the United States, becoming an American citizen in 1940. He taught at the University of California at Los Angeles until his retirement. His musical activities continued until his death in 1951.

Prior to 1908 his music stood firmly in the tradition of Wagner and Mahler. His best known composition of the period is *Verklärte Nacht (Transfigured Night),* a tone poem for string orchestra. The literary work that inspired the music is pure Romanticism. As a couple walks through the woods, the woman confesses that she has been unfaithful. The man assures her that he still loves her, and her gratitude transfigures the night.

Around 1908 Schoenberg began to turn toward smaller groups of instruments. He started to write more contrapuntally and to employ much more chromaticism. Slowly he

Arnold Schoenberg.

developed an atonal style. Such a step meant breaking away from the very foundations that had undergirded the music of previous centuries.

About 1923 he devised the tone-row system that was described earlier in this chapter. He followed tone-row principles for most of his works from that time on until the end of his life, departing from them occasionally in some of his later works. Schoenberg is as much remembered for his influence on twentieth-century music as he is for his compositions. His best known compositions are *Pierrot Lunaire*, Variations for Orchestra, and several chamber works.

Twenty-Seven

Music Now

With the end of World War II in 1945, the world moved into a new era. In a faltering manner the nations and peoples of the world started to rebuild in both a physical and emotional sense. Webern also died in 1945, and his influence was soon felt on the world of music. Partly because of him composers such as Stravinsky began writing in a different style. Also, a new generation of composers was soon to appear, and with them an interest in the new and improved means of producing and reproducing sound electronically.

From about 1945 to 1960 the struggle for musical predominance was between those who favored strict controls on music in terms of tone-row principles and those who favored few controls—chance music and improvisation. The most prominent person promoting controlled composition was the Frenchman Pierre Boulez (Boo-lez, b. 1925), who was for several years musical director of the New York Philharmonic. In addition to a row of pitches, one of his compositions contains this rhythmic row,

this row of articulations,

1	2	3	4	5	6	7	8	9	10	11	12
>	'	.	–	⌒	>̧	>	·̈	⌒̈	*sfz* ∧	*sfz* ♦	*normal*

and this row of dynamics:

1	2	3	4	5	6	7	8	9	10	11	12
pppp	*ppp*	*pp*	*p*	*meno* *p*	*mp*	*mf*	*più f*	*f*	*ff*	*fff*	*ffff*

So a tone row is controlled in four of its aspects: pitch, rhythm, articulation, and dynamics. Other composers also control timbre. Such compositions are usually frighteningly difficult to perform.

When tone-row principles are applied more broadly, the music is generally called *serial*. Other serial composers in addition to Boulez are: Karlheinz Stockhausen in Germany and Luigi Berio and Luigi Nono in Italy. An earlier version of controlled music was created by the Frenchman Olivier Messiaen (Mess-yun, b. 1908). In some of his music he uses one series for melody, another for dynamics, another for timbre, and another for rhythm. Each of his four series is of a different length.

Chance music and its leading proponent, John Cage, were discussed in Chapter 26. Other types of music allowing for some chance or unplanned elements include the "third stream" music of Gunther Schuller, in which some jazz improvisation is designated, and the "stochastic" music of Yannis Xenakis (Zeh-*nock*-iss, b. 1922). Xenakis was born in Athens and later studied architecture and composition in Paris. He believes that musical compositions should be based on the calculus of probabilities. In his music it does not matter if a particular note is played or not, since the ear cannot perceive every individual sound. *Metastasis*, written in 1955, used 63 instruments (mostly strings); but it consists of *glissandi* (slides) with only the upper and lower pitch limits specified. The effect is one of a "haze," or rain of sounds.

Electronic Music

As music moved into the 1960s, both the serial and chance types began to give way to a third type: electronic music. Today it is equally prominent in the art music being created. Even some advocates of other types of composition—John Cage, for example—have gravitated toward electronic music.

There are two types of electronic music. *Musique concrète* is one. Recordings are made of natural sounds and voices—parts of human speech, a fly buzzing, the wind, a motor roaring, a whistle. Then the tape is manipulated according to the desires of the composer. It can be speeded up or slowed down. It can be spliced. It can be recorded through a second or third recorder and thus the sounds combined. The composition in *musique concrète* is a segment of tape that contains selected and manipulated sounds in a planned sequence.

An American advocate of *musique concrète* is Vladimir Ussachevsky. He combines natural sounds and sounds from musical instruments, usually percussion, on tape. For instance, from the ring of a gong he may salvage only the last portion or "afterglow" of the sound. Then he may treat the taped portion in any of the ways previously described.

Musique concrète has functioned successfully as background for movies, plays, and ballet scenes, especially when eerie and unearthly music is required.

The other type of electronic music consists of sounds produced on electronic equipment (synthesizers and oscillators) and then recorded on tape. This music had its beginnings in the Studio for Electronic Music of the West German Radio in the 1950s. All sounds within the limits of human hearing are possible, even those too high or low to be identifiable as musical pitches. This range is considerably larger than the customary 88 pitches available on the piano keyboard. Furthermore, every level of volume and timbre can be reproduced. Also possible are machine rhythms, which are more complex and more accurately executed than those produced by humans.

Electronic music is not performed in the usual sense of the word. A button is pushed to start the machine. If the technician who prepared the tape has followed the directions accurately, the listener hears *exactly* the sounds the composer intended. The need for a performer is completely eliminated. The idea seems revolutionary at first. And yet in the visual arts no one expects to watch a painting being repainted by a "performing" artist. We see just what the original artist painted. The same principle prevails in electronic music.

The *Record Album* contains a portion of an electronic work, *Until Spring*, by the contemporary American Morton Subotnick. He considers creating such music with the synthesizer "like sculpting sound." *Until Spring* deals with three gestural qualities: thrusting out, becoming, and being. The opening minutes of the work are presented in the album.

A computer is not essential for electronic music, although it is often involved. The computer can "create" a musical composition from a prescribed program. The computer program can produce whatever type of music is desired—Mozart-like compositions, popular songs, or psychedelic synthesized sounds. Also, the music the computer specifies can, depending on the program, be played on a conventional instrument or sounded on a sophisticated synthesizer. Currently, the computer holds more promise as a research tool than as an aid to musical composition.

Creating electronic compositions is a highly specialized skill. To do it, one almost needs to study electrical engineering as well as music.

Instruction in electronic composition has only recently been offered in European and American music schools.

The potential of electronic music has barely been tapped. There is a vast world of sound manipulation possibilities to be investigated, and composers today are exploring a new area in search of musical riches.

Eclecticism-Consolidation

Although contemporary art music is pluralistic, with composers writing in widely divergent styles, there are some composers who use what they believe is the best of each style. They owe allegiance to no musical system or philosophy, and their compositions cannot be classified in any of the categories previously mentioned in this book.

In the opinion of many musicians, the leading composer today is Krzysztof Penderecki (Pen-der-*et*-ski), who was born in 1933 near Cracow, Poland. He is most interested in timbre and tonal effect, but he also uses the tape recorder in some of his compositions. His best known works are *The Passion According to St. Luke* and *Threnody to the Victims of Hiroshima*.

Other eclectic, experimental composers include the Italian Luigi Dallapiccola (b. 1904), the Pole Witold Lutoslawski (b. 1913), and the German Hans Werner Henze (b. 1926).

Crumb's Night of the Four Moons

In the discussion of each of the style periods and types, one or more works has been selected as an example of that kind of music. Deciding on the most representative works is difficult, and this is especially so in the case of very recent music. However, George Crumb's series of four songs entitled *Night of the Four Moons* appears to demonstrate well a number of the trends in art music today. It was composed during the Apollo 11 moon flight July

16–24, 1969. Crumb writes of the work:

> *I suppose that* Night of the Four Moons *is really an "occasional" work, since its inception was an artistic response to an external event. The texts—extracts drawn from the poems of Federico García Lorca—symbolize my own rather ambivalent feelings* vis-à-vis *Apollo 11.*

It was commissioned by the Philadelphia Chamber Players and involves a chamber ensemble consisting of an alto singer, alto flute (doubling on piccolo), banjo, "electric" cello (that is, amplified through a speaker), and one percussion player playing a number of instruments: a large drum, crotales (metal shells struck together), cymbals, tambourine, Japanese Kabuki blocks, bongo drums, Chinese gong, Tibetan prayer stones, vibraphone, and African thumb piano (Mbira). The singer's part requires *sprechstimme*, unvoiced singing, and whispering, in addition to normal singing.

The score is preceded by two pages of lengthy instructions to the performers. These directions include specifications regarding placement on stage, stage lighting, the dress of the singer (a Spanish cabaret costume), and stage entrance and exit ("should be solemn and suggest a somnambulistic, trance-like quality").

The text of the work consists of fragments of poems by Federico García Lorca, which are in Spanish. The text for the first song is:

> *La luna está muerta, muerta;*
> *pero resucita en la primavera.*
>
> The moon is dead, dead;
> but it is reborn in the springtime.

The other three songs are: *Cuando sale la luna . . .* (When the moon rises. . .), *Otro Adán oscura está soñando . . .* (Another obscure Adam dreams . . .), and *¡Huje luna, luna, luna! . .* (Run away moon, moon, moon! . .).

The music has some of the sparse quality developed by Webern, some of the aleatory techniques promoted by Cage, some elements of theater, and quite a bit of interest in timbres. The first two lines of the first song appear on pages 256–257. The unifying element in these lines is the figure circled in the example. The figure is inverted, or turned upside down, freely. Crumb writes of this song:

> *"The moon is dead, dead . . ." is primarily an instrumental piece in a primitive rhythmical style, with the Spanish words stated almost parenthetically by the singer. The conclusion of the text is whispered by the flutist over the mouthpiece of his instrument.*

The music has notated rhythm, but no metrical, steady beat. Dynamic markings and varied timbres add much to its effect, which seems to be a combination of intellectualism and mysticism.

The Future of Music

Where does music go from here? No one knows for sure, of course. Electronic music may turn out to be merely a passing experiment, although that does not seem likely. There may be a rebirth of interest in an earlier type of music, or some new type that is unknown today may emerge.

Only two predictions can be made with confidence about music in the future. First, there will be music. People have found sound and its manipulation too fascinating, too satisfying to abandon it completely. In fact, the indications are that music and other fine arts will mean more, not less, in the years to come. Second, music of the future will differ from music of the past. The creative mind is restless and forever unsatisfied with previous accomplishments. It wants to experiment with new ways, new materials. The truly creative artist is constitutionally unable to make imitations or be content with the efforts of others.

By definition, creativity involves the bringing forth of something new and unique. And in the art of music, as in any creative endeavor, there will always be something new under the sun. The product of an imaginative and skilled composer will always be a fascination to hear and a joy to understand.

Twenty-Eight

American Music

Music in America had a slow start, for several reasons. The nation began as a loose confederation of small, struggling settlements, isolated from the mainstream of European life by 3,000 miles of ocean. Physical survival was the uppermost concern. There was no stimulating contact with recent artistic creations. Furthermore, in those early days there could be no truly American music, since the settlers came from other lands and were steeped in the traditions of English, Dutch, or German music.

The Puritan influence, too, was strong in the colonies. These devout people thought that art and theater were morally wrong. At best, art and music were mere diversions; at worst, they were products of the devil. The only music permitted was the unaccompanied singing of psalms and hymns. The first book published in America was the *Bay Psalm Book*, in 1640. The first edition had no music, and none was added until the ninth edition in 1698.

The most sophisticated music written in America before the Revolutionary War was the product of the Moravian communities around Bethlehem, Pennsylvania. These people had come from the Moravian area of present-day Czechoslovakia, bringing with them a rich musical heritage. Besides music for church services, they also wrote chamber works. Mu-

sicologists are still discovering some of this fine music. There were several active composers in the Moravian community, but John Frederick Peter (1746–1813) was the most skilled. He came to America in 1770.

The first native-born American composer was an amateur, Francis Hopkinson (1737–1791), who was a friend of George Washington and a signer of the Declaration of Independence. His most famous song was "My Days Have Been So Wondrous Free." In 1788 he published some songs for which he also wrote the words. He dedicated the book to Washington.

If Francis Hopkinson's compositions did not sound particularly different from English music at that time, the works of William Billings (1746–1800) did. Billings was a tanner by trade, but he had an insatiable drive to write music. And he was a firm believer in American music for Americans. He explained in his first collection, *The New England Psalm Singer* (1770), that he would follow his own rules for composition. One of the techniques he used in his hymns was "fuguing," which was a high-class name for imitation. Billings was not modest in making claims:

[Fuguing] is twenty times as powerful as the old slow tunes. Each part striving for mas-

259

"Chester" by William Billings, as it appears in his Singing Master's Assistant. *The initials L. M. in the title mean "long meter" and indicate that there are eight syllables in every phrase of the text.*

tery and victory. The audience entertained and delighted. Now the solemn bass demands their attention; next the manly tenor. Now here, now there, now here again! O ecstatic! Rush on, you sons of harmony.

Whatever Billings lacked in training was offset by his native musical ability. Despite some crudities, his music has a quality that has attracted many musicians and lay people, especially in this century. The tune "Chester" is one of his best known. A version of it from Billings's *Singing Master's Assistant* is shown below. The melody is in the tenor part, the third line from the top. The music is plain and unadorned. "Chester" has reappeared in the annals of American music, specifically in the twentieth-century music of William Schuman.

Prior to the twentieth century, Billings wrote the only music that could be considered completely American. Even our national songs had their roots in Europe. The origin of "Yankee Doodle" is unknown, but it was first printed in Glasgow, Scotland, in 1782. The British sang it to ridicule the Yankees, who promptly took it over as their own song by adding new verses. The melody of "The Star-Spangled Banner" was adapted from a popular English drinking song, "To Anacreon in Heaven," which was composed by John Stafford Smith (1750–1836). The words were written as a poem by the American Francis Scott Key as he watched the British bombard Fort McHenry in 1814. It was not officially made the national anthem until 1931. "America" is sung to the same tune as the British national anthem "God Save the King," which was written by the English composer Henry Carey (1685–1743). The words as sung in this country were contributed by the American Samuel Francis Smith (1808–1895) at the suggestion of Lowell Mason.

The Nineteenth Century

The name Mason is important in American music. Lowell Mason (1792–1872) wrote many hymns, including "Nearer, My God, to Thee," and conducted the Handel and Haydn Society in Boston. His most significant achievement was the establishment of music in the curriculum of the public schools in 1838. He also spread the idea of music for the masses by organizing "conventions" for the training of music teachers. He made several lengthy trips to Europe to study. Two of his sons founded the piano-manufacturing company of Mason and Hamlin, and a third son became a well-known music teacher.

America imported not only much of its music but many of its musicians as well. Many European virtuosos found it profitable to tour the United States. The most sensational of these was the singer Jenny Lind, who was advertised by her brilliant promoter, P. T. Barnum, as "the Swedish Nightingale."

An American piano virtuoso was Louis Moreau Gottschalk (1829–1869). He was a handsome man who cultivated some of the mannerisms of Liszt. He wrote sentimental works with such tearjerking titles as *The Last Hope* and *The Dying Poet*.

Louis A. Jullien (1812–1860) conducted with a jewelled baton. He played some good music, including works by American composers. But his biggest success was a number entitled *Fireman's Quadrille*, during which, as flames burst from the ceiling, he brought the local fire department into the hall to quench the blaze dramatically.

For sheer spectacle he was matched only by Patrick Gilmore (1829–1892), a bandmaster who organized colossal extravaganzas. One was the Great National Peace Jubilee in Boston in 1869. The performance included a chorus of 10,000, an orchestra of 1,000, cannons, and 100 firemen pounding anvils in the "Anvil Chorus" from Verdi's *Il Trovatore*. The only way for Gilmore to top that was to organize a World Peace Jubilee. For this he brought Johann Strauss from Europe to lead his *Blue Danube Waltz*. Although the orchestra was held down to 1,000 players, the chorus was in-creased to 20,000 singers.

From Jullien's orchestra emerged a young German violinist named Theodore Thomas (1835–1905). In 1862 he organized his own orchestra. He maintained high standards of performance and sought to educate the audience; in so doing he laid the foundation for the symphony orchestras of today. He traveled throughout the United States and was for a while the conductor of the New York Philharmonic. Later he organized the Chicago Symphony and was its conductor for many years.

The revolutions in Europe, especially Germany, in the mid-1800s brought thousands of immigrants to America. Many were musicians who soon became affiliated with orchestras and opera companies throughout the country. The European immigrants constituted an interested audience for the German symphonic music that Thomas performed for them.

Stephen Collins Foster (1826–1864) was a native American composer both by birth and by compositional style. He was not a Southerner, as many people believe. He was born in Lawrenceville, Pennsylvania, of a middle-class family. His parents did not consider music a suitable career for a man, so they did nothing to encourage him. He was a dreamer and a failure at almost everything he undertook—work, marriage, and serious musical compositions. But he was a genius at writing popular songs. He wrote about two hundred of them, many for minstrel shows. "Beautiful Dreamer," "My Old Kentucky Home," "Old Folks at Home," "Camptown Races," "O Susanna," and others are still heard today.

Late in the nineteenth century a few capable American composers began to write longer and more sophisticated works. Most of these composers lived around Boston, and almost all of them had studied in Germany at one time or another. Consequently, much of their music sounded like works of the European masters with whom they had studied. The "Boston" or "New England" group included George W. Chadwick (1854–1931), Horatio Parker (1863–1919), Arthur Foote (1853–1937), and John Knowles Paine (1839–1906), who taught Foote. Little of their music is heard today.

Edward MacDowell (1861–1908) had excellent musical training. He studied at the Paris Conservatory when ·he was 11, and was a classmate of Debussy. He also played for Liszt at Weimar in 1882. After his return to America, he was a professor of music at Columbia University for eight years. Most of his works are for piano; *Woodland Sketches* and "To a Wild Rose" are representative of his style. He also wrote four piano sonatas and two piano concertos. His Suite No. 2 *(Indian Suite)* was a landmark because it was one of the first American works to use music from native sources.

The Twentieth Century

Soon after the turn of the century, the popularity of German Romanticism began to wane in America, only to be replaced by attempts to imitate impressionism. The best-known "American impressionist" was Charles Tomlinson Griffes (1884–1920). At first he wrote in the German tradition, but he later switched to the Debussy-Ravel style. "The White Peacock" from *Roman Sketches* is still frequently performed. Charles Martin Loeffler (1861–1935), who immigrated to America from Alsace at the age of 20, also wrote music of a somewhat impressionistic nature.

Thus as the twentieth century began, American music was in a dormant state. All around was a rich heritage of folk music in the songs of the blacks, the lumberjacks, the sailors, the cowboys, the Indians, and the mountaineers, as well as the ballads and folklore brought to America by its myriad immigrants. But except for MacDowell, no American composer had chosen to draw on the musical resources of this country. They apparently felt that the music of their own culture was inferior. Not only did it seem necessary for all serious musicians to study in Europe, it was considered advisable to pattern new compositions on European models.

One composer, however, was writing modern, innovative American music prior to World War I. At the time, however, virtually no one had heard of him. The name of Charles Ives meant nothing.

Charles Ives

Ives (1874–1954) was born in Danbury, Connecticut, and was the son of a bandmaster. His father was no ordinary town band leader. He encouraged his son to listen carefully and try to write different tonal effects. "Stretch your ears," was his advice. And so young Ives experimented with various acoustical effects, such as new tunings for the piano or two bands playing different music while marching toward and away from each other. He attended Yale as a music student, and upon graduation went to New York, where he literally made a fortune in the insurance business. He had a country home in Connecticut. In the evenings he sat at his desk and composed for relaxation. As he finished a page of music, he stacked it on the floor near him. When the stacks became too high, he carried them out to the barn for storage. Because he had no need for money, he did not bother to have his works published and sold. For years no one knew about them; they just sat there in the barn.

Shortly after the turn of the century, Ives was writing novel harmonies and rhythms that did not appear in Europe until a decade or more later. He experimented with such ideas as polytonality, dissonant counterpoint, atonality, polyrhythm, chords with added tones, unusual melodic intervals, and *sprechstimme*, the kind of singsong speech that Schoenberg used in several of his works. Ives's song "Autumn," presented in Chapter 8, is rather traditional compared to much of his other music.

Ives's Symphony No. 3, written between 1901 and 1904, won him the Pulitzer Prize in 1947. Another work that is often played is the Piano Sonata No. 2 *(Concord)*, which contains fragments of several well-known tunes heard in Concord, Massachusetts, between 1840 and 1860. The fragments Ives selected, the manner in which he employed devices such as polytonality, the character of his melodies, and his use of instruments produced music that was in no sense a copy of Stravinsky or Bartók. It was American music. At long last the seed planted by Billings, the tanner, was flourishing in Ives, the insurance man. But until the 1930s no one knew it.

Mainstream Nationalists

Most of the music that is considered "American" is somewhat nationalistic or Neo-Romantic in character. This type of music can be represented by two specific works: George Gershwin's *Porgy and Bess* and William Schuman's *New England Triptych*.

Gershwin's Porgy and Bess

Gershwin was impressed by DuBose Heyward's novel *Porgy*. The story deals with the poor blacks who lived on Catfish Row in Charleston, South Carolina. Gershwin could see the dramatic possibilities in the story, and he decided to write an opera based on it. To make his opera more authentic, he spent the summer of 1934 in Charleston observing the ways of the people. He heard the street cries of the vendors and listened to the songs the children sang as they played. Then he returned to New York and spent another nine months writing *Porgy and Bess*.

Porgy and Bess concerns itself with the common people. To make the story as real as possible, Gershwin has the characters speak most of their lines, instead of singing in recitative style. And he incorporates the music of these people—the blues and other features of jazz—into the opera. Although he does not include actual folksongs, he does maintain a folklike quality in the music. The jazz elements are written down rather than improvised.

The story of *Porgy and Bess* is filled with tragedy. Porgy is a crippled beggar who leads a lonely life. Bess, a loose-living woman, comes to town with her lover, Crown. Neither Bess nor Crown is accepted by the people of Catfish Row. Crown kills one of the local men in a fight, and Bess takes refuge from the police in Porgy's shanty. Their relationship grows to one of genuine love.

One day a big picnic is held on a nearby island. Because he's crippled, Porgy can't attend, but he encourages Bess to go. As she's about to catch the boat back to Catfish Row, she is abducted by Crown, who has escaped from jail and is hiding on the island. When Crown learns of Bess' love for Porgy, he sets out to kill his rival. In the fight between the two men, Crown is stabbed and dies. Porgy is taken off to jail on suspicion of murder.

Now is the moment Sporting Life has been waiting for. He represents the easy, evil life that Bess left behind when she moved in with Porgy. Because it's doubtful that Porgy will ever be freed from jail, Sporting Life is able to persuade Bess to go back to New York with him. But Porgy is released, and when he returns home he finds Bess gone. "Where is she?" he asks. "New York," answer his neighbors. The opera closes with the pathetic scene of Porgy climbing into his goat cart to go after Bess.

Porgy and Bess opens with the lullaby "Summertime." The mood is lazy and relaxed, and the accompaniment suggests a gently rocking motion. Short notes introduce each new idea, and the last syllable of each phrase is sustained. The effect suggests snatches of thought spoken at random. Later in the song Gershwin adds some vocal devices he heard that summer in Charleston such as a slide, or *glissando*, and a little catch on the word "cry." The rhythm on the word "jumpin' " increases the feeling of bounciness. The word "hush" is given a place of prominence so that the "sh" sound can be easily heard. Jazz harmonies are evident.

In "I've Got Plenty of Nothin'," Porgy displays a carefree spirit, telling everyone that he has everything he wants, so he doesn't have to worry about material goods.

"Bess, You Is My Woman Now" is a glorious duet between Porgy and Bess. It sounds more like opera than folk music. As is typical in such duets, the man sings first to initiate the exchange of feelings, the woman answers, and then they sing together. The two parts are quite different. Porgy's part is a counter-melody to what Bess is singing. This duet also contains some jazz elements.

In "It Ain't Necessarily So" Sporting Life tries to con the people over to his way of life. His words are not those of an honest skeptic but of a sly salesman. The pitches of the melody seem to slink about in a manner that is just right for Sporting Life's personality. The song is in an *A B A* form. The main portion is heard twice, then there's a contrasting section, which is followed by return of the main portion. The contrasting section features nonsense syllables rather than regular words.

Throughout *Porgy and Bess*, there's an attempt to duplicate black dialect by making some changes in grammar and pronunciation. The linguistic result is seldom accurate or realistic. But the content of the opera—its music, story line, and characterizations—is strong enough to make it an artistic success.

Schuman's New England Triptych

In 1956 William Schuman turned to the music of the early Boston tanner William Billings. He chose three of Billings's songs to serve as the basis for this orchestral work. The word *triptych* (*trip*-tic) comes from a Greek word meaning three layers or parts.

In the program notes—Schuman requested that they be included whenever possible —he pays this tribute to Billings:

The works of this dynamic composer capture the spirit of sinewy ruggedness, deep religiosity, and patriotic fervor that we associate with the Revolutionary Period. Despite the undeniable crudities and technical shortcomings of his music, its appeal, even today, is forceful and moving. I am not alone among American composers who feel an identity with Billings and it is this sense of identity which accounts for my use of his music as a point of departure. These pieces do not constitute a "fantasy" on themes of Billings, nor "variations" on his themes, but rather a fusion of styles and musical language.

The first movement of the Triptych is built from the anthem "Be Glad Then, America." The opening timpani solo is developed further in the strings:

Trombones and trumpets start the main section, which is a free and varied setting of the words "Be glad then, America, shout and rejoice":

The timpani lead into a fugal section based on the theme for the words "And ye shall be satisfied":

The music gains momentum and combines themes as it continues to a climax.

Playing melodic themes on the timpani became possible late in the Romantic period through the addition of pedals, which enabled the player to regulate the tension of the drumheads more quickly and thereby change pitch.

The excitement that can be created by exploitation of rhythm is illustrated in the fugal section of the music. In the following example, the regular beats have a number above them, and the syncopated notes are marked by an X:

The meter changes from $\frac{2}{4}$ to $\frac{3}{4}$ and back to $\frac{2}{4}$

The second movement is based on Billings's anthem "When Jesus Wept." The text of the original anthem is:

When Jesus wept, the falling tear
In mercy flowed beyond all bound;
When Jesus groaned, a trembling fear
Seized all the guilty world around.

The tenor drum with snares loosened opens the section. With its hollow sound, it imparts the feel of a funeral procession. The bassoon begins Billings's melody, followed by the oboe:

The melody is a moderately long round. Schuman probably chose these two instruments because their timbres suggest melancholy. The tune would not sound nearly as plaintive if played by a flute or clarinet.

After the oboe-bassoon duet, the strings play in the same mournful mood. The duet returns again to complete the three-part form. The funeral cadence of the drum closes the movement.

The final movement is based on Billings's marching song "Chester," and it is dazzling. A simplified score for it is included in the *Study Guide and Scores* book. The tune is played by the woodwinds in a straightforward hymn style. But suddenly the tempo doubles. Flashy runs are heard, and fragments of the theme appear from time to time. There is even a "fife and drum" duet between the piccolo and snare drum. The percussion instruments add conspicuously to the fireworks that conclude the Triptych.

Mainstream Composers

Walter Piston (1894–1976) was somewhat classical in his writing. The music for his ballet *The Incredible Flutist* is often performed as an orchestral suite. Most of his works are instrumental and include several symphonies. For many years he taught at Harvard, and he wrote several textbooks in music theory.

William Grant Still (b. 1895) is the first black American composer to receive international recognition. He has had varied experiences as a jazz musician and as a director in music publishing and recording. He studied with the composer Edgard Varèse. During his 50 years as a composer Still has produced a variety of works, including popular songs and some experimental pieces as well as motion picture scores and religious music. Probably his best known work is *Afro-American Symphony*, which was composed in 1930.

Howard Hanson (b. 1896) is one of the outstanding names in American music. He is noted both as composer and teacher, and he served for many years as director of the Eastman School of Music. He has promoted American music in many capacities. His works are romantic and rather heavy in nature. Hanson's Symphony No. 2 *(Romantic)* is a moving work. His opera *Merry Mount* is based on an early American story. He writes well for all mediums.

Virgil Thomson (b. 1896) was for many years the music critic for the New York *Herald Tribune*. He was not a prolific composer, but the works he composed tend to be witty, sophisticated, and objective. He cooperated with Gertrude Stein on two operas: *Four Saints in Three Acts* and *The Mother of Us All*. Some of his film scores are played often, particularly *The Plow that Broke the Plains* and *The River*. He has also written some abstract instrumental works.

Roger Sessions (b. 1896) generally writes in a complicated manner. He maintains that instrumental music is a medium for expressing

Mainstream Composers

highly serious thoughts (not verbal ones, however). His music takes on the characteristics of depth and complexity. His not-lengthy list of compositions includes two operas as well as orchestral and chamber music. Like Piston, he was a university professor, although he is now retired. His teaching positions included Boston University, Princeton, and the University of California.

George Gershwin (1898–1937) had little musical training. His early efforts were confined to popular songs and musical comedies. In 1924, when he wrote *Rhapsody in Blue,* he did not feel competent to write for instruments other than the piano, so he had Ferde Grofé do the orchestration. Gershwin's writing style matured rapidly, only to be cut short when he died from a brain tumor. Other well-known works include *An American in Paris,* for orchestra; *Concerto in F,* for piano and orchestra; and *Porgy and Bess,* which was presented earlier in this chapter.

Roy Harris (b. 1898) is a westerner in education and outlook. He has some interesting ideas about music, and he has written some outstanding compositions. He believes that music should be emotional but not romantic and that emotion is best achieved when the tempo is kept close to that of the normal heartbeat (72 to 80 beats per minute). His most successful work is Symphony No. 3. It was written in 1937–1938 and is in one movement.

Samuel Barber (b. 1910) is highly regarded as an American composer, as evidenced by his commission to compose an opera for the opening of the Metropolitan Opera House in Lincoln Center. His music frequently shows evidence of Neo-Romanticism, as in the lush *Adagio for Strings.* He is equally successful in vocal or instrumental mediums. Besides having written several symphonies and concertos, Barber combines vocalist and orchestra well in *Knoxville: Summer of 1915.* His opera *Vanessa* is

considered one of the best written in the twentieth century.

Elliott Carter (b. 1908) developed slowly as a recognized composer. Since 1950, however, his work has assumed more importance and has received high praise from the critics. Most of his compositions are for instrumental groups. His style is complex and appears to be influenced by the music of Schoenberg and Stravinsky.

William Schuman was born in New York City in 1910 and entered the music world as a Tin Pan Alley song writer and song plugger. At the same time, he was enrolled in a business curriculum at New York University. He heard his first symphony concert when he was about 20 years old. It had such an impact on him that the next day he withdrew from his business course and quit the job he had taken with an advertising agency. He switched his major to music. By the late 1930s Schuman's music was being performed by major orchestras at home and abroad. In 1945 he became president of the Juilliard School of Music, a position he held until 1961.

Schuman is equally successful in writing for vocal and for instrumental groups. Most of his vocal works date from the early 1940s and include *Pioneers,* based on Walt Whitman's poetry; a "secular cantata" named *A Free Song;* and the short, vivacious "Holiday Song." His instrumental works are better known. They include a number of symphonies and chamber works. Some, such as *New England Triptych,* are based on national themes.

Alan Hovhaness Chakmakjian was born in 1911 in Somerville, Massachusetts, of Armenian-Scottish parents. Early in his career he dropped his long and complicated last name. From the beginning he seemed destined to bring together the best of two worlds, the old and the new, the Occident and the Orient. His musical training in his younger years was largely confined to Boston and the New England Conservatory of Music. He did, however, study astronomy and Eastern music and religions.

Hovhaness began to receive public attention in the late 1940s. Thereafter he received several awards and grants to study music and compose. These grants took him to India, Japan, and Korea. His creative work seems to have increased with these journeys. His opus numbers are well past 200.

Norman Dello Joio (b. 1913) combines old and new elements in his music. His *Ricercari, Variations, Chaconne and Finale,* and Concerto for Harp and Orchestra all employ old forms. He also reaches back in music history and selects portions of Gregorian chant for thematic material.

Vincent Persichetti (b. 1915) draws from any source and utilizes any technique that he thinks will contribute to his music. He is especially successful in writing for piano. His seven symphonies are worthy of careful listening, as is his Quintet for Piano and Strings.

Ulysses Kay (b. 1917) writes both instrumental and choral works. Probably his best known works in each area are *Sinfonia in E,* written in 1950, and *Choral Triptych,* written in 1962.

Ned Rorem (b. 1912) is one of this century's most talented art song composers. He studied for five years in France, and much of his music shows the French influence. *Poems of Love and the Rain* (1963) is a cycle of 17 songs, of which each text except one is set twice. Other groups of songs include *Two Poems of Plato* (1964, in Greek), *Hearing* (1966), and *Some Trees* (1968). He has written several choral works and some music for piano, chamber ensemble, and orchestra, as well as a few works for the theater.

Gunther Schuller (b. 1925) is the leading advocate of what he calls the "third stream" movement, which combines contemporary art music and jazz. Unlike the planned jazz writing of Milhaud and others, actual improvisation by jazz musicians is called for in Schuller's music. Among his works in this vein are *12 by 11, Concertino for Jazz Quartet and Orchestra, Densities I,* and *Night Music.* These four works were written between 1955 and 1962. Prior to that time Schuller wrote abstract instrumental compositions using tone-row techniques, and since 1962 he has turned to opera. The "third stream" concept is an idea that seems logical but in fact is not easy to accomplish. So far it has not caught on in a big way, and Schuller himself has moved to other types of music.

Lukas Foss was born in Berlin in 1922 and came to America in 1937. His early works were in the style of Hindemith, but later he became interested in improvisation. *Time Cycle* was written for soprano and orchestra with improvised interludes.

Intellectualism

Not many American composers have been attracted to the tone-row techniques of Schoenberg as their dominant type of composition. Many of them have experimented with the idea, and some have used the principles of tone-row compositions for a few works. Only two names are rather generally associated with such compositions: Wallingford Riegger and Ernst Krenek.

Wallingford Riegger (1885–1961) began composing in the tone-row idiom soon after Schoenberg developed the style. He was essentially a conservative tone-row composer in that the rows he created often resembled traditional tonal music. Several of his best compositions are written for modern dance companies and for dancers such as Martha Graham and Charles Weidman. He also used Latin-American rhythms in some of his works. His best known orchestral work is Symphony No. 3.

Ernst Krenek (b. 1900) was born in Vienna and immigrated to the United States as a young man. His style is much more severe and stark than Riegger's. He was much influenced by primitive music, and he has maintained some of this tradition while writing in the serial or tone-row idiom. He has written a wide variety of works including some for the stage, ballet, incidental music, film music, orchestral works, electronic music, and vocal and choral music.

Experimental Music

Since World War II American composers have turned more to experimental and electronic music. It appears that some of the fires of nationalism that flamed in the music by American composers in the 1920s, 30s, and early 40s have given way to more international and experimental styles. The techniques of these composers are discussed more thoroughly in Chapter 27, which devotes its attention to experimental and electronic music.

George Antheil was born in 1900 in Trenton, New Jersey. He was one of the pioneers in breaking away from conventional music and advocating "an anti-expressive, anti-romantic, coldly mechanistic aesthetic." This belief led him to create the famous (or infamous) *Ballet mechanique* in 1924. The score specified eight pianos, a player piano, and an airplane propeller, but he later revised this score to include more pianos as well as anvils, bells, automobile horns, and buzz saws. Such compositions earned him a reputation as "the bad boy of music." Antheil had a variety of nonmusical interests also. He wrote several books, including one in which he predicted (and missed by one month) the bombing of Pearl Harbor by the Japanese in 1941. He also wrote articles for

Esquire, authored a book on criminology, advised police departments in criminal endocrinology, and with movie star Hedy Lamarr invented and patented a radio torpedo. Somehow in his busy life he found time to write six symphonies and a number of other stage works. He died in 1959.

Like Ernst Krenek, Edgard Varèse (1883–1965) was born and trained in Europe but spent most of his creative life in the United States. He is remembered as much for his influence on other American composers as for his own compositions. He was very much interested in tone colors and unusual rhythms, and he built strange and perplexing compositions by adding one layer of sound to another. Some of his better known works are *Octandre* (1923), *Hyperprism* (1923), *Ionisation* (1931), and *Density 21.5* (1936). Varèse was dreaming of electronic machines before they became a reality. His culminating work was written for the Brussels Worlds Fair in 1958—*Poème électronique*, an eight-hour work played stereophonically through 425 loud speakers and accompanied by a series of images projected on a screen.

Henry Cowell (1897–1965) set about creating new sounds with the conventional piano. In some numbers he requires the pianist to play clusters of tones over two octaves with the left forearm. In another work he instructs the piano player to reach into the piano and strum the open strings. On other occasions he has a second person hold down some of the dampers on the keys throughout the performance of the composition.

Otto Luening and Vladimir Ussachevsky are considered here together because they have created a number of works jointly. Together they explored new avenues in electronic music in America.

Otto Luening was born in Milwaukee in 1900. He was a talented musician who studied flute and composition and later went to study music in Munich and Zurich. He returned to the United States in 1920 to become one of the cofounders of an opera company in Chicago. He later taught at the Eastman School of Music and Columbia University.

Ussachevsky was born in Manchuria in 1911 of Russian parents. He came to the United States in 1930 and attended Pomona College in California. He attended the Eastman School of Music, where he studied composition with Howard Hanson. He had written a number of compositions for conventional instruments and voices prior to moving into the field of electronic music.

Together Luening and Ussachevsky presented the first public concert of tape recorded music in the United States. The year was 1952. Since that time they have explored this area extensively and have contributed much to the development of this type of music in America.

Milton Babbitt (b. 1916) was a trained mathematician. After World War II he started working with the tone-row system. Later, however, he became director of the Electronic Music Center operated jointly by Columbia and Princeton Universities. Since about 1960 almost all of his compositions have included electronic sound.

Charles Wuorinen (b. 1938) was born in New York City. His father was a history professor at Columbia University and his mother was an amateur musician. His interest in music began early, and at the age of 16 he won the Philharmonic Young Composer's Award. Since that time he has enjoyed a steady succession of awards, fellowships, and commissions. He has written some compositions in the tone-row system, but most have been in the electronic music area. Many of these works involve synthesized music coupled with conventional instruments.

John Cage (b. 1912) is undoubtedly the most experimental and controversial American composer. He was born in Los Angeles and received much of his early musical training from an aunt. Cage flirted with painting, literature, and architecture before deciding on a career in music. He studied for a while with Arnold Schoenberg, but he felt constrained by the rules of Schoenberg's type of composition. By the 1930s Cage was working with the "prepared piano"—tacks, bolts, and other foreign objects had been placed on the hammers and strings of the piano to produce different timbres when the keys were struck. About 1940 he became fascinated with oriental music and philosophy. This interest led to his chance or aleatory works that were discussed in the preceding chapter. His most famous work is 4'33", in which not a single sound is made! (The sounds will come, Cage claims, from our environment and our minds.) From chance and indeterminacy Cage has more recently tried his hand at computer music with a work entitled *HPSCHD*. Prepared with the aid of Lejaren Hiller, *HPSCHD* employs a complicated mathematical computer program that is broken into 59 channels of sound.

George Crumb was born in Charleston, West Virginia, in 1929. Among the awards he has won are the Pulitzer Prize in 1968 for *Echoes of Time and River: Four Processionals for Orchestra*, and the International Rostrum of Composers Award (UNESCO) and the Koussevitzky International Recording Award, both for his 1971 composition *Ancient Voices of Children*. His *Night of the Four Moons*, composed in 1969, was presented in Chapter 27. He currently teaches at the University of Pennsylvania.

American music has had a rags-to-riches history. From weak imitations of European styles, American music has progressed to a place of equal prominence in the world. America has developed a body of music uniquely its own. With the tremendous vitality of its cultural life and the increasing attention being paid the arts, music in America should continue to change and expand.

Twenty-Nine

Jazz, Rock, Country, Etc.

Jazz and rock are both American types of music. They are among our nation's most recognized contributions to the world of music. Both types have their promoters and detractors, and both developed under a cloud of doubt about their musical quality. Regardless of their artistic merits, or lack of them, no presentation of American music can be adequate without some discussion of jazz and rock.

Traditional Jazz

The roots of jazz reach back to black Americans' African heritage. But other elements have also influenced jazz: minstrel show music, work songs, field hollers, funeral marching bands, blues, French-Creole and Spanish-American music, and more recently, West Indian music. Jazz did not develop as a musical form until about the beginning of the twentieth century. Basin Street in New Orleans is traditionally considered its birthplace, and it was brought to public attention by the funeral procession. On the way back from the cemetery the band played its tunes in a way quite different from the somber sounds that

accompanied the march to the gravesite. They shifted the emphasis from the strong to the weak beat, and the players launched into a decorated version of the melody. When Storyville, New Orleans' red-light district, was closed down in 1917, many jazz musicians lost their jobs and sought work in other cities. Jazz moved up the Mississippi River through Memphis and St. Louis to Chicago and the rest of the United States.

Two types of Afro-American folk music existed with early jazz and later merged with it. One of these was *ragtime*. It featured the piano, occasionally in combination with other instruments. The music sounds like a lively march with a decorated right-hand part. Early musicians associated with ragtime are Scott Joplin in Sedalia, Missouri, and Ben Harvey, who published his *Ragtime Instructor* in 1897.

The other type of music involved with early jazz was the folk *blues*. Its musical characteristics will be discussed shortly. Some of the most famous names associated with blues are Leadbelly, a Texas convict whose real name was Huddie Ledbetter; W. C. Handy, who was known for his "Memphis Blues" and "St. Louis Blues"; and Ferdinand "Jelly Roll" Morton, whose first published blues appeared in 1905—the "Jelly Roll Blues."

Like folk music, jazz was created by mostly untutored musicians who could not have written down what they had played and sung if they'd wanted to. But jazz is different in two respects. It has sprung from the cities rather than the fields and forests; it's an urban form of music. And for most people it's a spectator experience. Usually only a few people perform, although listeners may contribute a little hand clapping and foot stomping.

But what is jazz? It has several elements.

Melody. The most significant feature of jazz melodies is the *blue note*. These notes are derived from an altered version of the major scale. The blues scale merely lowers the third, fifth, and seventh steps. Many times performers shift between the regular note and its lower counterpart as if they were searching for a sound. And in truth they may be. The blue-note interval is an approximation of a microtone, roughly half of a half step in this case. The African heritage is the influence behind its use in jazz. Blue notes are a source of subtle color. Their effect in jazz is further enhanced by the fact that the chord in the harmony usually contains the particular note at its conventional pitch, while the lowered blue note appears simultaneously in the melody. This combination creates an interesting and characteristic dissonance.

Harmony. Early jazz harmony was as conservative as any church hymn. The typical chords were the same three that form the backbone of traditional tonal harmony: tonic (I), dominant (V), and subdominant (IV). More recently more modern versions of jazz have employed the advanced harmonic idioms of Debussy, Bartók, and Stravinsky. The appeal of jazz, however, does not lie primarily in its harmony.

Rhythm. Here is one of the most important features of jazz. Although its meter is nearly always two beats per measure, with irregular meters occurring only rarely, the jazz musician employs an endless variety of syncopated patterns and rhythmic figures over this regular pulse. Syncopation—the redistribution of accents so that the rhythmic patterns do not conform to the meter as the listener expects—is the life-blood of jazz.

Jazz rhythms do not fit well into the traditional divisions of time according to sixteenths, eighths, and quarters. Jazz musicians perform rhythm with small deviations of timing and accent that cannot be adequately conveyed through notation. They even make slight alterations of the patterns of conventional notation when they read them. In some styles of jazz, the accent pattern is almost the reverse of that found in traditional music. These deviations in rhythm are one reason that explains why well-trained musicians often do not achieve a true jazz sound.

Timbre. The basic tone color sought by jazz instrumentalists is perhaps an unconscious imitation of the black singing voice: a bit breathy with a little vibrato (rapid and slight variance of pitch on a single tone). Certain instruments, therefore, have become associated with this idiom. The saxophone was intended to be a concert instrument, but it was taken up by jazz musicians because it can produce the desired quality. Besides, it's not so difficult to play, and it has a loud tone. Mutes—metal or fiber devices inserted in or over the bell to change the tone quality—are often used on brass instruments, and their names are as distinctive as the sounds they produce: *cup, wah-wah,* and *plunger,* the last of which can be duplicated by the end of a rubber sink plunger. Many jazz trumpeters use a particular type of mouthpiece that helps them produce a more shrill sound and makes high notes easier to play. In jazz style the clarinet is played in a manner that produces a saxophonelike quality. It differs from the orchestral clarinet's tone. The tone qualities of other instruments also vary according to whether they are playing orchestral music or jazz.

Some jazz timbres, like the bongo and conga drums and the Cuban cowbell, are from Afro-Cuban sources; others, such as the Chinese woodblock, cymbals, and vibraphone, have an oriental flavor.

Repetition of material. Jazz has no form that is applicable to all its styles. Generally it is a series of stanzas based on the chords to a popular tune. The form of the blues is more definite. A line is sung and immediately repeated, and then a third line concludes the stanza. Sometimes the singer does not sing all the way through a section, and an instrumentalist fills in with a short solo called a *break*.

Text. The metrical scheme of the text is often one of the standard poetic meters. It's not uncommon to find iambic pentameter in verses of the blues. The texts seldom have literary significance, but some are quite moving.

Improvisation. Improvisation is a fundamental component of jazz. Traditionally jazz is not written down because it's made up on the spot. This improvisation is what gives it its ever-fresh quality. Sometimes people confuse a lively popular song with jazz. A popular song does not become jazz until it is improvised upon.

What happens is this. The musicians agree that they will play a certain popular song in a certain key. They also agree generally on the order of each player's featured section. Then the first player, while keeping in mind the harmonies and melody of the song, improvises a part that reflects the rhythmic and melodic characteristics of the style of jazz being played. This procedure is followed as each player takes a turn. On the final chorus all play together in simultaneous, semiaccidental counterpoint. It's like an improvised musical conversation. Throughout the number no player knows exactly what the others will do, but each follows his musical instinct and fits his part in with the others. Nor is he entirely certain what he himself will do, because each time he takes a "ride" on the number, he will play it somewhat differently.

In several types of jazz a number of players improvise at the same time. This results in a type of "accidental" counterpoint that is held together only by the song's basic harmony and the musical instincts of the players. The presence of simultaneous improvisations in both African music and jazz can hardly be a coincidence. Sometimes there seems to be so much improvisation that the melody is no longer identifiable. Why does that happen? Because the player improvises on the basic harmony as well as the melody. For example, if the song starts on the tonic chord, as it usually does, and if the piece is in the key of C, then the notes of the tonic chord will be C E G. The improviser may play any or all of these three notes and can play tones that are nonharmonic in relation to that chord. In other words, the player can weave other tones around the notes of the chord. That is why the melody of the popular song may no longer be recognizable in the new embroidery of sound.

The particular song may get lost for another reason. Most popular songs have simple chord patterns, so there is often little difference between the chords of one popular song and another. When the melody is being improvised upon, the harmony is often not distinguishable from that of other songs. And the rhapsodic nature of jazz improvisation also leads to a sameness of mood that makes it more difficult to distinguish the basic song.

The Development of Jazz

The 1920s saw the real emergence of jazz, which was given impetus in 1918 by Joe "King" Oliver's famous Creole Jazz Band in Chicago. Other musicians soon became prominent: Paul Whiteman, whose band presented the first jazz concert in 1924, featuring the premiere of George Gershwin's *Rhapsody in Blue*; Bessie Smith, the famous blues singer; Fletcher Henderson and his band; Bix Beiderbecke, who started "white" jazz with his cornet and the band called the "Wolverines"; and the notable Louis Armstrong, who began his music-making as a boy in a New Orleans waif band. Through his trumpet playing and vocal renditions, Armstrong had much influence on the basic sound and style of jazz.

The prevailing style in the 1920s was *Dixieland*. It is characterized by a strong upbeat, a meter of two beats to the measure, and certain tonal and stylistic qualities that are impossible to notate. It has a "busy" sound, since there is simultaneous improvisation by perhaps four to seven players. Dixieland style used to be de-

Duke Ellington in 1943. Reproduced from the collection of the Library of Congress.

scribed as "hot"; it's fast, furious, and usually loud.

During the depression of the 1930s, the hiring of bands became prohibitively expensive. So pianists enjoyed increasing popularity, especially as they developed a jazz piano style called *boogie-woogie*. It features a persistently repeated melodic figure in the bass, or, in musical terms, an ostinato. Usually the boogie-woogie ostinato consists of eight notes per measure, which explains why this type of music is sometimes called "eight to the bar." Over the continuous bass the pianist plays trills, octave tremolos (the rapid alternation of pitches an octave apart), and other melodic figures.

The *swing era* in jazz lasted from 1935 to about 1950. It featured intricate arrangements and big bands of about 17 players, under the leadership of such musicians as Benny Goodman, Count Basie, and Duke Ellington. It was also the era of the featured soloist—Gene Krupa, Fats Waller, and Tommy Dorsey, to name a few. Other notable figures from the period include Artie Shaw, Harry James, Glenn Miller, Coleman Hawkins, and Fletcher Henderson. Musically, swing has four beats to the measure and rhythm with a "bounce." The swing era was one in which the audience danced. Its "concert halls" were such places as the Roseland Ballroom in New York and California's Hollywood Palladium.

Following World War II there emerged a style called *bebop*, or more commonly, *bop*. It was developed chiefly by Charlie "Bird" Parker and Dizzy Gillespie, who once defined the term by saying that in bop you go *Ba*-oo *Ba*-oo *Ba*-oo instead of *Oo*-ba *Oo*-ba *Oo*-ba. What he was describing was the nearly continuous syncopation that occurs in bop. It also features dissonant chords and freely developed melodies. Often the performers play in unison at the octave instead of presenting the traditional improvised counterpoint. In bop the fifth degree of the scale is lowered, which is a carryover of the blue notes discussed earlier. The bass drum does not sound all the time—a change from earlier styles. Instead, the string bass is given the responsibility for keeping the beat. Bop bands were much smaller than the bands of the swing era.

Stan Kenton was the leader of *progressive* jazz, which is characterized by big bands and highly dissonant chords. In a sense, the progressive style is an updated, intellectual version of the swing style that prevailed about 15 years earlier.

With Miles Davis and Dave Brubeck, jazz turned toward a "cool" style, still intellectual and well-ordered, but performed by much smaller groups. Charlie Mingus, Ornette Coleman, and John Coltrane led a movement toward *free form* jazz, in which all restraints were removed. No longer was improvisation held together by the harmony.

Over the years jazz has become more of a "listener's" type of music, in contrast to its early history. Gone is much of jazz's image as a "music of the people." It has "grown up" in

The Grateful Dead.

the sense that it's not always played just for fun, at least not by many jazz musicians. It is now serious business, performed by musicians who have studied Stravinsky and Bartók. Jazz represents the rediscovery of the art of improvising, which was largely neglected after the time of Bach and Mozart. Perhaps it was a better counterbalance to the deadly seriousness of nineteenth-century music than were the arty, chic attempts promoted by Satie and his followers.

Rock

Rock is generally considered to be a combination of the rhythm-and-blues music of America's blacks and the country-western style associated with Nashville, Tennessee. The people most associated with early rock (then called rock 'n' roll) in the 1950s are Elvis Presley, Jerry Lee Lewis, Little Richard, Chubby Checker, and Bill Haley and His Comets. The music was as forceful and untamed as the image Presley projected with his leather jacket and swaying body (earning him the title "Elvis the Pelvis"). The pounding beat of rock led one critic to define it as "Music in which the bass drum carries the melody."

As rock developed in the 1960s, it became somewhat more complex. The twist and discotheques came in about 1960, followed two years later by the "surfing" music of the Beach Boys and Jan and Dean. The "English invasion," as some writers refer to it, took place about 1964 with the appearance of the Beatles and the Rolling Stones. That was also the year that the "Motown sound" was born with the Supremes and other groups. Folk rock appeared about 1965 with Bob Dylan, the Byrds, and the Mamas and the Papas. Psychedelic or "acid" rock appeared in 1966 with such groups as the Jefferson Airplane (now known as Jefferson Starship) and San Francisco. By the early 1970s there were many types of rock, including combinations of rock with religious, theatrical, blues, jazz, and other styles. The Beatles were representative of the changes that took place in rock during the 1960s. They moved from the early "funky" sound to music that contained elements of electronic music, Baroque style, oriental music, and nineteenth-century art songs. However, the group's final recording, before they broke up in the late 1960s, was a return to the early rock sound.

How does rock differ from jazz? One characteristic of rock has already been mentioned: the heavy beat.

A second characteristic is frequent use of the modal harmonies that had fallen into disuse after the Renaissance. By 1970 more popular songs and rock pieces were in modes than were in the traditional major-minor system.

A third characteristic of rock is the departure from the standard formal schemes of the popular songs of previous decades. Most popular songs had been in an *a a b a* form, with eight measures for each portion. Rock phrases are more irregular, perhaps to fit the blank verse of many of the texts.

A fourth and very significant feature of rock involves the different timbre of the music. The dance band of the preceding decades, with its saxes and trumpets, was replaced by the small group, with its electric guitars and electronic organ or piano. Rock is often played through amplifiers that are turned up to a loud level. The singing, which is usually done by males, is generally a little higher in pitch and lighter in quality than the singing in earlier pop music.

A fifth change in rock is the use of different chordal progressions. The traditional dominant-to-tonic progression is less favored than adjacent or parallel chord movement (e.g., I-II-I-VII-I). Other somewhat nontraditional patterns are also found. The use of the modes gives the chords a different quality.

A sixth feature of rock is the dominance of small groups (many times composed only of males) instead of the individual "idol" of the preceding decades. The appearance of the groups is different too. From the dinner jacket of the 1930s and 40s and the leather jacket of

the late 1950s, the style of performers' clothes has changed to highly individual attire that ranges from denim to very bizarre outfits.

A seventh characteristic is the dependence on recordings. Rock music exists primarily on records and tapes. "Live" performances are limited, and some performers never perform in person. The sound of a recording is affected significantly by recording engineers.

An eighth characteristic of rock is its folk qualities. Some actual folk melodies have been revived, and much folklike music has been created. Like folk music, rock is often learned by imitation and is not written down.

A ninth characteristic of rock is its great diversity. For many people rock has become synonymous with popular music, so the word *rock* has lost some accuracy in definition. Some rock is in a quite conventional ballad style (The Carpenters, for example) and is hardly rock at all; some borrows freely from art music (Emerson, Lake, and Palmer); some is known as "punk" rock, which features males wearing lipstick and wigs and sometimes handling boa constrictors (Alice Cooper and David Bowie); some is a form of social protest against injustices in society; some involves the dubbing in of electronic sounds (the Beatles' "Sgt. Pepper" album); some is in a folk style; some is surrealistic or intentionally absurd; some is barbaric and psychedelic and is performed to flashing lights; some involves exaggerated emotions on the part of the performers; some is violent and animallike in its primitive sounds; some is strongly oriental in character (Mahavishnu Orchestra). There is also "bubble-gum" rock for early adolescents.

Rock has developed its own canons of criticism in such magazines as *Rolling Stone*, *Rock and Pop*, and *Crawdaddy*; and by such writers as Richard Goldstein, Lillian Roxon, and Jon Landau. It has also pervaded and influenced many areas of American popular culture: background music in cartoons and commercials on television, posters and pictures, hair and clothing styles, and the "do-your-own-thing" attitude.

Like jazz, rock has now been around long enough for nostalgic revivals of earlier rock styles and stars.

Rock is as much a social as a musical phenomenon. It is often identified as the music of youth. The large number of people between the ages of 10 and 25, the affluence that allows them to buy records and clothes of their choice, the youth orientation of American culture, the rapid rate of technological and social change that has increased the differences in viewpoint and orientation between young and old, the advent of mass communication, television, and especially the prevalence of recorded music—all these factors and more have contributed to a musical situation that is unlike anything ever encountered before.

Another fact that makes the present popular music situation different from previous times is the importance of the recording sound engineer. Most popular music, especially rock, is nearly as much the technician's creation as it is the performer's. The development of the 16-track tape recorder allows for the easy addition of accompanying parts and additional sounds. Also, a great deal of music judgment is required in reducing or "mixing down" the 16 tracks to the final stereo or 2-track version. In addition to adjusting the loudness of the various tracks, the sound engineer can add or subtract reverberation, control the sense of presence in the sound, and alter the timbre of instruments and voices. Errors can be spliced out and corrections inserted. The final record is usually quite different from the original sound—the record is likely to be far more impressive. This is one reason many rock stars avoid live performances unless similar amplification and sound enrichment is available.

Other Types of Popular Music

Rock was the predominant type of popular music since 1960, but by the middle 1970s that situation began to change.*

---

*There are several kinds of information to evaluate in determining the most popular song or type of music: record sales, gross earnings, playings on the radio, etc. Sometimes the evidence is conflicting. Also, the classifications are not precise, which adds to the difficulty of making an accurate judgment.

Country-western. The country-western music associated with Nashville, Tennessee, has been popular for many years. The musical qualities of the country-western style reveal an ancestry in the southern mountain folk songs, which in turn grew out of English folk songs. The texts are sometimes narrative in form, and they often express sadness. The harmony, rhythm, and phrase patterns are simple and direct. The songs are often accompanied by electric guitars and fiddle, except in the bluegrass style, in which only acoustic (nonelectric) instruments are acceptable. The singing quality contains little vibrato or dynamic range, and there is a tinge of melancholy in the tone. Notes are seldom sustained.

As with any popular style, the sociological factors are as significant as the musical factors. The increased interest in country-western music correlates to the renewed interest in "nostalgia"—the looking back with favor on the past when life seemed simpler and happier. The primary audience for country-western music is the white working-class population. The enthusiasm and loyalty to its stars, such as Johnny Cash, the late Hank Williams, Buck Owens, Mel Tillis, Dolly Parton, Loretta Lynn, and others, is great. In country-western music soloists are more significant than groups.

Rhythm-and-blues. Rhythm-and-blues is the popular music associated with America's black population. Its musical qualities reveal some aspects of African music, especially in the style of singing. It is emotional and forceful, with calls and exclaimed words. Open chords and parallel chord movement are characteristic of its harmony. The dynamic levels are often loud.

Some writers include soul and gospel music in the rhythm-and-blues category, and the relationships are close among these styles. Prominent names in rhythm-and-blues music include James Brown, Smokey Robinson and the Miracles, Wilson Pickett, and the groups associated with the Motown sound.

Sometimes the same song will reach the top of popularity charts in the rhythm-and-blues, country-western, and general popular music listings, but only occasionally. For example, the Beatles were never particularly popular with blacks. The ethnic associations of popular music influence its acceptance with various segments of the population. The preference is based on the style and timbre of the music rather than on the message of the words, although the background of the performer makes some difference. A few songs with a message about war, poverty, or ecology achieved limited popularity in the late 1960s and early 1970s, but the trend then returned to the overwhelmingly favorite topic of popular songs: love and its pain and joy.

Broadway musicals.   The Broadway musical is an American tradition extending back well into the nineteenth century, although it has distant ancestors in the *vaudevilles* of France and the Beggar's Opera of Handel's London. An immediate predecessor was the operetta, which was usually based on long-ago-and-far-away subjects, such as the ones in Sigmund Romberg's *The Desert Song* and Victor Herbert's *The Red Mill* (which takes place in Holland). By today's standards the operetta seems stilted. In the past 40 years musicals have become more contemporary and substantive.

West Side Story, the musical by Leonard Bernstein and Stephen Sondheim, is an example of this change. It is about the gang fights and prejudice between ethnic groups on the West Side of Manhattan. The plot is an updated version of the Romeo and Juliet story. It features Tony, a young man of Polish descent, and Maria, a Puerto Rican girl. Instead of a balcony, as in Shakespeare's version, they meet on a fire escape. Before the story concludes, Tony unintentionally kills Maria's brother in a gang fight, and Tony is killed in an act of revenge by the Puerto Rican gang. He dies in Maria's arms.

The setting allows Bernstein, who was for over a decade the Musical Director of the New York Philharmonic and a recognized composer and pianist, to write in the varied styles of his cosmopolitan musical interests. Latin-American music is represented by the song "America," a number in the style of a *huapango* with alternating meters, and by portions of "The Dance at the Gym," which was mentioned in Chapter 4. Jazz is especially evident in the "Jet Song" and "Cool." Popular ballad style is well represented by "Tonight" and "Maria." Operatic influences can be heard in "I Have a Love" and "One Hand, One Heart." Humor has its moment in "Gee, Officer Krupke!" The musical opens typically with an overture, which is a potpourri of the songs in the show. *West Side Story* also contains dances woven naturally into the action.

Because it is live theater, the Broadway musical is tailored for its audience. A musical is normally tried out in Philadelphia, New Haven, or other "out-of-town" city prior to opening in New York. Portions of the musical that appear not to please the audience are deleted or rewritten. No one worries about being faithful to an artistic goal or theory because the main concern is: Is it good box office? Such a situation would appear to be harmful to creative artists and writers. Interestingly, this has not usually been the case. Composers, writers, and stage directors have been able to work around limitations of audience preferences, and have many times produced imaginative and worthy productions. The Broadway musical is thriving.

By no means have all the types of popular music been covered. In addition to jazz, rock, country-western, rhythm-and-blues, and Broadway musicals, there are the songs of Burt Bacharach and other music for films, the big band sounds of Buddy Rich and Doc Severinsen, the staid music of Lawrence Welk, who has outlasted all other music shows on television, and many more. The world of music is larger and more interesting because of the many types of popular music.

Appendix

How Music Is Written Down

The ability to read or at least follow written music is not necessary for understanding what is heard, but it certainly helps. It's something like getting across town on foot. It can be done, but it's easier and faster on a bicycle or in a car.

How does reading notation help you learn more about music? Mainly by reinforcing visually what you hear. What you see *and* hear is usually remembered better than what you only see *or* hear. Two senses are generally better than one. The relative values of seeing and hearing differ for each person. Some people find a visual image (including written words) to be of limited value, while others rely strongly on sight.

Notation is educationally useful because you can look at the symbols and gain some idea of how the music will sound. You can tell if the notes go up or down or stay at the same level. And many people have a general notion about how rhythmic values are represented in the notes. So you can often follow a line of music, even if you can't read it in the sense of singing or playing it.

Importance of Notation to Music

Music is an art that depends on re-creation. When you look at a painting, a piece of sculpture, or a building, you experience exactly what the artist created without involving an intervening person. Not so with music. Someone must bring it to life; it requires an intermediary. A few compositions exist only on discs or tape, and in such cases there is no performing intermediary. In some types of music, such as jazz, the performer is the creator of the music because, to a degree, it is made up as the performer goes along. However, in most cases even composers can't remember or render their own music completely. They can't play several instruments at once, and they can't perform their music if they are not physically present. So other performers are needed.

Until notation was developed, all music had to be remembered, and human memories are only partially accurate. Furthermore, works that exist only in people's minds are generally short. It's almost impossible to remember extended compositions without the aid of notation. Some folk pieces are long, especially the music in African and Indian ceremonies, but these usually repeat basically the same music over and over with slight variations.

Until the twentieth century, notation was the only means of preserving music accurately. Even today with the means to record music, notation is almost always necessary if a performer is to render what someone else has written. Learning a piece by listening to a recording is only moderately successful, and it is usually limited to short works.

Limitations of Notation

People have found it difficult to devise a system of musical notation. Systems of writing were in existence at least 2,000 years before the present system was developed. The earliest attempts at indicating music were "cue cards" that reminded the performer what to do. They were about as useful as telling someone how to find a particular place in a city by saying, "Go south for a while, then turn east for a short distance, then go further south, then a little more to the east—you can't miss it."

A more specific system was developed in the eleventh century by a monk named Guido d'Arezzo, who came up with the idea of establishing relationships between pitches. With only minor changes his ideas appear today as the *solfa* syllables—*do, re, mi, fa, sol, la,* and *ti.* These syllables imply a fixed relationship between any two notes. *Do* to *re* is a standard distance, *re* to *fa* is another, and so on for all combinations of pitches in a given key.

Guido's idea is effective in learning to read music, but it's inadequate as a system of notation, for two reasons. One, it doesn't specify exact pitches; it indicates only relationships. Two, it fails to account for rhythm.

Notation of pitch. Modern notation specifies pitch by placing marks on horizontal lines somewhat like a graph. Each line and space represents a specific pitch. Only five lines are grouped together because more than that would make it harder for the eye to locate notes. The exact pitch is indicated by a *clef* that tells the musician what note names are assigned to each line and space. The five lines in the clef are called a *staff*. Three types of clefs are used in America: 𝄢 called the F, or *bass*, clef (pronounced base); 𝄞 called the G, or *treble*, clef; and 𝄡 called the C clef, which serves as both the *alto* and the *tenor* clef. The clefs indicate definite pitches, all named for letters of the alphabet from A to G. Here are the note names indicated by the treble and bass clefs:

The pitch G is indicated by the treble clef at the point where the curl goes around the second line. The two dots of the bass clef appear on either side of the fourth line, which is F; the large dot of the bass clef begins on the same F line. In the alto and tenor clefs the line on which the two bows meet is the pitch C.

Small changes of pitch are indicated by the *sharp* sign (♯) or the *flat* sign (♭). The sharp placed before a note raises the pitch one half step, while the flat placed before a note lowers the pitch one half step. Sometimes the *natural* sign (♮) is seen. It cancels a sharp or flat previously applied to the note.

When certain notes in a piece are flatted or sharped consistently, the composer writes the appropriate sharps or flats at the beginning of each staff of music to save writing the sign each time that particular note appears in the music. These clusters of sharps or flats at the beginning of each line are called the *key signature*.

The pitch range of a staff can be extended upward or downward by adding short horizontal lines called *leger lines*. Some leger lines appear in the example on page 280.

Pitches on the keyboard. Most instruments are constructed in such a way that the pitch relationships of the notes are not visible to the eye. Keyboard instruments like the piano and organ are different because the pattern of pitches is visible. The black keys on the piano are found in groups of twos and threes. All white keys are identified in relation to these groups of black keys. For example, every C on the piano is a white key immediately to the left of a two-black-key group; every F is a white key immediately to the left of a three-black-key group. The white keys are named consecutively from left to right, using the letters A to G:

lower pitches ← → higher pitches

To find the sharp of any white key on the piano, find the black key touching it on the *right*. To find the flat of any white key, find the black key touching it on the *left*. If there is no black key on the side where you are looking, the nearest white key in that direction is the sharp or flat.

On the keyboard below, notice that each black key has two names. For instance, the key can be called G sharp (because it is to the right of G) or A flat (because it is to the left of A).

Middle C, the note midway between the treble and bass staffs, is also the C nearest the middle of the piano keyboard. Using this as a guide, you can look at any note on the staff and find the exact tone it represents.

represents the first
G *above* middle C

middle C

represents the first
G *below* middle C

middle
C

Rhythm. In addition to indicating pitch according to its placement on the staff, each note indicates a duration. Basic to the notational system for rhythm is the 2:1 ratio that shows comparative durations. For example, a whole note (○) lasts twice as long as a half note (♩), which lasts twice as long as a quarter note (♩). An eighth note (♪) is half as long as a quarter note, and a sixteenth note (♬) is half as long as an eighth note. In the following chart of note values, the dotted arrows represent the passing of time. They do not appear in actual music.

Consecutive notes may share flags (wavy lines on the stems) for ease in writing and reading.

The notes represent sound; *rests* indicate silence. The 2:1 ratio also applies to rests. The symbol for the whole rest is ▬ (hanging from the fourth line of the staff). The symbol for the half rest is ▬ (sitting on top of the third line).

Notes are sometimes seen with a dot to the right of the note head. A dot on the right (*not* over or under the note head) adds *one half* of the note's value to the note. If a half note receives two beats, a dotted half note lasts for two beats *plus* half again as much (one beat), for a total of three beats.

Measures are set apart by vertical bar lines on the staff. (In fact, measures are sometimes called *bars*.) Each measure contains all the notes to be sounded over the span of time designated by the meter.

Two-beat meter:

	beat beat	beat beat
	measure	measure

Any type of note can equal one beat. The type of note is indicated in the *meter signature* (also called *time signature*). The meter signature appears at the beginning of nearly every piece of music. Most meter signatures aren't hard to figure out. The *top* number indicates the number of beats in each measure: A 4 means four beats, a 3 means three beats, and so on—usually.

The *bottom* number in the meter signature tells which note value lasts for one beat: 4 means a quarter note, 8 means an eighth note, and so on—usually. The 2:1 ratio mentioned earlier is maintained no matter what note value represents the beat. Therefore, it's possible to write music by choosing any one of two or three different note values for the beat; each version will sound exactly the same but the notation will look different.

The meter signature is *not a fraction;* $\frac{3}{4}$ does *not* mean three-fourths because it does not represent a portion of anything. Two abbreviated meter signatures are seen frequently: C (common time) means $\frac{4}{4}$, and ₵ (cut time, sometimes called *alla breve*) means $\frac{2}{2}$.

Meters are of two types. One has beats that are subdivided into a background of twos, and it is called *simple* time. The other, called *compound* time, subdivides the beat into threes. The meter signature for compound time is more complex. Since the common note values subdivide in multiples of *two,* some type of *dotted* note must represent multiples of *three.* (Since a dot adds half the preceding value—or one-third of the note's total duration—a dotted beat note creates the 3:1 ratio necessary for notating compound meter.) Furthermore, the meter signature must somehow indicate to the performer that the meter is compound. A signature such as $_1\frac{2}{1/2}$ is impracticable, so the number of beat *subdivisions* is indicated in the top number, and the note value of each of these subdivisions is indicated in the bottom number. A meter signature of $\frac{6}{8}$ usually means that there are two beats per measure, and a dotted quarter note lasts for one beat:

Tempo. The meter signature says nothing about the tempo of the music—the speed at which the beats recur. Tempo is indicated in two ways. One way is to specify the number of beats per minute. Some pieces display a marking like this at the beginning: ♩ = M.M. 120. The initials M.M. stand for Maelzel's Metronome. (Maelzel patented the work of another man and had the device named for himself.) The number refers to the number of ticks that are to be produced per minute. The quarter note means that in this particular piece each quarter note should last for one tick, with other note values in proportion to this norm.

The other way to give an indication of tempo is to provide verbal directions, such as

fast or slow. These provide only a general idea of the speed of the music. The words are traditionally written in Italian, although in the last 100 years some composers with strong feelings of nationalism have chosen to use their native tongue. These words are significant for the listener because they are often listed in concert programs to identify the large sections of a piece of music. Here are some of the most common terms:

Italian Term	Meaning
Largo	Very slow, broad
Grave	Very slow, heavy
Adagio	Slow, leisurely
Andante	"Walking," moderate tempo, unhurried
Moderato	Moderate speed
Allegretto	"Little allegro," moving easily
Allegro	Moderately fast, moving briskly
Allegro molto	"Much allegro," very brisk
Vivace	Lively
Presto	Very fast
Prestissimo	As fast as possible

Composers often couple other directives with the tempo marking. Usually the additions have more to do with style than with speed (such as *con fuoco,* with fire or force; *sostenuto,* smooth, sustained). Within the broad framework of a specified tempo there may be indications of lesser tempo changes: *meno,* less (as in *meno allegro*); *piu,* more; *poco,* a little; *rit.* or *ritard,* gradually slower; *accel.* or *accelerando,* gradually faster.

Dynamics. The notes themselves provide no indication of the dynamic level at which they should be sounded. To inform the performer about this, the composer places small letters at appropriate places in the music. Two Italian words are basic: *p,* or *piano,* which means soft; and *f,* or *forte,* which means loud. (The instrument known today as the piano was originally called the *pianoforte* because it was able to make gradual changes from loud to soft.) The descriptive words can be even more extreme: *ff*, or *fortissimo*, means very loud; and *pp*, or *pianissimo*, means very soft. Or they can be made more moderate by adding the prefix *mezzo* (pronounced *met*-zo), meaning medium; *mf*, or *mezzo forte*, means moderately loud; and *mp*, or *mezzo piano*, means moderately soft.

Gradual changes of volume are indicated by *cresc.* or *crescendo*, meaning get louder; and *decresc.* or *decrescendo*, meaning get softer. The latter term can be indicated equally well by *dim.* or *diminuendo*. Frequently the *crescendo* is represented by the sign ◁ and the *decrescendo* by the sign ▷ .

Indications about dynamics are not the only marks telling the performer how to interpret a certain passage in the music. Some markings tell the performer to "punch out" a note, some direct holding a note longer than normal, and some call for a particular style in sounding a passage. Occasionally words de-

scribing the desired expression are written on the music.

Our present system of music notation is a significant accomplishment, but it is inadequate in many ways. It is rather specific about pitch and rhythm, but it can't show the subtle deviations that make a performance musically satisfying. A performance that adheres slavishly to just what the printed music specifies will sound mechanical and dull. Also, some styles are especially difficult to put into notation. Jazz rhythms are one example. The performer of jazz plays certain figures in a way that's quite different from what the notation calls for. The limitations of printed symbols place quite a bit of responsibility on the performer, for whom the page of music is about as complete as the script of a play is for an actor. It provides the bare essentials. It is the performer who must bring the notes on the page to life as music.

Glossary

A cappella   unaccompanied choral music.

Accidental   a sharp, flat, or natural sign written in the music to show a departure from the prevailing key signature.

Acoustics   the science of sound.

Air   a song or melody.

Antiphonal   two groups performing "against" each other and stationed apart.

Appoggiatura   a musical ornament occurring on the beat and consisting of a nonharmonic, dissonant note that resolves to an adjacent harmonic note.

Arpeggio   in "harp" style; a broken chord in which the notes are played one after another instead of simultaneously.

Atonal, atonality   not in any key or tonality.

Bitonal, bitonality   two keys occurring simultaneously.

Cadence   a progression of chords (usually two or three) giving the sense of phrase ending. In poetic usage, it sometimes refers to "beat" or "tempo."

Cadenza   a solo passage of an improvised, free nature, usually found in concertos.

Canon   strict imitation carried on between two or more lines of music for a significant amount of time.

Cantabile   in singing style.

Cembalo   harpsichord.

Chanson   song (French).

Chromatic   melodic movement by semitones.

Clavecin   harpsichord (French).

Consonance   concord; a group of sounds that the listener considers restful or pleasant.

Continuo   a bass line for keyboard in which the player is given only a succession of single notes and other symbols from which to fill out the remainder of the harmony. Also, the instruments that play that part.

Dissonance   discord; a group of sounds that the listener considers restless or unpleasant.

Enharmonic   the characteristic of a pitch whereby it can have two names; for example, on a keyboard instrument E flat is also D sharp.

Ensemble   a group of performers or the effect of unity achieved when they perform together.

Equal temperament   a system of tuning in which the octave is divided into twelve equal segments or semitones.

Fugal   suggestive of a fugue in style but not actually a fugue in form.

Glissando   ascending or descending notes occurring quickly. Played on a piano by rapidly moving the hand across the keys; on a harp by plucking many strings consecutively in a single sweeping motion. Other instruments achieve the sliding sound in a variety of ways.

Grace note   an ornamental note preceding another more important pitch and printed in smaller size. It is performed quickly and does not usually affect the rhythm of the music.

Harmonic   a note produced by lightly touching a string at a proper place to divide it into segments. The sound is high and light in quality.

Harmony   the effect created when tones are sounded simultaneously.

Homophony   music consisting essentially of a melody with accompanying chords.

Improvisation   music that is performed without prior planning.

Inversion   turning a melody upside down so that an ascending interval descends and vice versa. Also, rearranging the notes in a chord so that its basic note is no longer on the bottom.

Intonation   the quality of sounding "in tune."

Key   the centering or relating of pitches around a particular pitch.

Legato   smooth.

Leitmotiv   a motive or theme that is associated with a particular character or idea, especially in the music dramas of Wagner.

Libretto   the text of an opera.

Lied   song (German).

Manual   organ (or harpsichord) keyboard played with the hands, as opposed to pedal keyboard played by the feet.

Melody   a series of consecutive pitches that form a unified and coherent musical entity.

Meter   the pattern created by stressed and unstressed beats in music.

Meter signature   time signature; numbers at the beginning of a musical work that indicate the meter.

Modulation   changing key as the music progresses, usually without a break.

Monophony   a single unaccompanied melody.

Motive   a short melodic or rhythmic fragment that achieves structural importance through its frequent recurrence.

Mute   a device for muffling or damping the sound of an instrument.

Octave   a pitch that has twice or half the frequency of vibration of another. The two pitches, if sounded simultaneously, blend into a sameness of sound.

Opus (Op.)   work. The opus numbers of a composer's music are generally in chronological order.

Ornament   a decorative note, or a rather unimportant melodic figure.

Ostinato   a persistently repeated musical figure.

Overtone series   harmonic series.

Pedal point   a note sustained above or below changing harmonies.

Pitch   the highness or lowness of a musical tone, as determined by the frequency of its sound waves.

Polyphony   music in which melodies of more or less equal importance occur simultaneously.

Polyrhythm   several rhythms occurring simultaneously.

Polytonal, polytonality   several keys occurring simultaneously.

Range   the upper and lower pitch limits of a voice or instrument.

Retrograde   a theme performed backward, last note first.

Rhythm   the sensation of movement in music; a factor regulated by the duration and strength of the various sounds.

Rubato   a performer's slight deviation from strict interpretation of rhythm.

Sequence   the repetition of a phrase at successively higher or lower pitch levels than the original.

Sforzando   a sudden accent on a tone.

Slur   a curved line grouping notes together and indicating that they are to be performed smoothly.

Staccato   notes disconnected from one another; usually indicated by a dot over or under each note.

Suite   a collection of stylized dances; or a collection of music from a ballet or opera.

Suspension   a nonharmonic, dissonant tone that was consonant in the preceding harmony and that eventually resolves downward to become consonant in its present harmony.

Syncopation   displacement of accent, so that accents occur where they are not normally expected and/or are lacking where they *are* expected.

Texture   the basic setting of the music: monophonic, homophonic, or polyphonic.

Timbre   tone quality or tone color.

Through-composed   a melody without repetition of phrases.

Tonality   key.

Transcribe   to arrange a piece for a performing medium other than the original.

Transpose   to rewrite music or perform it at a pitch level other than the original.

Tremolo   "trembling"; produced in two ways: by rapid back-and-forth motion of the bow on a stringed instrument or by rapid alternation between two pitches.

Trill   an ornament in which there is a rapid alternation between the written note and the note immediately above it.

Turn   an ornament consisting of several notes that move above and below the main note.

Vibrato   a very slight but rapid fluctuation of pitch.

Index